T0352501

Praise for *Felicity George*

'A dark and seductively dangerous Regency world –
think *Bridgerton* meets *Moulin Rouge* – where everything,
especially love, has a high price'
EMMA ORCHARD

'In George's irresistibly sexy Regency, a fiery courtesan
must outwit a devilish duke, and a tender-hearted
clergyman stands ready to fight for his true love. Kitty and
Sid break the mould – I adored every scintillating page'
JESSICA BULL

'What a joy it was to read! I don't think I've ever rooted
for a hero in a novel like I rooted for Sidney. And Kitty
was just the right amount of feist and fire. Loved her!'
JODI ELLEN MALPAS

'A heart-warming and richly emotional debut that shines
with sparkling wit, passion and fun'
NICOLA CORNICK

'A delightful romance in which the spirited heroine has
to decide if there are some things more important than
love-or if, in fact, love encompasses them all'
MARY BALOGH

Felicity George is a writer and teacher from Toronto, where she lives with her husband, her two teenage children, a large cat, and a tiny dog. A lifelong devotee of Jane Austen and Georgette Heyer, Felicity adores a happily-ever-after. *A Courtesan's Worth* is her second novel.

Connect with Felicity

🐦 Felicity George @ElizabethWelke
📘 Felicity George, Author
@FelicityGeorgeRegencyRomance

Also by Felicity George

A Lady's Risk

A Courtesan's Worth

Felicity George

First published in Great Britain in 2023 by Orion Dash,
an imprint of The Orion Publishing Group Ltd,
Carmelite House, 50 Victoria Embankment
London EC4Y 0DZ

An Hachette UK company

1 3 5 7 9 10 8 6 4 2

Copyright © Felicity George 2023

The moral right of Felicity George to be identified as the author
of this work has been asserted in accordance with
the Copyright, Designs and Patents Act 1988.

All rights reserved. No part of this publication may be
reproduced, stored in a retrieval system, or transmitted,
in any form or by any means, electronic, mechanical,
photocopying, recording or otherwise, without the prior
permission of the copyright owner.

All the characters in this book are fictitious,
and any resemblance to actual persons, living
or dead, is purely coincidental.

A CIP catalogue record for this book
is available from the British Library.

ISBN (Paperback) 978 1 3987 1594 3
ISBN (eBook) 978 1 3987 1047 4

Typeset by Born Group

MIX
Paper from
responsible sources
FSC® C104740

To Amanda and to Olivia,
who first read my novels.

Prologue

July 1813

After the Wedding of Lord and Lady Holbrook . . .

The Reverend Sidney Wakefield hopped down from Dr Alexander Mitchell's carriage, his booted feet landing squarely on the pavement before number twenty-nine Half Moon Street. He stretched his long legs. Seven hours on the road had left his muscles tightly sprung, eager for movement. He would run later that night, he decided, once he had settled whatever business awaited after a week's absence in Suffolk for his friend Nicholas's wedding to the former Lady Margaret Fairchild.

Sidney shifted a flowerpot of sweet peas from one hand to the other as he glanced at the lowering sun. He wanted to deliver the blossoms to Mount Street soon, so he could give them to his favourite four-year-old before she snuggled into bed. Tonight, the sweet peas could rest beside Ada-Marie's cot and fragrance her dreams; tomorrow, she could plant them in the jardinière outside her nursery window. Although Ada-Marie's eyes wouldn't see the pink and purple blooms, she'd delight in their sweet perfume and the softness of the frilled petals.

I

With a bit of luck, Sidney would also have a chance to talk with his dear friend Kitty Preece, Ada-Marie's guardian, and assess how she'd fared in the past sennight. Kitty's mind had been troubled lately, and Sidney worried for her.

As his housemates John Tyrold and Lord Edward Matlock disembarked from Alexander's carriage, a miaow arrested Sidney's attention. He smiled at the massive ginger tabby rubbing himself against the iron railing in front of the five-storey brick terrace.

He reached down to ruffle his pet's thick fur. 'Did you miss me, Marmalade?'

The cat purred but otherwise didn't deign to answer.

The front door of number twenty-nine swung open, and Mrs Smith, the housekeeper, emerged, followed by her husband and their niece, Ellen. Together, they comprised the staff of the bachelor abode, serving John, Edward and Sidney.

Mrs Smith put her hands on her hips as Mr Smith attended to the portmanteaux. 'So you lot are back, are you? Well, don't scuff up the floor with your filthy boots, for I've given this house a top-to-bottom and back again in the last four days, and Gad's me, it needed it.' Her gaze fell on Sidney, and her eyes softened. 'Your quarters weren't too dreadful, lamb. It's them I despair of.' She glared at John and Edward. 'Lord Edward's got his paints and brushes in *such* disarray and his studio reeked to the heavens of turpentine, and as for you, Mr Tyrold, I couldn't find the top of your desk for your stacks of dusty papers—'

2

'Which,' John interrupted, a thundercloud upon his brow, 'you'd better not have touched, Mrs Smith, lest you've jumbled my fortune and we end on the streets because I cannot set it to rights.'

Sidney smothered a smile. John was only teasing, and Mrs Smith knew it. There was no chance of John's fortune being lost; his assets totalled to about four million pounds, making him one of the richest men in Britain. But grey-haired Mrs Smith loved to badger her employer. John allowed it (although he'd take no such thing from any other soul), but he retaliated relentlessly.

When Marmalade meandered off, evidently tired of being petted, and Dr Mitchell's carriage departed, Sidney bounded up the stoop with Ada-Marie's blooms in hand. The heady scent of Mrs Smith's beeswax polish hit him as he crossed the threshold into the wood-panelled entrance vestibule with John and Edward at his heels. Edward ran upstairs without a word, but John perused a stack of correspondence on a side table. Sidney placed the flowerpot by the door, ready for his imminent departure for Mount Street, and headed towards the narrow stairs to change his clothes.

John halted his progress by tossing him a sealed letter. 'Something for you, Sid.'

Sidney caught it, glanced at the unfamiliar hand, ripped the wafer seal, and read – *Duffy and Ward, Publishers, Paternoster Row.*

Sidney's heart pummelled his chest – he hadn't dared hope for this response yet. Breathless, he skimmed the words.

Dear Mr Wakefield,
   Mr Duffy and I . . . pleased to offer . . .
exclusive publishers and distributors of the three
enchanting manuscripts which you delivered last
month . . . propose an August publication date for
first . . . readers will delight in the love story of Mr
Villeur and Charlotte as much as we did . . . trust
you will find our terms of settlement more than
satisfactory . . . I have the honour of being, etc.,
Mr C Ward.

Too elated to read comprehensively, Sidney clasped the letter to his heart and whispered his gratitude to the heavens. Here, at last, was the answer to countless prayers, and not a moment too soon.

'All well, Sid?' John peered over his own post, his green eyes sharp.

Sidney's chest expanded. 'Oh, John, it's never, *ever* been better!'

John's eyebrows shot up, but he didn't get excited. John *never* got overexcited. 'Best let me have a look at that letter, my boy.'

Sidney shook his head. 'Later, John. There's someone else I must tell first.'

John's lips thinned. 'Off to Mount Street with you, then,' he said gruffly as he returned to reading.

With warm blood coursing to his every extremity, Sidney dashed up two flights of stairs to his spartan chambers. Clearly, Nicky's lovely wedding was a harbinger of joy. The world was a beautiful place. Love and goodness abounded.

Still beaming like a boy, Sidney plucked his finest coat from his wardrobe and laid it upon the thin mattress of his wooden bed, along with a pair of buff trousers. He peeled off his travelling clothes, washed his lean body, and checked his reflection in his tarnished mirror. He could do with a fresh shave, he decided.

From a drawer, Sidney withdrew a Wedgwood bowl of sandalwood shaving soap, a luxurious gift which he used only on special occasions. He'd look his best tonight, come what may.

Sidney enquired for Kitty when the butler opened the cherry-red door of the Preece sisters' grand house on Mount Street, but Mr Dodwell shook his head.

'I'm sorry, sir, but Miss Kitty and her sisters are out for the evening.'

'Where?' Sidney asked eagerly, as he stood on the stoop holding the sweet peas and a recently purchased present for Kitty. He'd meet up with them wherever they'd gone.

Mr Dodwell hesitated, and Sidney was about to reach for a precious coin when a familiar man appeared on the grand central staircase beyond the butler's shoulder.

'*Mon Dieu*, *Monsieur* Dodwell,' cried Kitty's dresser, Philippe, his blue eyes shining under his forward-brushed sandy locks. 'Miss Kitty would not like you to leave her good friend *Monsieur* Wakefield waiting for an answer.' The tall Frenchman, who dressed with

5

an understated elegance to rival Brummell, glided to the door. '*Mon bon monsieur, les mademoiselles* left for Vauxhall half an hour ago.'

Ah, all was not lost. Sidney could join Kitty at the Pleasure Gardens.

Philippe extended his hands. 'Would *monsieur* like Philippe to place the flowers and package in Miss Kitty's chambers?'

'The flowers are for Ada-Marie. Might I take them to her if she is not yet abed?'

'Alas, the children are asleep, *monsieur*.'

Sidney couldn't take a flowerpot to Vauxhall. 'Would you ask Nanny Ashcroft to put them beside Ada-Marie's cot? To give her sweet dreams?'

Philippe accepted the sweet peas, burrowed his nose among the blooms, and inhaled. When he glanced up, his face shone. '*Les beaux rêves en valent la peine.*'

Sidney grinned.

Beautiful dreams were worth it, indeed.

I

That same evening . . .

Kitty Preece stepped from the bow of a Thames wherry and planted her gold-slippered feet on the shingle. Her four dark-haired sisters, gowned in silks which glistened in the amber rays of the setting sun, clustered together near the Vauxhall stairs as passengers emptied from dozens of lantern-lit boats along the Lambeth bank.

Kitty gathered her breath and squared her shoulders.

Tonight was the night.

She strode towards the stairs as lilting music and peals of laughter emerged from behind the Pleasure Gardens' walls. Among Vauxhall's myriad of multicoloured oil lamps and shadowy paths, Kitty must find a yet-unknown gentleman *tonight* and secure an offer of arrangement – a left-handed marriage, as it was termed – and thereby free herself from the despicable Duke of Gillingham, set to take her as his mistress in a month.

It ought to be a minor feat for the most desirable courtesan in London, but for the last month, Kitty hadn't had a single stroke of luck. The marquess she'd hoped to hook had stopped calling, gentlemen shied away when she promenaded in Hyde Park, and no man but Gillingham had stood up with her at the last three of the Preece sisters' famous Thursday evening entertainments.

Now time was running out. Her arrangement with Gillingham was set to commence in August, but if she didn't ensnare a wealthy keeper this week, her chance would be lost. Within days, the *haut ton* would abandon London's stifling heat for the shade-dappled parkland of country estates.

A wind swelled along the Thames, intensifying the river's stench, and ruffling the single layer of translucent silk gauze that comprised Kitty's gown. Matilda, the eldest of Kitty's four courtesan sisters, leaned on Kitty's arm as they trudged up the moss-damp steps. When they reached the top, Matilda paused under the glow of a street lamp and shivered as she examined Kitty from delicate laced slippers to gold-ribboned coiffure.

'Philippe outdid himself tonight,' she said, breathless from the climb.

'He calls it Venus in gold and white.' Kitty laughed as she elevated her arm skyward and posed like a marble statue, as her dresser, Philippe, had demonstrated earlier. The gold armlets positioned halfway between Kitty's elbow and shoulder blazed momentarily as the last rays of the sun slipped behind the distilleries and lumber yards on the far side of the river.

'Your gown is near as wispy as gossamer.' Matilda tilted her head, and the corkscrew curls which framed her plump face bobbed. 'But so cleverly draped as to not give it *all* away. Lovely, of course, for your figure is as pert as ever, Kitty-cat. If the duke is here tonight, he'll be beside himself, the old goat.' Matilda chuckled and coughed as the pedestrians spilling over the Vauxhall stairs thrust the sisters towards the elongated aquamarine awning of the Pleasure Gardens' water-gate entrance.

Kitty bristled among the jostling merrymakers. For the first time in the thirteen years of her profession, Kitty disagreed with Matilda about her choice for Kitty's next keeper – the man Kitty would reward with exclusive rights to her elegant body for as long as he desired, in exchange for her upkeep.

The Duke of Gillingham was wealthy and powerful, but he'd maltreated his eldest son. Kitty's stomach heaved when she remembered how Gillingham had wrenched the frightened young man from her bed and sent him quaking to Spain to fight for Wellington. The day Richard had sailed, the duke had paid Matilda a thousand pounds upfront for Kitty, with an offer of one hundred more monthly. It was a fortune much needed by the sisters now that Matilda and Barbara – both well past thirty and with twelve children between them – attracted less attention.

Only after days of Kitty's pleading did Matilda request a two-month reprieve, allegedly so Kitty's heart could heal from the severance of her year-long arrangement with the duke's son. But Kitty had deceived Matilda and the duke with that lie, for while she'd liked Richard well enough, she wanted the reprieve to find *anyone* other than Gillingham to replace him.

As Kitty and her sisters stood in the entrance queue, Matilda's cough intensified. She hacked until her blue eyes watered and dampness glistened on her forehead. Kitty's heart twisted. Her eldest sister suffered from an infection of the lungs that had been exacerbated by a cold during her most recent confinement.

Kitty burrowed a hand into Matilda's red reticule and drew out a flask. 'Here, dearest.' She pulled Matilda aside near the double-door entry and motioned with her chin for her other sisters to wait. 'A sip or two as needed, Dr Mitchell said.'

She rubbed her sister's back as Matilda swallowed the herbal brew. The aroma of liquorice, hyssop, and honey permeated the evening air.

Kitty restored the flask to the bag and dabbed away a tear on Matilda's pink cheek, careful not to smudge her sister's rouge. 'Ready now?'

Matilda nodded. 'You go first, my beautiful Kitty-cat.'

It was time for five ladies of the night to enter the Garden of Pleasure.

Kitty flashed her bronzed-medallion season token at the tailcoated ticket-taker, and, with her sisters following, she sashayed through the doors into a burst of light, music and laughter. Vauxhall glittered like a star-strewn sky. Tens of thousands of illuminated glass globes nestled in trees and draped pavilions. A two-tiered orchestra box sparkled as the musicians played jigs for dancing couples, while acrobats performed before wide-eyed children who clung to their parents' hands.

In a semicircle around the entrance, other customers' heads turned. Their jaws dropped at the delicate gown which displayed most of Kitty's spectacular bosom. With

her chin aloft, Kitty assumed her position in the formation she and her sisters had perfected: a vee, with Kitty in
the front like the proud figurehead of a ship, Matilda and
Barbara flanking her two steps behind, a pair of queens
slipping past their prime but noble yet in their diamonds
and silks, and Jenny and Amy in the back, fresh-faced
butterflies blowing kisses to slack-jawed youths.

The crowds parted before them. Debutantes flushed
scarlet, their eyes bulging as their pursed-lipped mamas
grasped their elbows and propelled them away. Plumed
dowagers peered down their long noses with curled lips.
Bewigged waiters winked cheekily as they bustled from
the kitchens towards the tables, white towels slung over
their forearms and silver platters held high.

A modish society lady, draped in pearls, fluttered her
fan. 'Sluts,' she exclaimed to a scarlet-cheeked friend.
'Have they no shame?'

'Think nothing of them,' her friend replied. 'They
are like chamber pots – merely a place for men to
dump their waste.'

Kitty blinked. *That* was a new one, cruder but no
more cutting than what she'd heard for years. She blew
the ladies a kiss, whereupon the ruddy one said, 'Soon
enough you'll be haggard and old, and no man will
want you,' before whipping around and hastening away.

It was true – and the reason why Kitty must earn
now. Her value was like that of a shiny toy, picked up
and discarded at will, soon to tarnish and break.

But the ladies' opinions needn't affect Kitty because
her sisters protected her from heart wounds. Besides,

Kitty was at Vauxhall for the gentlemen. From the port-fed papas to the straight-backed youths, any deep-pocketed one of them would do, provided he wasn't vicious like Gillingham.

From the direction of the cone-roofed rotunda approached a cluster of scourers – wealthy young roisterers who spent their summer nights breaking windows and attacking the Watch. Amy's long-legged keeper, Mr Spencer-Lacey, emerged from their ranks, his rakish face splashed with a grin, and Amy, the doe-eyed baby of the Preece sisters, floated to his arms. Kitty's heart warmed. Spencer-Lacey was a devil-may-care young buck – no doubt well on his way to running through his family fortune – but he was kind to Amy and an affectionate father to their infant son. It wouldn't last, of course, but for now Amy was happy.

The scourers split into two groups: Spencer-Lacey and others ventured towards the dinner boxes, while a faction led by the firebrand baronet Sir Vincent Preston trailed Kitty and her three remaining sisters through the fairy-lit Covered Walk, their boots crunching on the gravel.

Jenny, with genuine delight sparking in her long-lashed green eyes, squealed as they encountered a slack-wire walker juggling six colourful balls, while a flautist frolicked about him. 'How marvellous,' she said, clasping her hands to her bosom as if she'd never seen the like.

Kitty threaded an arm about Jenny's waist and kissed her second-youngest sister's satin-smooth cheek. Effervescent Jenny was frequently giddy, sometimes silly, but always ingenuous, despite having borne three children to as many different men.

Sir Vincent snorted, ruining the tender moment. 'If you wish to see a marvel, gentlemen,' he announced to his friends, 'observe Kitty Preece's tits. There are no finer mounds in Britain.'

The crudity recalled Kitty to her urgent mission to find a keeper other than the Duke of Gillingham. Since many scourers possessed abundant funds, she cast a smouldering gaze at Sir Vincent and his friends, hopeful a contender stood among their ranks. But, sadly, only none-too-wealthy Sir Vincent met her eye. Two of the others examined their boots. One rubbed his neck and stared at the blackening sky. The fifth, an obnoxious and gossipy lout named Bonser, whispered something in Sir Vincent's ear.

Still, it was worth a try, so Kitty batted her lashes. 'A worthy gentleman may climb these mounds, sirs.'

Matilda inhaled sharply and pinched Kitty's arm, but she plastered on a smile when she turned to the young men. '*Kitty* isn't available, my lovelies. Nor is Jenny. But you may call at Mount Street to make arrangements for Barbara or myself—'

Sir Vincent guffawed. 'You're ready for the knacker's yard, Matilda. Besides, as Bonser here' – he jerked his head at his whispering friend – 'reminded me, why pay a fortune for what costs two shillings in the Dark Walk? Come, gentlemen.'

As he sauntered past, he smacked Kitty's arse. It smarted, leaving her skin raw and stinging.

Bonser brayed with laughter. 'Take care, Vince, or her duke will avenge himself on you.' While the group rambled away, a last snippet floated back. 'Rather than wasting your money on whores, you should find yourself a rich dowd as I have. I shall be a wealthy and well-satisfied man soon.'

Kitty peeked at Matilda, who blinked rapidly, her colour high. Sir Vincent's cruel words had hurt more than his bruising smack. 'Oh, Matilda, don't let him—'

Matilda's eyes flashed. 'Kitty, kindly remember we rely on you. Stop playing fast and loose with Gillingham's goodwill.'

With that, Matilda turned on her heel towards The Grove, where Vauxhall's tiered orchestra box glittered like a gem-encrusted queen at the opera. Under strewn stands of many-hued lights, couples swirled to the tune of 'The Lass of Richmond Hill'.

Jenny spotted her keeper and danced into his arms.

Heavy-hearted, Kitty circled The Grove with Matilda and Barbara, her resolve growing with each step. Yes, she must earn, but there were plenty of rich men other than Gillingham. Vauxhall was teeming with them. And Kitty only needed *one*.

She batted her lashes to catch the eye of a popular young viscount as he ambled past the dancers towards the supper boxes. As Lord Britnell's eyebrows lifted, Kitty glided the tip of her tongue along the bottom of her top teeth.

The nobleman froze. His gaze melted down, his features tightening as he took in her body, naked under the film of flimsy silk. While he watched, Kitty slipped a fingertip under her neckline and slowly stroked one of her nipples, which hardened into a pert peak beneath her gown.

When Britnell raised his eyes to hers again, frank lust smouldered.

Kitty half-smiled. Oh, yes. There were enough rich men at Vauxhall for her purpose. She'd start with the viscount. If she could manage five minutes with him in the Dark Walk, she'd allow the young lord to fondle and caress until he begged to keep her.

Matilda brushed against Kitty's side. 'The Duke of Gillingham.' She fluttered her jewelled fingers in the duke's direction. 'He's watching you.'

Matilda's words wiped the smile from Kitty's face.

Lately, Gillingham always watched, as if one of the most powerful politicians and courtiers in Britain had nothing better to do than spy on Kitty's actions.

The spell between Kitty and Britnell fizzled, and the viscount scurried on his way. Kitty cut her eyes in the direction Matilda indicated. Gillingham strode through The Grove with his daughter Lady Caroline, who was engaged to marry a foreign prince in a week's time. Under the duke's formidable black brows, his heavy-lidded eyes blazed, and his thin lips sneered.

The duke was a snake, and Kitty was no Cleopatra to hold a viper to her breast. Gillingham *wouldn't* slither into her bed.

Kitty shuddered.

A shawl as soft as down slipped around her. 'I'm not cold,' she said over her shoulder. What was Matilda doing, covering her? Kitty had wares to display.

'The night has only begun. It may yet be chilly.'
The familiar voice rumbling in Kitty's ear sent delighted
ripples throughout her body. 'And you always forget
your wrap.'

With a gleeful squeal, Kitty spun around, the evening's anxieties washing away. She wanted to grasp the
speaker in a bear-like embrace, but it wouldn't do to
make a public display of her unlikely friendship with
the Reverend Sidney Wakefield. She squeezed his warm
hand instead, her heart fluttering as it always did when
his strong fingers enfolded her slender ones. 'Sid. You're
never at Vauxhall.'

Sidney flashed a grin, his features gleaming under
the oil lamps. 'Good evening, Kit. Matilda, Barbara.'
He released Kitty's hand and swept off his tall-crowned
black hat. He bowed in a grand, old-fashioned manner,
revealing his thick blond hair which lay in waves above
his straight brows.

It was a rare treat to see Sidney without his stark
parson's coat and flat white collar. He wore a simple
but well-tailored olive-green tailcoat, cut short in the
front across his trim waist. Tight buff trousers, pulled
taut by the instep strap under his polished black shoes,
encased his slim but muscular legs. A crisp white cravat
cascaded below his full mouth and cleft chin. His light
brown eyes shone like amber as he kissed the sparkling
fingers of Kitty's sisters. Barbara flocked to his side and
clung to his arm, fluttering her lashes.

Kitty frowned, reality descending to smother her
momentary delight. Without question, Sidney was one

of the handsomest young men in London – his golden good looks attracted nearly as much attention as Kitty herself did – but Barbara should mind her behaviour. Sidney might be as graceful and athletic as an out-and-out Corinthian, but he was also a mere curate who couldn't afford to displease his vicar at St George's Church in Hanover Square. And despite certain whispered rumours, Kitty remained convinced Sidney was almost as innocent as a new-born babe.

'When did you return to town, Sid?' Kitty asked with a shake of her head at Barbara, who stroked Sidney's waistcoat-clad chest. Barbara crinkled her straight nose with a laugh, disregarding Kitty's silent scold.

'I arrived this evening, and I rushed to Mount Street, only to have my heart crushed when I learned all the Preece sisters had left for Vauxhall, and Ada-Marie was already abed.'

Sidney's warm manner brought a small smile to Kitty's lips. He was always a darling; throughout their six years of friendship, they'd bolstered each other. 'So you dashed here to cover me as I walked through the gate, even though Philippe intended my arms to be bare tonight?' she asked teasingly as she removed the shawl he'd given her. But when the rich azure Kashmir slid like liquid lapis in her hands, Kitty's smile fell away. 'Why, good heavens, Sid! Wherever did you . . .' She hushed, flushing. What she'd almost asked might hurt his feelings. The shawl must've cost at least five guineas and Sidney barely had two farthings to rub together.

Sidney's amber eyes twinkled. 'Wherever did I find the money for such a present for my muse?' His grin deepened; he was like an adorably naughty boy with a secret up his sleeve. 'That is what I want to tell you, Kit. I have news—'

Barbara interrupted, fluffing the folds of Sidney's cravat. 'You're more handsome than ever without your Geneva collar, but what would your bishop say? Would he call you improper? *Are* you improper, lovey?'

Sidney cleared his throat. 'N-no, Barbara. You know that.'

Kitty glared at her sister. 'What did you want to tell us, Sid?' she asked, wishing to hurry Sidney's communication so he could escape Barbara and return to company more suitable for a respectable gentleman. Surely one of his friends had accompanied him to Vauxhall – the wealthy businessman John Tyrold, or the kind obstetrician Dr Mitchell, or the artist Lord Edward – although Kitty didn't see them anywhere.

'Er, that I . . . I have n-news.' Sidney stumbled on his words, his eyes flitting between frowning Matilda and simpering Barbara. 'I . . . I . . .'

Kitty patted Sidney's hand. The news must relate to his writing. He was trying to gather the courage to speak on a subject that always made him shy, and no doubt Barbara's petting unsettled him. If Kitty didn't have a mission to accomplish, she'd have asked Sidney to take a glass of wine with her at a supper table. But there wasn't time. Kitty must strike before the gentlemen were senseless from drink or poorer from the card tables. Sidney's news could wait, and Barbara needed to stop her flirting so Kitty could return to her hunt.

But dreamy-eyed Barbara was clearly enjoying herself. She petted Sidney's flat abdomen, disturbingly close to the waist of his trousers. 'Kitty told us you were in Suffolk for Lord Holbrook's wedding,' she said. 'The marquess is a divine man, but his marriage is no loss to us, is it, Matilda? I never expected he'd offer an *arrangement*. Holbrook is so handsome, there were plenty who gave it to him for free. Rather like you, Sidney, my love.'

Matilda grunted in disapproval. 'Preece sisters don't *give it* for free, Barbara.'

Sidney rubbed the back of his neck, his cheeks decidedly pink.

Kitty scowled. 'Stop it, Barbara. Sid's blushing.'

Barbara grasped Sidney's chin and moved his head from side to side, sighing. 'He's more handsome for it. Why are impoverished younger sons always more beautiful than their ennobled fathers or elder brothers?' She slipped her other hand behind Sidney's coat and slapped his bottom.

Sidney jumped, and a flame ignited in Kitty's breast. Barbara was as crude as Sir Vincent in her way, and Sidney was a lamb.

'Barbara, take your hands off Sidney immediately. Half his congregation is here, and while a curate speaking with courtesans – presumably attempting to save our souls – might be tolerated, if you paw at him like a starving tigress, you'll subject him to malicious gossip, and get him in trouble with his vicar.'

Barbara jutted out her bottom lip, but she released Sidney with a huff.

Ever polite, Sidney thanked Barbara for his liberation before turning once more to Kitty. 'Might I speak with you privately, Kit—'

'Hush.' Matilda held up a hand. She stood on tiptoes and looked over Kitty's shoulder. 'Kitty, distance yourself from Sidney. The duke is positively glowering.'

Kitty glanced over her shoulder. Gillingham, no longer with his daughter, stood at the edge of The Grove beside a giant man in leather breeches and hobnailed boots. The goliath was *not* a gentleman, but he *was* the duke's acquaintance all the same, for the nobleman whispered into his ear as they both glared at Sidney. The henchman rubbed a stubble-darkened cheek, nodded and spat.

Kitty tensed. As much as she wanted to repel Gillingham, she wouldn't put anything short of murder past the duke, and the man at his side clearly intended no good towards Sidney. Kitty held out the shawl, ensuring Gillingham had a clear view of her returning the gift. 'I mustn't accept such a present, Sid.'

Sidney's broad shoulders slumped. 'Oh.' His voice was flat, and he tugged at the knot of his cravat.

Matilda snatched the shawl and wrapped it around herself. '*I'll* take it. The wind is picking up.' She glanced at the duke. 'Come, Kitty. Bid Sidney adieu and let us away. I don't care for the look on Gillingham's face. He doesn't like your friendship with Sidney, and I wouldn't want him to suppose you intend to break the terms of our arrangement.'

Kitty fully intended to terminate the agreement, but if she riled Gillingham, he'd likely demand an instant commencement to their arrangement, and Matilda mightn't hold off. Kitty needed every available hour to catch another keeper.

'We'll talk later, Sid,' she said in a low voice. 'Visit me and Ada-Marie tomorrow, and you can tell us both your news.' Kitty met his eyes and smiled, thinking of the little girl they were raising together.

Despite having men in her bed since the age of fifteen, Kitty, alone of the Preece sisters, had never conceived. From the beginning of their friendship, Sidney knew how much Kitty longed to be a mother; thus, when an infant with white moons covering the pupils of her eyes was abandoned outside the Mayfair Maternity Hospital, Sidney had brought her to Kitty rather than take her to the orphan asylum. 'My friend Dr Mitchell says the baby is blind,' he'd explained, his golden head bowing over the blanket bundle encircled in his protective arms. The baby's petal-pink cheek and shell-like fist had rested against his chest, and Kitty reckoned no bed in the world would be more secure and safe. 'Perhaps it's presumptuous to bring her to you, but the asylum cannot provide anything more than minimal care, and it's unlikely a family will adopt her.'

Kitty's heart had overflowed the moment she had cradled the baby against her breast, and that love flourished daily. Although Matilda had been reluctant to allow her to keep Ada-Marie, Kitty had insisted. It was the best decision of her life.

'Ada-Marie misses you, Sid,' Kitty said. 'She asked today when you'd return from Suffolk.'

Sidney managed a small smile. 'I brought her some flowers, hoping we could plant them together tomorrow.'

Darling Sidney. He was simply the kindest and gentlest man, and it was heart-wrenching to leave him when he wanted to talk, but Kitty had a mission. For Ada-Marie's sake, as well as her own, she *must* find a kind keeper.

After smiling a wistful goodbye at Sidney, Kitty faced the Grand South Walk. With a determined step, she strode forth. Somewhere at Vauxhall was a man other than Gillingham who could afford London's most desired woman warming his nights, and Kitty would find him.

With plummeting spirits, Sidney watched Kitty's retreating back. She was dazzlingly clad in luminous white silk which revealed her body's every contour. Her curvaceous hips swayed under the gossamer cloth. Kitty clearly wasn't wearing a *stitch* beneath that gauze. No stays, no petticoats, no stockings.

Sidney frowned. If only she'd accepted his shawl.

Men's heads pivoted as she passed, their minds undoubtedly filling with thoughts of fervid tumbles. They were disgusting blighters, every one of them, and

Gillingham the worst of the lot. The steel-haired duke smirked at Kitty, seemingly confident of his conquest. His cold-hearted smugness agonised Sidney, who knew Kitty was desperate to free herself from Gillingham's control.

Sidney kicked the trunk of a tree, eliciting a disapproving grunt from a mob-capped old woman tapping her toes as she observed the dancers.

'Let it out elsewhere, young man.' Her strident voice reminded Sidney of his mother. 'There're ladies about.' She jutted a pointy chin at a gaggle of girls giggling near the Turkish Tent, an open-sided dining area. 'A strapping fellow like you ought to employ his energy courting, not kicking at trees like a petulant child.'

Sidney suppressed his boiling blood, as he'd learned to do growing up with parents scornful of emotions and individualism. He loved one woman only, and she was no tittering schoolroom miss. Even if Kitty never returned his devotion with anything more than friendship, Sidney's heart was entirely hers. Other women held no appeal.

'Thank you for your concern, ma'am.' He tipped his hat before thrusting his fists into his pockets and striding towards the arched entrance to the Grand South Walk.

Dammit, he wanted to tell Kitty his news *tonight*. The last month had distressed her, and Sidney's news would provide relief.

As he skirted the Turkish pavilion, a cursory glance up stilled his progress. Both Gillingham and his unsavoury companion glared at Sidney.

Sidney clenched his jaw as he brushed the brim of his hat, although he'd far rather dispense with pleasantries and remind the damned lascivious old man to pay suit to his long-suffering duchess rather than to Kitty. A firm kick to the ducal arse would do the job nicely.

Gillingham's henchman stood like a statue, arms crossed over a barrel-like chest, but the duke flicked his index finger against his hat brim in acknowledgement. He leaned against a tree, evidently erecting himself as a barrier between Sidney and Kitty.

Sidney seethed. For Kitty's sake, he'd avoid a confrontation with Gillingham in a public spot. He slumped into a chair at an empty table near the edge of the dining pavilion. His news would have to wait.

Among the flurry of serving staff, a waiter materialised. 'Supper, sir?'

Sidney couldn't afford to eat supper at Vauxhall, where butter cost extra with one's bread, and the chefs shaved the overpriced ham to translucency. 'Only a glass of sherry, please.'

He tossed two shillings onto the table, for even sherry was costly. Sidney oughtn't waste money on a drink, but he wanted to sit at the pavilion. If he couldn't be with Kitty, he'd write about her as he waited out the duke's guard.

When the waiter disappeared in the bar's direction, Sidney withdrew a scrap of paper and a pencil from his pocket. He despised the fact that Kitty was forced to sell herself for a living, but she *was* mesmerising tonight, and Sidney felt the familiar spark of inspiration Kitty always aroused.

He shifted in his seat, adjusting his trousers. Kitty aroused more than just inspiration.

The swell of her luscious breasts under the diaphanous silk had energised Sidney's loins, but he dishonoured Kitty if he dwelt on her body without her consent to *eráõ* her (Sidney lamented the shortfall of verbs for love in the English language). He contemplated innocent moments instead. Her delighted squeal. The sparkling reflection of the hanging lights in her blue-green eyes. The maternal love when she spoke Ada-Marie's name.

Sidney called Kitty his muse for *pure* reasons. He'd written his best novels and poetry in their six years of friendship.

Tonight, Kitty was a Greek goddess: her skin as white as marble; her graceful arms supple; her dark tresses arranged in glossy curls interlaced with gold ribbons. And her face . . .

Sidney sighed, propping his elbow on the table and pressing his chin into his palm.

Oval perfection, with long-lashed, almond-shaped eyes, arching dark brows, and generous, oh-so-kissable lips.

Lips that other men kissed.

Never Sidney.

He rubbed his temples, clearing his mind. Kitty deserved his pure thoughts.

The waiter delivered his sherry, and Sidney savoured it, rolling it around on his tongue as new poetry crystallised in his mind. He placed the tip of his pencil to the paper and scratched out the words before they fled his thoughts.

A blinding smack on the back of Sidney's head sent his hat flying onto the table. His stemmed sherry glass tipped, and the expensive drink splashed across the snowy linen. A hand seized the paper he'd been writing on.

Sidney recognised the hand's signet ring – and its split and scarred knuckles. He rose, glaring into the bloodshot eyes of his elder brother Cornelius, the sixth Lord Eden, who'd lived a wild, riotous life since inheriting their father's earldom five years before.

Cornelius's arms and shoulders bulged under his tailcoat, and his waistcoat buttons strained to withstand the girth of his chest. His powerful size was the product of nights spent prize-fighting in London's most depraved taverns.

'Fancy meeting you here, Sid,' Cornelius grunted. 'You remember Hawkins and Murden, I suppose.' He jerked his head towards his two swaying and hiccupping friends, who clasped their arms about one another's shoulders as if for support.

Sidney snatched at the paper in Cornelius's hand, but his brother held it aloft.

'Not so fast, Sidney. As head of the family, I ought to see what you're writing. Best be the Sunday sermon,' he quipped with a leery wink.

'I don't preach the Sunday sermon, as you well know.' Sidney was one of several curates serving the parish of St George's, but the vicar employed him for one specific reason: to solicit money and charity sponsorships from the wealthy widows and matrons sprinkled throughout the exclusive neighbourhood of Mayfair.

Cornelius sucked his teeth. 'True, little brother. You are too busy *praying* with old ladies.'

'Kneeling by their bedsides, anyway,' Hawkins said, and the trio guffawed.

While they howled, Sidney grasped for his poem, but Cornelius was too quick. He ceased laughing, whipped the paper behind his back with one hand, and pummelled his fist straight into Sidney's gut.

Caught unaware, Sidney stumbled and collapsed, struggling to breathe. He knelt on the stone floor of the pavilion with his arms wrapped around his stomach. When they were boys, Cornelius had pounded Sidney until the world darkened, and telling their father had only earned Sidney another clout. 'Fight him back, you fool,' the former Lord Eden had said. 'I won't have a white-livered scarebaby for a son.'

'What is this scribbling?' Cornelius asked as Sidney struggled upright. 'Writing poetry, are you, you fribble?'

'Give it back.' Sidney spat each word through clamped teeth. Cornelius ridiculed Sidney's writings, and these musings were *especially* private.

'I don't think I will, brother.' Cornelius held the paper under a light and snorted. 'Love lines to Kitty Preece, eh, Sid? Damn, perhaps you aren't the fool I took you for.' He leered. 'Does this nonsense get you between those fine legs? I hear she hasn't any hair on her cunny. Is that true?'

A roar ripped from Sidney. Mindless of where he was or who saw him, he barrelled into Cornelius.

His brother buckled, but he didn't fall.

Cornelius shoved Sidney in return. Sidney stumbled before renewing the assault, but this time Cornelius had prepared. Only Sidney's lightning-quick dodge prevented Cornelius's fist from smashing Sidney's nose. Instead, it grazed his chin, but it hurt like the devil all the same.

Spectators circled – some cheering, some gasping – but the fluttering arms of Mr Simpson, the Vauxhall manager, halted Sidney's return strike.

'Gentlemen, gentlemen. No fighting here if you please.'

The crowd booed and hissed.

'There are children present.' Mr Simpson held out his palms, beseeching the brothers and the onlookers alike. 'Vauxhall is a wholesome, safe place.'

Amidst the ensuing jeers, Sidney focused on one thing: his crinkled poem lay on the pavilion's stone floor. Cornelius had dropped it during the brawl.

Sidney dived to retrieve it and crammed the paper into his pocket. He located his hat, plopped it on his head and turned his back to the company. He intended to leave Vauxhall and return to his modest rooms on Half Moon Street, but he glanced once more towards the South Grand Walk arch.

Gone were Gillingham and the henchman. A swift survey of The Grove filled Sidney with renewed purpose. They were nowhere to be seen.

With a grin, Sidney slipped into the crowds, manoeuvring his way towards the walkways. The evening needn't be wasted. He could still find Kitty and relay his news.

If all went as Sidney planned, she needn't ever work as a courtesan again.

Kitty neared the end of Lovers' Lane, venturing into the hedge-flanked Dark Walk which ran along Vauxhall's eastern wall. She glanced over her shoulder. Her sisters were no longer behind her.

She peered down the tree-lined lane she'd traversed. Lamps dangling from overarching branches illuminated clusters of arm-linked lovers, but Matilda's and Barbara's sparkling diamonds and glistening silks were not among them.

Kitty bit her bottom lip, contemplating her best course of action.

The Dark Walk was dangerous. Pickpockets and prostitutes lurked in the shadows. Gentlemen generally risked the former only to benefit from the latter. Kitty had envisioned turning that carnal mindset to her advantage in securing an arrangement: a gentleman seeking pleasure would duck into darkness, only to spy a goddess. He'd fall at Kitty's feet, worshipping her. But without her sisters' protection, the situation *might* escalate in the unlit niches of the notorious path. Not that Kitty couldn't manage a swift kick to a man's bollocks, but she didn't wish to rumple her appearance.

With no alternative but to retrace her steps and pass the courting couples, she set forth.

Her hurried stride hadn't carried her far when a bruising clasp on her upper arm yanked her into the Dark Walk, cutting her armlets into her flesh.

She screamed, twisted and parried, but her assailant hauled her off her feet. A calloused hand reeking of tobacco clamped over her mouth and pressed her back against a massive and malodorous chest.

A thief. No doubt after her gold.

Dammit. Not only would this assault ruin her long ringlets and the rouge, powder and kohl Philippe had painstakingly applied, but Kitty should smell of her jasmine perfume, not unwashed male stench. If she emerged from the Dark Walk muddled and musky, everyone would assume she allowed men to have their way with her in the shadows like a common trollop.

Kitty might be a whore, but she sold her body for a king's ransom – and only between silk sheets. If rumours otherwise circled, it would damage her chances of finding a suitable arrangement.

She writhed, kicking her assailant's legs with her heels and digging her elbow into his colossal trunk, but held in such proximity, she had no leverage to inflict pain.

She'd have to employ her nails.

Kitty reached out, gathered the full strength of her long arm, and aimed for the stale-beer breath grunting in her ear.

A bellow. 'Argh! She scratched me, Yer Grace.'

Kitty ceased struggling. Of course, it was Gillingham's henchman who grasped her.

At least this was a situation Kitty could manage. She despised the duke, but he didn't intend to steal her gold and toss her murdered corpse into the Thames. He likely wanted to paw at her as he had the day he had paid Matilda – the day after he had sent Richard to war. Kitty shuddered; the moment she'd realised Gillingham derived pleasure from hurting his own son was the moment she'd set every fibre of her body against him.

The duke emerged chuckling from the gloom, his teeth flashing in the light of the crescent moon in the now-ebony sky. 'Living up to your name, eh, Kitty-cat?' Kitty bristled; that was her sisters' pet name for her. How dare Gillingham ruin it? 'Sheathe your claws, and Butcher will release you.'

Kitty's reply was unintelligible. 'Tell him to take his foul hand off my mouth' was a jumble of sounds against Butcher's rough palm.

Gillingham flicked his hand, and Kitty was free from the mangy paw.

Kitty inhaled a lungful of crisp air. It was a sweet relief, but she also needed freedom from the henchman rubbing her breasts with his arm as he pinned her.

She strained her neck, staring into the man's beady eyes to demonstrate he hadn't cowed her. 'Your name is *Butcher*?'

He smirked, displaying several gaps among yellowed teeth. 'I'm *called* Butcher, love.'

Kitty cocked an eyebrow. 'An unconventional application of an occupational surname, but presumably apt all the same.'

The henchman's grin vanished. 'Wot?'

Gillingham laughed. 'Butcher, release the delightful Miss Preece.'

Butcher placed Kitty on the ground.

With a huff, she smoothed her skirts, rearranged her curls, and sniffed her shoulder. She still smelled of intoxicating exotic jasmine with hints of musk and citrus, but Kitty's nose twitched at a whiff of sour beer and tobacco. Disgusting.

Kitty lifted her eyes to Gillingham, who observed her with a warmer smile. 'Is there any particular reason your grace's meat carver manhandled me tonight?'

Gillingham chuckled again. 'Leave, Butcher. Your presence is inconvenient now.' As the henchman skulked off, Gillingham offered his arm. 'Stroll with me, Kitty Preece.'

'No, thank you. I wish to return to my sisters.' She had a mission to accomplish. One that didn't include Gillingham. And time was running out . . .

'You may, momentarily.'

A bell chimed, signalling the beginning of the Cascade, Vauxhall's mechanical landscape attraction which operated for fifteen minutes every evening. Others would flock to see the agrarian scene laid out on a stage: cottages and waggons and villagers, all in miniature, with an artificial river made of countless moving metal plates which appeared to spill off the edge of the platform into the cascading 'waterfall' that gave the feature its name. But Kitty had seen it many times, and she wasn't at Vauxhall for pleasure.

'First walk with me while everyone observes the amusement,' the duke said. He tucked Kitty's hand into the crook of his elbow and leaned towards the murky shadows farther into the Dark Walk. 'I want a word.'

Kitty held her ground and tugged against him. 'Let us stroll in the lit lanes, Your Grace.'

The duke's smile vanished. 'Out of the question.' His voice was sharp. 'I'm here with my family, and you haven't a shred of virtue to preserve, my girl. Now stop playing.'

Kitty's nostrils flared, but an argument would accomplish nothing. Better to charm Gillingham into releasing her. Fifteen minutes in the Dark Walk – giving the duke the kisses he likely wanted – while most others watched the Cascade was no significant loss to Kitty's mission. She'd be sweet, pacify him, and then return to work.

Kitty softened, sliding next to the duke and peeping through her lashes. 'As you wish, Your Grace.'

Gillingham's grip slackened, but his expression darkened – his black brows drew together like shadowing hoods over his eyes, and his jaw tightened, his cheeks undulating with the effort. He strode forth, and Kitty accompanied him, seeking to mollify him with her breast pressed into his upper arm.

'What did your grace wish to discuss?' Her voice purred.

'I've heard many tales about the magnificent Kitty Preece, my girl.' Gillingham's step quickened, leading

33

them deeper into the dark. The hedges encroached on the path, forming niches and crevices where shadowy figures lurked. 'Her lily-white body, as smooth as satin. Those famous blue-green eyes which sweep a man to sea like the call of a siren. Her smile, warm enough to melt the burdens of the world from one's shoulders.' Gillingham stopped abruptly, pulling Kitty into a hollow in the boxwoods. Branches scratched her upper arms as the duke loomed, his lips thin. '*Never* have I heard it said that she's an unfaithful slut. Yet that is what I see before me tonight.'

No man spoke to Kitty in such a way. 'How dare you?' She wrenched her hand back, but the duke grabbed her wrists and clamped them in one hand. He pressed so viciously that the rounded bones of her joints ground together, confirming Kitty's intuition that he'd be a cruel keeper. 'Release me,' she said, refusing to allow him to intimidate her. 'I shan't listen to impertinence.'

'You'll listen to me, my girl. I've already paid a thousand pounds for you.' Gillingham pushed Kitty into the clawing boxwoods and leaned against her, his brandied breath and cloying fragrance, like over-ripe pears, assaulting her nose. 'You belong to *me*. Thus, I cannot imagine why you feel the need to practically pull down this . . . this *scrap* posing as a gown and all but expose yourself to every young cub at Vauxhall tonight.'

Of course. *Gillingham* was the reason Lord Britnell had fled Kitty's advances. He was likely why Sir Vincent's friends had resisted her lures. Whenever she'd progressed with a gentleman during the last month, Gillingham's foul spectre emerged *somehow*. His name whispered in her companion's ear, or the duke himself creeping in on a tête-à-tête.

With his free hand, Gillingham seized Kitty's breast and kneaded it through her gown. Kitty writhed, fuming, but the duke was as heavy as a horse and surprisingly strong. Squirming merely provoked him to press harder and tangled Kitty's hair in the shrubbery.

'London knows you're mine,' the duke said, panting hot, moist breath onto her neck. 'But you don't yet understand. I decide how to flaunt my property, Kitty. Not you.'

Kitty pulled her arms. Gillingham's vice-like grip held, so she threw an air of bravado into her speech. He wouldn't cow her. 'Your grace paid a thousand pounds with the understanding I shall be your mistress in August. Until then, you have no claim on me.'

'No, Kitty. You're mistaken. Out of the kindness of my heart, I allowed you two months to recover from your supposed love for that useless whelp of mine.' The duke's voice deepened, and his slimy tongue licked the groove of her collarbone. 'That was a ruse on your part. Not that I blame you for not loving my son – he hasn't an ounce of pluck – but I *do* blame you for using my money to finance your hunt for a new lover.'

Kitty's chest heaved as she struggled against Gillingham. It was unfortunate the duke had perceived her plan, but she was acting well within her rights. 'We had no such arrangement of exclusivity yet. I am my own

35

woman until the end of this month, and if I choose to seek another gentleman, I shall do so with a clear conscience. The agreement you made with Matilda is that she must refund your money before I take any other man to my bed.'

Gillingham released Kitty's wrists, only to clamp his arms around her waist, squeezing her against him. 'You won't find another gentleman. I've ensured that every man in London knows you're my possession, and no one dares cross me.'

'So, you admit that you're interfering.' Kitty ground her teeth, seething. How would she find a man willing to defy Gillingham? 'I would've imagined a duke plays fairly, but, then again, you hurled your own son into battle so you could steal me from him.'

Gillingham gripped the nape of Kitty's neck. 'It is not your place to criticise my actions, woman.' His eyes bored into her. 'By God,' he said, his voice thick and his breath heavy. 'What would a magnificent creature like you want with the pup when you can have the sire? You should thank me. You *will* thank me before I'm through with you.' He rubbed his erection against Kitty's thigh; her gown and his trousers chafed her skin.

Kitty ceased wiggling – it clearly excited the duke, who needed to be doused in cold water.

She must think.

Gillingham's power aroused him more than Kitty; belittling him might shrivel the pointy penis he ground against her.

Kitty rolled her eyes. 'Oh, boasting of your sexual prowess. How original. Yet in my considerable experience, those that boast have the least to show for it. The more swagger, the less swag.' She wiggled her little finger.

Gillingham drew back but didn't release her. 'I assure you, that is not the case. In fact, I've half a mind to show you right now.'

'You refer to the half of your mind controlled by your cock, I imagine.' Kitty laughed merrily, although her heart pounded. If she played this wrong, he might overpower her. 'I suggest you rely on the more rational parts of your brain. You won't support your claim of magnificence by shagging me in a hedge. Your grace might be the most accomplished lover in the world, but all I shall think of is how the boxwoods are scratching my back. They've ripped me half to shreds already while you humped my leg.'

Gillingham's lips twitched. 'One kiss then, my amusing Kitty — but make it magnificent. Show me you're a good girl who will behave herself now.'

'Oh, very well.' Kitty puckered up, relieved. She'd appease him with a kiss and return to her mission, hopeless though it might be. *This* time, as she prowled Vauxhall for someone with the bollocks to defy Gillingham, she wouldn't lose Matilda and Barbara.

As Gillingham crushed her lips with his smothering moist mouth, a hand plunged between Kitty and the duke and ripped Gillingham away.

Kitty stumbled back against the hedge, huffing at her golden-haired saviour. 'Sidney, why have you come?' His presence was the last thing she needed. It would only aggravate matters, for Sidney would incite the duke's anger again, and cost her more time when she'd handled the situation neatly herself.

Neither Sidney nor the duke gave any indication of having heard her. Sidney gripped the nobleman's lapels and bared his teeth. 'Damn you, duke! The lady doesn't want your kisses.'

Gillingham snorted, evidently unruffled. He was shorter and stockier than Sidney, but he remained calm, while Sidney fumed like a wide-eyed madman. 'Whatever are you talking about, Wakefield? There are no *ladies* present.'

Sidney whipped his hand back, gearing for an attack.

Kitty sprang between them. 'Stop this nonsense.' With a frown, she faced Sidney. 'Don't defend my virtue, for I have none. His grace is correct. I'm no lady.'

Sidney dropped his fist. His face softened, and he gazed at her with moonlight reflecting in his eyes. 'Kit, you are a lady. Believe that about yourself.'

'Oh, Sidney,' Kitty said, resisting the urge to embrace him. 'Your devotion is harmless as long as you realise it's all pretence.' She was not *truly* a classical muse.

Gillingham tossed his head back, roaring with laughter. 'My God, this is pathetic. A curate and a courtesan wooing in the moonlight.'

'It's no such thing,' Kitty said. 'Sidney and I are friends, and that is all. I'd never consider the advances of a penniless curate.'

Sidney flinched as if she'd slapped him, which didn't help matters in the least.

'Damned likely story,' Gillingham said, straightening his coat. 'Do you think me a fool?'

Sidney surged forward. 'Do you call the lady a liar, sir?' He spat the words into the duke's face.

Kitty shoved Sidney's arm, wedging herself between the men. '*Stop*, Sidney.' She addressed Gillingham: 'To answer your question, Your Grace, I *didn't* think you a fool, but if you persist in believing nonsense, I shall have no other choice. I acknowledge that Sidney's ridiculous behaviour resembles a stag during the rut, but it's not as it seems. He's an innocent and has confused notions about my honour.' Kitty ignored a strangled exclamation from Sidney. 'I assure you, Sidney and I are merely friends.'

'Well, tonight is the end of that friendship.' Gillingham's hooded eyes darted between Kitty and Sidney. 'I won't have Wakefield mooning about you ever again. He's not as saintly as you suppose.'

'Now, see here, duke—' Sidney began.

Kitty threw up her palm. 'Sidney, *enough!*' No good would come of Sidney infuriating the duke, since Gillingham might send Butcher to settle the score. 'When will you understand, I'm not a maiden in need of your defence?'

Sidney recoiled like a kicked puppy, but he snapped his mouth closed at last.

Kitty confronted Gillingham with her hands on her hips. 'If your grace is to be my keeper, you must accept that I choose my own friends. No gentleman has dared to question my faithfulness, nor has any dictated with whom I may or mayn't socialise—'

'I'm not *any* gentleman.' Gillingham flicked the back of his hand across his shoulder, as if removing a fleck of dust. 'I am the Duke of Gillingham, and you *will* obey me. While you possess my money, I forbid you from spending a moment alone with Wakefield. Don't imagine I shan't know if you break my command.'

Kitty stiffened, but she held her tongue. The situation was escalating, as she'd anticipated. How best to curtail it?

'Don't threaten her, duke,' Sidney said, squaring up to Gillingham again.

That wouldn't help. What possessed Sidney tonight? Over the years, Kitty had witnessed the occasional hot-headed burst from her friend when he perceived injustice or bullying, but he'd never interfered with Kitty's work before. He needed a muzzle.

'I'll do as I damned well please, Wakefield,' the duke said. 'This woman is my possession, bought and paid for. If I find she's been unfaithful to the terms of our agreement, I'll ensure no Preece sister *ever again* receives an offer from any man of consequence.' His eyes shot daggers at Kitty, whose heart hammered as her mind raced, sifting through the few options remaining. 'You and your sisters will feel fortunate to work on your knees in a back alley before I'm done with you, if you're disloyal. The breadth of my influence is immense.' He glared at Sidney. 'And as for you, Wakefield, I know someone who'd enjoy rearranging your handsome face. How then will you charm the widows and whores, my boy?'

Sidney clenched his fists. 'Duke—'

Gillingham held up a finger. 'Silence, boy. Kitty and I understand one another now. Don't we, Kitty?'

Two sets of eyes bore down on Kitty. The evening was no longer a hunt. The fates of Kitty, her sisters, and Sidney, now tottered on the edge of disaster. But the wisp of a plan had formed in Kitty's head, and she schemed, sorting the details. The duke could indeed destroy her and her sisters, and Kitty must *never* allow that. Gillingham was too dangerously cruel to have as her keeper, but he was also too dangerous *not* to have, unless Kitty could ensnare a gentleman with wealth and influence so immense that he'd be immune to the duke's power.

There was one such man in London: John Tyrold, the gentry-born businessman with a Midas touch, who was barely thirty and yet had already turned a considerable fortune into the colossal wealth of a king. He controlled vast portions of every growing industry in Britain. No one – not even duke or prince – underestimated the power of Tyrold's purse.

Kitty exhaled, her tense shoulders relaxing at last. Her attempt to find someone at Vauxhall had been futile, but the idea of Tyrold presented a glimmer of hope.

She'd never seriously considered Tyrold before because the conquest would be both difficult and problematic. He was a notorious miser, far too cheap to keep a mistress, and rarely in company.

But worse, he was Sidney's dearest friend. They kept lodgings in the same townhouse, and an arrangement between Kitty and Tyrold would devastate Sidney. Draped across his friend's lap, Sidney would certainly see Kitty for what she truly was.

Well, Sidney would simply have to cope. In fact, Kitty needed his help.

First, she must appease the duke. Then she'd speak privately with Sidney.

She took Gillingham's hand. 'You and I understand one another, Your Grace. Please forgive my behaviour tonight.'

'I say, Kit!' Sidney exclaimed.

Kitty shook her head, silencing him.

The duke smirked. 'There's a clever girl who knows what's good for her.'

She trailed a fingertip along Gillingham's jaw. 'Sidney and I have been friends for many years, sir. Please allow us ten minutes alone to say goodbye.'

Gillingham blinked; then he roared. 'Not so clever after all,' he said, when he'd recovered his breath. 'Good lord, woman. Certainly, I shan't leave you alone with Wakefield. You want one last shag, of course.'

Sidney tensed, but Kitty purred, pressing herself against the duke. 'Not at all, sir. I've already voiced my opinion on shagging in hedges, and as your grace said earlier, I'm known for my faithfulness. I *swear* to you, my friendship with Sidney is, and has always been, platonic. If you'll allow me to say goodbye, I shall be in The Grove again soon, and the moment I find my sisters, I shall return home and await your claim upon me like a virgin anticipating the altar.'

'No,' Sidney said. '*Don't*, Kit. He's not worthy of you.'

Kitty held up her hand, silencing Sidney, but the damage was done. The duke snarled. Within moments, there would be a fight or a challenge. Or Gillingham would summon Butcher to rip Sidney to shreds. And, in the end, there would be nothing but the same choice: Kitty would have to go with the duke or face his retribution.

Kitty must gamble. When nearly all was lost, there was only one thing to do: increase the stakes. Double or quit.

She whispered her next words in the duke's ear. 'Grant me my request, and as a reward for your generosity, you may claim me next week. Visit me the night of your daughter's marriage.' Gillingham's breath deepened. As Kitty suspected, the revolting old goat liked the idea. 'A sort of wedding night of your own, Your Grace, but with a woman of exceptional skill.' She ran her tongue along the contours of his ear. 'I shall give you magnificent bliss at the end of that tedious day.'

Gillingham growled greedily and pulled her close. As Kitty allowed the duke's thrusting tongue to seek the back of her throat, she perceived Sidney shudder from the corner of her half-closed eyes. It discomfited her to disgust him, but he knew what she was. He should've left her alone if he didn't want to see her at work. After all, she didn't interfere in whatever he did with the widows and matrons he visited. She'd never once queried him about the rumours.

43

To compensate for Sidney's fury, Kitty kissed Gillingham more vigorously. She must convince him of her enthusiasm for her plan to work.

The duke was panting when he finally paused his slobbery exploration. 'My God, woman,' he breathed against her cheek.

'See how agreeable I am when you're kind, sir?' Kitty purred. 'All I ask is ten minutes.'

The duke studied her through lust-filled eyes. 'Very well,' he said at last, his voice husky. 'But if I don't see you in The Grove in ten minutes, I shall send Butcher to fetch you both.'

Kitty forced a smile. 'You have my word.' *You bastard.*

She waited until Gillingham turned a corner. Then, with her eyes narrowed and her jaw clenched, she grabbed Sidney's hand.

'We've barely any time, and I must explain my plan.'

3

Kitty gritted her teeth as she dragged Sidney deep into the hedge and thrust him against Vauxhall's eastern wall. The silver shard of a moon shone in an ink-black sky above Sidney's golden head, hatless after the shuffle with Gillingham.

There was little time and much to communicate, but first, Kitty smacked Sidney's arm. 'You infuriating man.'

Sidney held up his hands, palms out. 'What did *I* do?'

Kitty stomped her foot. 'You interfered, and matters are worse than ever.' Now she must pursue Sidney's friend – and if her plan failed, she'd be Gillingham's mistress in mere days.

'What was I supposed to do with that old lecher assaulting you?'

'You're supposed to leave me alone.' Kitty hit Sidney's broad chest.

She struck it again. And again.

He possessed rigid muscles, exquisitely sculpted under her palms.

Sidney glowered, the moonlight shimmering on his handsome face. 'Stop hitting me, please, Kit.'

Kitty reluctantly dropped her hands. Perhaps because of the heated blood coursing through her veins, Sidney's nearness thrilled her more than it ever had before. Although he'd always been delightfully pleasing to gaze upon, his presence was typically more comforting than exciting.

Tonight, his proximity aroused Kitty.

And infuriated her.

She leaned against Sidney's solid body to avoid scraping the boxwoods which shielded them from prying eyes. A brisk breeze, conveying the harmonies of Handel from the orchestra, prickled her arms like gooseflesh as it whistled through the leaves.

'But I *want* to hit you,' she said. Sidney needed to understand the gravity of the situation. 'I shall be furious until you apologise.'

Sidney crossed his arms and stuck his nose in the air. 'Then smack me as much as you please, Kit, for I shan't apologise for protecting you.'

How maddeningly sanctimonious.

'I haven't time to beat you, with Gillingham's brute on his way.' Kitty inserted her icy hands into the elbow crook of Sidney's crossed arms to benefit from his body heat. 'I have a plan to rid myself of Gillingham, and since you interfered, you must perform your part.'

'You needn't worry about Gillingham anymore,' Sidney said, chin aloft. 'I have a plan of my own.'

Kitty's breath caught. *That* was unexpected.

Sidney stood tall, with his jaw set. Had he always had such a confident gleam in his amber eyes? Had he always smelled so heavenly – like sandalwood and citrus? 'That's what I've sought to say all evening,' he continued, uncrossing his arms, and taking Kitty's cold hands in his strong, warm ones, beautiful and veined. 'I can save you from Gillingham.'

As Sidney caressed Kitty's fingers with his thumbs, her mind muddled; it was difficult to breathe, challenging to think. 'I can't imagine what you're talking about,' she said, her voice a whisper.

A lovely smile spread above the firm cleft chin. 'Because you haven't allowed me to speak, my precious muse.' Sidney's tone teased sweetly. 'A month ago, when Gillingham first troubled you, I sent three of my manuscripts to Duffy and Ward – the publishers, you know – and when I arrived back in town today, there was a response. They want to publish them.'

Kitty yelped, covered her mouth, and then flung her arms around Sidney's neck, squealing. 'That's marvellous, Sidney. Of *course*, a publisher wants your clever books.' She clung tighter. Sidney returned her embrace, enfolding her in his muscular arms. Joy surged as Kitty nestled her face into his broad shoulder. 'I've told you for years that you're the most talented writer in all the world.'

Sidney's low chuckle tickled Kitty's ear. 'I don't know about that. I'm stunned, to tell you the truth.' He released the embrace but retained her hands, beaming as he played with her fingers. Tingling sensations ran up Kitty's arm. The night had turned cold, and she was underdressed. Sidney's hands heated hers, but she missed his sheltering embrace. 'Kitty, I want to support you with the earnings from my books.'

Kitty's heart leapt to her throat, pounding like a drum inside her. 'You wish to keep me?' she asked, breathless. The fringes of Kitty's mind had occasionally indulged dreams of a Sidney rich enough to be her lover.

Bliss. Paradise.

It was impossible, of course – Sidney's books would never earn enough money. But it thrilled Kitty nonetheless to know he wanted her.

Sidney's eyes widened. 'I . . . Oh, God, Kitty. N-not that.'

Kitty's hopes dropped like a stone. Sidney was honourable, of course, but did he truly not desire her at *all*? 'Then what are you talking about?'

Sidney pressed her hands. 'I want you to have independence. To be free to make your own choices for yourself and for Ada-Marie.' He placed her palms against his chest. 'I want to provide that for you with my writing.'

Warmth infused Kitty. Sidney was an angel. The busy nursery in the Preece sisters' house on Mount Street, crammed with boisterous and tumbling children, sometimes overwhelmed Ada-Marie, and Matilda resented every penny Kitty spent on the little girl.

If only the solution was as simple as Sidney thought.

But it wasn't.

Kitty stepped closer, drawing their clasped hands to her breasts. 'You are the kindest man in the world, but your plan is utterly impossible.'

Sidney's smile faded. 'Why?'

Kitty parted her lips to explain that the earnings from Sidney's writings couldn't possibly match what the duke had offered and what Matilda expected, but no words surfaced.

A golden lock had fallen across Sidney's smooth brow. Kitty brushed it back, dragging her fingers through his hair. She delighted in its luxurious thickness as her eyes dropped to Sidney's mouth.

His full lips parted.

His breath quickened, his chest rising and falling rapidly against their entwined hands. Sidney was responding to her intimacy, which exhilarated Kitty. Her own breathing instinctively followed suit. His gorgeousness set fire to her core, fuelling a desire to feel his lips against hers.

Had Kitty *ever* kissed a man simply because she wished to? If she had, she didn't recall – and it assuredly hadn't been like *this* all-encompassing urge.

She rose on her tiptoes and pressed her mouth gently against Sidney's.

Her eyes locked with his.

His lips gasped against hers.

His eyes widened, then hazed with heavy-lidded lust as their amber colour darkened.

He *did* desire her.

Electrifying.

Not so saintly at all.

It made Kitty want him. *Now.*

She grasped her friend like a wild animal, and he responded in kind. Sidney's powerful arm clamped around her waist as Kitty's lips met his again, but this time it wasn't soft. It was Sidney's gorgeous mouth, hot and wet on hers. He tasted of sweet wine and vigorous *man*. Kitty spread her lips, inviting his tongue to explore.

Sidney's hand slid under her gown, drawing down her neckline so her breasts spilled into the night air. Kitty's fingers glided across his silk waistcoat, exploring the ridges of his chest through the smooth fabric.

He grasped one of Kitty's breasts as his broad chest pressed against her. Kitty, burning for him, moaned as they kissed. He responded in kind. It had been ages since Kitty'd had a lover who excited her. How shocking and yet how thrilling that Sidney should be the man to enflame her now. He'd been her handsome, comforting friend for six years without demonstrating corporeal passion, and now he was a raging golden stallion and Kitty's body was responding as if she'd been waiting for this moment.

She shifted her hands and seized his firm arse, pulling Sidney against her, mindless of the hedge scratching her back as she glided her leg up his and tilted her pelvis so that her slick cunt – wet and engorged already through her gown's gossamer gauze – slid over the bulge in his trousers. She rubbed Sidney's girth, his eagerness, his readiness.

When had a man last satiated her?

Far too long . . .

And speaking of long . . . *Sidney* was long. Long, thick and hard.

Kitty broke their kiss and pushed down Sidney's head. 'Suckle me.' She leaned her bare shoulder against the cold stone of Vauxhall's perimeter wall. The throbbing between her legs intensified as Sidney's lips slid without hesitation across her bosom. His breath quickened on her tingling flesh. He murmured love words against her burning skin, poetry against her desire. Whispered her name, moaned something in Greek.

Sidney was heat and hardness.

Kitty moaned as his mouth caught her nipple. His tongue encircled her pert nub, teasing, tantalising. He encased it with his mouth and suckled her, flaming the fire inside Kitty so that she shoved her fist over her mouth to contain the cry that burst from her throat. Oh, God, perhaps Sidney wasn't an innocent lamb at all. He knew *exactly* what he was doing, and his skill was driving Kitty to desperation.

Frantic, needful, she rubbed herself harder against his bulge, pleasure shooting through her body. She was ripe, aching to rip open his trousers and impale herself on his cock. In her present state, a few thrusts against the wall would bring her to climax.

The fuck would be two earth-shattering minutes of unrivalled bliss. Two minutes of defying the duke and Matilda by gratifying her own desire for a change.

Her own woman. Her own choice. Exhilarating pleasure—

It could never be. It would complicate everything. Kitty needed Sidney's friend Tyrold, not Sidney. She needed money, not pleasure, as much as the thought pained her during this exhilarating experience.

'Sid. Sidney, stop.' She choked in the cool night air to clear her fevered mind and placed her palms against Sidney's chest, prepared to push him aside, for lust-fuelled men were sometimes difficult.

But Sidney froze at her command, with his lips at her nipple and his palm grasping her breast.

He stepped away. Two steps back, against the hedge, his hands to his temples, and his trousers bulging. 'Oh, Kitty. Forgive me.'

Kitty forced herself to concentrate. She settled her breasts into her gown and tidied her hair as best she could, ignoring the agony of her unfulfilled desire. 'There's nothing to forgive. *I* kissed *you*.'

Sidney fell to one knee. 'Marry me, my beloved Kitty . . .'

Oh, good lord!

Those words cooled Kitty's fire. This is what came of kissing idealistic young men – Gillingham's son had proposed frequently. She didn't have the time for her practised speech explaining why gentlemen don't marry courtesans.

'Get up, Sidney, and let your ardour cool.'

He rose. 'My proposal is in earnest.'

'No doubt it is, at this moment, but it cannot be.' Kitty smoothed Sidney's coat. 'We haven't another moment to spare, and I must have your help. As kind as your offer to support me is, it will never work, Sidney. I need John Tyrold. And you must help me get him.'

Sidney's forehead creased. '*John*? Why on earth, Kit?'

'He's the only man I can think of powerful enough to defy the duke. I need him to keep me, Sid.'

Sidney drew back, his jaw dropping.

What shimmered in his eyes? Hurt? Betrayal? Kitty's throat clamped.

'You're refusing my proposal to be my wife, and you expect me to help you become my friend's mistress?' Sidney asked, his wounded voice scarcely a whisper.

Kitty swallowed and nodded.

'What . . .' – Sidney blinked – '. . . why then did you kiss me, Kit?'

Kitty licked her lips, still tender from Sidney's passion. His taste lingered on her mouth. 'We haven't time to discuss that now. It has assuredly been ten minutes, and I don't want Butcher to find us still together. Listen, Sid. Arrange a private audience with Tyrold for me. Everything depends upon it – for me, for my sisters, and for Ada-Marie.'

'Absolutely not.' Sidney's eyes blazed. 'I shall pay for you now, Kitty. You needn't do this.'

Kitty sighed. Sidney didn't understand the stakes. The sisters' home, their staff, the ever-expanding throng of offspring . . . and Kitty was the biggest earner. 'Sidney, how much money do you suppose you need to pay for me?'

Sidney lifted his chin, and moonlight again illuminated his confidence. 'Whatever it is, I shall earn it with my writing.'

'My friend, I admire your optimism, but you cannot.' Kitty took his hand in hers, pushing aside the recollection of how his fingers had elicited such decadent desire mere moments earlier. 'Not in time, at least. My new keeper must reimburse Gillingham one thousand pounds within the week.'

Sidney blanched. 'One *thousand* pounds?'

Kitty nodded. 'And one hundred a month after that to Matilda.'

She paused to let him absorb the gravity. Sidney likely made less than a hundred per annum, and even with added income from his writing, there would be no guarantee of approaching anything like those sums.

'Do you understand now, Sid?' Kitty continued, squeezing his hand. 'I must earn a fortune. Our expenses are beyond comprehension – the children, the house, the servants, the incessant entertaining, with gentlemen expecting the best of everything – and Matilda and Barbara cannot earn like they once did. I *must* do my part, and for that I need either Gillingham or Tyrold.' Her heart melted at Sidney's heartbroken expression. She put her palm to his cheek. 'And I don't want Gillingham.'

'So, you want to screw my friend for his money?' Sidney asked, his voice breaking.

The words cut, despite their truth.

'You know what I am, Sidney,' she said as she stroked his cheek. 'I'm sorry it must be this way. Your offer of unconditional financial support is the most considerate thing any man has ever done for me, but unless you can refund all of Gillingham's money and pay Matilda one hundred every month without fail, it is out of the question. If you truly want to help me stay out of Gillingham's clutches, get me an audience with Tyrold tomorrow.'

Sidney drew in a ragged breath and turned aside, hiding his face in shadow.

He needed reassurance.

Kitty placed a chaste kiss against his broadcloth sleeve. 'You asked why I kissed you earlier, and I shall answer now. I kissed you because I'm proud of you, my dearest, loveliest Sidney. *I* know your writing is marvellous. Now the world will know.' Kitty pressed his hand. 'I must go.'

She stepped away.

Sidney pulled her back. 'Kitty, wait.' His voice was confident again – his heartbroken expression vanquished, his chest thrust forward, his shoulders broad. He was a golden-haired Sir Galahad, wishing to rescue her.

A mad thought erupted in Kitty's mind. What if Sidney put his foot down and declared that she wasn't to be a courtesan anymore? If he insisted on taking her and Ada-Marie away from this life of endless performance and cradling them both in his secure embrace forever more?

Of course, Kitty could never agree, *but* . . .

Her heart pounded. 'Yes, Sid?' she asked, telling herself she enquired out of curiosity alone. She *didn't* hope. She couldn't.

Sidney smiled. 'Tyrold *is* the answer. I shall arrange it all.'

Kitty's innards coiled tighter than a spring, and for a moment, she couldn't breathe. Then she shook her head, ridding her mind of its nonsense, returning herself to reality. Sidney had merely reconciled himself to the facts. Naturally he had; he was idealistic and romantic, yes, but he was a sensible man. Of course, he wouldn't take her away from her life as a courtesan. He knew what she was. His concurrence was precisely what she needed, for it would help her snag the raven-haired, green-eyed eccentric John Tyrold, a prize which courtesans had pursued unsuccessfully for years.

What a triumph for Kitty Preece to draw Tyrold's money into her bed – but a fitting triumph. After all, everyone said she was the most desirable courtesan in London.

Yet her throat ached too much to thank Sidney. Instead, she blew him a kiss, turned on her heels, and ran down the Dark Walk.

Her feet fell heavy on the path.

Everything had changed the moment Kitty's lips touched Sidney's in the moonlight. Not only had desire struck like lightning, but she'd also confronted a years-long attraction which was far more powerful than she'd thought.

She lusted after Sidney. Kitty had never experienced such fierce desire. Orgasms weren't easy to achieve, although she tried, both to please her keepers and to make her work more palatable. But when she'd stroked herself against the bulge in Sidney's trousers as he'd suckled her breast, Kitty had neared ecstasy.

Or were her feelings more than lust?

Kitty's heart raced faster than her running feet as she recalled how Sidney caressing her hands had warmed her scantily clad body, inside and out. That hadn't been lust, but it wasn't mere friendship either.

Kitty halted and faltered, throwing her hand against the hedge to steady herself.

Did she *love* Sidney Wakefield?

No. No. No.

Utter ridiculousness.

She couldn't love her friend. Courtesans weren't allowed to love.

'Kit,' Sidney's voice called from the darkness behind. 'What's the matter?'

She forced a light laugh and waved her hand to reassure him. 'Nothing, Sid. Goodnight.' Without looking back, she picked up her skirts and ran forward with renewed vigour.

Kitty must control herself. If she entertained lustful or loving thoughts about Sidney, she'd never survive being his friend's mistress – and she must survive that, for a woman like her had no other choice.

She turned the corner out of the Dark Walk and into the lights of Lovers' Lane, towards Gillingham's watchful eye.

4

With a spring in his step, Sidney trailed Kitty as she hastened towards Lovers' Lane after her slight falter.

She'd lifted her gown, exposing magnificent shapely calves as she scurried. Ardent desire surged within Sidney, but he pushed aside his lust. His was a noble love, and after years of inaction, the decisive moment had arrived.

Tyrold *was* the answer. But not in the way Kitty thought. John's sharp business mind could negotiate an advance for Sidney from Messrs Duffy and Ward, Publishers. John would grumble about doing Sidney a favour – it was difficult to convince him to do anything that didn't plump his pockets – but John possessed a heart, deep inside. His misty eyes at Nicky's wedding the day before had exposed it.

Once Sidney enlisted John's support in obtaining the money to reimburse the duke and pay Matilda's monthly sum, Kitty would be free to make her own choices.

Sidney's spirits soared. For the first time, he dared to dream she'd choose him, because Kitty had feelings for a penniless curate, after all. Although she didn't express it in words, love had blazed like fire between them when they'd melted into the heat of passion.

She'd wanted him. She'd moaned at his touch.

More than that, Kitty was *proud* of him.

Sidney's face split into a grin so broad his cheeks ached. If he attained this advance payment – no, *when* he attained it – she'd be prouder yet. The next time he proposed, she'd realise the depth of his love.

Kitty disappeared around the corner of the hedge, into the glow emanating from Lovers' Lane, and Sidney jogged to catch up. Once Sidney ensured her safe return to her sisters, he'd go home and speak with Tyrold tonight.

Nothing would stop him now.

Gillingham's henchman emerged from the shadows, rooted a hobnailed boot on either side of the path, and crossed his log-like arms over his chest.

Sidney craned his neck to see where Kitty went, but the giant filled his view.

Dammit.

He'd had enough of swaggering bullies for one evening. Cornelius, Gillingham and now this brute.

'Good evening,' he said, with narrowed eyes. 'Mr Butcher, I believe.'

A chuckle – or perhaps a growl – rumbled from the beast. '*The* Butcher, more properly.'

'Indeed? How charming.' Swap Butcher's rough apparel for Cornelius's fashionable but too-small togs, and it might be Sidney's brother before him. 'Sadly, I haven't time for conversation. If you'd be so good as to step aside—'

Butcher spat on the ground between them. 'I don't think so.'

Sidney clenched his jaw. 'I merely wish to ensure the young lady's safety.' He forced a quick smirk. 'On the odd occasion, one finds surprisingly unsavoury characters at Vauxhall, and Gillingham wouldn't wish Miss Preece to come to any harm.'

Butcher sneered. 'Miss Preece is no longer your concern. Her sisters are with her now.'

'Ah, excellent. In that case, I'll bid you goodnight.' Sidney lifted his hand to tip his hat before recalling he'd lost it. He shoved his fists in his pockets instead.

Butcher didn't budge.

'If you'll move aside,' Sidney said, 'I'll be on my way.'

'Not this way, you ain't.' Butcher jutted his chin. 'Back the way you came, and I'm coming along to keep you from that pretty canary bird.' He leaned forward with a gap-toothed leer. 'His grace thinks you want her for yourself. I can't say as I blame you, but the trouble is, she belongs to the duke. Bought and paid for.'

Sidney raised his brows. 'I'm afraid I don't agree, Mr Butcher.'

'That's why his grace don't trust you. And that's why I'm coming everywhere with you until that highflyer is dancing the blanket hornpipe with his grace.' Apparently to illustrate his point, he pumped one of his sausage-sized fingers through two circled fingers of his other hand. 'That's the jig what goes like this, parson.'

Bitter bile burned the back of Sidney's mouth. Damn Gillingham, who'd pawed at Kitty's body and thrust his forked tongue down her throat earlier.

But Sidney wouldn't reveal his feelings to Butcher. He shrugged, as if untroubled, and carelessly picked a leaf off the boxwood. 'It's quite unnecessary for you to accompany me anywhere, Mr Butcher,' he said, letting the leaf flutter to the ground. 'I assure you I lead a dull life, and besides which, I've not invited you.'

'I goes where I wants.' Butcher poked Sidney's chest. 'And where I wants is number twenty-nine Half Moon Street, residence of the *Honourable* Reverend Sidney Wakefield. Where you will go while I follows, and where that pretty puss ain't *coming*, if you takes my meaning.' He groped his groin and laughed at his ribald pun. 'Now turn around.'

Sidney's hackles rose. Butcher filled the width of the path, his shoulders brushing the hedge on either side. Sidney was no match for the bruiser's bulk; thus, he daren't attempt to squeeze past. Sidney had no choice but to comply, but he wouldn't allow his compliance to look like submission.

When charm didn't suffice, speed was Sidney's best weapon.

'We shall see if you keep up,' Sidney said, before pivoting on his heel and sprinting into the shadows.

Butcher grunted. His heavy boots thudded on the hard-packed dirt behind Sidney.

Kitty's words purred in Sidney's memories as he'd dashed down the path between the dark hedges.

Sid, you're the kindest man in the world.

Suckle me.

Moans. Pleasure.

And best of all, *I'm proud of you* – words no one had said to Sidney before.

Rapture hastened Sidney's feet. His beloved Kitty had feelings for him.

With a fresh burst of speed, he rounded the corner of the Dark Walk and darted past strolling groups on the illuminated, tree-lined Grand Walk as he bolted towards the Water Gate, with Butcher's leaded footfalls pounding closer than Sidney would like.

Now to win Kitty's heart . . .

Preferably without Butcher breathing down his neck.

Butcher proved to be a fleet-footed mountain and remained behind Sidney all the way to the riverside. Sidney threw himself into a wherry already packed with the usual maximum of six passengers, hoping there'd be no room for the giant, but Butcher jumped in after him, his weight shaking the boat. The other passengers gasped and grumbled, while the boatsmen dug their oars into the shore to stabilise it.

Butcher positioned himself beside Sidney, his breath laboured. 'What're you running for? I knows where you live.'

The boat slipped into the current of the Thames, gliding across water which mirrored the crescent-moon sky.

Sidney breathed deeply, the cool, misty air filling his lungs, and relied on his charm again. 'I ran because it's wonderful to be alive. Wouldn't you agree, Mr Butcher?'

Butcher sneered. 'You keep thinking about how much you enjoy life, parson. The alternative sometimes happens to those what take what ain't theirs.'

'Good heavens.' Sidney lifted his chin, employing an aristocratic hauteur he knew as well as any earl's son, but rarely used. Perhaps Butcher would respond to *that* sort of intimidation. 'Don't threaten *my* life unless you wish to dance at the end of a rope.'

Butcher's laugh thundered. 'We're just having a friendly chat.'

Clearly, Sidney's intimidation worked no better than his charm.

Sidney turned his shoulder to the henchman as the wherry slid over the river alongside the looming iron skeleton of the under-construction Regent Bridge. The movement pressed him closer to a handsome middle-aged woman who misjudged his intentions. She smiled encouragingly, inviting Sidney to view her ample bosom by trailing her fan along the lace edge of her gown. With her other hand, she reached under his coat-tails and stroked his bottom.

'Forgive my nearness, madam,' Sidney said, pointedly, hoping she'd cease the unwanted touching. 'My large neighbour presses me too close to you, I'm afraid. If I could, I'd give you more room.'

She spread and fluttered her fan, shielding their faces from the other passengers. 'I don't mind.' Her eyes trailed to his lips. 'What's your name, sir?'

Sidney shifted, attempting to escape her fingers, but he was wedged against Butcher's solid bulk. 'The *Reverend* Wakefield at your service, madam.' Would she perceive the emphasis and receive his implied message?

'Oh, the handsome curate of St George's. I'm not of your parish, but one hears such tales of you.' Her fingers slid under Sidney's waistcoat along the top of his trousers. Either his message had not been understood or she was wilfully ignoring it. 'My husband is away from town tonight.'

Sidney pressed his lips together. 'I am a man of the cloth, madam.'

She laughed. 'That may be, but I heard you hop from bed to bed the moment husbands turn their backs.'

Sidney set his jaw, fuming. Why could he never escape these rumours? 'You mustn't believe gossip.'

She snorted. 'There's usually truth to it.' But, at last, her hand dropped from his bottom. 'I suppose you think you're too grand for me. A shame, but it's your loss,' she said, curtly, before turning her own shoulder.

Butcher chuckled.

Good God, what a miserable boat ride.

Thankfully, the glow of Westminster and Mayfair grew close. A queue of carriage lanterns snaked a course to the shore to pick up ferry passengers when they landed.

The moment Sidney alit from the wherry, he sprinted again. He wove between the hackneys towards Mayfair's halo of light, as the invigorating exercise pumped his blood through his veins. He cared not if Butcher followed. Let him. It would take more than a Cornelius facsimile to stop Sidney in his mission to help Kitty.

Sidney pushed through a wrought-iron gate, which creaked upon its hinges, and ducked into Green Park, cutting across the shadowy meadows towards Piccadilly. The loamy scent of cows tickled his nose as he dashed past the dairy farm where he and Kitty took Ada-Marie once a week to drink frothy fresh milk from a tin cup.

Ada-Marie loved the cows. She giggled when they lowed as she threaded her fingers in the tuft of hair on the tops of their heads.

Sidney stopped in his tracks.

That was it!

If Kitty agreed to marry him, he'd take Kitty and Ada-Marie to the country, where they could start afresh in a cottage. Sidney would write to support their simple life. Gawks and ogling needn't trouble Kitty. Ada-Marie could have the peace she needed, and she'd thrive in the wholesome country air. Theirs would be a life of agrarian perfection, tapping into the essence of England of old. With Kitty – his love, his muse – at his side, Sidney would awaken refreshed and inspired every morning.

Thundering footsteps behind Sidney shattered his reverie. 'I see you, parson,' Butcher's ragged voice called from the dark.

Sidney had a quest to accomplish. He could dream later.

No, he wouldn't *have* to dream later, because if Kitty loved him, he would make this his reality.

With more vigour than ever, he sprinted towards the rumbling carriage wheels of Piccadilly. After passing through another wrought-iron gate, he stood amidst the brilliant chaos of a Mayfair summer night.

Street lamps illuminated the hackneys, crested carriages and sedan chairs weaving along the wide thoroughfare. Buff-trousered, tail-coated gentlemen crisscrossed Piccadilly on foot, carefree laughter on their lips. Peddlers hawked posies and fruit from the white stone pavement. Red-capped prostitutes hovered in shadow, ready to slip into Green Park at the flash of a coin.

Sidney dodged traffic, aiming for the corner of Piccadilly and Half Moon Street, where noise and laughter spilled from the open ground-floor windows of a public house. Above the door swung the sign of a half-moon, for the public had given Half Moon Street its name nearly a century earlier. Scents of roast meat, tobacco and ale permeated the air. Sidney's stomach rumbled; he hadn't eaten since breakfast at Holbrook's estate in Suffolk.

It was a lifetime ago. When he awoke at Alton Park that morning, he hadn't realised that this day would change everything.

Sidney trotted up the stoop to procure meat pies for himself and Tyrold. The food would appease his friend, and Sidney wouldn't go to bed hungry. The Smith family retired to their quarters early.

As Sidney swung open the heavy oak door, Butcher grabbed his elbow from behind. 'What're you doing, parson?'

Sidney yanked his arm back. '*Supper*. And I'll thank you not to touch me again, Butcher. Don't imagine I don't know how to deal with the likes of you.'

Butcher *was* Cornelius all over again.

With the henchman lumbering beside him, Sidney strolled into the smoke-laced tavern, muggy from dozens of ale-swigging bodies, and ordered three pies from a ruddy-cheeked barmaid, who wrapped the steaming pasties in newspaper.

Sidney shoved one in Butcher's hands. 'Something to keep you warm, for I'm afraid I shan't invite you in.'

Butcher grunted.

Sidney shouldered his way through the sweaty patrons and into the night, allowing the door to swing back on Butcher's face. He turned north, striding up Half Moon Street.

Marmalade sat on the stoop of number twenty-nine, licking his paw and washing his face. As Sidney fumbled for his key under the glow of a street light, the tabby miaowed.

Sidney grinned. 'You smell the pies, do you, Marmalade? Well, come in.'

He opened the door to admit himself and his cat before slamming it and twisting the key in the lock.

Then Sidney leaned against the wall in the entrance vestibule – dark but for the dim light which filtered through the windows – and exhaled, his shoulders shedding tension. Thankfully, he'd escaped more trouble from Butcher. Sidney peered through a wavy glass pane. The henchman stood aimlessly on the cobbled

67

street, shifting his hefty weight from one hobnailed boot to the other.

Strains of Beethoven's latest, Allegretto in A major, thrummed down the narrow staircase. Sidney smiled. Tyrold, whose private rooms were on the first floor, was awake and at his pianoforte, which meant he was likely in an amiable rather than ruthless mood.

Marmalade mewed from the entrance to the shared dining room, wanting his dinner.

'Very well, I'm at your command, *monsieur le chat*.'

Sidney shed his tailcoat and tossed it on a chair, over one belonging to Lord Edward. Sidney's coat slumped to the floor and pooled next to a coat of Tyrold's as Sidney crossed the vestibule.

The dining table and surrounding chairs were shadows, but after six years of lodging in Tyrold's house, Sidney knew their placement well. He riffled in the sideboard and withdrew three plates as his eyes adjusted to the gloom.

Sidney arranged the pies on two plates. He cut a section from one and diced the gravy-soaked meat and flaky pastry onto the third plate for Marmalade.

'Not that you haven't already had your fill of mice, I've no doubt,' Sidney said as the cat rubbed his trouser leg. 'Unless you've been with the lady cats, of course.'

Marmalade's eyes glimmered, picking up the faint street light from the vestibule. '*Miaow*.'

'No kissing and telling, eh? I admire your principles. That is the way of a gentleman, but you must know I shan't tell *you* anything either.'

Sidney grinned as he remembered the moments in the hedge. No longer was Kitty's body a marble statue. He'd held her soft and willing; the memory seared upon his mind.

Not only his mind.

Sidney's cock tingled.

There was no time for that now. First, he must procure a fortune and earn Kitty's love if he didn't have it already.

Then he'd ask her to marry him.

And only *then*, if she accepted, would he make love to her. To his wife.

Sidney set the bowl on the floor.

He scratched Marmalade between the ears as the cat lapped at his meal. 'I shall see you later. Warm the bed for me.'

Sidney grabbed the pies and shot up the stairs two at a time. He kicked at the base of Tyrold's door until the music ceased.

The door swung open, revealing a scowling Tyrold attired in his waistcoat and shirtsleeves, his long hair loosened from its customary queue and falling about his shoulders. His shaggy wolfhound Jolly wagged his tail beside him. 'What the dev—? Oh, it's you, Sid.' Tyrold's green eyes brightened as they dropped to the plates in Sidney's hands. 'Did you bring me food?'

Sidney grinned. 'Yes. Aren't I a pleasant fellow?'

Tyrold frowned. 'Depends. Who gets the half-gnawed one?'

'I'll eat it. I shared my dinner with Marmalade.'

Tyrold motioned with his head for Sidney to enter. 'To what do I owe the dubious honour of this late-night visit?' he asked once they'd settled into leather armchairs in Tyrold's book-lined study.

Sidney leaned forward with his hands clasped together. 'I've come to ask an absolutely enormous favour.'

The next morning, Sidney stepped out the door of Messrs Duffy and Ward, Publishers, and onto alley-like Paternoster Row as the bells of St Paul's tolled the ten o'clock hour. As he breathed in the summer morning with Tyrold at his side, the bells of St Sepulchre-without-Newgate and St Bride's joined the chorus.

Sidney embraced his friend. 'You are, without doubt, the best chap ever to live.'

Tyrold wriggled out of Sidney's hug. 'Good God, man. Save that for Kitty.'

Sidney beamed, his chest expanding. 'Come with me to tell her the news now, Johnny.'

Tyrold stomped down the three steps to the street, and Sidney followed. Together, they headed west to return to Mayfair, pressing through the pedestrians and horses jammed into the narrow laneway. Paternoster Row, with its towering bow-windowed publishing houses on each side, was no broader than the arms-width of three men, and it was heavy with the scent of paper and ink.

Behind them, Butcher lumbered. Apparently, he'd remained outside Sidney's lodgings all night, and he'd followed them the entire way along the Strand and Fleet Street, and up Ludgate Hill into the shadow of

St Paul's towering dome when they'd travelled into the city earlier.

'Do you know what your problem is, Sidney?' Tyrold shoved his hands in his pockets and wore a thundering cloud upon his brow.

'I have no problems, dear friend.' Even Butcher wouldn't plague Sidney much longer. 'The world is magnificent.'

Tyrold scoffed. 'Good lord. Put a few pounds in your pocket and you think the world's thine oyster.'

'Which I shall with love open,' Sidney added, intentionally misquoting the line.

Tyrold rolled his eyes. 'A true oyster one must open with a knife, Sid. As for love's effect on symbolic oysters, well, I wouldn't know. But, as a rule, I suspect it's money that opens those as well, whether on the wrong side of the sheets or the right.'

Sidney, accustomed to Tyrold's jaded attitude, ignored the cynicism. 'Bah! – and, anyway, how can you call it "a few pounds"? *Five hundred*, John. It may seem nothing to you, with your millions, but it's enough for Kitty and me to start a life.' He patted the pocket in which he carried the banknotes.

Sidney hadn't fully grasped the negotiations at the publishing house. A red-faced Duffy and a dour Ward had seethed through Tyrold's incessant demands for half an hour as Tyrold leaned back in his chair with his feet propped on their desk and a pipe between his teeth. But when John threatened to take Sidney's manuscripts elsewhere, Sidney objected profusely, and the events took a turn. Somehow, Duffy and Ward had the upper hand until Tyrold, with a clenched jaw, offered to stand as a guarantee against any loss Sidney's books incurred. They'd ended with only five hundred from the well-pleased publishers. The additional thousand to reimburse the duke would come from Tyrold, with Duffy and Ward repaying John after publication.

It made little sense to Sidney, but he had the money Kitty needed and that was all that mattered.

'The problem with you, Sid,' Tyrold continued, as they passed the stationers' guild, 'is you believe all the nonsense your brother and father fed to you years ago about your writing being rubbish. Thus, you don't believe your books are *worth* fifteen hundred. You don't fight for yourself.'

'That's hardly fair. What do you call our errand this morning?'

'I call it me fighting *for* you.'

Sidney threw his arm around Tyrold's shoulder. 'Why shouldn't I employ the best businessman in the kingdom to negotiate on my behalf?'

Tyrold raised his eyebrows. 'Employing me, are you? Perhaps we should discuss my rates. I thought I was acting out of the goodness of my heart. A bit of charity for my romantic friend.'

They turned into the carriage and pedestrian traffic of Ludgate Street. 'True, it is! I'm afraid I cannot afford your rates, Johnny.'

'Precisely. And yet here you are, demanding I move mountains so you may purchase yourself a wife. A handsome man like you, second son to an earl, might've counted on, oh, a bride with a dowry of at least ten thousand – fifteen if she were past thirty or plain – rather than paying greedy Abbess Matilda an annuity for the rest of your life. It's a damned wasted opportunity, Sid. Are you certain you don't wish to think the better of it?'

Sidney laughed. 'Come now. You aren't so parsimonious that you haven't a heart. Even you must admit love is worth more than money.'

Tyrold pulled a face. 'Worth more than money? Nonsense. Not unless you can eat love.'

'I don't believe for a moment that's your true sentiment.' Sidney sobered. 'And, John, don't call Matilda an abbess. She's *not* a brothel owner.'

Tyrold snorted as he ploughed past a waggon laden with citrus fruits. 'There we must disagree yet again. That's *exactly* what she is – and selling her own sisters, no less.'

Sidney recoiled. 'Damned disgusting way to think of it. Matilda never had a choice, for they were very poor indeed when they were orphaned.'

'I don't know the particulars, so I shan't attempt to dispute that Matilda entered the profession out of absolute necessity. But I've been in this world a few years longer than you, and I assure you, the elder two were running a damned successful business already when Matilda hand-picked London's wealthiest men for a dinner party and ordered a fifteen-year-old Kitty to pour us wine wearing nothing but flowers in her hair.'

Tyrold shook his head, with his lip curled in disgust. 'She was a nude virgin sacrifice for the highest bidder; as frightened as a mouse but trying her damnedest to put on a brave face. I thought I'd retch my meal, and so I told Matilda, but I was apparently alone in my sentiments. I left as the other gentlemen clawed their offers forth like a pack of wolves.'

'Good lord, John!' Sidney exclaimed, shocked. 'Why have you never told me this story before?'

John threw his hands up. 'What purpose would it have achieved? Personally, I wish I could forget it. But now that I have told you, do you still defend Matilda?'

Sidney rubbed his chin as they walked through throngs of dark-suited barristers milling under the Temple Bar. While it was nauseating to imagine all those lustful eyes on a frightened fifteen-year-old Kitty, there must be more to the story than his friend realised. Kitty adored Matilda. 'It's not fair to judge Matilda when you and I cannot possibly know her struggles in life.'

'Fair or not, I don't like Matilda, and that dinner party was the first and last time I graced the Preece sisters' establishment with my presence.' Tyrold's eyes cut to Sidney. 'And not, I assure you, without considerable effort on my part to resist, for I like to fuck as well as the next man, and Matilda would love to sink her jewel-laden claws into my money. In that regard, at least, she's no different from every unmarried woman in Mayfair.'

'Well, you've stated your opinion, and I've stated mine,' Sidney replied, hoping to draw the fruitless discussion to an end.

A fashionable young couple meandered arm-linked directly towards them, each so lost in the other's eyes, they failed to notice anyone else. Sidney and John stepped to the building side of the pavement, pressing against the stone façade of a public house.

Sidney's spirits soared as the doe-eyed lovers passed. Perhaps soon he and Kitty would walk together in such a way.

He lifted his chin and smiled at the cloud-dotted sky which stretched like a blue ribbon above the Strand.

'What a glorious world this is, John,' he said, waving a hand at the bustle before them. From upper storey windows of the terraced stone buildings lining the street, chambermaids poked out white-capped heads to water geraniums and marigolds in jardinières. On the ground floors, the panes of the shop windows sparkled with reflected sunlight. Proprietors hovered at the doors under jewel-coloured signs.

'Look down, my poetic friend,' Tyrold said with a wave of his own hand. Filth-covered children dodged between horses and carriages, sweeping manure from the cobblestones, and extending bony hands to beg a halfpenny from passers-by. 'What a damnable world this is.'

'No, not damnable while there's love,' Sidney said, although his heart ached at the sight of the poor mites.

Tyrold shook his head. 'Love again. It's your answer to everything, I suppose. But while we're on this subject, Sidney, I feel compelled to remind you a wife will cost more than you reckon. Quite apart from this suffocating sum you propose paying Matilda annually, where will you get the money to support your family if you give up the curacy and move to the country?'

'Three books a year at five hundred each, John. Twelve hundred to Matilda, and three hundred for me, Kit and Ada-Marie.'

'Three hundred a year!' Tyrold scoffed.

'Many families do it on far less.'

'But your wife won't be accustomed to frugal living. And how can you be so certain you'll produce three books annually?'

Sidney smiled, envisioning the cottage where he'd live with his wife. 'With Kitty by my side, I can accomplish anything.'

Tyrold snorted. 'Foolish naivety, Sid. This idealistic love will vanish the moment creditors bang on your door.'

And then Sidney snapped, whipping his head to face Tyrold with a violent scowl, for Tyrold's words tapped into his deepest fear: that under his noble intentions, Sidney was a worthless dreamer who would never amount to anything, as his parents had told him countless times over the years. 'Why should I listen to ruthless John Tyrold? I'd rather die poor and beloved than rich and alone, as y—'

Tyrold's lips parted.

Sidney stilled his tongue, calming at once. He oughtn't to lash out at his friend.

'Is that my destiny?' Tyrold asked quietly, as the corners of his mouth curved down. 'To die alone?'

Sidney grasped his friend in a tight embrace. 'Forgive me, John. I should never have spoken so – I owe you everything. But until you've experienced a love such as this, you cannot know the power it wields. I *can* and I *shall* provide for Kit and Ada-Marie.' After all, his love for Kitty had inspired him to write his best works and, at last, to sell the manuscripts. With Kitty at his side, he *wasn't* a worthless dreamer. 'I've never been more confident of anything in my life.'

Tyrold cleared his throat, patted Sidney's back, and disengaged from the embrace. 'I daresay you're correct. I know nothing of love. Let us think no more of it.' He offered his hand, and Sidney shook it. 'Now, is my role in this matter complete?'

'One more favour.' Sidney nodded his head towards Butcher. 'You really must accompany me to tell Kitty the news. That monster will never allow me alone near her.'

5

The morning after Vauxhall, Kitty lay upon silky sheets with her eyes closed, curled like a shell around four-year-old Ada-Marie's small body. Their fingers entwined as they caressed the satin blanket covering them.

They were *feeling* and *listening*, their breath rising and falling together as the late morning sun's warmth poured over the bed.

Kitty relished the moment, for there were only a few days left before a man's demands must again be the centre of her life. She buried her nose in Ada-Marie's feather-soft tresses. The child smelled of milk and honey, of fresh cotton and health. 'I love you, poppet.'

Ada-Marie sighed, a whispered exhalation. 'I love you, Kitty.'

Kitty had never asked Ada-Marie to call her mama. Matilda had forbidden it.

'She must call you Kitty,' Matilda had said three years earlier, when toddler Ada-Marie spoke her first words. 'I won't have men thinking you gave birth to that . . . that child. Your barrenness is desirable, for nothing is better than a mistress who doesn't produce the burden of bastards.' Matilda had sighed, lines furrowing her brow as she'd glanced over the boisterous Preece nursery. Most of the children received money from their fathers, but all faced a difficult path in life, for the stain of illegitimacy endured. 'Furthermore,' Matilda had continued after a toss of her dark curls, 'we must ensure there are no rumours that the Preece sisters bear imperfect children. If you insist on keeping her, *I* insist you're clear she's an orphan child, unrelated to any of us, whom you pitied. You may call her your ward.'

It was the hardest of all Matilda's dictates over the years, but Kitty acquiesced, for Matilda wasn't wrong. It was troublesome enough for men to provide for their by-blow without the added strain of a disability, and Kitty commanded the highest prices of any courtesan in London largely because of her infertility.

But there was no need for such grim thoughts in this moment of perfection.

Kitty inhaled. Breath expanded her chest, and Ada-Marie matched her.

They exhaled, and their bodies melted into the feather mattress.

Kitty's room was on the second floor, but the street noises blew through the open windows. Hooves clomped on the stone-paved streets. Carriage wheels churned. A ballad girl sang, no doubt standing outside Grosvenor House's garden wall, as usual. Vendors called: 'Oranges, lemons!' 'Quills! Pens sharpened!' 'Lace and ribbons!' 'Hot pigeon pies!'

When Kitty lay with Ada-Marie, she imagined the world as Ada-Marie experienced it, without sight. Horses were heavy-breathing and musky-scented. Their lips tickled one's palms as they gummed apple treats. Carriages swayed and jostled, bouncing one on upholstered seats. Oranges were sweet juice bursting inside one's mouth, and lemons were puckering tartness spiked with the essence of a summer's day. Pies were gravy, meat and pastry which melted in the mouth, warmed the throat, and lay rich and comfortable in the stomach like a thick blanket in winter.

Ada-Marie hummed along to the ballad outside, for she loved music and passed hours at the nursery window listening to the ballad girl's songs.

Kitty sang:

'One Friday morn as we'd set sail,
And our ship not far from land,
We there did espy a fair mermaid,
With a comb and a glass in her hand, her hand, her hand,
With a comb and a glass in her hand.'

Ada-Marie joined in for the jaunty chorus. The merry tune belied the tragedy of the song:

'While the raging seas did roar,
And the stormy winds did blow,
And we jolly sailor-boys were up, up aloft,
And the landsmen were lying down below,
And the landlubbers all down below, below, below,
And the landlubbers all down below.'

Heels clicked down the corridor.

Ada-Marie tensed and ceased singing. 'Miss Matilda is coming.'

As the door opened, Kitty opened her eyes, letting her gift of sight flood back. Why was Matilda invading her precious moments with Ada-Marie? When not working, the sisters could spend the mornings resting or pursuing individual activities. It was a rule of the house.

Matilda, attired in flaming orange silk and draped in pearls, with her dark hair bound in a plumed turban, looked Kitty up and down. 'Lord, you aren't even dressed.' She cleared her throat, stifling a cough.

Kitty sat up, wrapping her dressing gown tighter. 'Is there any reason I should be?'

Matilda strode to the bedside, her skirts whipping between her legs, and yanked the brass lever by Kitty's bed, signalling for a servant. 'Yes, so get up. And that child must return to the nursery at once.'

Kitty frowned. *That child* rankled her every time. 'Why?'

Matilda winked. 'Someone has business with you.'

Kitty tensed. 'I shan't see Gillingham today, Matilda.' She still had a week, and if Sidney got her the interview with Tyrold, she'd never speak with the duke again, if she could help it.

A mischievous smile danced across Matilda's face. 'I said nothing about Gillingham, Kitty-cat.'

Kitty started, surprised. 'Who is it, then?'

A housemaid rapped upon the door, and Matilda's smile evaporated. 'Take that child to the nursery, Sally, and send for Philippe.' She marched across the chamber and vanished into Kitty's dressing room.

Kitty embraced Ada-Marie once more, suppressing her annoyance with Matilda. Kitty wanted to preserve the child's innocence regarding Kitty's profession for as long as possible, although the day would come when Ada-Marie would learn the truth. Perhaps it would disgust her.

'Go with Sally, my sweet love, and find Nanny Ashcroft.' Kitty kissed the top of Ada-Marie's head. 'I shall be with you as soon as I may, although I know not when it will be.'

Ada-Marie patted Kitty's cheek. 'I love you.'

Kitty increased her squeeze. 'I love you more.'

The child giggled. 'No, I love *you* more.'

Kitty basked in the glow of their cuddle. 'Impossible, poppet.'

'We love each other the same.' Ada-Marie grinned, her rosy cheeks balling under her sightless eyes. It was an exchange they had often.

Kitty tucked wispy strands of golden hair behind Ada-Marie's ears. 'Yes, we love each other the same.'

She relinquished Ada-Marie to Sally's arms with a sigh. Her moments with her ward were the best part of her day.

Matilda re-emerged with gowns draped over her arm. She stood in a beam of light cascading from the tall windows and held them up one at a time – a wispy white muslin, a frothy raspberry tulle, a primrose organdie, and a cerulean satin with tiffany silk overlay – before depositing them over the back of Kitty's sky-blue sofa.

A rainbow of luxury, all so Kitty could spread her legs and earn more.

'These are lovely,' Matilda said. 'I shall leave it to Philippe to decide which will make you the most magnificent.'

Kitty wilted into her mattress. She'd been magnificent last night, and it had landed her only in trouble.

In trouble and . . .

Kitty smiled at the silver damask bedcurtains above her head and trailed a finger along her upper chest, tracing the edge of her dressing gown. Her body tingled as she recalled landing in Sidney's embrace the night before. Sidney's strong, warm arms, securing her to his dense hardness.

Kitty closed her eyes. Despite her intention to forget her lust, she'd barely slept thanks to her new but fiercely raging desire for Sidney. Would it be possible to slip him into her room *once*? She'd strip his black and white parson's clothes off what must be a chiselled, golden body. His beautiful mouth would slide down her nakedness, teasing her, tormenting her, nipping her breasts, suckling her nipples. Pleasure would swell everywhere his firm hands touched – grasping her bottom, slipping between her legs, caressing her wet throbbing cunt. Converting her aching agony into heavenly bliss. He'd give Kitty one magnificent night before she went to Tyrold . . .

The thought of Tyrold was cold water on her daydream. Tyrold was the reason Kitty had stopped Sidney last night. Kitty couldn't make love to her dearest friend and then put herself into the arms of *his* friend. Such a situation would devastate everyone.

Her arm flopped on the mattress.

Then she bolted upright.

Tyrold. Was *he* the reason Matilda hummed as she fluffed and smoothed the gowns?

'If it's not Gillingham who has business with me, Matilda, who is it?'

Matilda's eyes glittered. 'I still cannot believe it myself, but who do you imagine appeared at the door not ten minutes ago and attempted to send a note – a *private* message, he said – to your room?'

Kitty twisted her rumpled sheets, resisting the impulse to cry. It must be Tyrold. Who else would delight Matilda so much? How had Sidney convinced his friend this quickly to meet with Kitty?

Matilda crossed the room, plopped on the bed, and clasped Kitty's hand. 'John Tyrold. That's who.' She beamed. 'Tyrold offered for you, Kitty-cat.' She squealed and bounced her bottom on the bed. 'I cannot conceal my delight.'

He'd already *offered*? Kitty didn't need to persuade him?

'I see your surprise,' Matilda continued. 'But I assure you, it's true. Imagine, dearest: the great Tyrold is only a man after all, despite his bluster. I shall make him eat his words before he . . .' She trailed off, glaring.

'What words?' Kitty asked, head tilted.

Matilda fluttered her hands. 'Never mind. It was many years ago, but I've not forgotten his impudence. Kitty, make him burn when you meet with him, but don't give him *any* satisfaction.' She coughed, then smirked. 'Send him to *me* to talk business. I shall make him pay.'

'I thought you said he'd presented his offer?'

Matilda scrunched her nose. 'He as good as did. You know the man: no manners in the least. First, he demanded his note go directly to you – said it was for your eyes only. When I pleasantly explained all the business of the house must pass through me, he looked like the devil himself and insisted on speaking to you first. Alone. At the copse of elms by the Ring in Hyde Park in an hour.'

Kitty frowned. 'But why are you so certain he intends to make me an offer?'

Matilda jumped to her feet. 'Ah – that was a bit of cleverness on my part. I said I couldn't possibly permit you to meet alone with a gentleman unless the gentleman promised to present you an offer. Well, Tyrold growled and cursed, but at last, Kit, at *last* he admitted an offer awaits you in the park.' She broke into another grin, waggling her eyebrows. 'He's given his word, and Tyrold doesn't go back on his word. It's the only gentlemanly trait he has.'

A pit opened inside Kitty. That was that. She'd be mistress to Sidney's friend. She'd be free of Gillingham, but there was little relief.

Matilda clasped her hands to her breast and gazed at Kitty fondly. 'What a triumphant moment. You'll be the envy of every woman in London, virtuous or not. With my Kitty-cat's charm and beauty working on his mouldy heart, Tyrold will tumble over himself to spend his gold.' Matilda smoothed the back of her fingers down Kitty's cheek. 'How proud I am of you, dearest sister.'

At one time, those words would've melted Kitty's heart. But something had changed in the hedge the night before.

Along with arousing her physical desire, Sidney had awakened a yearning for love, which was something a courtesan could never allow herself. A courtesan's *affaires* were fleeting, meaningless things.

'Truly a triumph, Kitty,' Matilda repeated as she kissed the top of Kitty's head.

Kitty squeezed her eyes closed and breathed deeply, willing herself away from self-pity.

It *was* a triumph.

It was also shattering.

But she must make the best of it.

After all, Tyrold wasn't a vicious man. Once, Kitty had hoped he'd offer for her. When she was a frightened virgin shivering naked before two dozen potential keepers, only an eighteen-year-old Tyrold — by far the nearest to her age — had looked at her without lust. His green eyes had shimmered with sorrow, and she'd longed for him to save her. Had he done so, Kitty would've handed him her heart in exchange.

Instead, he had walked out of the Preece sisters' house and never returned.

Until now.

At five minutes to the appointed time, Kitty traversed the eastern meadow of Hyde Park under a pink silk parasol. Her dark hair framed her face with ringlets under a rosy bonnet, rouge reddened her lips, and her pink satin slippers whispered through the daisy-strewn grass.

She inhaled to calm the butterflies fluttering inside

her. Her free hand, encased in a kid glove, clutched at the tiffany silk overlay of her long skirts.

Philippe had chosen the cerulean satin. 'The blue-green colour,' he'd said, 'brings the maritime into your eyes. Paired with these pink sapphires' – he'd slipped a sparkling rose-gemmed necklace around Kitty's exposed bosom – 'it is reminiscent of the sea.' He'd stood back and observed, his freckled face pursed under his forward-brushed sandy locks. 'You are *une reine de la mer*. Queen of the mermaids.'

Kitty had smiled, despite her nerves. Philippe, whose salary she paid from her personal allowance, was a ray of sunshine.

Philippe had winked. 'There, *ma chérie*. I made you smile, which was my purpose, for the mermaid queen must appear welcoming before she drags the sailors to the bottom of the sea.'

But those playful moments were past. With leaden steps, Kitty approached the thundering noise of the Ring, a vast circular dirt track full of young bucks on high-bred horses racing at break-neck speeds while their friends cheered them from the shade of the surrounding elms, whose leafy green boughs reached high into the blue sky.

Tyrold, unmistakable in his worn tailcoat and loose-tied cravat, leaned against a tree on the northern side of the track, his shaggy black wolfhound panting at his feet. He'd given no indication he noticed Kitty. His customary brown hat shadowed his face, and he appeared to study his scuffed boots.

87

Kitty's stomach quivered. She paused, squeezing her eyes closed and breathing until a compulsion to retch abated.

Everything was wrong.

The moments with Sidney in the hedge were a dreadful mistake, for they'd exposed a detrimental weakness. Yearning for love destroyed courtesans. If one loved one's keeper, a broken heart awaited the inevitable end. If one loved a man *other* than one's keeper, a courtesan's job was noxious.

Kitty's eyes stung behind her closed lids, but she forced them open. She concentrated on the figure ahead, now apparently trimming his fingernails with a penknife. She shuddered. Although he wasn't unhandsome, Tyrold's shabby apparel and careless personal habits left a great deal to be desired, and Kitty wouldn't be able to change them. Perhaps wives could influence their husbands, but a mistress must pretend a man was perfect. That was the fantasy, the illusion, the magic. Kitty inhaled, squared her shoulders, and strode forward. She could do this. She'd pretended to like men much worse than Tyrold. Besides, her only alternative was Gillingham, and she'd take miserly eccentricity over cruelty any day.

A low whistle from her left – in the racetrack's direction – distracted her.

'By God, gentlemen,' a voice said. 'It's Kitty Preece.'

A lanky, debt-ridden young baron named Murden cut in on Kitty's path. A group of his friends followed him; among them was Sidney's massive brother Cornelius.

Kitty cast down her eyes. She was never disagreeable, but she had no time for conversation with men who couldn't afford her when Tyrold awaited.

'Don't look away, sweetheart,' Lord Murden said, lifting her chin with his forefinger. 'Stand with me in the shade and put your hands in my pockets. You can have whatever you feel in there.'

His friends laughed.

Kitty turned her head and tried to walk past, but Murden grabbed her upper arm.

'Please release me, Lord Murden. I have an appointment.'

Murden tsked. 'Don't break my heart, Kitty Preece.'

A dull pounding commenced behind Kitty's temple. 'My lord,' she said, tugging at her arm, 'you and your friends are always most welcome at the Thursday night entertainments my sisters and I host, but you must release me now.'

Murden's grip tightened. 'Amusing how you put on missish airs.'

'Come now,' Cornelius said. 'Let her go, Murden, and watch the race.'

Kitty blinked. Sidney's brother had never impressed her as anything other than a savage brute. Did he have a kind streak, or did he merely wish to return to his sport?

Murden curled his upper lip, but he released her. 'Perhaps I should write her poetry, as your brother does, Eden,' he said to Cornelius. 'What was the one last night? "Ode to Kitty Preece's Hairless Cunny"?'

Kitty flinched as if Murden had struck her.

The men guffawed as they left.

Had Sidney written erotic poetry about their precious minutes in the hedge?

Kitty fought the urge to cry, but if Sidney was just like any other man after all, it made her current task easier. This was exactly the dose of reality she needed.

With renewed purpose, she strode forward until Tyrold lifted his head.

When their eyes met, he snapped shut his penknife. Days' old stubble shadowed his cheeks, and a pipe dangled from the corner of his mouth. Although he looked for all the world like his shaggy wolfhound wearing a hat, Kitty gazed coquettishly through her lashes.

'Good afternoon, sir,' she breathed, her voice deep and throaty as she curtsied low. Kitty ensured Tyrold had a lingering view of her breasts as she hovered before him. Still with her knees bent, she shifted her gaze along his body and hovered at his groin as she licked her lips with the tip of her tongue.

She rose.

Tyrold stared, blinking. He removed his pipe and gulped. 'I–I . . .'

Was ruthless businessman John Tyrold shy under his crusty exterior?

Kitty batted her lashes. 'May I walk with you, my dear sir?'

'W–with *me*?' His eyes darted.

The man was daft, but Kitty forced a sweet smile. 'I assure you I don't bite.' She dragged her top teeth slowly over one side of her bottom lip. 'Unless you want me to.'

She rose on tiptoes, threaded her gloved fingers around the queue at the nape of his neck, and pressed her lips to his, shielding their kiss with her parasol. But as her tongue probed Tyrold's tight mouth, she stiffened. He wasn't kissing her back.

Perhaps he wanted her to work harder.

She leaned closer, pressing her breasts and pelvis against his body.

But her advances were thwarted when Tyrold pushed her away, sputtering as if *she* were the one with tobacco and coffee breath. 'What the devil? Are you a lioness to pounce on every man?'

Kitty's jaw dropped. Tyrold was an abomination. 'You know perfectly well I'm not, John Tyrold, for you've ridden with me and Sid many a morning. *You* set this assignation.'

'For Sidney, woman!' Tyrold shoved his pipe back into his mouth. 'Come.' He seized her wrist rather than offering an arm like a gentleman. 'He's waiting near the bridle path. I set up a guard here in case Matilda came with you.'

Kitty's thoughts swirled. 'I don't understand in the least.'

'Well, *I* shan't explain.' Tyrold huffed as he marched forward through the grass. 'I've had a damned ridiculous waste of a morning already, and Sidney can do his own talking this time.'

Kitty jogged to match Tyrold's long strides. Her mind raced, seeking answers and finding none. 'So, you don't intend to make me an offer of arrangement?'

'Good God, no. I'm merely here to take you to Sidney.'

Kitty's innards knotted as Tyrold dragged her past the racetrack. Sidney hadn't helped her after all. And now his interference would escalate the crisis a thousand times more.

Beneath a nearby elm, Lord Murden pivoted his gaunt face. His brows shot up, and he called unintelligible words to a group of gentlemen. Like a wave, a dozen heads rotated. Jaws dropped. Snickering commenced.

Nausea washed over Kitty. Gossip about Kitty and the gruff King Midas who never kept mistresses would infuse Brooks's and White's within hours, and soon Gillingham would know. Without an offer from Tyrold, Kitty would have no choice but to placate the duke in precisely the way he desired when he stormed to Mount Street to yell at her and Matilda . . .

Matilda.

Kitty's throat constricted. Matilda's soaring hopes would be crushed when she discovered Tyrold wasn't offering for Kitty.

She'd be wrecked.

No, she'd be livid.

Kitty attempted to wrench her wrist back; she must flee to Mount Street and appease her sister. 'Let me go at once, Mr Tyrold.'

'Not until you're with Sidney,' he said, pulling her harder yet.

Kitty stumbled up the grassy slope, her head throbbing. She'd be forced into Gillingham's keeping before the night was out . . .

'I have no interest in seeing Sidney,' she said. 'His interference in my life makes everything worse, and . . .' – the words stung as she thrust them out, but they were the truth – 'and he betrayed me.' Perhaps all was not lost. Perhaps Kitty could still convince Tyrold to keep her. 'Please, Mr Tyrold, you aren't unkind. Don't take me to Sidney. Help me instead. Escort me back to Mount Street.' Her heart pummelled her chest. 'I shall serve you wine and refreshment in my private room where no one will trouble us.'

Dear God, let him accept.

But he didn't.

'You're spouting utter nonsense,' Tyrold called over his shoulder as he yanked her forward until she crested the rise. He nodded his head. '*There's* your saviour.'

Kitty ground to a halt. Gillingham's henchman stood, arms crossed, beside Sidney.

The world closed in. It was a trap.

6

Tyrold tugged Kitty's wrist again. 'Well, woman? Go to Sidney.'

Kitty rooted her feet to the grass. Nothing made any sense. Her head throbbed, wrenching her skull apart.

With Butcher shadowing him, Sidney approached, golden and smiling in the leaf-dappled sunlight, looking exactly like the Sidney she thought she knew so well – the man who'd been a comfort to her for six years. Kitty yearned to fling herself into his widespread arms and burrow her face into the folds of his cravat. She also wanted to run in the opposite direction, for Sidney had betrayed her. He'd told his brother's friends about their encounter in the hedge, and rather than arranging a tryst with Tyrold, he'd delivered her to Gillingham's henchman.

Movement in either direction was impossible. Kitty's feet were stone, and the weight of the world pressed down like a boulder. Had Sidney done these things out of spite for being rejected? She would never have thought her dear friend capable of maliciousness, but, then again, she never thought him capable of arousing her ardent passion either.

'My dearest love.' Sidney's amber eyes shone like the sun.

How could Sidney call Kitty his love when he'd forced her into a situation where she must bed a dragon before nightfall?

Butcher loomed over Sidney's side. 'You're not to talk to his grace's ladybird, parson. I told you already.'

Sidney fluttered his fingers in front of Butcher's face as he held Kitty's gaze, his smile unruffled. 'Do shut up, Butcher,' he said. 'Better yet, tell Gillingham to go to the devil.'

Kitty struggled to piece together the puzzle before her.

Butcher turned crimson. 'I'll send you to the devil first.' He snatched at Sidney's shoulder.

Kitty's arm flopped to her side as Tyrold dropped her wrist and ploughed between the henchman and Sidney. 'Do you know who I am, you foul cur?'

Butcher stepped back, palms up. 'Mr Tyrold, my argument ain't with you, sir.'

Tyrold poked the henchman's barrel chest with the stem of his pipe. 'Your argument is with me if you touch my friend. At the best of times, I'm *not* a forgiving man, but I especially loathe mean-spirited ruffians and power-randy cowards.'

Under the shade of her parasol, Kitty blinked at the trio. Clearly, Tyrold and Sidney were not working with the duke, but what *was* happening? And why was it happening *outside*, within sight of dozens of young bucks who'd carry the tale to the clubs? Confusion and distress bubbled over, overcoming Kitty's inertia.

'Will *someone* explain what is happening?' She threw down her parasol so the pink silk spun like a top across the green carpet of grass. 'What is *he* doing here, Sid?' she asked, pointing at Butcher. 'No, what are *any* of you doing here? I might still be at home with . . . with Ada-Marie, but for . . .'

The words sawed at her tight throat. Kitty was humiliated, Matilda would be livid, the duke would win, and somehow Sidney – the gentlest man in the world – had produced this disaster.

Kitty covered her face with her hands.

Strong arms slipped around her and secured her in an embrace warmer than summer sunshine. 'My love, I have news.'

Kitty ought to wrestle free, but her knees were suddenly too weak to stand alone. 'I'm tired of your news, Sid. You haven't the least notion of my distress—'

Sidney chuckled.

'And now you *laugh*.' But Kitty had little fight, for Sidney's warmth melted her stone-heavy body. She buried her face in the folds of his cravat, her throat on fire. 'You wretched man,' she said, heedless of her overloud voice. 'You promised me you'd help me speak to Tyrold, to . . . to see if he could ever want me, and—'

'I say, what?' It was Tyrold's incredulous voice.

Sidney's grasp slackened. He drew back from Kitty, studying her with a furrowed brow. 'Kit, do . . . do you *want* John?'

Kitty crumpled.

96

It wasn't about what she wanted. In all her life, it had never been about what she wanted. She *needed* Tyrold. If Kitty were in his keeping, her sisters would have provision, and Ada-Marie would be safe from Gillingham's potential cruelty.

Everything was ruined if Tyrold didn't want her.

'I made it perfectly clear to you last night that I do.' Kitty's voice cracked. She was a desperate fool, falling apart before Tyrold and Sidney and Gillingham's slack-jawed anthropoid ape. 'I've never been so humiliated in all my life, and it's because of you, Sidney. The one person I thought I could trust.'

Sidney recoiled, dropping his arms. 'Kitty, forgive me. I-I thought . . .' He faltered before apparently gathering his resolve with a deep breath. 'No, never mind what I thought. I mistook matters. My original intention was to provide you with the financial inde-pendence to make your own choices. I stand by that; I shall celebrate your choices, whatever they may be. I' – he lifted his quivering chin – 'I shan't come between you and John.'

Tyrold blanched. '*What*?'

Butcher scrunched his forehead and scratched his chin.

Tyrold extracted his pipe. 'This is a goddamned farce worthy of Drury-blasted-Lane.'

Sidney's brows drew together. 'Watch what you say, John. You're a fortunate man.'

Kitty smiled weakly. Sidney *was* fighting for her, and everything would be perfect, if only her heart weren't

97

breaking in two, because she'd far rather return to Sidney's comforting arms than go to Tyrold's.

Tyrold blinked. 'Good God, Sidney, you fool. I ought to go home and leave you and Kitty to enact your star-crossed lovers' tragedy to its natural conclusion, for I have *profitable* business which needs my attention, but I'm invested now, and so I shall see this through. While you're an attractive woman, Kitty,' he said, jabbing his pipe's mouthpiece in Kitty's direction, 'I wouldn't touch you if *you* paid *me* a thousand pounds. I'm not such a cursed shifty cur that I'd lech on the woman my friend loves.'

The woman my friend loves.

Sidney loved her. The pounding of Kitty's heart deprived her of breath, but sense soon suppressed her elation. Sidney's love couldn't reimburse Gillingham and support Matilda, and Tyrold wouldn't take her because Sidney loved her.

Kitty put up her hands as if she could push away the disaster these two men, who possessed all the advantages of the world, had caused her. 'Don't talk to me of love when I must soon welcome cruelty into my bed. Neither of you understands the gravity of my predicament. If you won't keep me, what am I to do?' she asked, beseeching Tyrold, as if the magnate might yet solve her struggles, but even as the words left her mouth, she knew there was only one solution.

She must go to Gillingham, although the thought made her violently nauseous.

'Don't look at *me*,' Tyrold said, throwing up his own hands dismissively. 'Sidney, do your own talking.' He turned to Butcher. 'And as for you, walk with me by the racetrack.' He nodded in the Ring's direction. 'Tell me what line of business you're in, and I shall make it worth your while.'

Butcher hesitated, his eyes darting between Sidney and Tyrold. 'How much worth my while?'

Tyrold chuckled. 'How much? Ha! Do you think I mean to *pay* you to walk with me? Nonsense, my good man.' He clapped a hand on Butcher's arm. 'I shall honour you with a free consultation. There are many who pay me hundreds of guineas for the same . . .'

Tyrold's voice trailed off as he navigated the giant towards the Ring. Butcher balled his fists and glared at Sidney, but he followed.

Kitty slumped. Her head no longer pounded, but she was as empty as a wasted desert.

Tyrold wouldn't have her because of Sidney's love. If she were a different woman, with a different role in the world, Sidney's love would be more than enough.

But she was Kitty Preece, the most desirable courtesan in London.

A worthless whore.

Sidney squeezed Kitty's hand, but it didn't comfort her. Her limbs were numb.

'You *do* know how much I love you, don't you, Kit? How much I've loved you for years?'

'As friends, Sid.' The words scratched her raw throat. 'You know it can be no other way.'

'Not anymore.' Sidney pressed her hand to his chest, over his heart. 'Now it can be however you wish. With

Tyrold's assistance, I negotiated an advance from Duffy and Ward. I have the money to reimburse the duke, and I can pay Matilda one hundred pounds a month. I shall pay her three hundred today.'

The world swirled like watercolours in the rain. Sky and ground tumbled over each other, and Kitty might've collapsed if not for Sidney's arm swooping behind her as her knees buckled.

Relief welled up, nearly suffocating her. Was she truly free from Gillingham?

'You can keep me?' she asked, her heart soaring. 'Darling Sidney, shall we really and truly be lovers?'

It was too much happiness to be borne to have a keeper like Sidney.

Sidney clasped her tighter, his gentle but powerful arms supporting her, shielding her from the world. Gone was shy, timid Sidney whom Kitty had protected for years, and in his place was assertive Sidney, virile, vigorously masculine, as he had been since the moment in the hedge when he'd first explained his plan.

A plan Kitty never should've doubted.

Sidney grazed Kitty's cheek with his fingers. 'I wish to provide you with the freedom to make whatever choices you want, Kitty. But if you love me in return' – his eyes shone – 'please do me the honour of becoming my wife.'

Idealistic naivety again.

It grounded Kitty but didn't dispel her joy. For now, Sidney could afford to keep her as a mistress, which was the only way for a gentleman to love a woman like her. Kitty simply must help him understand why they couldn't marry. 'Sidney, a man of your class doesn't marry a woman like me without terrible, unbearable consequences. Everyone would ridicule and despise us. We'd be accepted nowhere.'

'I shall take you and Ada-Marie to live in the country, outside the reach of London society.'

A quiet home far from men's gropes, smacks and control, with Ada-Marie as her daughter and Sidney as her husband, was a dream Kitty couldn't allow herself to dwell upon. It was both too good to be true and too tempting to resist. 'We'd never be outside the reach of society, Sid. Furthermore, I cannot leave Matilda after all she has done for me. It would break her heart.'

'Then we shall stay in town.' Sidney smiled. 'And we shan't be without friends. John, Alexander, Nicky, Edward – society's dictates don't matter to them. I wager Nicky's wife Meggy would be your friend, Kit – she's a rum sort. And you will have your sisters—'

'Sidney, stop.' Kitty sighed. 'You don't understand. Perhaps you are correct about Tyrold and Holbrook and the others – men of power and position have nothing to lose from a friendship with a whore. But Lady Holbrook?' Kitty shook her head violently. Even if the brand-new marchioness wanted an acquaintance-ship – and of course she *wouldn't*, however highly Sidney thought of her – society wouldn't tolerate it. 'A noblewoman cannot be friends with the likes of me. And as for my *sisters* . . .' Kitty shuddered, her stomach as tight as a nut. Courtesans depended upon each other when their looks faded. They despised those who deserted the ranks to marry, because they'd traded the security of sisterhood for the security of a man. 'My sisters would consider my marriage an act of betrayal, as if I were telling them their way of life is not good enough. They'd loathe me pretending to be a lady.'

'You are a lady, Kit.' Sidney pressed his lips to her forehead.

In that moment, clasped against the most gentlemanly heart in all of London, Kitty almost believed him.

But no – it was a fairy tale.

'Sidney, I sell my body for money. I have done so for nearly half my life. I'm *not* a lady.'

'You're my lady.' He trailed kisses along her face – her brow, her eyelids, her cheekbones. 'None of the rest matters.'

'It will always matter, Sidney.' She wanted to float into his fairyland, but she couldn't. 'Love has clouded your sense. How will you feel the first time you walk with your courtesan wife, and a man calls out for me to give him a blow or—'

Sidney pulled back. Fury flashed in his eyes. 'I'd call the villain out.'

'You cannot call out every man in London. Besides, I don't want you to call out *any* to defend my honour, for I have none.'

'Stop, Kitty.' Sidney's jaw clenched.

'I shan't stop, because that is what it will mean to be married to me, Sidney. Society will mock you as a fool and despise me as a glorified slut, giving herself the ultimate airs.'

Sidney's breath quickened.

Kitty kept her last reason against marriage secret: she must be free to leave Sidney once the money ran out, because Matilda would demand it of her.

That reality was a stab to the heart, because if Kitty went to bed with Sidney, leaving him would destroy her.

Kitty turned aside her head as she at last comprehended the extent of her sentiments. She'd loved Sidney for years, and now, whatever happened, there'd be no happy ending.

'You care for me, Kitty. I know you do.' Sidney enfolded her in comfort and strength. 'I love you and Ada-Marie so much. Allow me to provide for my two girls.'

'Oh, Sidney,' Kitty said into his shoulder, 'stop speaking of marriage, and we can be together.'

If only for a short while.

Sidney's breath stilled.

'Ask me, Sid,' Kitty whispered, tilting her head to look at his face. 'Ask me to be your mistress.' Her heart hammered – surely its thump pounded Sidney, as close-pressed as they were. 'I want you desperately.'

His amber eyes darkened. 'I wasn't imagining your sentiments last night, was I?'

'No, dearest darling. You weren't imagining anything.' She marvelled at the splendour of sincerity. None of her customary pretence with men marred this interaction. 'I want you to make love to me today.'

Sidney's eyes glazed. 'My God, Kit.'

Kitty kissed his parted lips. 'Ask me to be your mistress,' she breathed, her lips touching his with each word.

Sidney's eyes fluttered closed. He sighed against her mouth, enflaming Kitty. She throbbed for the erection hardening between them, and she laced her fingers into his hair below his hat.

'Ask me,' she said again, tilting her hips so he'd feel the pressure against his groin.

Sidney moaned. 'Oh, my love, will you' – Sidney stuttered, wavered, and stumbled on – 'will you be my m-mis . . . my mistress?'

Kitty rejoiced. 'Yes, Sidney Wakefield. Yes, yes, yes.'

She clasped her lips to his. They were in a world alone, floating above everyone else.

Sidney would keep her. Sidney would be hers.

For a time.

As Sidney's tongue slipped into her mouth, Kitty deepened the kiss. One day, her heart would break, but that was even more reason to savour every moment while it lasted.

7

Sidney's tongue slid into his beloved's mouth as his heart filled his chest.

Kitty was honey and fire, angel and enchantress. He could kiss her forever, drinking her sweet taste, cradling her luscious curves.

She broke the kiss to trail feather-light caresses on his neck, over his high starched collar.

His lips skimmed her jasmine-scented cheek. 'I love you,' he said, offering his essence, his *everything* with three words.

Kitty's blue-green eyes glistened. 'I love you, too, Sidney.'

'Do you truly?' he asked, breathless with joy.

'Oh, yes.' She exhaled her response against his skin.

Words were on the tip of Sidney's tongue – if we love each other, that is all that matters, so marry me – when a rough hand seized his shoulder and heaved him to the ground like a fall from a horse. The impact thudded throughout Sidney's body.

Butcher's looming presence blocked the sun. 'Get your hands off his grace's property, parson.'

This, *again*?

Kitty knelt beside Sidney, smothering him in kisses and concern.

Tyrold approached, running from the Ring, but trailing him were more potential threats: Cornelius and his friends, Murden and Hawkins.

Sidney braced himself. He must vanquish his four aggressors and protect Kitty. Even with John's help, it would be no small task, but Sidney wouldn't capitulate.

He stood and dusted off his clothes, shielding Kitty by putting his body between her and Butcher. Her sweet hand found one of his, and her cheek rested against his coat, over his shoulder blade. 'Tell Gillingham I'll call with his money, Butcher. He has no claim to Miss Preece anymore.'

Butcher, almost purple, readied his fists. 'Get away from the woman, Wakefield. I'm going to beat you to a pulp. What's left of you can speak to his grace yourself.'

It was the response Sidney had expected.

'Stand with John, my love.' Sidney kissed Kitty's upturned face, seeking to soothe her distress. 'Once I deal with Butcher, we'll go together to talk to Matilda.' But Kitty clung to his coat, so Sidney extracted her fingers and handed her to Tyrold. 'I grew up with Cornelius. I can handle Butcher.'

Sidney *hoped*.

He faced his adversary with his fists raised.

Butcher snarled. 'I'll enjoy knocking every one of your teeth out of that pretty mouth, parson.'

As they squared off, Cornelius arrived, but Sidney focused on Butcher. If he lost eye contact for a split second, the brute would strike.

'What's this?' It was Cornelius's bark. 'Sid, why are you fighting?'

'Not now, Cornelius,' Sidney said, eyes still glued to Butcher. 'I'll deal with you next.'

'No, I say, Sid. You can't beat this bruiser.' Cornelius stepped between them, jabbing a finger in Butcher's face. 'I know you. I saw your bout at Fives-Court a fortnight ago. What's your name? Blunder, isn't it?'

The henchman growled. 'Butcher, Lord Eden.'

'How do you know me, man?'

'You fought the Reaper and Mendoza.'

Cornelius smirked. 'Yes, and I won, as well, although some consider Mendoza the greatest pugilist of all time.'

Butcher spat on the ground. 'Mendoza's an old man. My sister could beat him.'

Cornelius's eyelids drooped as his lips curled. It was an expression that had haunted Sidney's childhood. The lazy gaze belied a latent power, like a crouching tiger ready to pounce.

As a boy, that expression had signalled one thing to Sidney. Run.

But Butcher didn't know that.

'She could, eh?' Cornelius looked the giant up and down. 'If she's anything like you, I don't doubt it. I'll keep your sister in mind if I ever fancy a shag with a beefy heifer.'

Butcher lunged forward, but Cornelius was ready.

It was something to see his brother fight when Sidney wasn't the target of his fists. Cornelius's lightning-quick first blow was a neck-snapping left hook to the jaw which caught Butcher unaware. A stream of blood shot from the henchman's mouth as his body jolted askew. Sidney grimaced. His brother had often been vicious with Sidney, but clearly Cornelius had never beaten him with the same force he employed with other pugilists.

Whatever Cornelius's reason for fighting Butcher, he certainly didn't need Sidney's help, so Sidney reclaimed Kitty from Tyrold. She nestled her face into his shirt when Cornelius struck the next knuckle-splitting wallop, a follow-up right hook, while Butcher remained mid-throes.

Kitty clung to Sidney. He folded her in his arms. Butcher, Cornelius, and other men might display bravado through swaggers, boasts and fights, but the true mark of manliness was being a safe harbour for those one loved.

A series of sickening thuds drew Sidney's eyes back to the match. Butcher braced himself in a defensive position, with his forearms shielding his head, but Cornelius rained blows on the henchman's torso.

'I think,' Cornelius said between clouts, 'you mistook your man earlier. If it's a Wakefield you want to spar with, it's me you want, not my scrap of a little brother.'

Sidney's jaw dropped. Cornelius had *never* defended him.

Kitty raised her head and quirked an eyebrow.

Sidney lifted his shoulders. 'I'm as astonished as you, Kit.'

'I should think so,' she said with an adorable sniff. 'To call you *little*, of all things!' She smoothed her hand over Sidney's biceps, but her eyes fell to his crotch. 'You're not little in the least, darling.'

Sidney's cheeks warmed as he shook with silent laughter.

Kitty caught his eye; her own twinkled. She giggled, smothering her amusement in the folds of his shirt linen.

Love overflowed from Sidney's heart. 'I want to take you away with me, my angel.'

Kitty's blue-green eyes grew hazy. 'Where would we go?'

The words almost slipped out: *to Scotland*. As much as Sidney despised the idea of a clandestine elopement, it would be better to face everyone – his brother, Kitty's sisters and, worst of all, his mother – with the fact of their irrevocable union rather than with a proposed marriage.

Sidney didn't say it. His attention returned to the bout, for at last Butcher had managed a wallop to Cornelius's gut. As his brother stumbled, the henchman called out through his thickening lips: 'My fight is not with your lordship. It's with *him*' – he pointed at Sidney – 'what can't keep his hands off the Duke of Gillingham's woman.'

Kitty broke from Sidney's embrace. 'This nonsense must cease at once, Butcher. I am *not* the Duke of Gillingham's woman. I never have been, and I never, ever will be.' She crossed her arms under her bosom. 'You may tell his grace so at once.'

Butcher spat a bloody wad onto the grass. 'Damned if I'll do any such thing.'

Cornelius looked from Sidney to Kitty with a broadening grin as he recovered his breath and straightened his tight waistcoat. 'Are you *Sidney's* woman, Kitty Preece?'

Sidney scowled. 'Kitty is her *own*—'

'Yes, I *am* Sidney's woman.' Kitty lifted her chin, glaring at each of the circled men. A smile played at her lips as her gaze returned to Sidney. 'He's magnificent.'

'Oh, Kit,' Sidney breathed. '*You're* magnificent.'

Her arms encircled him, binding them as one. Sidney wished everybody else a million miles away so he could be alone with Kitty to marvel in this new mystery. He brushed his lips over hers; her long lashes fluttered over her sea-coloured eyes. He could fall into their depths, sink into her body . . .

Cornelius whooped, drawing Sidney back to reality. 'Ha! Well done, Sidney.' He smacked Sidney's back. 'My little brother, gentlemen,' he cried to his friends, 'possesses the finest damned filly in London.'

Sidney ought to object to the crassness, but the words were unexpectedly thrilling. His brother had never boasted about him. Cornelius was . . . almost *friendly*.

Even after Butcher had slunk into the shade of an elm tree to nurse his wounds, presumably aware he couldn't defend Gillingham's claim with Cornelius around – and Tyrold and the spectators departed – Cornelius hovered.

Despite himself, Sidney warmed to his brother. 'Thank you for your assistance with Butcher.'

Cornelius shrugged. 'Head of the family, aren't I? Can't allow a gallows-bird like that block my brother's chance at a good fuck.' He laughed. 'Besides, you can reimburse me; let me know when you're willing to share her.'

The nascent warmth shattered like glass on brick. Sidney tensed, fury rising fast, but Kitty held him closer and caressed his cheek with the back of her fingers.

'Shh, darling. Don't. This is exactly what I spoke of earlier, and it's not worth a fight. Take me home instead.'

Cornelius clasped a beefy hand over his heart and roared with laughter. 'Lord, she's as saccharine as you are, Sid, but with a body and face like hers, I still see the appeal. I can't blame you for wanting her to yourself. Put in a good word for me with Matilda or Barbara instead, will you?'

Sidney remained silent, glowering at his boorish brother, but Kitty smiled charmingly. 'Matilda *is* the handsomest of us, Lord Eden.'

'*You're* the handsomest,' Cornelius said, 'but she's well enough. Better than the heiress my mother wishes to shackle me to.'

A possible marriage was such surprising news that Sidney responded despite his anger. 'What heiress?'

'Nabob's daughter, banker's widow,' Cornelius replied. 'Wispy blonde thing. No meat on her.'

'Mrs Overton?' Sidney asked, astonished. He'd visited her Mayfair home often at the vicar's request. Eliza Overton was an amiable, exceedingly wealthy young widow with two delightful little daughters, well provided for by the terms of their father's will.

Cornelius grunted. 'That's the one.'

Warmth filled Sidney's chest. Mrs Overton possessed an affable, gentle disposition. She'd fill Paradisum Park – the seat of the Earl of Eden – with a kindness it had never had in Sidney's lifetime. 'Why, she's lovely, Cornelius.' He turned to Kitty, sharing a smile with her. 'You've seen her too – she's sometimes at Green Park when we take Ada-Marie for fresh milk. Do you recall?'

Kitty nodded but said nothing. Naturally, she and Mrs Overton hadn't spoken, but they'd certainly peeped through the corners of their eyes at each other. Ladies frequently glanced covertly at Kitty.

Sidney clapped his brother on the shoulder. The news that Mrs Overton would be the next Lady Eden heartened him. While Sidney's mother would certainly never accept Kitty, Mrs Overton might. 'This is truly joyous, Cornelius. Mrs Overton will make a magnificent Lady Eden, and her daughters are precious. But I knew of no connection between you. Is it quite serious?'

'I suppose.' Cornelius rubbed his chin with the back of his hand. 'Once the solicitors finish squabbling over the settlements, I might as well let her drag me to the altar. Mother's champing at the bit; the whole affair's her doing, but, in truth, I don't much object. Eliza's flat as a wall, but positively rolling in blunt. She'll enliven my pockets to the tune of eighty thousand. I shall have plenty for a sweet bit on the side to enliven my *loins*.' He winked at Kitty.

Sidney's flesh crawled with revulsion. Poor Mrs Overton. 'If you mean to marry,' he snapped, 'be faithful to your wife. Don't be like . . .' He bit his tongue, too ashamed to complete his thought aloud.

But evidently Cornelius understood. 'What? Don't be like our old man?'

Sidney wished he hadn't brought it up in front of Kitty, although of course she must be aware of his father's infidelity. *Everyone* knew the previous Lord Eden had kept a string of mistresses and yet still seduced housemaids under his wife's nose. Until shortly before the late earl's death, *he'd* often frequented the Preece sisters' Thursday evenings. 'Yes, Cornelius,' Sidney said. 'You can be a better husband than he was.'

Cornelius guffawed. 'Lord, Sid, your sanctimonious act doesn't ring true with Kitty Preece on your arm. But this is enough chattering. I'll bid you both a good day, for I've something to discuss with that bruiser.' He pointed at Butcher.

After Cornelius left, Kitty leaned her cheek against Sidney's shoulder. 'Never mind your brother, darling. Let's not allow anything to disturb our perfect happiness.'

Her voice calmed him, her touch soothed. Balm to his wounds, as their friendship had always been, although now he hoped it would be so much more.

'Is that what it is for you as well, Kit? Perfect happiness?'

'You cannot imagine.'

He smiled tenderly. 'I think I can.'

She put her hand to his cheek. 'Then kiss me again. Kiss me here, where everyone can see. I want the world to know I'm yours.'

'That I can do.' Sidney cupped her chin and gave himself to bliss.

Sidney's bliss shattered when they stepped through the cherry-red front door of the Preece sisters' townhouse on Mount Street.

Matilda smouldered like an orange flame before the carved oak central staircase of the carmine flock-papered entrance hall, her slippered foot tapping on the lush red and gold Turkish carpet.

Sidney passed his hat to Mr Dodwell. 'Good afternoon, Matilda.'

She scowled. 'Kitty, why were you wandering through the streets draped on Sidney as if you're his lover? I watched you walk along Mount Street – everyone could see. Gillingham will be furious.'

Kitty's colour heightened.

Sidney took her hand, prepared to announce their news. 'Kitty and I—'

'Silence, Sidney! I wasn't speaking to you.' Matilda seethed, her eyes aflame, and Sidney obeyed, hopeful Kitty could ease her sister into rational behaviour. Matilda jerked her head at Kitty. 'Where's Tyrold?'

Kitty's hand trembled within Sidney's, but she held her chin aloft. 'Sidney is my keeper, not Tyrold.'

Matilda's face flushed as red as the wallpaper. 'Since when is the business of this house arranged behind my back?' She spat out the words before dissolving into hacking coughs.

Kitty released Sidney's hand and crossed the hall to grasp her sister's. 'Matilda, Sid has the money to pay everything the duke offered.' She rubbed her sister's back until the coughing calmed. 'You cannot say no.'

Matilda's eyes darted between Kitty and Sidney. She directed one word at Sidney. 'How?'

At last, permission to speak. 'I sold my novels. I shall reimburse Gillingham his thousand pounds, and here.' Sidney withdrew a bundle of banknotes from his pocket. 'Three hundred for you.'

Matilda glanced at the money, but she didn't move. 'And after three months?'

'There will be more. I will write more.' Sidney ignored the quiver of self-doubt in his gut. He *had* to write more, so he would. 'Please, take this money.'

Matilda clicked her tongue behind her pursed lips instead of reaching for the banknotes. 'Go, Kitty,' she said at last, her eyes never leaving Sidney's face. 'Sidney and I shall speak alone.'

'But you cannot say no, Matilda.' Kitty threw her arms around her sister. 'Please don't say no, dearest. Don't make him pay more – you agreed to these terms with Gillingham, and Sidney's—'

'Hush now.' Matilda patted Kitty's shoulder. 'I shall decide based on your best interests, Kitty-cat.'

'Yes, but please, Matilda, please. Other than Ada-Marie, I've never asked for any—'

'Enough!'

Kitty's usual confident posture stooped as she accepted the scold, and Sidney bristled. He returned the banknotes to his pocket and walked forward, prepared to intervene.

Matilda's eyes cut to him.

She addressed Kitty in a milder manner. 'Have tea with Ada-Marie in the garden. The honeysuckle smells sweet; it will delight your little girl.'

Kitty glowed. 'She loves it above all else. I hadn't thought you'd noticed.'

'Of course, I noticed.' A razor-edge of hardness scored her kind words.

Kitty didn't appear to perceive it, for she grinned at Sidney. 'Find me and Ada-Marie in the garden, Sid, after you've chatted with Matilda.' She slipped through the door, blowing kisses as she went.

Sidney faced Matilda.

Gone was every semblance of affability. Antagonism glinted in her eyes. Clearly, she was yet *another* adversary.

Sidney frowned. 'Why am I a villain to you, Matilda?'

Matilda lashed like a cobra, seizing his arm, and hauling him into the lavish gold-papered receiving room – furnished with clusters of upholstered sofas and a gilded pianoforte – where men initiated their visits to the Preece house. The brocade drapes were closed against the summer's day; once Matilda slammed the door behind them, gloom darkened the room.

'Because,' Matilda said, shadow gouging her features, 'you'll break her heart.'

'Upon my word, I won't.'

Matilda backed Sidney against the wall, her bosom heaving. 'I've tolerated your friendship with Kitty – strange though it is – because until now, you respected the boundaries. But this is intolerable. Kitty will fall in love with you.'

116

Warmth and pride swelled Sidney's chest. 'I think . . . rather, I *know* she already has.' He lifted his chin against Matilda's scathing glare. 'But it is no more than what I feel, Matilda. I love her with all my heart.'

'You do *now*.' Matilda spat each word, flecks of saliva assaulting Sidney's face. 'But one day – likely soon now that you have a bit of money in your pocket – you'll meet a high-born little virgin, cosseted from birth by her wealthy papa, and you will give up Kitty like that.' She snapped her fingers. 'You will leave without a second thought for my tender-hearted sister, because that is what men do, time and time again without fail. And Kitty will languish for love once you desert her.'

'If that is your only concern,' Sidney said, pleased to win Matilda over to his true objective, 'I can set your mind at perfect ease. I want to marry Kitty.'

Matilda clutched her hand to her chest and stumbled back. 'Marry *Kitty*.' She crumpled onto a gold silk sofa, coughing fitfully.

Sidney sat beside her, lifted her ringed hand, and held it between his palms. 'Marriage is what I want above all else. I proposed, but Kitty wouldn't have me, out of fear of disloyalty to you. Please, Matilda, tell her you approve. Tell her, and you will bring us both great joy.'

Matilda extracted her hand and lay it upon her lap. 'Gentlemen don't marry courtesans. What will your bishop say?'

'What he says doesn't signify. I intend to give up the curacy.' He'd decided the day before. 'I shall meet with the vicar tomorrow.'

'You intend to give up your livelihood?'

'Writing is my livelihood now.' He smiled, hope rising that she'd become his ally. 'I shall take care of Kitty, I promise you. I've loved her for six years; I shall cherish and honour her until my dying day.'

Matilda stood, twisting her hands as she paced the carpeted floor towards the gilded mantelpiece. Before the fireless hearth, she halted and peered at her reflection in the gold-framed mirror.

She faced Sidney. 'Don't marry Kitty, Sidney. In fact, I forbid you to tempt her by speaking of it again.'

The words were terse, and Sidney's blood boiled. Who was Matilda to dictate the actions of two adults, both nearing thirty years of age and both perfectly capable of understanding their own hearts and minds?

'Your family will despise her,' Matilda continued, 'and your friends will scorn her, and that will destroy her as surely as your desertion. A marriage between you and Kitty must never happen.'

The words sliced through the room like the fall of a sword.

Sidney tightened his jaw, preparing for a battle from which he would *not* retreat. 'I'm uncertain why you think you have the authority to forbid it. Kitty is well past the age of majority.'

Matilda's fingernails tapped on the mantel. 'Kitty respects my wisdom.'

Was this wisdom? Or jealousy? Or something else?

Whatever it was, Matilda was no ally.

Sidney crossed his arms and stilled his tongue. There was no sense telling Matilda about his plan to take Kitty and Ada-Marie to the country.

'Very well,' he said, pretending to acquiesce. 'You forbid marriage between us. Kitty and I shall content ourselves with the usual arrangement in that case.'

He waited.

Matilda's nails tapped.

'No,' she said, cold and flat. 'You mayn't have her at all. It is best for her long-term happiness.'

Rage ignited within Sidney. He rose to his feet, suspicion about Matilda's motivation writhing in his mind like a twisting viper. 'Your concern for your sister's happiness is commendable, Matilda,' he said, advancing with each word as he returned her blazing stare. 'But I daresay now her happiness depends upon me. Why don't you tell me the *true* reason you deny us joy?'

Even in the dark room, Matilda visibly paled, but she recovered herself with the shake of her turban and a quick swipe of her sparkling hands, smoothing her creaseless skirts. 'I've told you everything there is to tell. This conversation is over.' She stepped towards the door.

Sidney blocked her path. 'Not over yet, Matilda.'

She coughed fretfully. 'I don't like you like this, Sidney. I thought you were a kind man, until now.'

He was the unkind one?

'And I thought you gave a damn about Kitty's happiness. It seems we've both lived with misconceptions.'

Matilda inhaled sharply, as if gearing up to chide him, but she didn't hold power over Sidney as she did over Kitty.

'Whatever else you have to say, Matilda, I have no interest in hearing.' He withdrew the three hundred pounds and pressed it into her palm. 'There is my money. Now I shall go to Kitty. She and Ada-Marie expect me in the garden.'

'I didn't—'

'Stop!' Sidney seethed. 'I shan't listen to another word from you unless you wish to bestow your blessing – for what it's worth, if it *is* worth anything – on my marriage to your sister. You can have nothing else to say to me.'

He stalked to the door, but as he reached for the handle, Matilda's voice called out: 'I've not given my permission for an arrangement. Perhaps, if you pay a bit more, I might overlook your boorish—'

More? Already, he must give Matilda almost every shilling he earned for the foreseeable future in order to pull Kitty from her clutches. She'd get nothing else from him.

Sidney turned. 'Enough.'

Matilda floundered.

At last, Sidney comprehended Tyrold's revulsion. Matilda cared nothing for Kitty's well-being. She cared only for how much money she could squeeze from men who desired her sisters. 'Your chance to negotiate with me is over. I've paid you the value you assigned to three months of Kitty's . . . companionship.' It was a disgusting sentence to utter. 'Now she and I shall do as we please. Kitty doesn't need her sister's permission to act in a manner which constitutes her own happiness, and you assuredly have no authority over *me*.'

Sidney turned the brass door lever and swung open the door. He fumed as he marched across the entrance hall and through a drawing room, but he halted before the exit to the courtyard garden. He gathered his breath to calm himself.

When he opened the door, Sidney blinked at the brightness. Before a honeysuckle-laden trellis, Kitty and Ada-Marie snuggled upon a wrought-iron bench, sunbeams shining down as they shared tea and laughter. Despite the troubles with Matilda, Sidney's heart soared. His two ladies were a vision of paradise, the embodiment of his hopes and dreams.

Kitty raised her head. She smiled and beckoned.

Ada-Marie slid off the bench. 'It's Sidney,' she squealed. Her red slippered feet landed on the brick pavement. She walked forward with her arms outheld, and her white muslin gown fluttering. 'Where are you, Sidney?'

Sidney strode forth. 'Here, sweet mousey,' he said, swinging Ada-Marie up in the air. She shrieked joyfully and kicked her little legs towards the sky. Then Sidney clasped her to his chest and laid his cheek against her blonde hair, inhaling her child-fresh scent of sunshine, soap and sweetness. He needed to protect her from Matilda, as well. Now more than ever, he comprehended the dangers of the house on Mount Street.

Ada-Marie reached with her fingers and patted his face, her way of seeing him. Sidney smiled, and when her fingertips brushed his lips and teeth, she smiled too. 'May we plant my new flowers now?'

'Yes, my darling. You, me and Kitty.'

Holding Ada-Marie close and feeling the trust and love in her squeezes, Sidney knew exactly how to persuade Kitty to let him care for her and their child, properly.

8

From the garden bench, Kitty's heart soared as Sidney enveloped Ada-Marie in an embrace. The little girl laughed as she snuggled her flaxen head against Sidney's shoulder.

Sidney held Ada-Marie in secure arms, as if he'd protect her until the end of time.

Like a father.

During the precious few years before darkness descended on Kitty's childhood, her own dear papa had greeted Kitty and her sisters in such a manner at the end of a long day's work. Meanwhile, Mama – sweetest, loveliest, gentlest Mama – would stir a stewpot, a soft smile on her beautiful lips, and their two-room lodgings became more magnificent than a palace.

Now, in the courtyard of this prison-mansion, sunlight shimmered across Sidney's brow and danced over the tender lips which had so recently kissed Kitty with heated passion. He was virile, yet gentle, and whenever Kitty took Sidney to her bed – soon, hope-fully – the love they'd make would be real instead of forced. With Sidney, Kitty needn't pretend she was someone else. She needn't fake her sentiments.

Kitty smiled as they approached her bench. Simpered, no doubt, but she didn't care. She wore her heart proudly on her sleeve, relieved she could finally display feelings she'd suppressed for six years.

Ada-Marie bounced in Sidney's arms. 'Come, Kitty. We're going upstairs to plant my new flowers.'

'Mousey's orders.' Sidney winked at Kitty after employing the adorable pet name he'd given Ada-Marie when she was a bundled infant.

Beaming, Kitty put down her teacup. 'Aye, aye, Captain Mouse.' She stood and smoothed her cerulean skirts as Ada-Marie wiggled down from Sidney's arms.

Kitty took one of Ada-Marie's hands, and Sidney took the other. With direction, Ada-Marie led them, as she liked to do, sliding her slipper along the brick to feel her upcoming step before confidently moving forward. In this way, they progressed out of the courtyard, through a darkened drawing room, into the entrance hall and up four flights of stairs, while singing Ada-Marie's favourite songs.

Meanwhile, Kitty basked in the delightful realisation that, for the first time in her life, she was simultaneously working *and* spending her time exactly how she would've chosen to. The phrase 'Sidney is my keeper, Sidney is my keeper' repeated in her head – too good to be true, and yet, there he was beside her, with Ada-Marie secure and beloved between them, and *no other man* would come and demand Kitty's attention. That was Sidney's privilege alone.

Kitty's joy was so intense, her chest ached, burned, flamed with happiness. How could she bear such bliss?

And how could she bear to relinquish it, one day? She'd barely set her lips to this cup of joy, and already she knew no other draught could ever quench her thirst. It was all very well to think – as she had at the park – of savouring every moment, storing memories for future loneliness, but, in truth, Kitty wanted to sink her claws into this ecstasy and never, ever relinquish it.

When they arrived at the third-floor corridor, Sidney opened the door to the children's spacious chamber, still called – out of habit – the 'nursery'. Matilda's and Barbara's eldest sons went to school, and three of the Preece sisters' offspring were raised exclusively by their fathers' families, but twelve children still occupied the jonquil-papered, dormitory-like space.

Yet, at the moment, the nursery was relatively quiet, with most of its inhabitants absent – likely at Green Park or on a carriage ride. Ada-Marie's ever-diligent attendant, steel-haired and grey-eyed Nanny Ashcroft, was setting the nursery to rights by directing two chambermaids to tidy books, puzzles and toys. She greeted Ada-Marie in her customary warm but business-like manner, as she straightened the blue eiderdown duvet on Ada-Marie's corner cot. A dozen other narrow beds and cradles were scattered in niches throughout the room, separated by bookcases, cabinets and trunks. On the far wall were two brass beds for the night-time attendants.

Kitty had been lucky to entice Nanny Ashcroft – a dependable and trustworthy woman – to work at the infamous Preece sisters' home. The forty pounds Kitty paid the grandmotherly nanny per annum – six times more than the nursemaids earned – certainly helped retain her, but Nanny Ashcroft also genuinely loved Ada-Marie. Having once raised a boy who had lost his sight to smallpox, she capably supported and encouraged Ada-Marie's self-determination.

Kitty wouldn't have it any other way. And, like Philippe, Nanny Ashcroft held a position of power in the servant hierarchy at the Preece sisters' establishment. Yes, Matilda was queen, but everyone from butler to scullery maid knew Kitty earned the lion's share of the income, so Kitty's personal servants reigned supreme in the servants' hall.

In a beam of light by one gabled window sat thirteen-year-old Tess, Matilda's eldest daughter, rocking Amy's infant son. Upon Kitty's progression farther into the nursery, Tess's dark eyes grew overlarge. The girl peeked at Sidney from behind her thick curtain of auburn hair, a decidedly pink stain to her round, pretty face.

Tess seemed terrified of Sidney, so Kitty sought to put her niece at ease. 'Do you recall the Reverend Wakefield, Tess?'

Tess shook her head as her eyes ducked down to the baby.

Poor child. Tess was often timid.

Kitty murmured to Ada-Marie that she'd soon join her and Sidney at her jardinière and traversed the room to kneel beside her niece's wooden swing chair. 'You didn't want to go out on this lovely day, Tess?'

Again, Tess shook her head. 'No. There's sun enough for Hughey and me here, by this window.' She trailed the tip of a finger over the baby's rose-petal cheek.

Kitty embraced her niece, her heart twisting for the child's sweet and timid nature, which often got Tess in trouble with her mother.

Tess nestled as close to Kitty as she could without disturbing baby Hugh.

'Ada-Marie and I are planting flowers in her jardinière if you wish to join us.'

Tess quivered, as fearful as a cornered mouse. 'No, thank you. Hughey likes me to rock him.'

Kitty considered telling Tess that Sidney was safe — that he wouldn't tease or touch her or make confusing comments — but she decided against it. What did Tess gain by knowing kind men could also flit in and out of a courtesan's life, although less frequently than the unkind ones? It might raise the poor child's hopes . . . encourage her to yearn for something very different from her mother's intentions. And for what? Yes, some men were safer than others, but they were all transitory.

Even Sidney, eventually. If not by his nature, then by the constraints of his purse and Matilda's financial expectations.

Kitty kissed Tess's cheek. 'Enjoy the baby snuggles, dearest.'

When she joined Sidney and Ada-Marie, they were kneeling on a woven linen rug next to a wooden Noah's Ark. Sidney had given Ada-Marie the carved mahogany toy for her second birthday, slowly adding to it over the following two years by purchasing a new set of wooden animals every few months. Miniature toys – doll's houses, animals, carriages – allowed Ada-Marie to feel the shape of objects otherwise too large to take in.

Ada-Marie bounced her bottom on her heels. 'Tell me all about the country, Sidney. Were there animals?'

'Yes, indeed, mousey.' Sidney lined up a pair of doves, the cow and bull, and the ram and ewe, as Kitty watched, her heart full. He ran Ada-Marie's fingers over each as he spoke. 'I heard birdsong, the lowing of cows, and the baaing of sheep without the grating noises and shoving crowds of the city.' He lifted Ada-Marie's arms and held them out by her sides. 'There were wide spaces where one might spread one's arms and twirl, with no carriages or buildings to block one's delight.' He drew both of her hands into one of his. 'Because it's summertime, the breezes smelt of fresh grass and sweet peas, which are a darling flower, *not* the little round vegetable which rolls about on one's plate. You can smell the ones I brought you.'

Ada-Marie inhaled deeply. 'They tickle my nose with their perfume.'

Sidney smiled. 'But they aren't as sweet-smelling as you, mousey.'

Ada-Marie giggled. 'Let's plant them outside. They love the sun's warmth as much as I do. Come, Kitty, and help.'

Kitty had no objection. Philippe might waggle a teasing finger later if any dirt muddied her fine gown, but he'd understand. And because *Sidney was now Kitty's keeper*, no other man could demand she present an impeccable appearance. Thus, she dug her hands into the moist soil of Ada-Marie's window garden with *almost* as much enthusiasm as Ada-Marie and Sidney.

The nursery door clicked open as they knelt together. Kitty turned, expecting to see some of her beloved nieces and nephews, red-cheeked and sweaty and laughing from boisterous adventures.

But only Matilda stood framed in the doorway.

Her eyes flittered towards Kitty, and although they didn't linger, poison laced her brief gaze.

Ice ran down Kitty's spine.

Why was her sister angry? Why did she look . . . almost *hateful*? As if she despised Sidney. Or Kitty. Or the sight of them together with Ada-Marie, their hands inches deep in dirt.

Kitty retracted her fingers from the soil and furtively wiped them on her handkerchief. 'Matilda, how lovely you've come,' she said, standing, intending to ask her sister to observe the sweet peas, hopeful that if Matilda witnessed their joy, the unpleasant scowl which made Kitty quail would vanish from her sister's face.

But Matilda *ignored* her, not granting Kitty a chance to issue the invitation.

She spoke to Tess instead, in a curt, sharp voice. 'Teresa, your dancing master has been awaiting you in the drawing room these last fifteen minutes. Put that baby in his cradle and come down at once.'

Tess seemed to shrink in on herself even as she rose and handed Hugh to Nanny Ashcroft, who'd marched across the room in anticipation.

'Don't slouch,' Matilda barked at her daughter.

Chin quivering, Tess straightened her back and tucked a thick strand of dark red hair behind her ear.

Matilda grunted. 'That's better, but far from perfect. You must learn to stand and walk as your Aunt Kitty does, to display your figure to best advantage. No man wants a maudlin, slump-shouldered meekling for a mistress.'

Kitty pressed a hand to her aching heart as Tess followed her mother from the room. She longed to help her niece, but what power did she have to alter the child's fate? Other than to earn as much as she could for as long as she could, and hopefully delay the inevitable day when Matilda would auction Tess's virginity.

'What's a mistress?' Ada-Marie asked after the nursery door clicked closed.

Kitty's stomach dropped like a rock in water. The moment she'd dreaded had arrived: Ada-Marie would soon realise what Kitty really was.

Sidney answered smoothly. 'A mistress is like a master, but a *lady*-master. Thus, a woman who has charge of something, whether it be a household or a coffee shop or Queen Charlotte's robes or a man's heart.'

Heart? Ha!

A mistress had charge of a different organ.

But Kitty didn't dispute Sidney's definition. According to *his* understanding, it wasn't a lie, and Ada-Marie needn't know the complete truth yet. Kitty breathed easier, grateful for another reprieve.

Ada-Marie wiped her nose with a dirty paw, leaving an adorable smudge of soil across its tip. 'Is Kitty your mistress, Sidney? Since you love her?'

Sidney's face took on a peculiar expression. But Kitty marvelled, astonished at Ada-Marie's intuitive understanding. How had the child sensed something Kitty herself had realised only hours earlier?

Sidney wiped his hands on his own handkerchief and wrapped his arms around Ada-Marie. 'She is indeed mistress of my heart, which reminds me of something I wanted to tell you, mousey. A glorious dream is about to come true. Would you like to hear about it?'

'Oh, yes,' Ada-Marie said, her milky blue eyes widening, her questions about mistresses hopefully forgotten.

Sidney lowered his voice to a near-whisper. 'I sold three of my novels to a publisher, and with the money I received, I can take care of Kitty and you – our little daughter. I hope to take you both to the country, where we can live together in our own snug cottage forevermore. Just *us*, mousey, with Nanny Ashcroft and my cat Marmalade.'

Kitty wished Sidney hadn't said such a thing to Ada-Marie. Of course he could take them to the country if he wished – Kitty belonged to him now – but it wouldn't, *couldn't*, be 'forevermore'. Sweet idealistic Sidney didn't understand the temporary nature of a keeper-mistress relationship. Kitty would have to explain later – in private.

Ada-Marie clapped enthusiastically. 'Truly, Sidney?' she asked, squealing. 'Are we to have a home together? Am I to live with you and Kitty as my papa and mama?'

The backs of Kitty's eyes prickled.

Poor Ada-Marie.

It couldn't last. It wouldn't last.

'That is what I want, mousey,' Sidney said, 'but you and I shall do what Kitty feels is right.'

Ada-Marie leaned her head closer to Kitty. 'May we *please*, Kitty?'

Kitty swallowed the tightness in her throat. 'Sidney and I shall discuss, poppet.'

Ada-Marie clasped Kitty in a hug, and Sidney slipped his arms around them both. 'Say yes,' Ada-Marie whispered. 'Please say yes.'

Kitty closed her eyes, trying to relish the family embrace.

When would these sweet moments become memories as achingly painful as those brief, perfect years when Kitty's papa and mama had lived? And how would she and Ada-Marie withstand the pain of severance one day?

When Kitty stepped outside the nursery half an hour later, she faced Sidney in the third-floor corridor. Several children had just returned from the park, and their shrieks and laughter were audible through the oak door.

Kitty rubbed her hands, seeking to reduce the tingling of her palms. Thoughts of Matilda's anger, Tess's fear and Ada-Marie's joy writhed inside her brain. 'Sid, why did you say those things about living in the country?'

'Because I want to give you and Ada-Marie the best life possible, Kit, and neither of you have that here. Even with Nanny Ashcroft's constant attention, Ada-Marie can't thrive here like she could living in a quiet family home. I can provide that for you both.'

Kitty squeezed her hands together; the tingling wouldn't go away. It was tempting to give in to Sidney's dream, as if she were a respectable woman with the right to an honourable life. But a temporary taste of joy might render a return to Mount Street unbearable for Ada-Marie.

Sidney tucked one of Kitty's curls behind her ear. 'Kit, what is Matilda's plan for Ada-Marie?'

Kitty's cheeks burned; she turned her face aside so Sidney couldn't peer into her eyes. 'Not what it is for the other girls. Not like what she has in mind for Tess.' She swallowed and forced herself to look at Sidney. His gaze was kind, but troubled, and Kitty sought to reassure him. 'Matilda *promised* she'd never expect Ada-Marie to become a courtesan. In her own way, Matilda is good to Ada-Marie. After all, she allows the pianoforte lessons Ada-Marie loves so well.'

Matilda permitted the lessons so the child could one day provide music during the Preece sisters' famous evenings of entertainment. 'She's an extraordinarily pretty girl,' Matilda had said after watching the precocious child sing with her master, 'and her voice is remarkably tuneful. Her *condition* won't disturb anyone if she's at the instrument.'

But Kitty didn't tell Sidney that.

'And if Matilda changes her mind because a man offers, Kit?'

Bile burned in Kitty's mouth. 'She'd never. I'd never allow it.'

133

'But can you always protect Ada-Marie here, in this house full of men? A beautiful blind girl—'

Kitty threw a hand to her throat, for Sidney's words strangled her. 'If you had these horrid, filthy concerns, why did you bring her here when she was a baby?'

Sidney deflated, rubbing his temple. 'I acted impulsively because I wanted to give her the best chance of surviving, and I knew you'd have the means and the desire to provide that. She likely would've died at the asylum – we both know that, even if we haven't said it aloud. Instead, she's thrived in your care, Kit.'

Kitty's lips turned down. 'I've tried my best. I love her beyond comprehension.'

'I know.' Sidney took her hands in his. 'As do I. Thus, I'm committed to giving her the best future possible. Besides her music, she can learn to read and write. We can hire a tutor from the Royal School for the Blind to teach her Monsieur Haüy's method. We've spoken of these things for more than a year, but the time to act is *now*. You and I want to be together, and I can support you. Let us give our daughter a home with *married* parents.'

Kitty swallowed. *Marriage* again . . .

Sidney held her hands tighter. 'Kit, Ada-Marie isn't safe here. I can no longer share your confidence in Matilda. She wanted to keep us apart.'

The confirmation of Matilda's disapproval was a stab to Kitty's heart. 'Why?'

'She claims to think I'll hurt you. My love, you've known me for six years – have I given you any reason to suppose I'd *ever* hurt you?'

'No, of course not.' Kitty frowned, studying Sidney's beautiful fingers caressing her hands. 'But . . .' She hesitated. They couldn't marry. Sidney mustn't ruin his life by uniting himself irrevocably with a woman like her.

A nursemaid opened the door, bobbed a curtsy, and bustled down the corridor on her errand.

'But what?' Sidney asked.

'We cannot discuss this in a corridor.' They needed privacy, so Kitty tugged Sidney's arm, leading him down the stairs, her free hand sliding across the polished oak railing. Her heart hammered as she pulled him along the second-floor corridor. She was taking *Sidney* to her *room*. As much as she needed to talk, there was something else she desperately wanted, and she required privacy for that, as well.

Her bedchamber was the grandest in the house. Matilda had granted it when Kitty's second keeper made her the highest-paid courtesan in London, and Philippe had refurbished it in silver, white, and light blue: the colours of a frosty winter's morning under a clear sky.

'To protect your heart, *ma chérie*,' Philippe had explained to a seventeen-year-old Kitty as they had peered at his beautifully rendered sketches. 'The men, they have your body, and they think it is warm and willing, but the icy room will shield your true essence.' As he'd studied his drawings, his blue eyes had glistened.

Now, as Kitty closed the door behind Sidney, they were alone in this spectacular ice-world. All traces of the gowns she'd discarded had been removed, and the bed neatened. No doubt Matilda had ordered the room readied for Tyrold.

Kitty's silver damask drapes were open, allowing thin late-afternoon sunbeams to filter through the crepe inner curtains. Shadow and light waltzed over the pristine white carpet. Snowy hydrangeas spilled from blue jasperware vases on the Carrara marble mantelpiece.

But Sidney stared at the bed.

That didn't surprise Kitty.

It was a work of art. A bed for a queen of the night. Under scalloped silver bedcurtains, the thick feather mattress stretched wide enough for a tall man to lie *any* way he chose. A mountain of pillows lay before the pale blue upholstered headboard. Under the shimmering satin counterpane, the sheets were cool silk.

For the first time, Kitty would take a man she desired into her bed.

Sidney's breathing deepened. His amber eyes darkened, and his eyelids grew heavy. No doubt he needed a shag as much as Kitty did.

Kitty's body throbbed as she drew close to him. 'Sidney, look at me.'

He swallowed before meeting her gaze.

'We can have that' – Kitty indicated the bed – 'and our life in the country, without marriage, darling.'

Sidney shook his head. 'I only want *that*, as you term it, with you as my wife.'

So noble, and yet his voice was thick with lust.

They needed to make love. In the moments that followed, Kitty would explain again how they could live together outside of marriage. They'd be happy for months – or perhaps a few years if the money held – but when the inevitable day arrived when Sidney saw Kitty for what she truly was, he'd be free to seek a young lady of his class who could bear him children.

And perhaps Kitty would somehow find the strength to leave Ada-Marie in their care, to save her beloved girl from a destiny like her own. A destiny like Tess's.

After all, what would anything matter to Kitty then? She'd return to this ice-chamber with no warmth left to protect, a shattered shell of her former self, the only purpose of her existence to ease life for her nieces, even if it meant accepting Gillingham next. That would be the price of her temporary happiness, but it was the only way.

Gentlemen didn't marry courtesans.

She must convince Sidney.

Kitty lifted an eyebrow. 'Do you mean to tell me if I refuse your hand, you won't make love to me *ever*? Not even once?'

Sidney's breath grew heavier. 'I would attempt to resist my desire, out of respect for you.'

Kitty inched closer. He faltered.

Her eyes trailed down his body and hovered at his loins. His trousers revealed the tented outline of the massive erection she'd felt in the darkened shadows of the Dark Walk and while they embraced by the Ring.

Poor Sidney. He needed release. He'd think rationally afterwards.

'May I touch you?' she asked, breathing the words against his cheek.

Sidney nodded, albeit barely, and Kitty cupped his scrotum through his trousers and laid her forearm against the length of his cock as she pressed him against the door.

His eyes rolled back.

'You fail to consider,' Kitty said as she nipped his earlobe, 'my feelings on the matter.' She gripped his hard rod and manipulated it through his trousers. Sidney moaned, low and guttural. 'I want you as much as you want me. Perhaps *more*, for I'm unable to resist my desire.'

The throbbing between her legs grew painfully urgent.

Sidney's eyes were closed, his lips parted, his breath laboured as he leaned his head against the door while she rubbed him.

Kitty trailed her kisses to his lips.

His eyelids fluttered, opened. His eyes smouldered. Their intensity caused Kitty to tremble deliciously, her body aflame.

Sidney cupped one hand behind her head and threw his arm around her waist, and pressed into her, over her, kissing her so ardently he knocked the breath from her lungs. He crushed her lips with the power of his passion.

Blissful agony.

Her feet gave way under her as Sidney picked her up, one arm behind her shoulders, one under her knees, kissing her as he carried her, wilfully powerless in his solid embrace.

He laid her upon the bed.

Kitty moaned as Sidney's lips left hers. He half-knelt on the mattress, and she arched her back, wanting to draw him to her like iron to a magnet. She parted her legs, spreading herself, inviting him to lie on top of her. To mount her, to fuck her with vigorous thrusts. 'I need you,' she said, tugging at her skirts.

Sidney sat on his bottom, his eyes hard and his jaw tight, and rubbed his hand along her silk stocking. He slid his palm over the curve of her calf and past the garter-ribbons at her knee, pushing the cerulean gown up and studying her leg as if it were the most fascinating phenomenon known to man.

Kitty's cunt throbbed, engorged, desperate for him. '*Sidney.*'

'Marry me, Kitty.' His voice was husky, deep, authoritative. 'Be my wife.' His fingers caressed her inner thigh. 'And I shall worship your body as I already worship your mind and spirit.'

Kitty groaned. Her body glided across the satin bedspread as she writhed under Sidney's touch. She fisted the counterpane and lifted her hips, panting, willing Sidney's fingers up, up, up to her wetness. 'Please put me out of my misery, Sidney.'

'Marry me,' he said again. 'And when you are Mrs Wakefield, I shall make love to you for a week solid.' He grazed his fingertips higher on her thigh, but he stopped short of the place which pulsed with passion.

Kitty huffed. 'You impossible man!'

He chuckled.

Kitty narrowed her eyes. How *dare* he sit there so calmly while she squirmed and pleaded? 'Two can play your game, Sidney Wakefield.'

He raised his brows. 'Whatever do you mean?'

Kitty yanked his hand away from her thigh. She raised up on her knees and grasped his shoulders. 'I shall make *you* beg now.'

Sidney didn't comprehend the depth of her skill. But she'd show him.

9

Sidney fell into a pillowy pile as Kitty pushed him down onto her bed.

She leaned over him, her curls framing her lovely face. 'You'll never underestimate me again, Sid.'

'I don't underestimate you—'

Kitty grasped his cock through his trousers. As had happened at the door, a jolt of electricity shot through Sidney's body, depriving him of the ability to speak, and his eyelids grew too heavy to keep open.

She rubbed him, bringing him to peaks of pleasure with each stroke. 'You *do* underestimate me, you foolish man. Open your eyes.'

It was the tone of authority. Sidney obeyed.

She smiled wickedly. 'You mayn't close them again unless I say so.'

Kitty pulled out her hairpins, and her dark ringlets tumbled over her shoulders.

Exquisite.

Sidney twisted his finger in one that rested upon Kitty's décolletage. 'Your curls are perfect.'

Kitty giggled, softening into the darling Kit Sidney knew. 'Philippe spends hours making them so.'

141

'Does he?'

Kitty spread her arms wide, as if presenting herself to an audience. 'Everything perfect about my appearance is the product of Philippe's incessant grooming.'

Sidney trailed his palm across the twinned mounds of her splendid bosom. 'These aren't.'

Kitty's grin deepened. 'No.' Her fingers navigated the buttons at his waistband. 'They aren't.'

Sidney's breath caught when she opened the fall of his trousers. He'd stop her soon . . . but his cock strained against his shirt tail, craving her touch, and Sidney didn't want to resist quite yet. He moaned as she held him in her hand, skin on skin.

'Oh, Sidney.' Her voice was husky, throaty. 'How magnificent.'

She slid her hand up and down, peeking at him through her lashes, and his lids fell heavily across his eyes again.

Kitty fisted his cravat and gave it a none-too-gentle tug, startling him out of his daze. 'I told you to keep your eyes open. If you close them again, I shall lift my skirts and ride you with no further warning. Do you understand?'

Sidney nodded. 'I shall keep them open so I can savour your beauty,' he said, his voice thick. He would allow himself a few minutes to luxuriate in his beloved's attentions, but there couldn't be fulfilment yet. First, he must ensure the long-term wellbeing of Kitty and Ada-Marie.

Kitty's eyes glinted. 'Let's test this iron resolve of yours, you gorgeous man.' She bit her bottom lip as her eyes fell again to his cock. 'I want this shaft in my cunt, but you won't give it to me.' She rubbed her thumb over the tip of his penis, spreading its lubricant over the smooth head while Sidney burned with desire. 'I suppose my mouth will have all the fun.'

Sidney's breath quickened, fast, desperate. Kitty's mouth slid wet and hot over his cock, her tongue encircling its sensitive head. A groan ripped from his throat as she sucked, hard and vigorous, mimicking the motions of exuberant intercourse.

'Oh, God, Kitty.' Her hair fell like silk through his fingers as he cupped her scalp while she took him deep into her throat, her almond-shaped eyes locked with his and full of passion, full of feeling, full of desire.

He moaned loudly, intensely, careless of who overheard in this house of pleasure. The virile man in him triumphed at his position on Kitty Preece's bed, her mouth on his cock, her curls tickling his hips, her eyes united with his. He lay in the most coveted spot in Mayfair, on the verge of exploding in Kitty's mouth or throwing her on her back and thrusting into her with the vigour of a stallion.

But it was not enough, because he *loved* this woman.

'Stop, Kit, stop.' He pulled her off him, stroking her curls, her cheeks, her chin. 'You're magnificent, but stop, my dearest love.'

She blinked, but she did as he asked.

Sidney pulled her next to him, snuggling her body in a warm embrace. She nestled into his shoulder with her arms curled against her chest, no longer a seductress but a tender-hearted woman, uncertain if she deserved love.

After Sidney buttoned his trousers, he lifted her chin. 'Marry me.'

'Oh, Sidney.' Her sweet brow furrowed. 'You cannot truly want me to marry you.'

'I've wanted you to be my wife for six years.'

The corner of her lips turned down. 'Why did you never ask before?'

'I've never had the means to support you and Ada-Marie until now.' He brushed her curls from her face. 'And until last night, I never dared hope you returned my sentiments.'

Kitty fidgeted with the ruffles on his shirt. 'In truth, I didn't comprehend the true nature of our feelings for each other until today.'

Ah, perhaps uncertainty about *her* feelings towards *him* caused Kitty's hesitancy. Sidney stroked her cheek. 'Do you doubt your sentiments? Please tell me if you do.'

She smoothed the folds of his cravat. 'My sentiments aren't new. I've loved you . . . romantically, I suppose you'd say, since the first time you visited after bringing Ada-Marie here. You'd written her a poem – "The Scents of Night-time, the Sounds of Day" – to help her learn to distinguish one from the other. If I didn't know it before, I realised then you were the most wonderful man in the world.' She half-smiled, poignantly. 'But I repressed my sentiments because I thought we could never be.'

Sidney pressed his lips to her forehead. 'We're both free to follow our hearts.'

'But . . . your kind and mine don't marry.' Kitty's voice was less certain, as if she was considering Sidney's reasoning. 'Others will never let us forget we aren't equals.'

Sidney would continue to soothe her reservations away. 'Kit, you and I are equals in love, and therefore we're equal. Why should the opinions of society stop us from making a choice that hurts no one?' He pressed Kitty's head against his chest, holding her ear to his heart, willing her to hear his devotion.

Kitty gathered a ragged breath. 'If you marry me, you'll never . . .' – she covered her eyes with her hand before the words rushed out of her – 'you'll never have a child of your own. I cannot let you give that up.'

Ah, was that what held her back? Inadequacies tortured Kitty, but on this point, at least, Sidney could absolutely reassure her.

He brushed her hands away, met her gaze, and spoke from the heart. 'Blood doesn't make a family. My parents and my brother never loved me, but my friends, and you, and Ada-Marie do. I don't need children of my own begetting to be a father.' As Kitty glanced down and fiddled with the buttons on his waistcoat, Sidney rested his chin on the top of her head. 'We can adopt more children if you want a larger family.'

She looked up, wide-eyed. 'Truly?'

Her reaction was proof of what he'd suspected from the beginning of their six-year friendship: deep down,

145

Kitty longed to live simply as a wife and mother, but she'd never had that choice before.

'Yes. Not immediately, but soon. After Ada-Marie has adjusted to the new environment, after I've written another book or two. Perhaps a year from now?'

'Oh, Sid,' Kitty said, her voice fraught with emotion, 'I want to be a mama.'

'You *are* a mama.' Sidney stroked her cheek with his thumb. 'Do you remember how your love of children brought us together? Six years ago, when I mistook your sister Jenny's infant for your own . . .'

Sidney paused, recalling the memory of their first meeting. He'd been a recently ordained two-and-twenty-year-old, riding in Hyde Park with Tyrold and Holbrook when he'd spied Kitty sitting in the shade cradling a baby. She was breathtakingly beautiful in a ruffled, short-sleeved pink gown, with silky strands of dark hair escaping her elegant chignon. But it was her expression which had stunned Sidney. She'd cast her thick-lashed eyes downward, her face awash with love for the infant she held. A delicate glow seemed to emanate from her, like a Madonna with her child. Clearly, no one else existed to her at that moment.

Sidney had reined in his horse. 'Who is she?' he'd asked his friends. He'd assumed she must be married, but he couldn't resist.

Tyrold had laughed. 'Too expensive for you, my boy.'

Sidney hadn't understood.

He'd looked to worldly widower Holbrook for explanation.

Nicky's grey eyes had studied Sidney. 'Her name is Kitty Preece. She's one of several courtesan sisters. You see the others there, blowing kisses to men and neglecting their children.'

Until then, Sidney hadn't noticed the other beautiful dark-haired women, nor the nursemaids chasing several boisterous children.

'Let it go, eh, Sid?' Holbrook had urged gently. 'Don't lose your heart there.'

'I only want to write her a poem, Nicky.' Mindless of Tyrold's continued ribbing, he had dismounted, drew out a pencil and paper, and composed a sonnet he'd entitled 'Motherhood: Lines to Miss Kitty Preece as she Cradles her Child'.

Kitty's voice drew Sidney from the memory, but the mention of their meeting had evidently absorbed her as well. 'You wrote me a poem.'

Sidney smiled. 'It was the moment I realised I'd found a muse. It was my best work to date.'

'When you gave it to me, you said, "Forgive my boldness, madam", and you bowed and walked away. I expected love verses. Instead, it was as if you saw into my soul.'

'You told me so weeks later. Meanwhile, I thought you'd hated it, since you didn't respond.'

'It touched me so deeply, I *couldn't* respond sooner. I kept it beside my bed and read it every day.' She nodded towards a side table. 'There, in that drawer. If you look, you'll find it under a blue shawl.'

Sidney searched Kitty's eyes instead. 'Do you recall what you asked me when you thanked me for the poem?'

'I asked you to tell me your deepest desire. You didn't hesitate in your response. "For my novels and poetry to bring joy to others."'

Sidney nodded. 'You replied, "You've accomplished it, if my joy matters."' He stroked Kitty's cheek. 'Your joy matters more than anything else. Kitty, you're my everything. My very salvation.'

'Oh, Sidney,' Kitty said, pressing her fingers to her lips, 'your words make my soul sing. It's as if my mind has just let me accept something my heart always knew.'

Sidney's soul sang as well. 'Kitty, for six years we've comforted each other . . .'

'. . . Been there for each other,' she said, their minds thinking as one. 'You've bolstered me when men were unkind . . .'

'. . . And you've believed in my writing when no one else did.' Sidney smiled. 'For four years, we've raised our child together, Kit.'

Kitty nodded. 'She's been our chief delight, in a way no one else understands.'

Sidney held his love close, her body melding against his. 'Between us, there has only ever been kindness, respect and support.'

Amazement shone in Kitty's blue-green eyes. 'And love,' she whispered. 'There's always been love. First, the strongest of friendship, and then something stronger yet.'

Sidney's chest expanded, filling with adoration. 'The Greek language recognises different kinds of love. Friendship, passion, devotion, and enduring love, which

148

survives every trial and tribulation. Kit, I feel all of those for you.'

She nodded. 'I feel the same.'

He smiled. 'I know. I know because we are alike, Kit. That's why we've been the dearest, if unlikeliest, of treasured friends. We are two sensitive souls who've never fit into the worlds in which we were thrust. When we found each other, we knew we needed each other. Kitty, we *belong* together.'

She propped herself up on one elbow, her eyebrows peaked. 'You truly want this? Me, forever and ever?'

'With all my heart.'

She worried her plump bottom lip with her white teeth, as if thinking. 'Sid, if we marry, could we . . . could we, maybe, provide a home – a respectable home, in as much as any home with me in it can be – to Tess? And others of my nieces, should they not wish to be courtesans?'

A wave of financial worry pressed against Sidney's chest, but he forced it away. His dream was within his grasp – he couldn't let it go, even if he must provide for a dozen of Kitty's nieces. He'd do whatever he must to succeed. 'Yes, Kitty, of course.'

'Oh, Sidney,' she said, breathless. 'Darlingest of all men. You are truly my Sir Galahad.'

And Sidney, knowing he'd breached her reservations at last, smiled whole-heartedly, assuredly. 'Catherine Preece,' he said, now confident of her answer, 'will you do me the honour of becoming my wife?'

'Yes, Sidney.' Clear and precise, as he'd known it would be. 'Yes. I shall marry you.'

Sidney clasped her in his arms. 'You've brought me joy unimaginable,' he said, smothering her face in kisses as their tears and laughter mingled.

Then Kitty's mouth sought his.

And there was only their kiss.

Sidney couldn't drink deeply enough of Kitty's taste – the essence of the lady he loved.

His heart. His life. His muse.

His wife.

Somehow, she was under him, and her body yielded. Her back arched, her curves and softness moulding perfectly against his angles and hardness. Sidney's hands sought her luscious breasts; he yearned to free them from the gown, cup them, suckle them. His cock throbbed with the urgent desire to possess Kitty. To plunge into her. To bring their love to physical fulfilment. To peak the crest of passion with the woman he loved.

Kitty parted her legs, and Sidney pressed between them, the layers of their clothes the sole barrier between their union.

'Now will you make love to me?' Kitty's voice pleaded, heavy with desire.

Sidney shook his head, although his cock cried out against his decision. 'Not until you're my wife.' He doubted his own resolve as he said it, but he knew one thing for certain: he wouldn't have her *here*, on this magnificent bed where others had exploited her.

Kitty groaned. 'When can we marry?'

The question sobered Sidney.

He supported himself on his elbow. Kitty's hair fanned out around her, dusky waves against the quilted satin counterpane. 'I've thought about this a great deal since yesterday, Kitty. If we marry in England, it must be in this parish. Whether I go to the bishop for a common licence, or whether we wait three weeks for the banns—'

'There'll be trouble,' she said.

'Some . . . difficulties, yes.' Sidney spared her the truth: the bishop was his maternal uncle; he and Sidney's mother would do everything in their power to prevent the marriage, and they might succeed. 'Do you know what I must ask?'

Kitty's smile was pure perfection. 'An elopement will be thrilling, Sidney Wakefield.'

Sidney's shoulders eased. 'You truly don't mind, my love?'

'I've always wanted to visit Scotland.'

Sidney grinned. They'd vanish north for two weeks of paradise, and return man and wife, and no one – not his uncle, not Cornelius, not Matilda, not Gillingham, and not Sidney's mother – could change it. 'Give me a few days, and I shall arrange the journey. Tell Ada-Marie we'll be away for a fortnight – I meant what I said about spending a week in bed once you become Mrs Wakefield, and the journey each way will take two or three days. When we return, you and Ada-Marie and Nanny Ashcroft will live at my lodgings. As soon as I can lease a cottage, we'll move to the country.'

Kitty grasped his hand. 'What about Gillingham?'

'I shall visit soon and reimburse him.' Sidney paused, considering how little he trusted the duke. 'Try to stay at home – or go out in company with Philippe or *several* of your sisters.' *Not Matilda alone.*

Kitty nodded, but two lines marred her pretty brow.

Sidney smoothed them with a kiss. 'Do not distress yourself. I can handle Gillingham.'

Kitty's eyes widened, as if with a sudden thought. 'Sid, if we leave the night before Gillingham's daughter's wedding, he couldn't possibly follow us for another four-and-twenty hours. He won't be able to escape the festivities until the wedding ball has ended.'

Sidney's heart twinged. Gillingham had clearly frightened Kitty, despite her ever-brave face. 'We needn't plan our lives to avoid Gillingham, love. There's no reason to fear him anymore. You are my fiancée, and soon you will be my wife. I shall protect you.'

Kitty kissed his palm. 'Now that I've sampled joy, I shan't risk losing it. Please let's leave the night before Lady Caroline's wedding.'

Sidney nodded. 'Very well. We shall depart at midnight in five days' time. Send word at once if you have trouble from *anyone*.' Kitty feared the duke, but Matilda worried Sidney more, for she might poison Kitty's mind against him. 'I think it best if we keep our elopement a secret from *everyone* except Ada-Marie and Tyrold.'

'Nanny Ashcroft and Philippe must know as well, Sidney. We cannot expect Ada-Marie to keep such an exciting secret with *no one* else to speak to. Besides, I shall need Philippe's help.'

'Do as you think best, my sweetest love.' Sidney gave her a lingering kiss.

But before passion consumed him, he left, returning to Half Moon Street with his heart soaring.

Kitty would soon be his wife. Nothing would prevent their perfect happiness now.

Not while Sidney had breath in his body . . .

The next five days saw a shocking reduction of the two hundred pounds with which Sidney intended to support his new family.

The hire of a post-chaise to Scotland deprived Sidney of thirty pounds, and he'd require that much again for the return trip. He calculated ten pounds for inns and meals but couldn't gauge the cost of the ceremony itself. What did one pay a Scottish blacksmith to bind one's hands and whack an anvil?

And, of course, Kitty needed a ring. Twenty guineas disappeared at Rundell and Bridge in exchange for a gold wedding band set with turquoise.

Sidney proudly displayed that purchase in Tyrold's book-lined study on the day of his intended elopement, when he visited his friend to collect Gillingham's thousand pounds.

Tyrold was unusually foul-tempered, sitting dishevelled and brooding at his mahogany desk in front of double windows which overlooked Half Moon Street. At the sight of the ring, he clutched his chest and collapsed against the back of his leather armchair. His wolfhound ceased snoring on the hearthrug, perked his ears, and growled.

'There, there, Jolly,' Tyrold said as he waved a hand in front of his face, mimicking a dowager recovering from a fit of vapours. 'I'm not suffering an attack of the heart. It's Sid's foolishness which temporarily incapacitated me.'

Sidney snapped closed the jewellery box. Tyrold didn't deserve to see the ring if he must be an ass. 'In what way am I foolish?'

Tyrold threaded his fingers into his shoulder-length black hair, currently loose from its queue, and cradled his skull. 'In practically every way, but that trinket offends me at present.' His voice was that of a patience-weary parent admonishing a stubborn child. 'Kitty has more jewels than the Queen, and yet you spent ten per cent of your current funds on a *ring*? With, I might add, no chance of additional income until you complete a novel you haven't begun?'

Sidney scowled down at his friend. 'Those jewels are from . . . others. This ring is a symbol of our eternal love.'

Tyrold closed his eyes and sighed, still cradling his skull. 'Apparently you intend to test your theory on love's value over money.' He sat up and waved his hand dismissively. 'I wash my hands of you.'

'Not yet, you don't.' Sidney slipped the ring box into his pocket. 'I require the banknotes for Gillingham.'

Tyrold growled rather like Jolly, but he extracted a loop of keys from his waistcoat pocket. 'Does that bruiser Butcher still trouble you?'

'He never troubled me.' No more than Cornelius, anyway.

Sidney strolled to the window and squinted down at the passers-by and sedan chairs weaving along the street. If Butcher was there, he wasn't visible, but he had an uncanny way of popping up without warning.

Tyrold jiggled his keys. 'Butcher told me he desires wealth but decries this nation's lack of opportunities for fortune-building based on brute strength alone, which I don't dispute. I recommended he move to Upper Canada and try his impressive hands at the logging industry. I rather hoped he'd take up the suggestion at once, rather than lurking after you.'

Sidney half-smiled. 'Did he appreciate your recommendation?'

'Everyone appreciates my recommendations. Rather, everyone but addle-pated numbskulls like you.' Tyrold unlocked a stout metal safe behind his desk. 'So, *is* Butcher following you?'

'Unfortunately, yes – on occasion.' Sidney leaned against the window frame with his hands in his pockets. 'I'll demand Gillingham call him off, for I can't have him trailing me tonight.'

'I'll say. Not a wedding guest *I'd* want.'

As Tyrold withdrew a steel strongbox from the safe and placed it on his desk, Sidney pondered what type of wedding his friend would have. Something stark, no doubt, with a woman as miserly as he.

'I still need you to locate us a cottage,' Sidney said, returning to business matters. The notion of an adult Tyrold in love was beyond Sidney's imagination, although long ago, when they were boys, there had been a girl who'd inspired John into an adoration of sorts.

'Locating you a cottage is an impossible task at the price you demand.' Tyrold leaned back in his armchair and steepled his fingers. 'I cannot find anything better than the one in Devonshire you dismissed.'

'It was two hundred a year.'

'A damned decent price, all things considered.'

'I disagree. Why should I pay two hundred for a country cottage when I pay only ten pounds per annum for a sizable flat and my board in Mayfair? A few bedrooms cannot be such a difference.'

Tyrold remained silent, with his head hunched over his peaked fingers.

Sidney started. Had his friend charged him less than normal rates for his lodgings? 'Johnny,' he said slowly, as he stalked round to the front of Tyrold's desk, 'how much would one *typically* pay for lodgings like mine in Mayfair?'

Tyrold sat up, cleared his throat, and adjusted his cravat. 'How the devil should I know?' He took up the key again and turned it in the strongbox lock.

'As you own numerous lodgings in Mayfair, I should say you know damned well.'

Tyrold opened the lid of the box. 'Then ten pounds is likely positively extortionate.' He withdrew a stack of Bank of England promissory notes and counted out ten of the handwritten papers. 'I'm a stingy fellow, squeezing every drop from my business dealings, didn't you know?' He slid the money across his desk. 'Now, if you're *quite* done displaying the baubles you've purchased, I've work to do.'

Rather than taking the banknotes, Sidney collapsed in a leather chair before Tyrold's desk. 'No, dammit, I need your advice. Explain *why* I must pay so much for a home in the country.'

Tyrold closed his box. 'Because, despite your fanciful assumptions, you cannot live in a tenant's cottage. You're accustomed to servants waiting upon you—'

'I've lived spartan enough for these last six years.'

'Ha! The Smiths cook your meals, do your laundry, and tidy your rooms. Sidney, you leave your cat's dirty bowls in the dining room and your coats on the floor of the entrance hall—'

Sidney glowered. 'As do you.'

'Oh, I'm *far* worse. But I'd readily admit to anyone but Mrs Smith that I wouldn't survive a day without her care, whereas you appear unaware of your inabilities, likely because Mrs Smith simpers over you like you're her pet lamb. Do you expect the same of Kitty? Do you intend to ask your wife to scour your floors, roast your mutton, and wash your smalls?'

'Good God, no.'

'I didn't think so.' Tyrold ticked his fingers one at a time as he continued: 'You'll require a cook, a house-keeper, a chambermaid and a scullery maid. You must maintain a home large enough to house them comfortably. There's Ada-Marie's attendant as well, and perhaps a live-in tutor soon. I imagine Kitty's accustomed to her abigail—'

'He's a dresser and *coiffure*.' Deep despair doused Sidney's dreams. Kitty probably paid Philippe between fifty and a hundred pounds per annum. 'French.'

Tyrold raised his eyebrows. 'Lord, this gets better and better.' He returned the strongbox to his large safe. 'Will you sow the fields yourself?' he asked over his shoulder as he secured the steel door.

'What fields?'

Tyrold turned in his chair, blinking. 'The acres upon which you must grow or raise food for your household. You realise isolated cottages don't have Fortnum and Mason round the corner?'

Sidney slumped deeper into his chair. 'My God. I know nothing about farming.'

'Because your notion of living in the country is to be the son of Lord Eden of Paradisum Park.' Tyrold tucked away his ring of keys. 'You'll need a farmhand and a boy to help him. I'd also suggest a manservant, which will cost near ten pound a year, including the tax. You'll require beasts of labour for the farm, and, unless you expect Kitty to ride about on a workhorse, or drive herself in a donkey cart, you'll need a carriage, carriage horses and a groom.'

Sidney's throat thickened. An agrarian life no longer seemed so idyllic. 'Stop! I've heard enough. What shall I do, Johnny?'

'Plato would say that your need will be your inspiration, but that is exactly why I despise philosophy. If such were the case, no one would be poor.' Tyrold drummed his fingers upon his desk. 'Listen, I doubt you'll appreciate this suggestion, but every time I see Kitty, she's draped in at least a hundred guineas' worth of jewels. Unless they're paste, but I don't think they are.'

Sidney frowned. 'What has that to do with anything?'

'I can't imagine what use they'd be living in a country cottage. The sale of those pink sapphires she wore to meet us in the park alone would garner . . .' – he pursed his lips and looked towards the ceiling – 'well, I'm no expert, but I know a bit. I'd say four hundred quid.'

'Four hundred!' Sidney had no notion Kitty's jewels were so valuable.

'That alone would see you well set up,' Tyrold continued. 'If she sold the lot, I suspect you'd have a tidy sum to invest in the funds.'

Sidney recoiled. 'You'd have me ask Kitty to sell her jewels to support us?'

'No, merely to supplement your income. The old idea of sinking wealth into silver and jewels is foolish in this age of commerce, trade and invention. One must *invest* money for it to grow. Maximise one's assets. Sell the jewels, establish yourselves with some of the proceeds, invest the rest, and the interest will augment your writing income.'

'I'd be a devilish sorry sort to behave in such a way.'

Tyrold wagged his index finger. 'Be careful not to give your pride more consequence than your common sense. End in debtor's prison, and Kitty will sell her jewels anyway – and likely for a fraction of their value.'

'What a grim picture you paint on the day of my elopement,' Sidney said with a huff.

Tyrold held up his hands. 'If you don't like what I suggest, so be it, but you'd do well to remember there are many who pay a great deal of money to hear my opinion. Now, I'd be pleased if you'd let yourself out, as I have business to attend to.'

Instead of leaving, Sidney sank into the leather upholstery and rubbed his chin. Would Kitty be willing to sacrifice her jewels? After all, they planned to live a simple life in the country, and the money would solve their immediate difficulties. Perhaps Sidney should ask her to sell only the pink sapphires, no doubt a present from one of the foul blighters who'd used her and tossed her aside like a discarded toy . . .

'Sidney!'

Sidney jumped in his chair.

'I asked you to leave.' Tyrold pointed to the door with one hand and offered the banknotes with the other.

Sidney rose, folded the money, and put it in his coat pocket. 'Damned decent of you to support this advance, John.'

Tyrold picked up his quill. 'Don't tell a soul, you chub.' He extracted a piece of parchment and dipped the feather in ink.

'You'll remind Mrs Smith to feed Marmalade?'

'Of course. She likes your cat better than she likes me.'

Sidney smiled affectionately at the top of his friend's head. Mr and Mrs Smith and their niece were devoted to John, despite Mrs Smith's incessant chiding. And well they should be, for John was a rum fellow who meant well with his advice. 'And you'll keep an eye on Ada-Marie? Meet her and her nanny in the park at eleven every fine day, as you said?'

'When I give my word,' Tyrold replied, not glancing up from his correspondence, 'I give my blasted word.'

Sidney's heart filled. 'You are the best of men, John.'

'Don't utter those words ever again. I'm a ruthless devil.'

Sidney grinned. 'I shall see you in a fortnight. Wish us joy?'

Tyrold sighed, at last looking up. His green eyes were both kind and sorrowful. 'The greatest of joy to both you and Kitty, every day, and a long, long life together, my friend.'

Sidney winked and exited, closing the door to John's study behind him.

He'd seek out Kitty and ask about the jewels *before* he called upon Gillingham, he decided as he sprang down the stairs. As much as he hated to admit it, he didn't look forward to the discussion with the duke . . .

II

Fervent anticipation *and* tortuous anxiety filled the days after Kitty agreed to be Sidney's wife. Horrific images twisted in her imagination: Butcher beating Sidney in a dank cellar; Gillingham destroying the banknotes in order to claim Kitty still owed him; Sidney's irate mother forcing him to leave England by ordering him onto a frigate bound for danger, as Gillingham had done to poor Richard.

On the afternoon of her intended elopement, Kitty agonised. Surely *something* would prevent her joy. *Something* would stop Kitty from successfully trading her unfulfilling, constrained life for one of love and security with Sidney, in which Kitty herself could, in turn, be a safe harbour for Ada-Marie, for Tess, and others.

She paced back and forth in the bedchamber, until her worries reached a fever pitch, and she rambled frantically to Philippe.

Philippe put his foot down – literally – by stomping his high-polish Hessian on the white carpet. 'Enough! We go out, *chaton*. Shopping.'

Kitty paced the length of her room again, rubbing her palms back and forth across her churning abdomen. 'I need nothing which money can buy.'

Philippe's sandy brows rose. '*Non*? Then tell me, *chaton*, which of your intimate *déshabillé* will you wear for your husband's pleasure? Which duke or marquess's gift would *monsieur* also appreciate?'

Kitty jolted to a halt. 'Oh!' She blinked out the window at the hazy sky. She possessed countless lace, silk and feather dishabilles, but all were tainted by the memory of other men's lust. Kitty couldn't change the fact that she'd had many lovers, but she *could* buy delicate items for Sidney's pleasure alone. 'I see your point.'

Philippe lifted his chin, smiling. 'Philippe always knows best. We go to see Madame Desmarais. *Après*, Nanny Ashcroft can bring Ada-Marie to the toy shop, which you always so enjoy.'

Thus, less than an hour later, Kitty strolled with Jenny, Amy, and two smart footmen towards Bond Street. Philippe also accompanied them, much to Jenny's and Amy's delight. Philippe was Kitty's servant, but he was the indisputable favourite with all the Preece sisters, and Amy and Jenny danced about him like two dark-haired daisies in their dotted muslin gowns, seeking his advice on everything from perfume to petticoats.

To outward appearances, Madame Desmarais was a haberdasher. Her small shop's solitary bow window displayed a selection of kid gloves elegantly pointing pastel fingers at lace fans, with gossamer-thin silk stockings, embroidered garters, and yards of ribbon cascading like so many rainbow waterfalls over piles of folded handkerchiefs. Inside the rose-scented front room, a dazzling array of plumes and posies, ready for trimming bonnets, were laid upon tables, and on shelves behind the mahogany counter, Madame Desmarais had arranged exquisite Valenciennes and French point laces.

But Madame Desmarais kept the *real* treasures in a back room, and to this larger space she admitted Kitty, her younger sisters and their servants.

The chamber was a profusion of lacy, silky femininity – *if* one didn't open the drawers within the mahogany cabinetry along one wall. Jenny and Amy gushed as if they'd landed in paradise, but Kitty went to work at once, examining the lace peignoirs and silk nightgowns featured on mannequins or hanging from rows of pretty ribbons like frothy flags. She wanted only the most elegant, most tasteful items – intimate apparel appropriate for a *wife*, not a courtesan. She wanted to titillate Sidney without disgusting him.

Meanwhile, Jenny and Amy perused the secrets within the cabinetry, sliding open one drawer after another.

'These ones, Philippe?' Amy asked, holding up a linen condom with a ribbon tie.

Philippe raised his eyes from examining a silk crêpe nightdress. '*Non, ma chérie.* If you do not wish to conceive, *monsieur* must employ the ones made from animal intestines.'

Amy put the linen condom back with a sigh. 'Spencer-Lacey won't wear them, anyway.'

Madame Desmarais, who was a petite Frenchwoman with coal-black hair despite her sixty or more years, nodded knowingly. 'You must enquire of Dr Mitchell the obstetrician for more discreet items, which the gentleman needn't know about.'

Amy murmured her thanks, but clearly her interest in preventives had waned. She and Jenny burst into giggles as she opened another drawer.

'This one is Spencer-Lacey,' Amy squealed, holding up a colossal carved ivory dildo, rendered with astonishing realism, complete with veins.

'And *this* like Henson,' Jenny said, lifting a similar-sized polished wood penis. 'But none like my last keeper's prick, because no one would pay good money for *that* flaccid lobcock.'

Both dissolved into more giggles.

Kitty, who pressed a white peignoir to her shoulders as she gazed into a looking glass, frowned. 'Hush, darlings,' she said to her sisters. 'Save such talk for home.'

'Bah!' Jenny threw the dildo into the drawer and jutted out her bottom lip. 'We're only having fun.'

'But it's disloyal.' Kitty handed the peignoir to Madame Desmarais with a nod. The virginal-white garment was elegantly unadorned, but the gorgeous silk would cling to Kitty's curves. 'We Preece sisters are famed for our loyalty.'

Jenny scurried to Kitty, clung to her arm, and batted her lashes at Kitty's reflection in the looking glass. 'We Preece sisters are famed for our beauty, Kitty-cat.'

Kitty patted Jenny's hand. 'Our beauty is precarious, just like everything in our lives.' As she spoke, a measure of peace descended on Kitty. *If* all went well, one day she could provide a safe home for her sisters.

Amy's smooth brow furrowed slightly over her large, dark blue eyes. 'Nothing is precarious, Kitty,' she said, sliding the dildo drawer closed.

'Oh, but everything is precarious, Amy. You don't remember our life before Mount Street, but' – Kitty pressed Jenny's hand – 'darling Jenny, do *you*?'

Jenny grimaced. 'I don't *want* to remember.'

Realisation dawned on Kitty. Her two younger sisters didn't comprehend the precarious and transient nature of their wealth and status. To them, there had always been plenty, thus, there always would be plenty. They likely didn't worry for their children or their nieces, either. And with Matilda and Barbara seemingly too jaded to care, it truly *was* up to Kitty to provide a stable, respectable alternative for her family.

Amy danced over to Kitty, her eyes shining. 'No more dreariness, Kitty. Let us speak of cheerier things, such as how your handsome Sidney will *burn* when he sees you in the beautiful peignoir you chose.'

Jenny's eyes brightened. 'Oh, yes! I'm so happy, Kitty-cat, that you and Sidney are *finally* releasing the desire you've repressed for *ages*. How steamy your nights must be after six years of lovesick pining.'

Kitty's hand flew to her mouth. 'Did *everyone* know what I myself couldn't see?'

Philippe laughed, his arms full of lace and silk. '*Chaton*, it is not your fault. Some loves are so intricately woven into our hearts that we ourselves do not recognise them. After all, the sun does not know his own warmth, even while all around him bask in it.

But, come, let us complete our purchases. It is nearly time to meet Ada-Marie and Nanny Ashcroft at Russell and Sons.'

As Philippe directed the packaging up of the boxes and consulted with Amy and Jenny on their purchases, Kitty sat in a chair and breathed deeply to calm her nerves. With every passing moment, she comprehended more thoroughly how long she'd yearned for the stability and love Sidney offered . . . and how she'd yearned for Sidney, himself.

That they would soon be irrevocably bound was a joy beyond belief – and terrifying, lest something happen before the joy came to fruition.

Kitty stood, redirecting her thoughts. It didn't do to dwell on her anxieties. Instead, she'd enjoy the delight of shopping with Ada-Marie. She wanted to buy her little girl a perfect gift, something to tuck into her cot tonight, along with one last assurance that they'd start their new life in a fortnight.

Perhaps saying it aloud would make it come true.

Jenny and Amy returned to Mount Street with a footman and their purchases, but Philippe and the other footman remained with Kitty. They stood together with Nanny Ashcroft near the toy shop's door so Kitty and Ada-Marie could enjoy time alone.

Russell and Sons burst with families amassing town-made toys before going into the country for the summer and autumn. With Ada-Marie in her arms, Kitty weaved past glaring matrons and pinafored nurses, ignoring their whispered insults as she smiled at glossy globes, colourful picture books and cleverly pieced puzzles. Those were not the best toys for a blind girl, but Kitty described them to Ada-Marie in intricate detail.

'What toys were your favourites as a little girl, Kitty?' Ada-Marie asked.

Kitty's heart ached. Her childhood toys consisted of bits and bobs, such as the scraps of fabric her mother knotted into a doll, now tucked inside a blue shawl in Kitty's side-table drawer with Sidney's poems. Matilda had reversed the Preece sisters' fortune soon after their mother's death, but eight-year-old Kitty's childhood had ceased with the upward move.

'I had a doll,' she said quietly, placing Ada-Marie down in front of the carved animals. The child's fingers explored eagerly, picking up a pair of elephants, which Kitty named for her. As Ada-Marie delighted in the intricate tusks and long trunks, Kitty told her everything she knew about India and Africa – gleaned from years of conversation with nabobs and officers.

While Ada-Marie played with the elephants, the name 'Mrs Overton' caught Kitty's attention. She looked over her shoulder and spied the widow Cornelius had spoken of near the Ring – the one Sidney had addressed on occasion at Green Park.

Exceedingly curious about Cornelius's future bride, Kitty observed Mrs Overton closely.

Cornelius, she decided, had no grounds for complaint. Mrs Overton was very young – no older than Jenny – and her appearance was exceedingly elegant. A jaunty plumed hat topped her buttery blonde hair, which curled around a delicate face with large hazel eyes. She was *tiny*, it was true – she looked as if Cornelius could snap her like a twig – but her figure was proportional and displayed to fine advantage in a smartly tailored green silk redingote over a light green walking dress. Her two blonde daughters wore matching pink frocks, rosebuds next to Mrs Overton's slender, stemlike frame.

Despite her youth, Mrs Overton possessed a digni-fied, regal air as she greeted the acquaintance who'd called her name. *That* woman, expensively but not elegantly dressed, simpered and smirked, fawning over the Misses Overton as people do with the wealthy. The acquaintance pushed forward a small boy wearing a dark blue one-piece skeleton suit and tittered. 'My Samuel will be courting your pretty girls one day soon enough, I've no doubt.'

Mrs Overton stiffened.

Inhaled sharply, nostrils flaring.

And glared.

The tiny widow scooped up her daughters like a mother hawk, placing one child on each hip. Without even a nod adieu to her obnoxious acquaintance, she marched towards the exit. As she passed Kitty, she asked her daughters in a breathy, sweet voice, 'Shall we go to Gunter's or Webb's for ices, my loves?'

The girls squealed, declaring their preference for Webb's. With a jingle of the bells on the door, the widow and her daughters vanished.

Kitty smiled to herself. Mrs Overton was a fiercely protective and loving mother, and Kitty felt a surge of pride in the lady who would soon be her sister-in-law. Naturally, Mrs Overton would never acknowledge a relationship between herself and Kitty, but she *might* encourage Sidney to bring Ada-Marie when he visited his family estate, which would ease a path into elegant society for *their* daughter.

Their *daughter*.

Kitty savoured the thought. She was a *mama*, and together with Sidney, she'd provide a safe and loving home to their daughter. Suddenly, Kitty knew she wanted to give Ada-Marie something representative of what Ada-Marie gifted to Kitty: the joy of motherhood.

'Ada-Marie,' she said, more strongly than before. 'When I was little, I had a doll I loved very much indeed. I want you to have a doll, as well. She will be a friend you can hold close at night; a companion you can sing ballads to during the day.'

She led her daughter towards the shelves displaying magnificent dolls of all sizes, ignoring a turbaned matron's sneers. Ada-Marie's hands reached out, searching for tactile details, and she exclaimed joyfully when her fingertips brushed against the dimensional face of a small beeswax doll with glass eyes, rooted eyelashes and eyebrows, and real hair bound in plaits.

Smiling, Kitty lifted the doll, whose gown and petticoats consisted of frothy cotton layers decorated with velvet ribbons. The toy's delicate hands had moulded fingers, and tiny kid slippers covered stockinged feet. Kitty put the doll into Ada-Marie's arms, and the child instinctively rocked it like a baby.

Kitty's heart swelled. *This* was the perfect gift for Ada-Marie.

'Revolting,' the matron muttered as she prodded at various dolls. 'Buying toys for her bastard during *respectable* shopping hours.'

Although Kitty had learned to deflect insults directed at her, this barb struck deep, deflating her joy in one fell swoop. Why couldn't she purchase a present for her innocent little girl in peace? She clasped Ada-Marie and the doll to her breast, as if her arms could protect her daughter as Mrs Overton had protected *her* daughters, but, in truth, Kitty didn't have Mrs Overton's wealth and respectability – and *that* was what had truly protected the Misses Overton. Within London or among the *ton*, insulters would always taunt Kitty. By extension, they'd hurt Ada-Marie and Sidney.

Kitty's heart sank to her feet, pulled down by the weight of her worthlessness.

But *then* . . .

A familiar hand kneaded her shoulder. And *somehow*, Sidney was behind her with his golden smile, his amber eyes, and his secure arms – Sir Galahad in her time of anguish. Kitty might not be worthy, but Sidney loved her, and his embrace could efface the matron's cruelty. *He* possessed status and respectability.

Kitty threw caution to the wind and, with Ada-Marie on one hip, she flung an arm about Sidney's neck, and kissed him passionately, although hisses and muttering surrounded them.

'He's Lady Eden's second son.'

'The curate.'

'*Not* a curate any longer, and no wonder, the way he acts, and in a shop filled with children, no less.'

'Is that blind child his by-blow?'

'Lord knows; those Preece sisters have had half of London between their legs.'

Kitty broke the kiss, pulling away and shielding Ada-Marie by putting one of the child's ears to her shoulder and covering the other with her hand. With an aching heart, she realised she'd already ruined Sidney's respectability.

She longed to be far away from hateful London.

Sidney's eyes darted about the room before returning to Kitty and Ada-Marie. 'Come to me, mousey,' he said, taking the child in his arms. To Kitty, he said, 'Never mind them, my love. We shan't be in London much longer.'

Kitty beamed because they were exactly the words she needed to hear. 'We shall be at our snug coastal cottage in Devonshire.'

Ever since Sidney had – after much persuasion and with surprising reluctance – described it to Kitty a few days earlier, she'd daydreamed. At their cottage, Kitty would build sandcastles with Ada-Marie in the mornings. In the afternoons, she'd mend Sidney's pens and fetch him tea as he wrote. She'd plan weekly menus of wholesome meals with a kindly housekeeper who knew nothing of Kitty's past, and she'd learn to sew Sidney's shirts and Ada-Marie's frocks, as proper ladies did for their husbands and children. Evenings she'd spend by the hearth, first reading bedtime stories to Ada-Marie, and later alone with Sidney.

Revelling in their passion.

Passion she'd experience *soon*. Much earlier than Sidney realised, if Kitty got her way.

Sidney's face paled as his eyes settled on the footman laden with bundles. 'Been shopping?'

'Only a very little.' She pointed at the doll in their daughter's arms. 'Look what Ada-Marie and I have found.'

'Oh . . . how sweet.' Sidney cleared his throat. 'Do you know the . . . the price?'

Kitty frowned. 'No – why do you ask?'

Sidney shook his head. 'No reason, my love. Or, rather, I simply wonder if I carry enough coins.'

'We can put it on my credit.'

'No, no. I shall purchase our daughter's doll,' he said, moving towards the wooden counter.

The weedy young shop assistant's gaze latched onto Kitty's breasts, which burst from the low-cut neckline of her muslin gown. Too late, Kitty remembered respectable women wore fichus before the evening hours. She'd attired herself in one of her usual bosom-bearing frocks. Her stomach sank; she had so much to learn, but she must succeed for Ada-Marie and Sidney's sakes.

Sidney perched Ada-Marie on the counter and snapped his fingers before the assistant's gawking eyes. 'How much for the doll, man?'

The assistant jumped to attention. 'Er . . . one pound, six shillings, sir.'

Sidney recoiled.

He recovered himself swiftly, but *something* clearly was wrong. Was he troubled about money already?

Kitty put a hand on his arm. 'Is all well, Sid?'

'Perfectly so.' But two fine lines creased Sidney's brow as he reached into his pocket and withdrew a gold guinea and two silver half-crowns from among a handful of coins.

His words didn't reassure Kitty. Something bothered him, and if he wasn't concerned about money, perhaps he was reconsidering his rash proposal.

As the shop assistant wrapped the doll in paper, Kitty squeezed Sidney's forearm. 'Are you happy, darling?'

His face softened. 'I'm beyond happy, Kit.' He kissed Ada-Marie's cheek, and their daughter swung her legs and hummed. 'I always am when I'm with my girls.'

Kitty scrutinised his expression, unable to feel at ease although his eyes shone with genuine joy.

'Truly,' he continued with a smile. 'But I wondered . . .' – he hesitated – 'Kit, do you recall the jewellery set you wore when you met me in the park?'

'My pink sapphires?' she asked, surprised. 'Yes, of course.' Along with most of her extremely expensive sets, the pink sapphires had been a gift from her third keeper, the Duke of Wells. Wells had employed Kitty primarily as a tool to flaunt his wealth and power, much as Gillingham had wanted to do; unlike Gillingham, Wells had exploited Kitty without cruelty, although he'd been Kitty's most aloof keeper.

Sidney's gaze fell. 'It's a lovely set—'

The assistant handed Ada-Marie the doll wrapped in brown paper clinched with twine, and Sidney ceased speaking to hitch their daughter against his chest. Kitty nestled on his other side. When they turned, other shoppers recoiled from their family trio as if smallpox sores festered on their skin. Although this revulsion was like the reaction Kitty received when she was out with her sisters, it differed vastly from when she'd appeared on the arms of previous keepers. When a duke or marquess had escorted her to Bond Street, everyone simpered. Clearly, a connection between an impoverished curate and a courtesan offended society's sensibility – but what did that matter when Sidney would soon take her away from this misery?

A porter opened the shop door, and hazy sunlight bathed Kitty as she and Sidney emerged onto busy Bond Street, with Philippe, Nanny Ashcroft and the footman following behind. Kitty exchanged a glance with Philippe, held up a hand to tell him to wait, and pulled Sidney out of the paths of shopping ladies and their bundle-laden maids and into a niche near Russell and Sons' bow window.

'Why did you enquire about my sapphires?' she asked.

Sidney adjusted Ada-Marie more closely against him and smiled, genuinely and brightly, all the earlier concerns vanquished. 'Ada-Marie, tell your mama I enquired about her sapphires because I shall always remember she wore them on the day she promised to make me the happiest of men.'

Kitty's concern melted. How like Sidney to be sentimental. Now that Kitty wasn't a courtesan who must display her status and advertise her cost, her jewels meant nothing beyond their considerable monetary value. She'd keep them as security for Ada-Marie's future.

Sidney transferred Ada-Marie into her arms. 'If you can forgive my ungentlemanly behaviour, might I leave my girls here, in the formidable protection of Philippe and Nanny Ashcroft? I must deal with something urgent.' He nodded at a public house across the street.

Butcher stood outside its entrance with his arms folded. Terror flooded Kitty's chest. 'Does he still follow you?'

'Yes, but not for long. I shall call upon Gillingham at once.'

'Be safe, Sidney,' she said, through waves of fear.

'I shall.' Sidney leaned forward, his lips brushing her cheek. 'I shall see *you* later.' He kissed Ada-Marie. 'I love you, mousey, and I shall see you in two weeks.'

Kitty snuggled her daughter close to her chest as Sidney left them. She murmured reassurances to Ada-Marie's enquiries, while watching Sidney's black hat sail over the sea of female shoppers until he rounded the corner of Grosvenor Street. Butcher slunk behind.

Kitty's earlier disquiet had returned full force, but she breathed to calm her coiling innards. Since a courtesan couldn't possibly visit a duke's house – imagine Kitty knocking upon a duchess's door! – she'd do best to return home and cherish her last afternoon with Ada-Marie for a fortnight. Then, to keep her mind occupied with something other than worry, Kitty would direct her energy, with Philippe's help, in preparing herself for her *husband's* pleasure.

And her *own* pleasure.

Kitty's heart skipped a beat.

She didn't intend to spend two days in a carriage playing travel chess when there was a much more gratifying way to pass the hours.

Kitty stepped forward with fresh resolve.

Sidney wouldn't resist her *this* time.

12

After days of living in Butcher's shadow, Sidney recognised the henchman's heavy tread. Without doubt, the brute trailed him around the corner of Grosvenor Street.

The stalking must cease *now*.

Sidney pivoted. Butcher jolted to a halt, nearly toppling into Sidney as shoppers swished past them.

'Why do you still follow me, man?'

Butcher's old-fashioned cocked hat cast a triangular shadow over his stubble-darkened face. Only a split lip and yellowish bruises told the tale of the fight with Cornelius. ''Cause his grace pays me six bob a day to watch you.'

'Even though you've told him Miss Preece is with me now?'

The brute chuckled. 'I ain't told him anything of the kind.'

'Gillingham doesn't know?' Sidney asked, his nerves prickling.

'I cannot say what his grace knows or don't know, but he don't know it from *me*, and he ain't asked me to stop following you, has he?' Butcher's beady eyes twinkled; clearly, the situation amused him. 'But if he don't know, I wager he's excited about tomorrow night, and he won't appreciate your informing him he can't have what he wants.'

Indeed, the duke was a notoriously sour loser. Sidney had procrastinated the reimbursement in part to give Gillingham time to nurse his wounded pride. He'd envisioned an unpleasant but brisk call – one thousand pounds in the duke's hand, a curt goodbye, and the distasteful business would end.

It likely wouldn't be so simple, but it was best to get it done.

Sidney ground his teeth as he turned his back on Butcher. He crammed his hands into his trouser pockets, wrapping his fingers around the roll of banknotes, and proceeded west along Grosvenor Street.

Butcher fell into stride beside him. 'I'm starting to warm to you, parson.'

'Indeed?' Unfortunately, Sidney couldn't offer Butcher the same affirmation.

Butcher chuckled again. 'I admire your pluck, for such a little fella.'

'I'm not *that* little, Butcher. Six foot and thirteen stone, as a matter of fact.'

Butcher roared with laughter. 'You're a puny cove, but a right 'un all the same, and I'm glad it's you what gets the ladybird rather than his grace.' He lowered his voice, breathing beer fumes in Sidney's ear. 'I hear you're a top diver with the married ladies, eh? Like to lie like bread and butter with the widows and whatnot. A bit of rantum scantum, riding St George—'

Sidney threw his hand between himself and Butcher.

'I *quite* take your meaning, Butcher.' He didn't require a catalogue of sexual euphemisms. 'And I'd recommend you not give credence to gossip.'

Butcher shrugged. ''Twasn't gossip. Your brother told me.'

Sidney increased his pace, clenching his jaw as his boots pounded the pavement. He'd always suspected Cornelius's part in those revolting rumours. Not that there wasn't a grain of truth in them – but that was all years ago. Sidney had never defiled his sacred office. Parishioners deserved trustworthy, safe clergymen.

They progressed past two terraced townhouses before Butcher spoke again. 'Your brother wants to fight me at Fives-Court next week. If I win, I've a mind to use the prize money to sail to Upper Canada with my sister. England offers naught for the likes of us.' He spat on the pavement.

Sidney barely restrained his own torrent of laughter. Clever Tyrold – he possessed remarkable powers of persuasion for such a grouch.

At the end of Grosvenor Street, Sidney paused, the expanse of the grandest square in Mayfair stretching before him. Tall, terraced brick houses edged the four sides of Grosvenor Square like rows of uniformed officers standing to attention. Beyond the central oval green, with its leafy shrubs and glinting gilded statue of George I on horseback, stood Gillingham House.

'Well, Butcher,' Sidney said, eager to draw his discourse with the henchman to a close, 'if you win the prize money, I hope you thrive in Canada.'

Butcher raised his bushy brows. 'If you want me to win, how about you tell me your brother's weakness in the ring?'

Sidney half-smiled. 'I'm afraid you mistook me. I'd never inform on my own brother.' Even if Cornelius didn't extend the same courtesy . . .

'Might be worth your while,' Butcher said with a gap-toothed grin. 'Place a wager on me and make a few quid, eh? Buy your woman something sparkly?'

'No, thank you. I'm not a gambling man. Besides, if my brother possesses a weakness for anything other than violent sport and fast horses, I've yet to discover it. Best of luck to you, but I'd say the same to him.' Sidney extended his hand, and Butcher clamped it in his hefty rough paw. 'Although I sincerely hope we never meet again, I wish you well, Mr Butcher.'

Butcher chortled. 'Pay me for my day, and I'll disappear now. I'd rather not see his grace after your chat, anyway.'

Sidney pulled three half-crowns from his pocket. 'A bit extra,' he said, depositing the coins into Butcher's calloused paw. No doubt Sidney was a dupe, but losing seven and a half shillings was nothing compared to ridding himself of Butcher.

Butcher brushed his hat brim with a finger. 'I'll drink your health with it.'

After a last nod at the rogue, Sidney traversed the square, breathing deeply to steady his nerves as Gillingham House loomed larger and larger. With seven bays across and standing four storeys high, its pilastered front was splendid – even in a square which housed thirty-five noble families among its fifty residences. Three dukes, more than a dozen marquesses and earls, and nearly twenty viscounts and barons made Grosvenor Square their London address.

Sidney hesitated before the dark green front door. He was boy-Sidney again, trembling at the entrance to the Paradisum Park library while he summoned the courage to approach his father, who stood beside his ebony desk and swished a cane against his thigh, with his face contorted and his pale blue eyes blazing.

No. Sidney gathered his breath. He wasn't a helpless child anymore. He was a man with a fiancée and daughter to protect.

Before his resolve faltered, Sidney gripped the brass loop dangling from a lion's mouth and knocked.

A lofty-nosed butler decked in green and silver livery opened the door. 'May I help you . . . *sir*?'

From his previous visits to the Duchess of Gillingham to solicit for charity subscriptions, Sidney knew the butler – whose name was Mr Harper – disdained anyone below the rank of earl.

Sidney patted his pockets and extracted his card case. 'Mr Wakefield for the duke.'

Harper squinted at the card. 'Perhaps you aren't aware, *Mr* . . . Wakefield, but this is a busy day for the family.'

Sidney barely repressed an eye roll. Harper could likely recite Debrett's *New Peerage* from memory; he certainly knew Sidney's connections. Lord Eden's younger brother wasn't so far removed from society not to know of Lady Caroline's wedding. In fact, as one of the duchess's favourites, Sidney had received an invitation to tomorrow's evening ball, although he'd sent his regrets. 'Despite Lady Caroline's wedding tomorrow, the duke will want to see me. Now.'

The butler's nose rose an inch higher. 'Very well, sir,' he said at last. He opened the door a fraction further to allow Sidney to enter the white marble hall, abounding with green-liveried footmen carrying gilded chairs, glistening candelabra and stacks of folded linen. Chambermaids draped the balusters of the sweeping staircase in garlands of snowy roses.

Sadly, the welcoming face of the duchess was absent from the scene – or perhaps that was for the best. Although Sidney enjoyed her grace's company, he didn't have time for tea and a discussion about why he'd left the church. Neither was the duchess's presence appropriate for Sidney's business with her husband.

'If you would be so good as to wait in the library, sir?' Harper indicated double doors to the right. Sidney opened them for himself.

The book room contained more gilt-framed portraits of past dukes and duchesses than leather-bound tomes. As the pinched expressions of Gillingham's ancestors held no appeal, Sidney strode to the window and clasped his hands behind his back. On the pavement before him, footmen unloaded towering cream-coloured boxes from a Webb's Confectionery delivery coach and carried them down the narrow servants' stairs into the basement.

All the preparations were a gratifying sight. Gillingham would be busy indeed for the next day and a half. Meanwhile, Sidney and Kitty would be as far north as Stilton before Lady Caroline's wedding day even dawned.

The door clicked open and closed.

'This is inconvenient timing, Mr Wakefield,' Gillingham's icy voice drawled.

Sidney turned and bowed stiffly. Gillingham, attired in a gold silk banyan, blended with his gilt-framed, unpleasant ancestors. 'My business needn't take long, duke. In fact, the sooner it's concluded, the better.'

The duke narrowed his eyes. 'Ah. In that case, I'll not ask you to be seated.' His thin lips twitched. 'And you must excuse my state of undress. I've not stirred from the house today. We prepare for my daughter's wedding, as you must know, given your *employment* at St George's.'

Sidney's stomach tightened. Clearly, Gillingham knew something about Sidney's business. Likely, he knew a great deal.

Sidney mustn't reveal any secrets, but he also must demonstrate he wasn't frightened. 'I'm no longer employed at St George's, as I'm certain you are aware.'

The duke's expression remained as cold and impassive as marble. 'One hears many rumours, some more credible than others. I regarded it as inconceivable that the second son of an impoverished noble family would give up his only livelihood.' Gillingham's gold banyan shimmered as the duke inched closer, drawing his white fingers along the back of a gilded chaise longue. 'But your concerns are your own, Wakefield. As long as they don't conflict with mine, I couldn't care less what you do.' The duke stood still. 'Now, what is your business with me?'

Sidney withdrew the banknotes. 'I'm here to reimburse the thousand pounds you paid to Matilda Preece.'

A flicker crossed the duke's eyes.

Rather than taking the banknotes, Gillingham extracted a silver snuffbox from the sleek folds of his banyan and pinched the fine-ground tobacco between his thumb and forefinger. His nostrils flared as he inhaled.

He dropped the snuffbox back into his pocket and drew his lips into a smile. 'Keep your money, Wakefield. I shall make Matilda a new offer. One you *won't* top.'

Sidney's muscles tensed. 'Not for Kitty, you won't.'

The duke chuckled. 'Ah – there's the enraged young buck I recognise from Vauxhall. Wakefield, let me explain something which it appears your father – who was a great friend of mine – didn't teach you.' Gillingham's smile stretched into a smirk. 'Among *gentle* society, we don't fight over a fuck like strutting cockerels. Sexual conquest is made possible by wealth and influence, of which I have infinite amounts and you have . . . none.'

Sidney seethed, longing to slam his fist into Gillingham's vile face. 'I don't give a damn about your wealth or your influence. I shall soon put it out of your power *ever* to touch Kitty.'

Gillingham raised his brows. 'Will you indeed?' Mock sincerity dripped in his voice. 'I wonder how. Do you . . . do you mean to *marry* her, Wakefield?'

Sidney recoiled. Dammit – despite his resolution, he'd revealed the very secret he strove to protect.

The duke's brows lifted a fraction higher. 'Oh, dear. Evidently you do. My son also wanted to marry her. Did you know? No, I can tell you didn't. Like Richard, you'll discover the young woman has more sense than you do.' Gillingham frowned. 'Or perhaps she doesn't. She'd be a marchioness – and a future duchess – if she'd fled with Richard to Scotland.'

The duke's eyes cut to Sidney, who hopefully preserved a neutral expression despite his rage and anxiety. The duke mustn't discover their elopement plans.

Gillingham strolled so close that his cloying perfume assaulted Sidney. 'My son and I were in this very room when Richard tearfully confessed his undying, *honourable* love for Kitty. "I cannot live without her, Father," said he, as whiny as a child. He was not unlike you, Wakefield, although I'll grant you have more backbone.' The tip of Gillingham's tongue flicked across his lips, but his unblinking gaze never left Sidney's eyes. 'As Richard wept, I thought only of how much I wanted Kitty for myself. And I *shall* have her. You won't stop me.'

Sidney's innards twisted with fury. 'I'd give my life to protect her from you. Content yourself with another woman – or, better yet, be faithful to your poor wife.'

Gillingham's gaze wavered; his expression soured. 'How amusing, coming from—' He stopped and waved his fingers. 'But never mind. I *cannot* content myself with another woman. Kitty is . . . like an especially fine wine, full of complexity and intriguing contradiction.' His eyelids grew heavier. 'She's fierce and yet breakable. Pert and yet submissive. Honourable, but a whore.' The duke shivered as if with delight. 'I simply *must* have that, Wakefield. I confess, she torments my thoughts. I shall possess her.'

Sidney didn't disguise his revulsion. 'All your licentiousness achieves is to make me more determined than ever to prevent your access to the woman I love. My arrangement with Kitty is five days old; by now it's common knowledge, and if you infringe upon it, I shall consider it an offence against my honour. Now, take this money at once.'

Gillingham laughed. 'You're delirious if you believe I shan't convince Matilda to end your arrangement with Kitty in favour of my own. *My* wealth is boundless, whereas I suspect you have nothing beyond what you hold in your hand. In fact, how *did* you come across a thousand pounds, Wakefield? Did you earn it in bed with a dowager? Or did your debt-ridden brother actually convince the bank to extend him more credit?'

Sidney thrust the money into the duke's palm.

Gillingham squinted at the notes, each marked with '*The Bank of England promises to pay Mr John Tyrold or bearer on demand the sum of one hundred pounds*'.

The duke blanched.

Sidney triumphed. Determined to employ his temporary advantage to maximum effect, he forced an icy chuckle. 'There's plenty more where that came from.' Strictly speaking, Sidney's declaration wasn't a lie. The money had come from Tyrold's strongbox, which contained many more banknotes. Sidney would never ask John for more money if he couldn't repay it, but the critical point was to put the duke off. Within hours, Sidney and Kitty would be out of his reach forever. 'Mr Tyrold would like a receipt.'

An element of defeat showed in the duke's cold eyes. 'Very well, Wakefield.'

Gillingham stashed the notes in his banyan pocket and strode to his desk. After extracting a quill and paper from a drawer, the duke dipped the feather into a gold inkwell and scratched a few lines. He flourished his signature across half the page.

'Don't imagine,' Gillingham said as he held out the paper, 'this is the end of my quest for Kitty Preece, but, in the meantime, I wish you joy of your whore. From now on, whenever you marvel at her skill, recall how many have gone before you to teach her what she knows. I understand from a multitude of her past keepers that she bestows blows liberally, and always swallows mettle as if it were nectar from the gods—'

Sidney slammed his fist on the desk. '*Shut up.*' His chest rose and fell with thunderous fury.

The older man chuckled. 'Now, now. Strengthen your stomach, Wakefield. I thought you wanted to *marry* her? You must be aware how many have ploughed that field before you.'

'If you say one more word, duke, I shall demand you meet me at dawn, your daughter's wedding be damned.'

Sidney regretted the words the moment they left his mouth. He couldn't duel Gillingham without delaying his elopement, which would break Kitty's heart. Furthermore, the challenge conflicted with Sidney's promise to stay safe.

Then again, he *couldn't* stand aside while the duke slandered Kitty . . .

Fortunately, Gillingham shrugged. 'At present, I've wasted plenty of time on this folly without meeting an impudent pup at dawn. Besides, I've said all that's necessary. I daresay the image of those who came before won't leave your mind the next time you *make love* to your Dulcinea.'

Sidney's throat thickened. It wasn't true; the duke's taunting *wouldn't* affect his feelings. He and Kitty loved each other. Nothing else mattered. 'You haven't won, duke.'

Gillingham again withdrew his snuffbox and tapped a finger on the top. 'Not *yet*.' A cruel smile spread across his face. 'I trust you can see yourself out, boy?'

When Sidney stepped over the threshold into Grosvenor Square, with the dark green front door slamming shut behind him, cloud cover had smothered the hazy sun and a damp wind swelled.

Sidney shivered. He'd achieved his objective, but he was far from tranquil.

He trudged, slump-shouldered, towards Half Moon Street, but somewhere between Mount and Curzon Streets, Sidney – who was hardly aware of his surroundings – shrugged off his concerns. Within hours, he and Kitty would be out of Gillingham's reach. Within days, Kitty would be Sidney's wife.

Their union would be untouchable, even by the Duke of Gillingham.

191

13

At half-past eleven that evening, Kitty stood nude before her full-length looking glass. A fire crackled in her dressing-room hearth as Philippe applied heated tongs to the last uncurled segment of her hair. Dark ringlets cascaded unbound over her shoulders.

'Do you truly mean for me to wear *nothing* but my slippers and the white cloak?' Kitty asked, looking longingly at her portmanteaux. Within one case, she and Philippe had packed her wispy afternoon purchases, with which she'd intended to tantalise Sidney into making love to her the moment the carriage doors closed.

'Only the cloak,' Philippe said. 'When you're together in the carriage, you offer your body uncovered. This is the most vulnerable way, the most exquisite way, to declare, "I trust you, I love you", *oui*? Later, you wear the lace.' He waved his hand. 'But not the first time you *fais l'amour* with your husband.'

Kitty scrutinised her reflection. Thanks to Philippe, she *did* look lovely. Her nudity would assuredly be difficult for Sidney to resist, which was the point. She wanted to . . . well, seduce him, truth be told.

But would it be too bold? Too much like the behaviour of a courtesan, and not of a wife? Philippe was the definitive source on men's pleasure usually, but this time was different. Kitty came to Sidney not as a courtesan, but as a *bride*.

'What do you call tonight's creation?' she asked.

Philippe always named his artwork.

'For this creation,' Philippe said, 'I have no mythological reference.' He slid the snowy velvet cloak over Kitty's bare shoulders. It flowed to the floor in heavy folds. Philippe positioned the deep hood over her head and arranged her curls becomingly about her face. He studied her reflection in the mirror. 'You're Miss Catherine Preece, a pure virgin, ready for her husband.'

Kitty sobered. 'But I'm not.'

Philippe's sandy eyebrows shot up. 'Not ready for your husband?' He clamped a hand to his heart, as if horrified. 'Even after all Philippe does for you? Tell me, how have I failed? It was the *dépilatorie*, was it not? I tell you, you squirm too much.'

Kitty giggled. He was attempting to amuse her, and, as always, he'd succeeded. 'You're perfectly silly. You know that's not what I m—'

But Philippe continued his dramatics. 'So, it is not the *dépilatorie* she dislikes. *Mon Dieu*, how then did I fail to prepare her?' He addressed the ceiling, as if appealing to the heavens for an answer, and Kitty laughed again. 'I file and buff her nails. The white of the eggs I massage into her hair before I bathe her with rosewater. *J'applique du rouge et de la poudre sur sa belle peau*' – he lapsed into

193

rapid French and gesticulated wildly as Kitty strained to breathe between peals of laughter – '*jusqu'à ce qu'elle soit à la fois un lys et une rose*. Under my care, she has become tonight the most beautiful of virgins, and yet still she is not *ready*—'

'Stop, Philippe, please.' Kitty dabbed at the tears streaming down her cheeks. 'I shall ruin your handiwork if I laugh too much.'

Philippe gasped. '*Quelle horreur!* Has she destroyed my beautiful creation?' He cupped her chin and stared into her face. '*Non, ma chérie,*' he whispered, 'you have not, because it is your soul that is beautiful, not my handiwork.' He kissed the tip of her nose.

Kitty gazed into his blue eyes, her heart melting. 'Philippe, I love you so much.' She threw her arms about him. 'But I *meant* I'm not a virgin.'

'*Oui, je sais.*' Close-pressed as they were, Philippe tapped a finger to Kitty's heart, under her cloak, mindless of her nudity. 'But you come to your husband with a heart of love, so you are pure, *chaton.*'

Kitty clung to Philippe. She wanted her quiet country life with all her heart, and yet there was sorrow in change. Without doubt, her days with her beloved *habilleur* would soon end. Although Philippe hadn't yet given notice, Kitty knew he wouldn't enjoy life in a secluded coastal cottage. He was as much an artist as any member of the Royal Academy, although Philippe's preferred canvas was a woman, and his mediums were expensive clothes, jewels and the delicate powders, paints and lotions he blended himself. Regardless of whether he planned Kitty's evening wear, refurbished her bedchamber, or advised Matilda on the decoration of the common rooms employed to entertain gentlemen, Philippe designed his creations for display. He'd wither in the country dressing a housewife.

Kitty squeezed him tighter. 'You've been a comfort to me for so long, Philippe.' Her voice cracked.

'And you to me. But now you have *monsieur, oui*?'

Kitty's heart swelled at the thought of Sidney. He was her golden-hearted, golden-haired saviour – her own Sir Galahad – who loved her enough to disregard her past. 'I don't deserve him, Philippe.'

'There I must disagree. I have only recently decided he deserves you.'

Kitty didn't respond, for Philippe was biased. Kitty *didn't* deserve the sacrifice Sidney offered, and if not for Ada-Marie, she'd never presume to accept it.

But for her little girl's sake, Kitty would allow herself to live a fairy tale.

If something didn't prevent it . . .

After all, fairy tales don't come true.

Kitty released an unsteady breath against Philippe's chest.

Philippe murmured into her curls. 'Monsieur Wakefield is the only man I trust with the heart of *ma chérie. Il a pénétré*— but how do I say that in English? Ah, yes, he *penetrated* the ice walls I built to protect you.'

Kitty giggled into Philippe's cravat. 'Philippe, you're incorrigible.'

He drew back, blinking as if innocent. 'Do I mistake the word? Is it not *penetration*?'

But Kitty laughed too much to answer, and Philippe joined her.

'Come now, *chaton*,' he said, once their laughter subsided. 'It is only ten minutes until midnight.'

Kitty put her hand to her throat. Surely something horrendous had occurred with Butcher or Gillingham that afternoon. She squeezed her eyes shut, the horrible images which had haunted her for days flooding her thoughts once again.

But, this time, she allowed in another fear, which up until now, she'd kept in her mind's shadows. Perhaps Sidney had realised what Kitty truly was, and he wasn't coming for her at all.

Fairy tales don't come true.

'*Chaton!*' Philippe stood in the doorway, carrying her portmanteaux and her hat boxes. 'Do you want *monsieur* to think you changed your mind?'

'He won't come,' Kitty said, her voice a whisper.

Philippe grew misty-eyed. 'He will come, *ma chérie*. I know he will.'

Kitty clapped her hand over her heart.

Maybe fairy tales do come true.

With butterflies swarming in her stomach, Kitty tiptoed through the dark corridor behind Philippe. She clutched her cloak closed to hide her nudity, but the corridor draughts still chilled her bare skin. In her free hand, she carried a note for Matilda.

Philippe accidentally knocked a portmanteau against the newel post at the top of the stairs.

'We mustn't wake the others,' Kitty whispered urgently. A confrontation with her sisters was yet another potential danger to Kitty's happiness. She might not withstand Matilda's anger or disappointment.

'They're asleep or otherwise occupied, *ma chérie*. They do not hear us.'

Regardless, Kitty crept down the two flights of stairs, treading gingerly on those that creaked. When she reached the entrance hall, she hurried at last, for her feet fell silent on the Turkish carpet. As Philippe waited, Kitty placed her note on the silver platter by the front door. When Matilda awoke, Dodwell would put the post and papers on the platter and send it up with Matilda's breakfast tray. By that time, Kitty and Sidney would be . . . where? To Kitty, towns north of Mary Le Bone were dots on a map because, except for trips to Brighton and Margate with past keepers, she'd never left London. But wherever they were in eight or nine hours, they'd be too far for anyone to stop them.

Nevertheless, Kitty hadn't disclosed their destination in the note. She'd confess everything later, after she and Sidney returned.

Dearest Matilda – she'd written – *Sidney and I decided to travel into the country for a fortnight, so we may celebrate our love alone for a few fleeting days. Never fear, Sidney reimbursed Gillingham, so we are no longer under any obligation to the duke. I realise you disapprove of my choosing Sid because you do not want me to be hurt if ever he forsakes me, but I must choose him. If I suffer in the future, at least I shall have the memory of these days to cherish. I know you wouldn't deny me my one chance at happiness. Ever your devoted Kitty-cat.*

A gentle rap – almost a scratching – sounded, and Kitty's heart pounded.

Was it truly Sidney?

Philippe stood back while Kitty turned the key in the lock, rotated the deadbolt, and opened the door.

Sidney – her actual Sidney, unharmed and perfect – stood silhouetted against the glare of the street lights. He enfolded her in an embrace, and Kitty nestled against him. She lifted her mouth to his, but she held her arms under her cloak so as not to spoil his surprise.

'Is this truly happening?' Kitty asked, her lips brushing his.

'If it's not, it's the best dream I've ever had.' Sidney tasted of spiced toothpowder. His smooth cheeks smelled of sandalwood shaving lather, and a clean, masculine fragrance clung to his coat and shirt linen.

Kitty closed her eyes. 'If it's a dream, I don't want to wake up.'

Sidney's lips closed on hers. Tender, soft, sweet.

Safety and security.

Fervent desire lurked below the surface, but that wasn't something she could surrender to here.

When they were sealed into their cosy carriage, however . . .

Kitty broke the kiss, desperate to be alone with Sidney, on their way north, out of the reach of those who'd tear them apart. 'Philippe has my bags.'

198

Before lifting the portmanteaux, Sidney put gold coins – at least two guineas, and perhaps more – into Philippe's palm. Kitty smiled; that was well done.

She gave Philippe a last kiss, then she strode into the night with Sidney behind her.

The door clicked closed, and the lock turned.

It *was* truly happening.

Or was it?

Fog swirled on the near-deserted street – Mayfair was quiet on the night before Lady Caroline's wedding – but there was no sign of a black-and-yellow travelling coach. 'Where's the post-chaise, Sid?'

Sidney jutted his chin. 'In the mews, my love. More discreet.'

Oh! – of course.

The stable-lined mews were to the north along Park Street. Kitty trotted beside Sidney, ducking her head so that the broad velvet hood of her cloak shadowed her face, even though the street was nearly empty. The damp mist which hazed the air also slicked the pavement stones, and the earthy smell of rain mingled with London's stench. A watchman strolling on the far side of the street called the hour, some minutes late.

Kitty followed Sidney into the mews. A solitary post-chaise hitched to a team of two horses stood within the hazy halo of a street lamp.

A groom hopped off the rumble seat and grabbed Kitty's cases.

Sidney opened the door of the carriage.

Kitty stepped inside, sat on the single upholstered

bench, and pressed her trembling palms together. Through the wide front window, two oil lamps illuminated the postillion's back.

The carriage rocked as Sidney climbed in. He sat beside Kitty, his presence warm and *real*.

Kitty panicked. 'Are you *certain*, darling? Do you truly want to marry me? You know you can take me anywhere, even to Half Moon Street, and have me with no obligation—'

'Shh.' Sidney drew back Kitty's hood, lifted her chin, and gazed into her eyes. 'Not marry my dearest friend? My greatest joy? Not marry the only person who truly believes in me? The lady who made me a man? Loveliest Kit, this is the happiest moment of my life to date. Never doubt that.'

Kitty's body melted against him. Her trembling quietened. Sidney loved her and wanted to marry her, despite everything.

The post-chaise swayed into motion.

As they travelled on the relatively empty Mayfair streets, with the carriage wheels whirring and the horses' metal shoes striking on cobblestone, Kitty relished Sidney's embrace. But when they swung onto the Islington Road and the horses beat a steady trot against the hard-packed dirt, she lifted her head. Best to find out at once what Sidney thought of her surprise. Besides, she wanted him so much, she ached.

She licked her dry lips. 'Will you draw the curtains, darling?'

'Of course.' He leaned forward and closed the drapery

at the front window and the two side windows. The carriage darkened, but the glow of the lantern lights through the thin wool provided sufficient illumination for Kitty's purposes.

Sidney settled into the seat again. 'Do you wish to sleep?'

'No.' Kitty slid a hand through the opening of her cloak and placed it on his thigh. 'I'm not the least bit tired.' She drew her hand higher, into the fold of Sidney's lap.

His breathing deepened.

Kitty's heart pounded.

She unclasped her cloak at her neck. With a flick of her wrist, the velvet shifted off one bare shoulder, which gleamed white in the darkened carriage.

Sidney stared.

Kitty held her breath. Would he find her brazen or desirable?

Without speaking a word, Sidney pulled at the velvet. The cloak slipped to Kitty's elbow, exposing half her bosom.

She peeked through her lashes. 'Do you like your surprise?'

Sidney groaned as he grazed his fingertips under her breast, driving Kitty to madness. 'Oh, God, Kit. *Yes.*'

Kitty smiled as she grasped the steel rod of his erection through his buckskin breeches. 'Two days is a dreadfully long time to spend in a carriage unless we find a *satisfying* way to pass the time.'

Their eyes locked.

Then Sidney seized her with the same fervour he'd demonstrated twice before. He relieved her of her cloak with one deft movement and crushed her in his powerful embrace. His mouth clamped over hers, and Kitty gave herself over to pent-up passion.

For years, she'd desired this man.

Now she'd have him.

14

Sidney's body raged with desire as he drew Kitty into his lap.

He smoothed his palms down the soft skin of her back as he kissed her, plunging his tongue into her honeyed mouth, her own tongue answering back with equal hunger. Her perfume, her essence, and her contours were details he'd perceived a thousand times over the last six years. Now they overwhelmed his senses.

Kitty's fingers threaded into his hair, caressing, kneading, and knocking off his hat, which rolled into the darkness.

Sidney gripped the curves of her luscious bottom and slid her closer to his throbbing cock. She rubbed herself on him through his breeches, moaning into his mouth.

A jolt radiated from Sidney's loins, so intense he broke their kiss to recover. His passion was almost too much – so powerful he wanted to unbutton his fall and explode into her within moments – but that was no way to make love to Kitty for the first time. He must worship her, honour her, take it slowly . . .

Although Kitty seemed to have other plans entirely.

'Get this off,' she panted, clawing at his coat, yanking at his cravat. 'Get it all off.'

She leaned back to allow Sidney to struggle out of his tight coat. Sidney's gaze melted down her body, her beauty intoxicating him more than strong drink. Her long ringlets spilled past her shoulders and over her bosom. Her nipples stood erect, begging for his suckling, his kisses. Her trim waist rounded into full hips, and her lush thighs straddled him.

And her centre of pleasure spread before him in his lap, its coral folds glistening with readiness – as smooth and hairless as a Greek statue.

I hear she hasn't any hair on her cunny.

You must be aware how many have ploughed that field before you.

Damn Cornelius and Gillingham. Damn them, damn them, damn them for their dishonourable talk. Kitty's past didn't matter. She'd survived as best she could in the world, and she'd retained her beautiful, noble, generous spirit through it all, and no one could poison Sidney's devotion. He needed her to know that before they made love.

Sidney squashed Kitty in a smothering embrace. 'I love you, I love you, I love you,' he murmured as he showered her head in kisses.

'I love you too,' Kitty said, her words muffled against his shoulder, 'but I can't breathe.'

Sidney loosened his grip. 'Forgive me.' He gazed into her long-lashed eyes. 'But I want you to understand the purity of my sentiments. How I cherish and adore you.'

Kitty's face was tender in the shadows. 'I feel the same, Sidney. That's why I've chosen to give you my heart, something no other man has ever possessed.'

Full of adoration, Sidney took Kitty's hands in his. 'If we are to make love, there are words I must say first.' He inhaled, and with his breath's release, he began, 'I, Sidney, take thee, Catherine, to my wedded wife, to have and to hold . . .'

Kitty put her fingers to his lips. 'Shh, Sidney, there will be time for vows later.'

He retrieved her hand, pressing it once more between his. 'Please let me speak, Kitty, for the blacksmith won't say *these* words. I planned to say them in Scotland, before we consummated our union, but God will hear them just as well here. I, Sidney . . .' And he recited his share of the vows from the Book of Common Prayer, although the lump in his throat rendered speech difficult.

'Oh, Sid,' Kitty murmured when he'd finished, 'what did I ever do to deserve you?' She leaned forward and kissed him, her breasts brushing against his waistcoat. 'But when,' she said, breaking from his lips and bringing his hand into the slick fold between her legs, 'will you stop being so *angelic* and give me what I want?'

Sidney's cock lunged, craving release from his breeches.

'I'll give it to you now,' he said, deftly exploring the treasure at his fingertips.

Kitty whimpered as he slipped a finger into her hot, wet opening, dripping for his cock's thrusts. He caressed her clitoris with his thumb.

Kitty trembled in his arms. She rocked with his movement, her breath panting, her thighs rising and falling as she rode his hand. 'I could come now, Sidney. *That* is

205

how much I desire you.' She removed his hand. 'But I want us to climax together.'

The fire inside Sidney raged. 'I'm yours to command.'

Kitty lifted her eyebrows. 'You will obey all my demands?'

'By God, yes. Every one, a thousand times over.'

'Take off *everything* while I watch you.' She shifted onto the bench beside him. 'Show me what I'm getting.'

Sidney grinned. He was confident of his physique: the one thing he had in common with Cornelius and their father was the need to exercise himself frequently, although Sidney preferred non-violent sport, such as field tennis with his friends or riding, swimming and running.

Sidney winked as he unknotted his cravat. 'You won't be disappointed.'

Kitty's lashes fluttered. 'I won't?'

'Not at all.' He unwrapped the strand of linen, draped it around the back of Kitty's neck, and used it to draw her towards him for a kiss. 'Keep that lead,' he said as he released her. 'You mustn't escape.'

Kitty giggled as she played with the cravat. 'There's not much room in this carriage to escape, even if I wanted to.'

Sidney unbuttoned his waistcoat. 'And do you want to?' He tossed it to the floor to join the mound of discarded clothes.

'Not in the least,' she purred. 'I'm your captive forevermore.'

Sidney pulled his shirt over his head. 'It's only fair, as you captivated me years ago.'

Kitty's eyes drifted across his torso, and Sidney flexed his muscles for her amusement.

'How do you like what you see?'

Her eyes gleamed. 'Outrageously well. My fancy man is an Adonis.'

'Fitting, as you are *clearly* Aphrodite.'

'Take off the rest.' Kitty leaned against the side of the rocking carriage and slipped her fingers between her legs. 'While I enjoy the view.'

Sidney kicked off his riding boots and yanked off his stockings. He unfastened the buttons at his knees and his fall, wrenched off his tight breeches, and tossed them on the mountain of clothing.

They were both nude in the shadowy light.

Kitty panted as she stroked herself. Sidney grasped his cravat and reeled her closer, focusing on her beautiful eyes.

She was his at last, to have, to hold, to protect, to adore.

The carriage slowed.

Kitty gasped. 'Are we stopping?'

Sidney kissed her wide-eyed face. 'The turnpike,' he murmured as the carriage rolled to a halt. 'Pay it no mind.' He hauled Kitty against him, her fever-hot skin enflaming his.

Once the postillion paid the toll, the carriage jolted forward, and their naked bodies jostled against each other, each movement an exquisite and torturous sensation.

'Do you think they'll hear us?' Kitty asked.

'No, my love.' The postillion had brought the horses to their fastest pace, and the pounding outside the carriage was loud enough to drown out the sounds of a vigorous pounding within.

Sidney kissed Kitty's jaw and down her lovely neck. She arched her back, offering herself fully. Her skin tasted of roses; it was silk against his hands and lips, against his chest, against his arms and his thighs.

His cock ached with need.

Not yet.

First, these magnificent breasts. His lips sought a nipple and suckled.

Kitty moaned, long, pained. 'Harder, more.' She threaded her fingers behind his head and pushed him against her. Sidney drank deeply, his mouth full of her nectar, his tongue encircling her hard nub.

Kitty slid her velvet-hot sex along his throbbing shaft, and he broke his suction, nestled his face into her pillowy breasts, and groaned.

'I need you, Kitty.' The words ripped from his throat as his hand found the dripping and engorged folds of her vulva, and she grasped his cock.

Suddenly it was all too much, Sidney suspected for her as well as him, and their need was at a breaking point which hands and fingers could no longer satisfy.

Sidney pulled back enough to view Kitty's face – there was no trace of amusement anymore.

'I need *you*, Sidney. Hard and deep.'

Passion erupted with the power of a volcano as he laid her back upon the bench, lengthwise across the upholstery, and stretched her legs into a vee on either side of his chest, her calves resting at his neck. He glided his hands up and down their marble smoothness.

'Say it again,' he demanded, as his penis poised at her slick entrance, anticipation cresting through his every extremity.

Kitty trembled as she trailed her fingers down her bosom, grazing over her nipples and clutching her own breasts as she commanded in a harsh voice: 'Hard and deep. *Now*, dammit.'

Her entrance squeezed the sensitive head of his cock.

There was no more waiting. For years, he'd loved her and kept his thoughts pure, all while desiring this union with a fevered lust. Now, under these circumstances, joining with the woman he'd soon marry, with whom he'd spend the rest of his life, fevered lust and true love united, and all their love required to achieve the ultimate fulfilment was this exquisite consummation.

He thrust deep, driving hard into Kitty's silky heat, that all-encompassing place of agonising pleasure. She cried out, angling her hips to meet him, so that they crashed into each other, moaning in harmony.

Sidney withdrew and steeled himself, and plunged again, farther into the molten paradise. She matched his thrust, squeezing tightly so pleasure shot like flames through his body.

After that, there was only vigour and fire as repeatedly Sidney thrust and Kitty parried, their moans escalating, their cries unconstrained. Their bodies slicked with sweat, the place of their union grew wet, and the aroma of arousal permeated the post-chaise.

Passion rose from Sidney's heart and reverberated throughout his being. How much more intimate and intense the physical act of love was when it united two hearts as well as two bodies.

'Sit back,' Kitty cried at last. 'I want to ride you.'

Sidney complied and collapsed against the seat, the upholstery sticking to his damp skin, as Kitty straddled him. She controlled the rhythm, first deliberately, then swift and strong as Sidney clasped her breasts, and Kitty's warm wetness squeezed his shaft.

All thought faded from Sidney's mind. Pleasure was his only sensation.

Kitty panted in his ear as she leaned into him, wrapping her arms around him, uniting them as one. 'Now,' she moaned, breathless and urgent. 'Explode with me now, Sid.'

Passion peaked into that final crest as Sidney delved into Kitty. His cock burst deep inside her, and he cried out as he pulsed, the force of his orgasm devastating in its ecstasy.

Before the waves of Sidney's rapture subsided, Kitty threw back her head and called his name, trembling as she climaxed. She collapsed into a damp heap upon Sidney's chest, their bodies satiated beyond reasoning, their strength expended.

'Oh, my God,' she murmured into his sweat-soaked shoulder. 'I never imagined it would be *that* bloody amazing.'

Sidney's heart swelled with love and pride. He knit his fingers into her hair and held her close. Gillingham had been wholly and completely wrong. This consummation had only increased Sidney's devotion to Kitty. 'You and I are meant to be, my muse.'

Kitty sat up, still impaled on his hard shaft, and searched his eyes.

Then she grinned. 'Let's do it again.'

Sidney raised his eyebrows, momentarily uncertain of his abilities, but she squeezed him, and his cock responded with a jolt, signalling its enthusiasm.

'Adonis is yours to command, Aphrodite.' He smiled as they began anew to rock with the rhythm of the post-chaise as the horses thrummed forward on the Great North Road, transporting them to an irrevocable union – one which would defy conventions, destroy society's grip on them, and demonstrate the invincible power of love.

No one could hurt them, ever again.

15

Two days later, a vibrant blue afternoon sky spread above verdant slopes as the post-chaise rumbled over the River Sark bridge.

'Are we in Scotland now?' Kitty asked, leaning out the open window. The fresh air whipped her bonnet ribbons and cooled her cheeks. Twenty feet below the stone rail, the indigo water of the Sark gurgled over cascading steps; it frothed under the bridge before proceeding downstream in satin ripples.

'We are now,' Sidney replied, as the carriage passed off the bridge and onto the hard-packed dirt road.

Kitty sat back. Her palms prickled; she folded her gloved hands in her lap. How was it possible to be so excited and so utterly terrified at the same time?

The postillion drew the chaise to a halt at a tollgate house with wild roses climbing its weathered stone walls. A middle-aged man wearing a woollen suit took the toll from the driver as a barefoot lad opened the wooden gate.

The postillion called to the horses, and the carriage jolted forward. The tollgate keeper and his boy bowed their heads and bid them a good day.

Kitty pressed her hands more tightly together, but the tingle remained. 'I never left England before.'

Sidney smiled as he reached for his coat, which he'd shed after their luncheon stop in Carlisle. 'What do you think?' he asked, slipping the dark blue wool over his shirtsleeves.

'I thought Scotland was mountainous.' The sheep-dotted land rose in only slight inclines. The grey and white houses of a nearby village sat upon the highest slope.

Sidney straightened the ruffle of his shirt at his cuff. 'Farther north, it is.'

'The tollgate keeper spoke English and dressed like an Englishman.'

Sidney chuckled. 'Did you expect Gaelic and tartan?'

Kitty had, but she kept the thought to herself. Her images of Scotland derived from Scott's *The Lady of the Lake*, but there were no signs of 'heathery couches' or 'mountain and meadow, moss and moor', or any of the other wild, evocative description in the poem. Nor had the tollgate keeper sounded anything like Robert Burns's poetry, which the Scottish lord who had once kept Kitty laughingly quoted when he drank too much.

Kitty licked her dry lips and turned the subject. 'When do you suppose we arrive in Gretna Green?'

Sidney nodded his head in the direction of the village, now clearly visible as sturdy stone buildings built low to the ground. 'It's there, my love.'

Already?

Kitty squeezed her tingling hands into fists. She breathed deeply as the buildings grew larger, trying to calm her nerves. The news of Kitty's marriage would enrage her sisters upon her return to London, but Kitty would spend the rest of her life proving she hadn't married for selfish reasons. Eventually, they would forgive her, but if not . . .

She clutched Sidney's forearm. 'We'll provide a home for my nieces should they not wish to be courtesans, won't we, Sidney? Tess may live with us, mayn't she?'

Sidney kissed her forehead. 'Kit, we've talked about this incessantly for the last two days. Our home will be a home for anyone who needs it, and I shall support your family to the best of my ability. As you've requested, we shall go without before they do.'

Kitty relaxed her tight grip. Even if her sisters never forgave her, she *wasn't* selfish. Through her marriage, she could provide a safe alternative – a simple but wholesome life – for Ada-Marie, for her sisters, and for her nieces. Tess needn't be a courtesan unless she *chose* the life, and the same for the younger girls.

The carriage slowed.

And stopped.

Sidney grabbed his hat, covered his thick golden hair, and extended his hand. 'Shall we?'

Kitty released a slow breath and placed her hand in Sidney's.

As she climbed down the post-chaise steps, the clamour of metal striking metal drifted from the wide-open carriage doors of a lime-washed stone and timber-beam building.

She hesitated once she planted her feet on the dusty road. 'It's truly a smithy?'

Sidney's amber eyes saddened. 'You don't mind, do you?'

Kitty shook her head and curled her fingers tightly around Sidney's hand. 'No, darling. What fun.'

But although she smiled to reassure him, her thoughts were in turmoil. How could an impromptu marriage at a blacksmith's shop in Scotland constitute a legally binding union in England, where nearly everyone but royalty must marry within a church and even then only by licence or banns?

A brawny, brown-haired man wearing a black waistcoat and a leather apron emerged. He cast lazy-lidded eyes over the carriage, but when his gaze alit on Sidney and Kitty, his face broke into a wide grin.

He looked Sidney up and down. 'Well, well,' he said, hooking his thumbs into his waistcoat armholes. 'Jamie,' he called over his shoulder. 'A fine young gentleman has arrived with a bonny bride; fetch the bishop.'

Kitty started. A bishop in a blacksmith's shop?

A weedy youth with a shock of red hair popped around the open doors holding a metal hammer. His shirt collar was open, and a thick Adam's apple bobbed in his scrawny neck. 'Aye, Joe.'

He tossed his hammer down and loped across the village green towards a cluster of trim stone cottages.

'Come in,' Joe said. 'Nae need to be shy. We have a wedding most days. Sometimes two or three.'

Still clasping Sidney's hand, Kitty stepped through

the wide doors into the blazing heat of the smithy. Sunbeams cut through small dusty windows, but it took a moment for Kitty's eyes to adjust to the dark interior.

On the far end of a long room crossed with rough-hewn beams, a boy pumped the bellows of a massive iron forge. Sparks flew as a ruddy, strapping blacksmith with rolled-up shirtsleeves struck red-hot metal on a black anvil. In a corner, a young apprentice bent over a chestnut horse's hoof, hammering on a shoe as he held an iron nail between his teeth. A long-limbed mongrel bitch nursed a pile of wriggling pups on a woollen blanket on the dusty stone floor. Another lanky dog ran to greet Joe as he entered behind Kitty. Benches spread with tools and horseshoes lined the walls between ploughs and other heavy metal equipment.

The only sign that the shop operated as anything other than an ordinary smithy was a vast tree stump set up like a mock altar, with an anvil in the middle. Slim wooden boxes, a thick leather book, colourful ribbons, parchment and quills cluttered the stump around the anvil.

Kitty's heart sank.

But how fitting that she should marry in such a setting.

Joe opened one of the boxes and ran his fingers over two dozen gold bands which lay upon a dusty velvet lining. 'You need a ring, lad.'

'No, thank you,' Sidney said. 'I have a ring already.'

Joe's smile vanished. He narrowed his blue eyes, which darted between Kitty and Sidney. 'Most gentlemen that come here allow the young lady tae select her ring hersel', as she's the one who must wear it. But perhaps ye chose the ring he speaks of, lass?'

Kitty swallowed. She hadn't even thought of a wedding ring, and the gold bands were a solemn reminder of what she'd agreed to do. After today, she'd wear a visible sign on her body for the rest of her life declaring that she was a *wife*. 'I shall be happy with the ring my . . . my friend chose.'

Joe snapped the box closed with a grunt and laid it on the tree stump altar. 'Aye, well, but ye must choose yer binding.' He gathered a bundle of lengthy ribbons in a rainbow of colours. 'Unless ye've brought that as well?'

Sidney's cheeks pinked. 'No.'

Joe offered the ribbons to Kitty. 'Which one do ye fancy, lass?'

'What are they for?' Kitty asked.

'For hand-fasting, of course. When the bishop binds yer hands, ye'll be man and wife.'

Kitty furrowed her brow, but she selected one of the least grubby ribbons – a wide satiny silk the flaxen-yellow colour of Ada-Marie's hair.

Joe laid the other ribbons aside and smirked at Sidney. 'One last business matter, my good man, and ye'll be ready for the bishop. Today's services will be eleven pounds.'

Sidney recoiled, blanching. 'You . . . you *cannot* be serious. I am a clergyman, and within the Church of England—'

Joe crossed his arms over his chest. 'Aye, well, this isn't the Church of England. Eleven pounds, if ye want

217

to marry this beautiful lass. Otherwise, turn back around and marry in England.'

A deep voice spoke from the entrance. 'Joe, we shall grant a professional courtesy to our fellow man of the cloth.' A stout man with a black shovel hat pulled low over his dark hair extended a hand to Sidney. 'Bishop David Laing at yer service, and I shan't take a farthing over ten pounds from ye, lad. A small price indeed for a future of matrimonial bliss with yer lovely bride, eh? Now, let's have no more talk of money when there's love to celebrate.'

As Bishop Laing walked past Kitty on his way to the anvil, the unmistakable odour of strong drink assaulted her nose, but the man's keen eyes were sharp, and his words precisely articulated. He cleared his throat; the noise of the smithy ceased as both the smith at the anvil and the apprentice with the horse laid aside their hammers. The bishop folded his hands over his rotund middle, below his flat Geneva collar. Despite his protest about money, he stared pointedly at Sidney until Sidney withdrew a handful of silver and gold coins from his trouser pocket and handed them to Joe, who counted them into a box. Meanwhile, the red-headed youth opened the leather book to a page half-covered in script, withdrew a parchment certificate, and dipped a quill into an inkwell.

'State yer name and parish, my good man,' Bishop Laing said in a ponderous voice, as if addressing a large congregation.

'Mr Sidney Wakefield of St George's Parish, London.'

The red-headed boy stuck his tongue in the corner of his mouth and drew the tip of the quill slowly over a blank space in the parchment certificate.

Bishop Laing glanced expectantly at Kitty.

'Miss Catherine Preece of the same parish.'

As the boy wrote this information, Bishop Laing continued. 'Are ye both above sixteen years of age, not closely related by blood, not married to another living soul, and willing to receive each other for better or worse?'

Sidney confirmed he was; Kitty did the same.

'Put the ring upon her finger, lad.'

Kitty removed her gloves and tucked them into her reticule as Sidney produced a gold band set with turquoise.

Kitty's heart fluttered as he slipped the cool metal over the fourth finger of her left hand.

'Now, lad, place her hand with your own on the anvil.'

Sidney coiled his warm fingers around Kitty's hand and rested it upon the cool metal.

Bishop Laing tied their wrists with the yellow ribbon. Then he tapped a hammer on the anvil on either side of their bound hands. 'As a blacksmith merges metals upon an anvil, I unite these two individuals as man and wife.'

Approaching carriage wheels sounded. Joe perked up his head and sauntered outside. Bishop Laing peered over Sidney's shoulder.

'Well, then, a good day to ye both,' the bishop said.

'That's *it*?' Kitty asked, before she could stop herself.

Bishop Laing laughed. 'We keep the ceremony short here, as ye'll be longing to be alone. Either the Gretna Hall Inn or the King's Head will serve ye a fine dinner, with champagne, and ye'll find the bedsheets well-aired.' He snatched the certificate from Jamie and waved the parchment to dry the ink. 'The marriage lines for the wife's keeping. There's yer proof for whoever doesn't want this union.'

Revulsion arose as Kitty held the ink- and dust-smudged paper between two fingers of her unbound hand. The marriage ceremony was as unsavoury as the surroundings; surely it had offended Sidney's romantic sensibilities. He ought to have wed a beautiful heiress in Hanover Square with his friends at his side.

Bishop Laing patted Sidney's shoulder. 'Best to consummate it at once, lad. Remove the hand-fasting after the thing is done. Now, if ye'll move along, we have others wishing for their own happy union.'

Still staring at her paper, Kitty allowed Sidney to draw her from the anvil. Could this grubby certificate and that bizarre ceremony truly make her Sidney's wife? It seemed utterly impossible.

But, then again, did it matter? Kitty had been willing to live with Sidney outside of marriage; why therefore did the legality of the ceremony trouble her? If it pleased Sidney, wasn't that enough?

Or did Kitty wish to be married – truly and honour-ably married – more than she'd realised?

A braying laugh from outside the blacksmith made Kitty freeze, for she thought she recognised it. When it sounded again, her heart hammered. Good lord! Could it be, she wondered? It sounded exactly like the horsey, jarring laughter of the penniless gossipmongering scourer Mr Bonser, the obnoxious friend of Sir Vincent Preston and of Amy's keeper, Mr Spencer-Lacey, whom she'd last seen only days ago at Vauxhall.

The man's voice rang out. 'Name's Bonser,' he said, putting an end to Kitty's speculation. 'Which one are you, Paisley or Laing?'

'We must hide our faces as we exit,' Kitty whispered into Sidney's ear. 'I know this man, and I don't want to see him.' If Mr Bonser observed her and Sidney at Gretna Green, London would be rife with the gossip well before their return – and Kitty *must* be the one to tell Matilda what she'd done, if she had any hope of forgiveness.

Sidney placed his untied arm around Kitty and drew her close. She buried her face in his shoulder, tucking their bound hands together. She trusted him to direct her outside, past Mr Bonser's boisterous voice, louder now as he haggled over the price.

'I'll be damned if I pay even *two* quid. You're not the only drunken lout in Scotland to put on a slathering bib and declare himself a cursed clergyman. I hear your uncle Paisley'll perform the ceremony for a bottle of French wine, the old smuggler.'

Sidney inhaled sharply.

'Never mind,' Kitty whispered into Sidney's neck. He *did* worry about money, as Kitty had suspected in the toy shop, and the unnecessary loss of eight pounds undoubtedly hit hard. 'Let's flee from here.'

'You don't wish to stay at the inn?'

Kitty climbed into the carriage, still bound with Sidney. 'No, let's go somewhere where no one will know us, and no one will cheat us.'

'Where?'

She settled into the seat. 'For now, let's drive.'

Kitty peeked round the carriage curtains at Mr Bonser as the postillion readied the team. Mr Bonser's bride, dressed in silks and feathers, was older than Bonser, with lined cheeks and a sallow complexion. She, not Bonser, dropped two gold coins into Bishop Laing's waiting hand.

Was this woman – presumably a lady of fortune, if not youth – happy with her chosen husband?

The carriage lurched forward. As Kitty watched the diminishing forms before the blacksmith, Bonser smacked his bride playfully on the bottom, and a girlish blush spread over her face. She clung, smiling, to Bonser's arm as they entered the smithy.

To each her own, Kitty supposed.

Kitty's eyes fell to the marriage lines on her lap. Her ponderings begged a similar question of her. Was *Kitty* happy?

She chewed her bottom lip. At the moment, trepidation and confusion overpowered other emotions, but perhaps happiness would come on the first night she tucked Ada-Marie into bed in their country cottage.

Or maybe it would come a bit sooner, tucked into bed with Sidney, her *husband*, that night.

'Are there any mountains we might reach before dark, Sid?'

'Hills only, I think.'

Kitty nodded. 'Let's drive to the hills.'

'As you wish, Mrs Wakefield.'

'Mrs Wakefield,' Kitty repeated with a small smile. It sounded well.

Unpresumptuous. Simple. But well.

Kitty leaned eagerly towards the window. She'd enjoy her time in Scotland, come what may at the end of it.

After three further hours of travels – in which Sidney and his new bride made swift work of the consummation and then, hands freed, cuddled and gazed out the carriage windows – Kitty chose Langholm, a village of stone buildings nestled on the banks of the River Esk at the base of rounded hills.

Sidney bespoke the best room available at The Crown, a lime-washed stone coaching inn with black corner quoins. The second-floor chamber was low-ceilinged and the bed narrow, but a feather bolster topped the mattress, and the linen was fresh. Thick woollen blankets promised to provide warmth, despite the evening chill, which wafted in from the open window, carrying the lanolin scent of sheep and the crisp smell of the river.

But when Kitty stepped out from behind a four-panelled screen wearing the sheerest of silk nightdresses, Sidney, who lay upon the bed in his shirt and buckskin breeches, knew he needn't have worried about the chill. Their cosy bedchamber was suddenly hotter than the Gretna Green smithy.

'Oh, wife,' Sidney said, exhaling as his eyes trailed down her perfect body. 'Come to bed, my love.'

That night, their lovemaking was slow, not urgent. Luxurious and almost lazy, as their bodies stretched over the feather mattress. Kitty's gasps melded with Sidney's moans as he mounted her time and time again for hours, both of them needing love more than sleep. Their bodies entwined, fingers knotting together as they fisted the linens, legs tangled with the blankets, mouths against each other's necks, breath hot on fevered skin, with pleasure flowing over Sidney's body like ripples on a sun-kissed river.

When the dawn broke, and the sun extended red-orange fingers into a heather-purple sky, Sidney gazed down at his wife's dark head, which lay upon his shoulder. 'Are you awake, Mrs Wakefield?'

Kitty snuggled closer, her skin warm silk against his body. 'I don't want to sleep, because for the first time in my life, reality is more beautiful than any dream.'

Sidney's heart filled his chest as he kissed her jasmine-scented tresses. 'It's the same for me, Kit.'

He adjusted the pillow under his head, and observed the sun rise gloriously on his married life, with Kitty's breath steady against his chest.

'Kit,' he said after a time, his fingers brushing lazily through her long hair. 'What did you dream of when you were a child?'

Her breath hitched, but she answered readily. 'I wanted to change the past. Make it so my parents lived rather than died.'

Sidney held her closer. 'Will you tell me what happened?'

Kitty exhaled slowly, a soft breeze against his chest. 'When I was very young, my father had steady work as a clerk, and while we were extremely poor, we had each other and a warm meal every day. But the winter after Amy's birth was a hard one. Illness descended and didn't lift. Matilda and my mother suffered the worst. Infections settled in their lungs, much as Matilda has now, again. My father, desperate not to lose us, spent his savings on medicine and doctors, and when that was spent, he incurred debt. He fell ill himself, caring for us, but the debt was his death sentence. He didn't survive a year in the Marshalsea.'

'Oh, Kit. I'm so sorry.'

She placed her palm over Sidney's heart, as if feeling its aching beat. 'We lost our lodgings, of course, but Mama found an attic room in Southwark. She'd been a lady's maid, once, before her marriage, and her needle-work was exquisite. She'd already been teaching Matilda for years, so they took in what they could. Mending, mostly, but sometimes they'd receive a commission for a frock from a merchant's wife or daughter.' She trailed her fingertips over Sidney's chest as she continued. 'We never had enough to eat, and Mama didn't have time to teach me or Barbara needlework, so Barbara and I climbed down to the Thames when the tide was out and scavenged the riverbed for items to clean and resell.'

'Oh, my angel,' Sidney said, overcome. His own childhood had been loveless and lonely – and he'd

225

suffered vicious beatings from his father and brother – but he'd never lacked food or shelter. He'd never scrambled over filthy shingle, digging for his subsistence from river debris. 'I cannot imagine what you suffered.'

'It wasn't all bad,' she responded quietly, 'at least while Mama still lived. Jenny and Amy were good babies, never fussy, bless them, as effervescent as they are now, content to roll upon the floor at Mama's and Matilda's feet, playing with scraps of fabric. At night, Mama tucked us all into bed together and sang us to sleep, and that was the best of all. Our thin mattress was a safe, secure, loving island.'

'When did your mother die?'

Kitty's fingertip traced swirls on Sidney's chest. When she replied, it was short, to the point. 'A year after my father. I was eight.'

Sidney gathered a breath and asked a question he'd long wondered. 'And how . . . how did Matilda . . . change things so significantly for your family, Kit?' Many young women were forced by circumstance into prostitution, but none, to Sidney's knowledge, had risen from such poverty to such luxury so quickly.

Kitty's finger stilled. She lay like a stone beside Sidney's body, and it wasn't until her breath tickled dampness on his skin that Sidney realised she'd cried silent tears.

'Kit, never mind, my love.' He rubbed her back. 'I shouldn't have asked.'

She lifted her hand to her face, and although Sidney couldn't see, he suspected she wiped tears from her

226

cheeks. 'I don't mind that you asked. But there are some things I don't think I shall ever speak about. That past is past.'

'I shan't broach the topic again, my love.'

Kitty lifted her head, rising on one elbow and smiling wistfully up at him. 'All I want, right now, is to relish this time together.'

Sidney nestled her against him again, willing her to feel the strength of his love in his embrace. 'It shall be as you wish, Mrs Wakefield.'

He meant what he said.

Although financial worries and family troubles assuredly awaited his return to London, for the next week, Sidney would delight in his Kitty, his love, his wife. He could figure out the difficulties later.

After all, they'd overcome the greatest challenges already, had they not?

16

A glaring white sun striped with silver haze hung over the oppressively muggy afternoon a week and a half later when the post-chaise arrived at twenty-nine Half Moon Street. Throughout their travels that day, Sidney's clothes had clung to his damp skin as Kitty rested against his shoulder, her hand lying on his thigh, her breath warm against his neck.

Sidney was hot and tired as he toted their portmanteaux up the stoop, but he had many tasks to accomplish before the day ended. As he deposited the cases and boxes into a heap in the entrance hall, he mentally sorted his list: bathe and change his clothes; go with Kitty to Mount Street to relay their news and collect Ada-Marie and Nanny Ashcroft; settle his new family into his flat on the second storey; and arrange with Tyrold to lease the Devonshire cottage, since Kitty yearned for it.

Then he'd start his next novel. Tonight.

The time in Scotland had been paradise, but real life began now, and Sidney desperately needed to sell another manuscript.

Kitty crossed the threshold and closed the front door.

'Welcome to your temporary home.' Sidney swept his arm out, presenting the dark, wood-panelled entrance hall for her inspection.

She smiled wanly, her eyes darting about the space.

Sidney's heart sank. She didn't like it. Why would she, after the grandeur of her home with her sisters? 'I wish I could give you a palace, my love.'

Her eyes shot to his, and her face softened. 'Oh, my poor Sidney,' she said, untying her bonnet ribbons. 'My thoughts were elsewhere, so now you think I want a palace rather than this perfectly lovely home.' She smiled. 'But I don't, darling. I've lived in a glass-sided palace for years, caged like an animal at a menagerie. It was never *home*. I haven't had a home since my mother died – and, as you know, this *is* a palace next to that.' She placed her bonnet on a table near the door and looked around. 'Are we the only ones here?'

The house was often quiet.

'Edward's likely rusticating somewhere, this late in July. And as for John, unless he's playing on the piano-forte, one hardly hears him.'

'And your servants?'

A pile of unopened correspondence resting beside Kitty's bonnet caught Sidney's eye. 'They're out, I suppose,' he said, as he shuffled through the letters. Curiously, many of them bore Cornelius's name: *The Rt Hon The Earl of Eden.* Why had the senders directed them to Sidney's address rather than Eden House in Berkeley Square or Paradisum Park in Hertfordshire, where Cornelius likely was by now?

Kitty's hand touched Sidney's back, recalling him to her presence.

'I'm nervous,' she said. 'That's why I seem out of sorts. Actually, I'm more than nervous. I'm frightened.'

Sidney placed down the letters. 'Oh, sweetness.' He held out his arms, and she snuggled against him. 'Frightened of telling Matilda?'

Kitty nodded into his chest, and Sidney tightened the embrace.

'I understand. I'm not looking forward to informing my mother, to be perfectly honest.'

Kitty shivered in his arms. 'I can't bear the thought. Her ladyship will loathe me.'

Sidney didn't argue. His mother would certainly never approve of his choice of wife, but then again, nothing pleased her. 'Don't let it distress you.' He rubbed her back. 'Kit, our love hurts no one. Our happiness *ought* to be enough for our families. If they choose to bask in prejudice rather than sharing in our joy, it'll hurt them more than it hurts us.'

Kitty raised her chin and studied him, but she said nothing.

Sidney kissed her forehead. 'And, anyway, before the autumn, we shall be in Devonshire. Simple Mr and Mrs Wakefield and their daughter, living in our sea-breeze-cooled cottage.'

Kitty peeled herself away from Sidney. 'How lovely *that* sounds.' She fanned her hand in front of her face. 'I don't know when I've ever been so miserably hot and sweaty. I must look a fright.'

She *did* look different – she'd looked different since the first full day of their travelling. Without Philippe's perfect ringlets, Kitty's hair tumbled in tangled waves which fluffed into a cloud when Sidney brushed them. Devoid of cosmetics, her features were less defined, and her complexion was ruddy rather than ivory. Her rosiness deepened further when she laughed, when they made love, and now, when she stood before him, hot from the heat, her pink face surrounded not by orderly curls, but by a frizzy dark crown.

She'd never been more beautiful.

Sidney smiled. 'Aphrodite could *never* look a fright.'

Her eyes crinkled. 'Take off your rose-tinted spectacles.'

'Never – and never take off yours either, Mrs Wakefield. When your husband is gouty and grey and his waistcoat strains so much the buttons fly off, you must, of course, see only your Adonis.'

'Always.' She smiled tenderly. 'Although, when we're not being *passionate*, you are more of a Sir Galahad.' She gazed in that wide-eyed, admiring way she had – as if he were her hero.

Sidney *wanted* to be her hero, but how long until she noticed the cracks in the illusion? How long before she realised how close he frequently came to asking her to sell her jewels because little of his two hundred pounds remained? Once he'd put down the first quarter payment on their cottage, they'd have forty pounds on which to relocate and to survive until Sidney wrote another book. They'd have to hire servants with promises – and there'd be no money to buy even a donkey for the farm unless Sidney took out credit against his name.

Sidney steeled himself, forcing those thoughts from his mind. He had a wife and child. He *must* succeed. There was no other choice. He needed to start his work.

Which meant he should finish the other business of the day quickly, beginning with the call to Mount Street, but he didn't want to appear before Matilda smelling of sweat and dust.

'My love, before we fetch Ada-Marie, what say you to a proper bath with running water?'

Kitty's eyes brightened. 'Have you one?'

'Yes, although it's often rather tepid.' Sidney struggled out of his coat and tossed it on top of their cases. His shirtsleeves stuck to his skin like plaster.

'Tepid sounds *lovely* right now,' Kitty replied. 'Ice cold might be even better.'

Sidney led Kitty through the shared spaces – the dining room and parlour – and into the black-and-white-tile-lined lavatory at the back of the house. He plugged the bottom of the copper bathing tub and turned on the taps. The water roared and the pipes shook as the deep basin filled.

Sidney unlaced Kitty's gown. 'You mustn't tell a *soul*, for you know how closely John guards his reputation as a parsimonious miser, but he's passionate about modern inventions. He plans to fit all his properties with gas lighting and flushing close stools.'

Kitty lifted her gown over her head. 'So he *does* spend money?'

Sidney grinned. 'More than he'd ever admit, and most of it on charity. But on a new coat? Perhaps once a decade.'

Kitty laughed and offered her back again so he could untie her stays. 'Tell me more about your friends.'

Sidney loosened the knot he'd tied that morning. He'd become Kitty's dresser over the last fortnight, and – after tangling her laces a few times – he'd managed some proficiency. 'Nicky, as you know, was a devilish rake. He, *ahem*, never refused an offer, shall we say? And he was remarkably talented at securing them. He certainly wouldn't have mangled your stays as miserably as I've done repeatedly—'

'You've learned, darling. You're a first-rate dresser now.'

Sidney slipped the straps off Kitty's shoulders, and the corset fell to the floor.

'But now Meggy has thoroughly domesticated Nicky.'

Kitty slid her stays across the chequered tiles with her toes to join her discarded gown. 'Lord Holbrook always seemed cold and unfeeling on the few occasions he came to one of our evenings, or when he joined us for a ride in the park.'

Sidney unbuttoned his waistcoat. 'Guarded would be a better word, although he wasn't when we were boys together at Eton, and he's not anymore. Meggy's changed him back.' As Sidney took off his boots, he ventured cautiously into a topic Kitty disliked. 'I know you don't believe me, but Meggy will like you, Kit. She's not like the common run of debutantes. She has gumption. Had to have it, with Edwin Fairchild as her brother. Surely you recall that poor blighter? He drank himself into an early grave after squandering the family fortune.'

'Yes, I recall the late Lord Berksleigh.' Kitty frowned as she pulled off her chemise. 'But, Sid, we've spoken about Lady Holbrook before. You must understand that being married to you does not erase my past. I shall never be a respectable woman, fit to be friends with a marchioness. Please accept that.'

'But I don't agree—'

Her eyebrows snapped together. 'Stop it!' She turned her head aside, breathing rapidly.

Sidney's stomach sank. He'd angered her. 'Forgive me, Kit.'

The running water thundered, filling the weighty silence of their broken conversation.

At last, Kitty spoke again. 'Let's simply not speak of it.' Her voice was calm, measured. 'Tell me instead about your other friends, since I don't know them like you do.'

Sidney attempted to recover his own inner composure as he complied with her request. 'Well, as you've discovered, John is more tender-hearted than one would think, but he's bristly about anyone knowing it, and I've no idea why.' Sidney slid his braces off his shoulders. 'Alexander is brilliant, kind, honourable, and good fun, as well – but he works so much, I hardly see the man. And Edward—' Sidney shrugged. 'What can I say? He enjoys bachelorhood and nursing his artistic temperament. But they're all marvellous, really. Something *independent* about each of them – they're not afraid to be their own men.'

234

That's why Sidney admired his friends. He'd only begun not to be afraid of being his own man when he'd offered his books for publication, and he owed his new confidence to Kitty, who'd repaid him so trustingly with her heart and hand.

Now if only he could be worthy of her.

Kitty slipped off her stockings and shoes as Sidney continued undressing himself. She let down her hair and, naked, dipped a toe into the bath. 'Lovely,' she purred. 'I shall feel a new woman after this.'

Sidney smiled, grateful for the contentment in her voice. 'Careful,' he said, offering his hand to assist her to a sitting position. 'It's rather slippery.'

Kitty doused a sponge and squeezed it over her breasts. Delight infused her face. 'Paradise.'

It was an intensely erotic sight, and Sidney's cock hardened, despite their tiff.

As he kicked off his trousers, Kitty stroked her breasts. 'Something on your mind, Mr Wakefield?'

He grinned. 'The sight of my gorgeous wife bathing.'

Kitty gazed coquettishly through her lashes, squeezing more water over her sleek skin. 'Join me.'

Sidney needed no more encouragement. The cold water struck his body with a refreshing bite as he settled beside Kitty. He turned off the tap and submerged himself, the sweat and grime of travelling washing away.

Kitty's slippery-wet body sidled on top of his. 'I shall wash you,' she said, soap in hand. She lathered him, smoothing lavender-and-rosemary-scented suds over his shoulders and across his chest. Her palms glided over his arms like a sculptor shaping clay.

She dropped the soap into the water, slipped her arms around his neck, and rubbed her curvaceous chest over his torso.

Which drove Sidney mad with desire.

Sidney tried to thrust into his wife, but she twisted away like a slippery fish.

'I shan't make it *that* easy,' Kitty teased. 'Show me you want me.'

'Want you? I crave you.'

Again, he attempted a capture, but she grasped his cock instead and rubbed her thumb across its tip. Sidney groaned, desperate.

'You torment me.'

Kitty grinned wickedly. 'How can that be? You had me this morning.'

'Ah, but I could make love to you five times a day and not tire of it, you siren.'

Her naughty grin deepened. 'Calling me a siren while we're bathing is terribly daring of you. Hold your breath, sailor, while I drag you under to wash away these bubbles.'

Sidney followed her orders, and she pulled him below the surface of the water. The suds covering their bodies floated away.

They came up together, rivulets streaming off their hair.

Water pooled in Sidney's ear. As he tilted his head to drain it, a distant knocking, presumably on the front door, distracted him.

It was insistent. Urgent.

Oh, well. Whoever it was, the caller would have to return later if the Smiths or John weren't home.

Sidney returned his attention to Kitty, kissing her deeply.

She pushed him back until his head rested against the tub's curved metal rim.

Evidently, her teasing was over, for she straddled him and positioned herself over his shaft. 'Now that the sailor has suffered his drowning so bravely, the siren wants to fuck him.'

She slid down, squeezing as she went, and Sidney moaned.

'The sailor is more than willing to give it to the siren,' Sidney gasped between waves of pleasure. He gripped her hips and thrusted to assist her as the cool water lapped around them.

Pleasure surged, ebbed, surged harder.

The knocking grew louder.

Kitty rode him faster. Water coursed over the rim, splashing onto the tiles. Sidney thrusted urgently, on the brink of ecstasy. Together, they approached the summit . . . it was in sight . . . a few more plunges . . . Kitty leaned her head back, gasping . . .

The knocking ceased.

Muted voices filled the silence. One was Tyrold's. The other was female, high and piercing, rather like Sidney's mother's voice.

No, exactly like his mother's voice.

Sidney's throat tightened, choking him.

237

His cock wilted, instantly unable to perform.

'Good God.' Sidney pulled Kitty off him. 'Forgive me, my love. Stay here.'

As he stepped out of the bath, dripping more water on the chequered tiles, the voices grew louder.

'I shall find him myself, Mr Tyrold.'

Sidney grabbed a linen towel from the stack on the table near the door. He fumbled with it, trying to tie it around his waist so he could flee the lavatory to protect Kitty's privacy. If his mother was on a quest to locate him, even John couldn't deter her. This was not how Sidney wanted his mother and Kitty to meet; he ought to call out that he'd come to the dining room in a moment, but his throat was thick, and he couldn't speak . . .

Tyrold's booted footfalls and Lady Eden's clicking heels were in the parlour now.

'If you'll wait here, *Lady Eden*' – Tyrold said the name unnecessarily loudly, no doubt to warn Sidney – 'I shall bring him to you.'

An exclamation sounded from Kitty.

The footsteps stopped; a body pushed against the other side of the door.

'Bathing, is he? Good lord, Mr Tyrold, do you suppose there's anything behind that door I haven't seen? Now, stand aside.'

Sidney tied the towel and found his voice at last. 'Mother, don't—'

But the knob turned, and the lavatory door swung open, framing Lady Eden, who was black-swathed from her plumed hat to the bottom of her stiff bombazine skirts.

Behind her, John offered Sidney a laden look – something like a distressed *forgive me*, perhaps – before skulking off.

Lady Eden's gaze flickered behind Sidney to Kitty, who crouched deeper into the water and covered her breasts with her arms. Sidney shielded her as best he could. He ought to ask his mother to wait in the parlour, but, once again, throat tightness prevented his speech. In his mother's presence, he became a terrified child, trembling and seeking approval he never received.

Lady Eden's face pinched. 'So, you and your . . . your *mistress* are back at last.'

Sidney gathered his courage. He must defend Kitty, and there was no better time than now to tell his mother the truth. 'Kitty's not my—'

His mother waved her hand. 'I've no intention of discussing *her*, son. I want to know what you intend to do about matters now you've finally returned.'

Sidney frowned, bewildered. Do about matters? Did she mean his livelihood? 'I don't need the curacy at St George's anymore, Mother. I've sold my novels—'

'Good lord.' Lady Eden sighed. 'Do you not know, son?'

Sidney blinked. 'Know what?'

'Your brother is dead.'

The edges of the world dissolved around Sidney, with colours draining away like dust in the rain. Somehow, he remained standing, aware only of the weight of his feet against the water-puddled tile. Cotton filled his head; a ringing plagued his ears; his vision blurred and wavered.

As if from another room, his mother's voice continued: 'Killed in a fight with some rabble last week. What was the name? Bruiser or . . .'

Sidney clutched at his damp chest as the walls closed in around him. He gasped a single word through his constricting throat: 'Butcher.'

His knees buckled. He collapsed on the cold, wet floor and covered his face.

17

A boulder weight pressed on Kitty's heart. Butcher had killed Cornelius while she and Sidney had cocooned themselves in selfish happiness.

It was ghastly. Sickening.

Poor tender-hearted Sidney would grieve long over this. At present, he huddled towel-wrapped on the wet floor with shaking shoulders, clearly in desperate need of comfort.

Kitty met Lady Eden's gaze, hoping the countess would at least turn around to give her a measure of privacy to step out of the bathing tub, but Lady Eden simply glared. If she mourned for her elder son or worried for her younger one, she concealed her sentiments well. She was an impenetrable fortress of frost – her handsome face an icy counterpart to Sidney's warm features. Her thick blonde hair glittered with silver, and her light brown eyes glinted like gold. If Kitty had any secret hopes that her mother-in-law would grow to accept her, they were instantly doused.

Sidney's sobs intensified. His mother evidently didn't intend to offer the love he needed, so there was nothing to do but get out of the bath. This was hardly the first

241

impression Kitty had planned, but her only concern was for Sidney.

Water slurped off Kitty's body as she rose. She dribbled streams onto the cold tile when she stepped out, meeting Lady Eden's gaze throughout.

After all, Kitty was a brazen hussy who could hold her own against supercilious ladies. She had a damned lovely figure, and if Lady Eden wished to gape at the notorious Kitty Preece . . .

The boulder weight plummeted to Kitty's gut.

She wasn't Kitty Preece anymore.

She was Kitty Wakefield, and she stood nude and exposed, with her hair plastered flat to her skin, before her well-dressed, high-born mother-in-law, like a sewer rat facing a queen.

Kitty's foot slipped on the tiles. She recovered from her stumble, but she stooped her shoulders and covered her breasts with her forearms. 'If your ladyship—' Her tongue was swollen. She nodded at the stack of linen at Lady Eden's elbow.

The countess pinched a towel between two black-gloved fingers and tossed it with a flick of her wrist. Kitty caught it awkwardly by a corner, as she was attempting to conserve as much of her modesty as possible with her other arm.

The thin linen clung to Kitty's wet body as she tied it over her breasts. When she knelt beside Sidney, he grasped her at once – as if he were drowning and she were a lifeline – and wept against her bare shoulder.

The countess tapped her toes. 'Do you intend to snivel on the floor all afternoon, Sidney?'

Kitty's jaw dropped. How could anyone speak so viciously to darling Sidney, the gentlest of men?

Lady Eden arched an eyebrow. 'Perhaps you can silence his crying, girl? I presume you can stimulate *some* manly capabilities in him, or you'd not be here?'

For Sidney's sake, outrage displaced Kitty's mortification. 'A man may cry without shame upon hearing of his brother's death, Lady Eden.'

'Nonsense, there was never an ounce of love between them.'

Even if that were true, guilt must gnaw at Sidney, like it did in Kitty. If not for her, Cornelius would've never met Butcher.

But *no*. Cornelius met Butcher because of *Gillingham*, who had no business sending a henchman after Sidney. None of this was Kitty or Sidney's fault. It was Gillingham's, and Butcher's . . . and, yes, perhaps even Cornelius's, for hadn't Sidney said the earl demanded the match with the prize-fighter?

These were the words with which Kitty would comfort Sidney once his mother left them alone. She'd reassure him tenderly, while letting him cry as long as he needed.

Sidney smeared the back of his hands across his cheeks. 'What happened, Mother? How did Cornelius die?'

Lady Eden snorted. 'Savagery, as that sport always is. No better than a cockfight.' The slightest flicker crossed her face – perhaps the countess wasn't as unaffected as she pretended. 'But it was merciful, at least. That brute hit him into a post; Cornelius cracked his head.' She raised her black-gloved hand halfway to her face before it sank back to her side. 'Never regained consciousness. He died within hours.'

Kitty covered her mouth, as if she could push away the waves of nausea.

Sidney stared glassy-eyed at the wall, his towel-wrapped legs still folded under him. 'He died at Fives-Court?'

Lady Eden fiddled with her onyx-bead necklace. 'No. His friends brought him to Eden House. I was with him when he died.'

Sidney closed his eyes and shuddered, as if consumed with nightmarish imaginings.

Only with the greatest difficulty could Kitty push away a visualisation of Cornelius's bruised and broken body, his strength, vigour and vitality eradicated in one devastating blow.

Perhaps Kitty was the one who should leave, to allow mother and son to grieve alone.

The countess drew herself up. 'Not that it matters who was with him,' she said curtly. 'He never regained consciousness, as I said. Might as well have died in the ring, for all he knew.'

Sidney bowed his head. Kitty embraced his hunched shoulders and pressed her lips into the damp skin at the back of his neck. He still needed her, after all.

The countess appeared determined to deny her grief.

'Tyrold sent an express after you,' Lady Eden continued. 'Wherever you were. Did you not receive it?'

'No.' Sidney mindlessly folded and unfolded a corner of his towel at his bent knees. 'We didn't stay where we originally intended to stay.'

Kitty cursed herself for suggesting they leave Gretna Green.

Lady Eden's eyes cut to Kitty and returned to Sidney. 'That was exceedingly inconsiderate, son. I've needed your presence for many days. You know that, as a lady, I can't attend the funeral, and considering the heat, we've delayed it too long already.'

Kitty's mind churned with childhood memories of bloated animal and human corpses along the Thames shore; she pressed her mouth into Sidney's shoulder, again as if the force would dispel her queasiness. And the barbarous tradition among the upper classes for ladies not to attend the funerals of their loved ones defied reasoning.

Sidney wept into his hands.

'We'll bury him at Paradisum Park, naturally,' Lady Eden continued. 'But before we leave for Hertfordshire, you're to attend to the matter of . . . of *that man*. He's at Newgate, charged with manslaughter, but, at my request, the judge will permit you to voice an opinion on the sentencing, and I want something more severe than what's customary in these cases of death during pugilism. A fine of a *shilling* at the last one. That's unacceptable. He ought to hang, but I'm told that's impossible. Regardless, accept nothing less than transportation. Remember, you're the Earl of Eden, so don't be such a weakling as you always are—'

Kitty's eyes flew open. Pounding commenced in her ears, drowning out the countess's words. Distraught about Cornelius, Kitty hadn't considered that Sidney was Lord Eden now.

But if Sidney was an earl, and Kitty was Sidney's wife . . .

No, no, no.

Kitty tasted the bile she'd forced back; it burned her throat raw. Her marriage was a ghastly mistake. For Kitty to dare to be Mrs Wakefield of a humble Devonshire cottage was audacious enough, but, with time and distance, people would've forgotten them, and Kitty's sisters probably would've eventually forgiven her.

But Kitty couldn't be a *countess*, couldn't bear the same title as the grand lady who stood before her now. Never, in a million years, would *anyone*, from any sphere or class, tolerate such a social rise. The brazen slut who displayed her body in wispy gowns, who strutted on the arms of various noblemen draped in their jewels, and who blew cheeky kisses at respectable ladies could never deck herself in hoops and ostrich plumes and bow before Her Majesty at the Court of St James, calling herself *Lady Eden*.

It was beyond comprehension.

The countess's voice cut through her writhing thoughts. 'Answer me when I speak to you, girl.'

Kitty looked up, startled, aghast, her movements thick and slow, like walking through water. 'I-I beg your ladyship's pardon. I didn't hear.'

'I asked if you're the barren Preece sister?' Lady Eden's words slashed the air like a whip.

They stung Kitty as badly.

'Y-Yes, my lady.'

'Thank God,' the countess said.

Meanwhile, Sidney sobbed, not even defending Kitty.

But why should he defend her? Countless times she'd asked him not to, and he was finally doing as she wished.

'No doubt you're expensive,' Lady Eden continued, 'but at least you won't produce *lasting* charges on Sidney's resources.'

Sidney spoke through his tears. 'Mother, don't talk to Kitty like that. She's my—' He stopped abruptly. His eyes were unfocused, confused. Or perhaps horrified.

Ah, Sidney had realised, at last. He'd attempted to defend her, and then comprehended the catastrophe of their marriage.

Fairy tales don't come true.

With her heart shattering into a million pieces, Kitty placed her palm against his cheek. 'Never mind.' *Don't defend my virtue, for I have none*, she added silently, hoping he could read the sentiment in her eyes. 'Never mind, darling.'

The countess spoke. 'Sidney, as you'll soon discover when you speak with the steward, our affairs are dire. What with your father's excesses and your brother's extravagance . . .'

'Tyrold can help.' Sidney's voice was strangely flat.

The countess frowned. 'No. We need an immediate solution. Tyrold's odd notions are too slow.'

'He's awfully clever, Mother. For years I've suggested Cor—' Sidney's face crumpled, and he dissolved into tears again. 'Oh, poor Cornelius.'

Lady Eden's nostrils flared. 'Stop blubbering. Cornelius wouldn't have shed a tear over you.'

Sidney cried harder. He nestled into Kitty's neck, kissing her through his tears, sobbing words into her skin. Words like *I need you* and *forgive me* and *my only love*.

Kitty's heart melted. Sidney loved her. He never should've married her, but he *loved* her. Was that love enough? Could it see them through the scandal and the ostracism they would face?

Lady Eden fiddled again with her black beads until the violence of Sidney's tears abated. When she spoke, her tone was kinder. 'Your brother was engaged to a worthy young widow of your acquaintance named Eliza Overton.'

Sidney sniffled into Kitty's neck. His hand gripped a chunk of her wet hair as if it were a rope holding him afloat. 'Yes, he told me.'

'Ah. I wasn't certain if you knew. There wasn't yet an announcement, as Cornelius never attended to his duties as readily as he should. In this case, however, perhaps the delay was for the best.' Lady Eden cleared her throat. 'Sidney, I considered Eliza an excellent match for your brother. Besides possessing a substantial fortune, she's ladylike, she's handsome enough, and she's a *proven breeder*.' The barb stung, as the countess no doubt intended. 'And she comes from good stock, despite her fortune's connection to trade. Her mother is the daughter of a baronet.'

Kitty's throat tightened. Why was Lady Eden cataloguing Mrs Overton's virtues, if not because . . .

Oh, God.

Sidney's breath heated Kitty's neck. 'Mother, if Mrs Overton is grieving for Cornelius, tell me. I shall pay her a call.'

'Good lord, she's not grieving. She barely knew him. No, the switch is natural, and there'll be no scandal, as few knew of her engagement with Cornelius. Fortunately, despite the *on-dit* about you and *her*' – Lady Eden nodded at Kitty – 'acting as if a Bond Street toy shop were a brothel, Eliza is clearly more content to have you than Cornelius, although she discussed it decorously, of course. I'm exceedingly well pleased with her.'

Kitty's heart raced. Her rash, selfish folly would ruin Sidney's life, as she knew it would. Mrs Overton was precisely the wife he needed. Sidney had said it himself on that momentous day in Hyde Park.

Sidney lifted his pale face. 'What do you mean, Mother?'

Did he truly not understand? Did he not recall the very words he'd spoken to his brother? '*Mrs Overton will make a magnificent Lady Eden*'. He'd been correct . . . he was *still* correct. Sidney needed dignified Mrs Overton as his wife. She'd fill the earldom's depleted coffers. She'd merge effortlessly with his society, hosting elegant affairs to support the political efforts which Sidney would surely have now that he must serve in the Upper House. And she'd give Sidney beautiful sons of his own, as blond, handsome, and kind as their father.

Sidney's mother smiled for the first time. 'No need to delay the wedding merely because of mourning. It's a second marriage for Eliza, so it's perfectly reasonable to keep it small. I told her next month should do. But you ought to be more discreet with *that woman*' – she pointed at Kitty – 'until after the ceremony, so as not to put Eliza off.'

Sidney's colour rose. 'No, Mother. No, no. I cannot marry Mrs Overton—'

Kitty interrupted, digging her nails into Sidney's palm to silence him. He wasn't thinking clearly, but Kitty was, so she needed to take control of the situation before Sidney ruined his life even more irrevocably. 'I shall make myself scarce, my lady. I know my place.'

'*Kitty.*' Sidney spoke her name with animated feeling. 'My love, your place is by my side.'

Sidney needed to be silent.

'Discreetly, yes, Sid,' Kitty replied firmly. 'But only discreetly.'

Sidney recoiled. '*What?*'

Kitty didn't explain. Instead, she lifted her chin proudly and looked straight into Lady Eden's golden eyes. 'I know my place,' she repeated. 'Your ladyship needn't worry.'

The countess glared. 'You have more sense than he does, girl. See to it you continue to know your place.

Sidney, wait on me at Eden House tonight. Before dinner, mind you, so don't spend long with your harlot. You had plenty of time for *that* during the last week, when we needed your help in London. You'll focus on duty now.' She glanced around the room. 'Naturally, you'll move out of these pitiful lodgings. The earl's bedchamber is ready for you, and don't you dare bring *her* to Eden House while *I'm* in residence.'

The countess turned on her heel, and before Sidney could utter any words – he inhaled as if he intended to call out after her – Kitty clamped her hand over his mouth. 'No, Sidney, don't tell her. She lost her son; don't distress her more.'

He pulled her hand away. 'Kitty, the secrecy was only for the elopement. We agreed we'd tell people about our marriage now that our union is secure. My mother needs to know, lest she continue to arrange a wedding for me. I cannot marry Mrs Overton.'

'True,' Kitty said.

Sidney couldn't marry Mrs Overton *yet*.

Kitty's chest compressed with pain, but she must help Sidney see the wisdom of ending their dubious Scottish marriage before he threw away his future on a childless union which would bring him scandal, shame and financial ruination. A divorce would be complicated and costly and there would be dreadful gossip, but it was the only feasible option.

Unless there was a simpler way out of a blacksmith's union . . .

But those were details for later.

For now, Kitty must simply convince Sidney not to reveal their news. She wouldn't attempt to persuade Sidney to end their marriage when his grief was raw. He would need time to adjust his sentiments, his duty, his sense of honour.

'We mustn't tell anyone about our marriage *right now*,' Kitty said, though her throat ached. 'I shall return to my sisters' house while you attend to your duties.'

'No.' Sidney pulled her into his lap, clinging again as if his life depended on it. 'Don't say you won't come with me to Eden House and Hertfordshire. I cannot bear separation from you.'

'I mustn't come, darling. It would be cruel to ask your mother to absorb such a shock on top of dreadful grief. Don't force her to face my presence as she buries her son.'

'But what about *my* feelings?' he asked, distraught. 'How am I to manage without my wife?'

Kitty's heart screamed in agony, but Sidney *must* manage without her from now on. 'You must think of your mother first. Assist her, as she requested.' Once he mingled with his kind again, the inevitable self-importance which accompanied titles would consume him. He'd become ashamed of Kitty, and he'd regret their impulsive union.

And, in the meantime, Kitty would plan. It would be torture, but she must repress her emotions and lead with her head, not her heart. Letting her heart rule had got her into this situation in the first place. Logic, not love, must determine her actions now.

First, she'd discover if there was a way to dissolve their Scottish marriage more quickly and quietly than an English one. But if not, she'd convince Mrs Overton to wait out the divorce and the accompanying scandal.

Kitty schemed; if necessary, she'd call upon Mrs Overton and appeal to her fiercely loving maternal heart by explaining Kitty had only dared to step outside her social sphere for the sake of Ada-Marie. Then Kitty would assure Mrs Overton she'd realised the error of her ways. She'd beg the widow to wait for the divorce to finalise, because, despite the scandal, Sidney was worth it. Sidney was honourable and faithful and kind. The best man in all the world.

Kitty's eyes stung.

She envisioned the widow's response.

'Faithful?' Mrs Overton might say. 'How do I know he'll be faithful? A woman of *your kind* would think nothing of continuing an affair.'

Then Kitty would kneel before the widow and swear to give up Sidney forever if only Mrs Overton would take in Ada-Marie and love her as her own. As Lord and – the *proper* – Lady Eden's adopted daughter, Ada-Marie would grow up a lady, accepted everywhere, her future safe and secure in a way Kitty could never provide. No one would mock her in a toy store. No one would ask her to play the pianoforte and sing for licentious men in a house of whores. No one would question her right to an honourable and decent life. Sidney would ensure she'd have the best education money could buy, and all the love a little girl needed.

She'd soon forget Kitty altogether.

Kitty stifled stinging tears. These were the sacrifices she must now make. They were the prices she'd pay for her audacity. If she hadn't married Sidney, she needn't have lost him yet. He could've married the widow and kept Kitty as his mistress, at least for a while. That was the proper order of things.

Kitty swallowed down her gut-wrenching pain. She must be brave for the two people she loved more than her own life.

'Go to your mother, Sidney. She's borne her burdens and grief alone for a week. Reassure her you'll take care of everything.'

The sorrow in Sidney's red-rimmed eyes struck deep into Kitty's core. 'I don't know if I can take care of everything, Kit. And I certainly won't succeed without you.'

Kitty threaded her fingers into his wet hair and pressed her lips to his. Their kiss tasted of salt from their mingled tears. 'Yes, you can. You *can* take care of everything, and you don't require me to succeed. You're' – the words stuck in her throat – 'you're my hero. Never forget that, darling Sid. Never forget.'

Just as Kitty would never forget the fourteen days and nights when her happiness had been complete. She'd cherish the memory for the rest of her days, for never again would she know such paradise.

18

An hour and a half later, Kitty lay beside a sleeping Sidney, with his golden head resting near her shoulder and his deep breaths tickling her bare breasts. Gloomy shadows darkened his sparsely furnished bedchamber at the back of the second storey, for outside the open windows, the sky had grown overcast. The house itself remained as quiet as a tomb, but the faint sound of hooves striking cobblestone drifted in from the mews.

One last time, Kitty kissed her beautiful Sidney's smooth brow as she rested her hand over his heart. 'I love you,' she breathed against his slightly salty skin. Under her palm, his chiselled chest rose and fell. 'But I must go, darling.'

At *once* – before he awoke and begged her to stay. Leaving was hard enough as it was; Kitty couldn't face Sidney's entreaties.

Carefully, she extracted herself from Sidney's loose embrace and slid off the thin mattress. The bed creaked as it had when she and Sidney made love earlier – an intimacy Kitty had encouraged, hoping the activity would calm and exhaust Sidney after forty minutes of crying.

Her success broke her heart, for now she must depart. The heart-wrenching tender moments she'd just shared with Sidney would be the last time he held her in his arms.

She dressed silently, loosely tying her laces and smoothing her damp hair with her palms. The tarnished mirror above Sidney's dressing table reflected a disaster — puffy eyes, frizzled tresses, splotchy cheeks. Kitty didn't care. She must speak with John Tyrold, but after that, she'd return immediately to Mount Street.

The knob glided as Kitty turned it. She opened the door enough to slide out, and she guided it closed until a soft click announced she'd secured the latch.

Her feet flew across the barren floorboards of Sidney's small parlour and down one flight of the narrow stairs. Her raised fist hesitated briefly before Tyrold's closed door.

She knocked.

'Come in.'

Kitty entered — but she froze in the doorway with her hand trembling on the knob.

In the book-lined room, Tyrold reclined in a leather chair with his feet upon his mahogany desk.

He wasn't alone.

Lord Edward Matlock sprawled before the fire-less hearth; Tyrold's sleeping wolfhound pillowed the artist's chestnut head. Familiar Dr Mitchell — who often attended to the Preece sisters' medical needs — leaned against the window frame, rubbing his temples, his auburn hair ruffled. Dark and handsome Lord Holbrook sat in an armchair with his boots upon a footrest.

Four sets of eyes met Kitty's.

As one, the three men not standing rose, and Dr Mitchell straightened his posture.

Tyrold indicated the chair across from Holbrook. 'Have a seat, Kitty. We were discussing which of us will accompany Sidney to Hertfordshire.'

Kitty shook her head. 'I cannot stay.' She stepped into the room and closed the door behind her. 'Please sit again. I have only one thing to say. As it happens, it's relevant to your discussion.'

The men returned to their previous positions with their eyes still on Kitty, who twisted her fingers in her long skirts as she struggled to find words.

Although she'd seen these men many times before, her stomach knotted. In the past, she was the spectacular Kitty Preece, the courtesan-muse Sidney had innocently placed upon a pedestal, and, in their own way, these gentlemen had respected her in that *rôle*. They were aloof and polite, and at least somewhat in awe of her beauty.

But now she was Sidney's secret, shameful wife, and she stood before his four grand friends without her cosmetics mask, wearing dishevelled clothes and with her dark hair in a tangled, loose mass. Ungroomed, ugly, disgraceful. A dirty street urchin, all over again.

Did they know she was – *ha!* – a countess, supposedly? Had Tyrold told them? If so, did they judge her as harshly as she judged herself? Were they discussing how she'd ruined Sidney's life? How revolting it was that Sidney, now an earl, was married to a whore?

Kitty searched Tyrold's face, but his expression revealed nothing.

'How's Sidney?' Holbrook asked, his deep voice severing the weighty silence. The marquess's grey eyes were sombre.

Kitty inhaled deeply. Best to say what she must and flee back to Mount Street before her quivering emotions collapsed like weak scaffolding. 'Sidney's sleeping soundly. Someone should wake him up in an hour or two, for Lady Eden requested his presence before dinner.' She glanced down. A thick lock of frizzled hair fell over her cheek, and she tucked it behind her ear. 'Naturally, I shan't go to Hertfordshire—'

Tyrold sat up abruptly. 'What did you say?'

Holbrook and Dr Mitchell's eyes darted between Tyrold and Kitty. At the hearth, Lord Edward sat up and rubbed his chin, joining the scrutiny.

Kitty mustered her strength. 'It's best I return to my home on Mount Street, Mr Tyrold. At once, for Sidney is clinging to me when he must stand alone.'

Tyrold drew back, curling his upper lip. 'You're a callous creature if you think this is the time to cut the apron strings. He's lived and breathed you for six years. Now he has you, and you desert him?'

Tyrold's words were a battering ram against Kitty's resolve.

With effort, she recalled Sidney's debt, his mother's viciousness, her sisters' fury should they ever know, and she lifted her chin. She couldn't falter at the beginning of an arduous road to freeing Sidney. 'I have no choice. A gentleman cannot bring his mistress into his mother's presence.'

Tyrold's eyebrows shot up. 'His m—' The businessman stopped himself, putting a hand to his untidy cravat. 'Sidney said that?'

'Lady Eden said it,' Kitty replied firmly. 'Sidney didn't dispute it because his mother is correct. He needs your help now, not mine.'

Tyrold blinked several times before throwing his palms in the air. 'Good lord. I should've never involved myself in this disaster.' He leaned back in his chair and flung his feet on the desk. 'A farce I called it that day in the park, but it's a cursed tragedy now. And you' – Tyrold pointed a finger at Kitty – 'are at the centre.'

Kitty staggered against the door.

'John.' Holbrook spoke with authority. 'Kitty isn't to blame.'

Tyrold's green eyes flashed. 'You don't know the half of it, Nicky.'

So, the others *didn't* know. Otherwise, Holbrook wouldn't have defended her.

'In that case,' Dr Mitchell said from the window, softer but somehow more imposing than Holbrook's scold, 'perhaps someone should tell us.'

Tyrold drew his lips into a thin line and stared at his lap. 'You won't hear it from me. Ask Kitty.'

'There's nothing to tell,' Kitty said, stabilising her voice with effort. 'Nothing to discuss. I merely wanted to ask Mr Tyrold if he . . . if he could take care of Sid now, since I-I shan't be able to do so anymore.'

Tyrold slammed his palm on the desk. 'Dammit, woman, don't tell me what to do. I was taking care of Sidney for more than a decade before *you* even met him. I love him as if he were my brother. I *thought* you loved him as well, but it appears I was gravely mistaken.'

'John!' Holbrook jumped to his feet and strode to Tyrold's desk, scowling. 'What the devil is the matter with you to treat Kitty like this?'

Tyrold growled low in his throat. 'She knows.'

Kitty turned her head to the side, unable to meet their gazes anymore. 'Mr Tyrold, think of me what you will, but convince Sid this is for the best. I've said all I wanted to say, and now I shall leave.'

Without another glance at the men, Kitty fled the room and down the stairs. In the entrance hall, she grasped her bonnet, shoved it on top of her wild mane, and yanked the ribbons into a knot. She thrust her hands into a pair of gloves and opened the front door. As she fumbled with her portmanteaux – one leg propping the door – a man's footsteps trod heavily down the stairs.

Before her pursuer reached the hall, Kitty dashed outside. She didn't want to know who followed her. Holbrook, Dr Mitchell, Lord Edward, that vile monster John Tyrold . . .

. . . Or Sidney, whom she couldn't bear to see.

The front door opened behind her as she descended the front stoop.

'Don't desert him, Kitty.' It was Tyrold's voice.

Kitty pivoted, ready for an attack, but Tyrold's

expression startled her. He stood in the open doorway, his green eyes glistening with emotion.

'I must,' she said softly, beseechingly. 'I cannot be anything but what I am.'

Tyrold's disappointed gaze was worse than anger. 'I thought better of you.'

'John,' a voice said behind the businessman. 'I sent you down to apologise, not to berate her more.' Holbrook swung the door fully open and shoved past his friend, who crossed his arms and set his jaw. 'I apologise on his behalf, Kitty,' the marquess said, hailing a passing hackney. 'I shall see you home.'

As the hackney driver pulled up his team, Holbrook relieved Kitty of her portmanteaux. He tossed the cases into the coach, but as he reached out to hand Kitty up, his eyes widened, and the faintest hint of colour tinged his high cheekbones.

Kitty knew what troubled him. Gossipmongers would delight in spreading a vicious report into the ears of Holbrook's young bride. It wouldn't do for the marquess to be seen speaking to her on the pavement, much less riding with her in a closed carriage.

Holbrook recovered himself, composing his face into a stiff mask. 'John, you're coming as well,' he said, somewhat gruffly.

Even that would set tongues wagging.

Kitty, not wishing to cause the new marchioness even a moment of pain, waved her hand dismissively. 'I don't need anyone to take me home. Take care of Sidney, not of me.'

With that, she stepped into the hackney unaided and closed the door herself.

When Kitty dragged herself up the front stoop of the house on Mount Street minutes later, it was impossible not to compare her heavy tread with the light steps with which she'd flown down these stairs to start her new life a mere fortnight ago, her naked body sleek under her enveloping cloak.

Dark clouds blocked out the sun, churning with the weight of a brewing storm.

Kitty turned the brass knob and pushed open the cherry-red door. She hoped to slip upstairs unseen and, as gently as possible, inform Ada-Marie there would be no cottage in the country, after all. Kitty would snuggle her little girl tight and assure Ada-Marie she'd always be safe and loved, and that, until Papa had a new home for them (she'd say *them*, although the home would be only for Ada-Marie), they must remain on Mount Street.

'Well, well, Kitty-cat.' Matilda stood at the base of the grand central staircase, much like the day when Kitty and Sidney had returned euphoric from Hyde Park.

The dreadful day Cornelius had met Butcher.

Kitty handed her portmanteaux to Dodwell. 'Good afternoon, Matilda.'

Matilda broke into a grin, her plump, rouged cheeks shining pinker than her rose-silk gown. 'You clever girl.'

Kitty blinked, surprised. 'Why do you call me a clever girl?' she asked, fumbling with the knot on her bonnet ribbons. She'd tied it so tightly, her gloved fingers couldn't loosen it.

Matilda swished across the entrance hall. Her jewelled hands took over Kitty's clumsy efforts. 'Because you've snatched up the newest peer before the matchmaking mamas or other courtesans could get to him.'

Kitty's heart thumped. Did Matilda know about Kitty's ill-fated marriage? And if so, was she indeed *pleased*? 'Why! – what do you mean?'

Matilda's brows arched. 'My dear sister, you and Sidney are the talk of Mayfair. Saint Sidney, the handsome curate, kissed courtesan Kitty Preece in a toy shop and then swooped her off to the country while his oafish brother got himself killed. You cannot expect people to ignore such riveting gossip. Why, it's the stuff of novels.' She removed Kitty's bonnet and grimaced. 'Lord, Kitty-cat, your hair is a fright.'

Kitty patted her tangled locks. 'I bathed at Sid's . . .' Her words stuck in her throat.

Matilda tossed the bonnet to Dodwell. 'Thank God no one's here to see you, for you certainly don't look like an alluring temptress now.' She smoothed Kitty's hair, coughing and chuckling intermittently. 'The most amusing thing about the *on-dit* is that it paints your placid Sidney as the wildest sort of roué. It's so diverting, I confess I've fuelled the rumours where I could by reminding everyone that a Preece sister transformed a lowly curate into a dashing devil.'

Kitty's eyes stung. Poor Sidney. Kitty had already destroyed his good name with her wanton behaviour

263

in the toy shop. 'Sidney's not a rake. He's the noblest and best of men.'

'Lord, Kitty, don't spoil the fun. Now, come.' She tucked Kitty's hand into the crook of her arm and led her towards the stairs. 'Let's take you to Philippe – and next time Sidney sweeps you away, bring Philippe with you. It doesn't do to have you look like a common drudge.'

Kitty's shoulders slumped. What did it matter how she looked?

Matilda chattered as she tugged Kitty upstairs. 'Truly, don't repeat all that "noblest and best" nonsense. Gentlemen like to imagine themselves as rakish cads. Makes them feel like men, and not the mollycoddled, spiteful babies they really are. They will model themselves after the handsome devil Lord Eden, and they will want to keep a Preece sister as well.' Matilda paused on the first landing and grasped Kitty's free hand. 'I'm really quite grateful to you, Kitty-cat. These rumours may help us out of our slump at last. We had twice as many men at our Thursday night entertainment this week as we normally have this time of year. Oh! – and Barbara received an offer, far more generous than her last keeper.' Matilda grinned. 'That dashing Colonel Dixon. I accepted on her behalf, and she's well pleased to rip the redcoat off his broad chest.'

Kitty forced her lips into a weak smile as they proceeded upstairs again. 'If she's pleased, I'm happy for her.' But, in truth, now that Kitty had experienced love, she couldn't fathom joy in a superficial affair.

'Yes, it's all worked out beautifully, despite my misgiving. To be perfectly honest, I was *livid* when you chose Sidney.' Matilda waggled her forefinger as if Kitty were a naughty child. 'A Preece sister the mistress of an impoverished curate-turned-novelist: what would *that* do for all our reputations? But I never should've doubted you. My Kitty-cat is a clever puss.'

Kitty frowned as they walked along the second-floor corridor. Something didn't make sense about Matilda's words, and the inconsistency awakened Kitty from her stupor. 'I thought you didn't want me with Sidney because you were scared my heart would be broken?'

There was the barest falter in Matilda's step. 'I-I . . . I *was* concerned about that,' she said with a cough. 'But, see, it's not a problem. He adores you. You were right all along.'

Kitty stopped in the middle of the corridor. She pulled her hand from Matilda's elbow and stared into her sister's blue eyes. Matilda's lashes fluttered, her gaze fell, and Kitty knew the truth.

'You're lying to me, Matilda,' she said, ripping the words from her burning throat. 'You didn't accept Sidney when he offered because he wasn't rich and grand enough for you. You don't care if my heart is broken. All you care about is money, money, money. So much so that you expected me to suffer viperish Gillingham because *your* last keeper took credit in your name.'

'Kitty, that wasn't my fault,' Matilda snapped. 'He absconded to France while I was ill, and I was accountable for his debts.'

'But it wasn't my fault either, Matilda. And, yet, even when Sidney paid that money – selflessly handing over the fruit of *years* of labour to pay your debts – it wasn't enough for you, because Sidney isn't a rich, asinine, tyrannical prick like Gillingham.'

Matilda knitted her fingers together. 'Kitty—'

'No! None of your excuses. *Damn* your prejudice.' She clenched her fists, too angry to say more. If Matilda had simply agreed to Sidney's offer rather than riling him up so that he worried for Kitty and Ada-Marie's safety, Kitty could've avoided the current disaster. She would've insisted on a keeper/mistress relationship with Sidney.

Or, at least, she *probably* would have.

'Dearest Kitty-cat, you know we have a certain reputation to uphold.' Matilda's wheedling words chafed Kitty.

'I'm not listening,' Kitty said, turning away and marching towards her room.

Matilda chased after her. 'We can't let poor men think they can afford us, or it cheapens everything. From our very beginning' – Matilda grabbed Kitty's elbow, slowing her progress – 'from *that event* only you and I know about, what has mattered?'

The words hit Kitty so hard, she staggered. Matilda was using an old tool against her, evoking memories best laid to rest . . .

'What matters?' Matilda asked again, more urgently, her eyes glinting as she pressed her advantage.

It worked.

The sudden pounding of Kitty's heart compromised her ability to breathe. She pressed her hand against the wall to support herself and pushed her forehead into it.

'Illusion matters,' she muttered, the words serrating her throat.

'*Yes.*' Matilda's breath heated Kitty's cheek. 'We must maintain the illusion of worth. When a powerful man possesses a Preece sister, he increases his status, his significance and his virility in the eyes of his fellow rich men. Illusion is why we earn hundreds of guineas rather than giving two-bob shags in Covent Garden.' She tugged at Kitty's arm. 'You know illusion saved us. Take away that illusion, and we're the worthless grubby urchins we once were.'

Kitty pressed her forehead harder against the wall. She closed her eyes as memories swirled, transporting her into her trembling, waifish eight-year-old body standing barefoot in a dim, dank corridor in Southwark not a week after Mama was carted to the paupers' grave . . .

Little Kitty's toes curled into the splintered wood of the cold floorboards as the gin-swigging landlord blocked her path. His odour was fouler than the river, and Kitty gagged, clamping her mouth closed to keep from retching. The landlord laughed, exposing brown teeth in swollen red gums as he lifted her thin skirts. When his rough cheek scratched her own, Kitty couldn't contain her vomit any longer. She hurled the watery contents of her stomach on his filthy shoulder.

His eyes – hazy and unfocused before – now burned with fire. 'You disgusting brat.' He yanked Kitty's hair so hard, her head spun as he pushed her towards the front of his soiled leather breeches.

A shriek sounded from the end of the corridor. Fifteen-year-old Matilda had returned from an errand, their mother's blue woollen shawl wrapped around her thick dark hair. She flung down the paper-wrapped bundle she carried and hauled Kitty into oh-so-thin arms, still brisk with an outside chill. 'Find Barbara and the others *now*, Kitty-cat, and stay in our room with the door locked until I return,' Matilda whispered urgently as the landlord seized her from behind. 'And take that bundle with you. It's worth more than our lives.'

Kitty ran up the first flight of stairs, towards their attic room, as the man dragged Matilda by their mother's blue shawl. 'You're late with the rent, you little cunt, and I told you I need payment. If it's not her, it'll be you.'

The other girls were asleep before Matilda limped into their attic room, but Kitty had stayed up, holding a tin bowl of pottage. 'Here,' she said, offering it to her sister. A darkening bruise stained Matilda's left cheek. 'I tried to keep it warm, although the fire went down hours ago.' The bowl was ice in Kitty's chilblained hands. The night had grown extremely cold indeed.

Matilda shook her head. 'I can't eat right now, Kitty-cat. But I do need your help,' she said, wincing as she squatted over the chamber pot. When she lifted her skirts, dark streaks smeared her thighs. 'Bring me the scrap bag, please.'

Kitty dragged the bag out from its spot near the hearth. 'Is it your monthly courses, Matilda?' she asked, rubbing the icy tip of her runny nose with the back of her hand.

'Something like that, Kitty-cat. Fetch the wash water, will you?'

Kitty broke a thin crust of ice on the wash water – already employed to scrub potatoes and cabbage for the pottage – and lugged the bucket to Matilda.

Later, when Matilda had washed, she held Kitty. 'Don't you ever be alone anywhere no more, and don't let the other girls be alone neither. You promise me that, Kitty-cat, and meanwhile, I shall find a way to get us far away from here.'

'Will you marry the baker's 'prentice who courts you, Matilda?' He was a handsome lad and occasionally gave them a loaf of stale bread.

Matilda's lips trembled. She looked over Kitty's shoulder towards the cold ashes in the grate. 'No, I can't marry him. He's a poor man. Besides, he won't love me now—'

'Why not?'

Matilda closed her eyes. 'Never mind, Kitty-cat. Maybe I don't want marriage. Mama was a respectable woman and look where it got her, so perhaps it's not such a bad thing I'm not respectable now.' She opened her eyes, a new determination shining in them. 'All the same, I won't be a common trull. No one will treat me like *that* ever again.' Matilda reached for the bundle Kitty had carried upstairs. She turned up a corner of the paper, displaying a silk that shimmered like new-fallen snow. 'Do you see this?

It's for the baker's daughter's wedding gown. I'm to sew it, you see. The baker's wife told me it cost two guineas, Kitty – two whole gold guineas! Papa starved at the Marshalsea for less than that.' Matilda released Kitty from their half-embrace and, standing, pulled the fabric out and wrapped it around herself. 'I'd look a princess in it, wouldn't I?'

'Oh, yes,' Kitty said, breathless. She'd never seen a more beautiful sight than her shapely sister with her long thick hair and large dark-lashed eyes swathed in clingy silk. 'You're the handsomest girl in London, Matilda.'

Matilda smiled. 'It's all about illusion.'

She began sewing that night, but it wasn't a gown for the baker's daughter. By the time her bruise diminished, she'd completed something worthy of Mayfair.

Matilda vanished for a fortnight, leaving thirteen-year-old Barbara with a handful of pennies and three sacks of potatoes. When she returned, it was in a crested carriage, on the arm of a duke. She wore a daffodil-yellow gown and a plumed bonnet, and she draped warm scarlet cloaks about her sisters' thin shoulders. Kitty grabbed her knotted rag doll, Mama's blue shawl, and took Matilda's kid-gloved hand. Matilda's duke tossed two gold guineas at the baker's wife as they left Southwark forever.

But if Matilda's gamble hadn't paid off, she would've hanged for theft after the butcher's wife arrived to collect a non-existent wedding gown. The images of what didn't happen – Matilda's body swinging on the gallows outside Newgate – haunted Kitty as much as the memory of her sister squatting over a chamber pot with dark smudges on her thighs, evidence of violence intended for Kitty.

A handkerchief on Kitty's cheek recalled her to the present, and she gazed into her sister's face. It was the same one that had comforted her in their filthy attic room, but now roundness replaced gauntness, and rouge gashed where once a bruise darkened. Philippe said Matilda's maid applied cosmetics with too heavy a hand.

'I'm concerned about you, Kitty-cat. Did you and Sidney quarrel?'

Kitty smeared her cheeks with the handkerchief, slowly regaining her composure. 'No, not at all. I'm exhausted from the road.' It wasn't a lie, but it certainly wasn't the whole truth.

'Come, let's get you to bed.' Matilda opened Kitty's door. The scent of jasmine – comforting and yet not – assailed Kitty's nose. 'Was it a terribly long journey?'

Kitty shrugged, not wanting to answer. She slumped onto her sofa, wishing she were at Sidney's cramped wood-panelled lodgings rather than in this palatial bedchamber.

Matilda renewed her questioning as she pulled back the satin counterpane. 'Where were you?'

The hair on the back of Kitty's neck prickled, warning her of Matilda's artfulness. 'Nowhere you know.'

Matilda wouldn't know Langholm.

Matilda pursed her lips. 'Do you know what I think?'

Kitty held her breath. Would Matilda say she suspected they'd been in Scotland? 'What?'

'I think Sidney must've worn you out,' Matilda said, giggling. 'Is he divine in bed?'

Although her tense shoulders eased, Kitty didn't reply. She would *not* discuss such precious things.

But Matilda didn't relent. 'Well, *is* he?' she asked, her eyes shining gleefully. 'Is he well furnished by nature, so to speak?'

Kitty scowled. With past keepers, she'd laughed over such details with Matilda, but her intimacy with Sidney was private.

Her sister's delight defused. 'Bah – you're strange today, Kitty, and not much fun at all.'

The words nettled. 'Well, forgive me if I don't wish to discuss intimate details when Sidney and I only just discovered his brother was violently *killed* in our absence.'

Matilda's face fell, and Kitty regretted her harshness.

She moderated her tone. 'I'm tired, Matilda. I want to rest.'

Matilda nodded, coughing. 'Naturally. Forgive me – I didn't realise you've only just heard.' She pulled the bell lever. 'Philippe will ready you for bed. Come here, and I shall help with your boots while we wait.'

Kitty arose. She plodded across the room and plopped on the edge of her bed. Matilda knelt and worked her boot laces, and Kitty's anger vanished. Perhaps she should tell Matilda the truth. Together they could consult about the best recourse for Kitty. It might be that one of the MPs or lords who visited the Preece sisters could advise . . .

Kitty tugged at the fingers of her gloves, removing first the right and then the left.

Matilda inhaled so sharply, her breath hissed. She grasped Kitty's left hand. 'What is *this*?'

It might've been a trick of the light in the darkening room, but for a moment, with the way the shadow slashed Matilda's glittering eyes, her sister resembled a monster.

Kitty had completely forgotten about her ring in the chaos of the afternoon. Now was her chance to confess, but those words didn't come. Instead, she stammered, 'N-Nothing.' She covered her left hand with her right. 'Only a ring Sidney gave me.'

'On your *left* hand?' Matilda asked, dangerously.

'He put it there.' It was the truth, but Kitty's face burned under her sister's intense scrutiny, until she snapped. 'What, Matilda? Why do you beleaguer me?' She was tired of her sister's presence, tired of relentless questioning, and her heart hurt so much, her chest couldn't bear the pain. 'I cannot help which hand Sidney chose to put it on.'

'True.' Matilda's voice was softer. 'Likely he wasn't thinking when he put it there – men are so careless and stupid, after all – but move it to your right hand now. We wouldn't want anyone to get the wrong impression, even for a moment. Would we, Kitty-cat?'

'N-No.' Kitty slipped the ring off her left finger – untouched since Sidney slid it on at the smithy – and moved it to her right.

Matilda smiled. 'Looks better.' She patted Kitty's knee. 'We Preece sisters know our place, don't we? No gentleman who comes here is in danger of our trying to rise above our station.'

The words fell against Kitty's heart with a thud, but their truth rang clear. A courtesan couldn't be a countess.

Matilda pulled off Kitty's boots.

The door clicked open. Philippe entered, his blue eyes dancing, but his face grew solemn when he met Kitty's gaze.

Kitty collapsed onto her feather mattress and turned her back to her sister. The tears would flow hard now. Philippe, who came around to the other side of the bed and studied her with a furrowed brow, could see them, but Matilda must not.

Matilda patted Kitty's shoulder. 'I'll leave you to Philippe's care.' Her footsteps faded, and the door closed.

Kitty looked up at Philippe. 'Bring me Ada-Marie?'

Philippe shook his head. 'Not yet, *ma chérie*. First, you must have your cry with Philippe.'

Kitty reached out her arms, and Philippe crawled into the bed.

'I feel I shall die, it hurts so much, Philippe. I can't breathe with the pain.'

'Ah, *chaton*,' Philippe murmured, kissing her forehead. 'Hearts do heal.'

Sobs racked Kitty's chest. 'No, Philippe. Not this time.'

He rubbed her back. 'It is how it always feels. Every single time.'

Kitty buried her face into his cravat as raindrops splattered her windowpanes.

The storm had broken at last.

19

On an afternoon in early September, six weeks after
Cornelius's death, Sidney shuffled through the letters
and ledgers covering the ebony desk in the oppressive
library at Paradisum Park, searching for a clean piece
of paper.

Even five years after his father's death, the desk
evoked memories as surely as if the broad-shouldered
earl's ghost hovered nearby with his arctic blue eyes
enquiring: 'Why do *you* sit at my desk, Sidney? You
were the disappointing son.'

Sidney shivered. The weather had turned cool and
wet after the storm which blew in on the day Sidney
learned he was the seventh Lord Eden, but it was the
phantom presence that chilled his flesh.

Maybe his next novel would be a Gothic horror.

Sidney rubbed his forehead, recalling himself to the
task at hand. There wasn't time to think of novels
now. He must write to John Tyrold, for he'd struggled hopelessly with the finances since John and Nicky
had returned to their own lives a month earlier, after
spending a fortnight in Hertfordshire assisting Sidney out
of his immediate pecuniary – and emotional – distress.

The estate brought in ten thousand a year, but his brother, his mother and his late father's spending had exceeded that income for decades. Lady Eden blamed Cornelius's extravagance, but when Sidney totalled her costs for the last year, including her gambling debts, they exceeded her widow's settlement by an additional three thousand pounds. All while Sidney had lived on less than one hundred per annum.

He needed more of Tyrold's help to sort through the mess he'd inherited.

'You might move,' Sidney told Marmalade, who licked his paw atop an open account book. Sidney's voice pierced a tomb-like quiet. For some time, the only sounds other than the cat's purring had been the ticking of the longcase clock and the crackle of the fire in the black marble hearth.

The Paradisum Park library was a dismal chamber. Even with the crimson damask drapes open and the September afternoon sun filtering through the lead-paned windows, light withered into shadow under the soaring ebonised ceiling. The room had terrified Sidney in his childhood. Despite his love of books, he'd crept in to slip oxblood-leather tomes off the dark walnut shelves because spending more than five minutes in the library risked attracting his father's attention. Sidney would clasp his chosen volume and tiptoe upstairs to hide wherever he was least likely to be found.

Sidney might be the Earl of Eden now, but Paradisum Park didn't welcome him.

'Why don't you take a chair by the fire, sir?' Sidney asked Marmalade, indicating one of the many blood-red leather armchairs dispersed about. 'How am I supposed to work with you sprawled upon my ledgers?'

Marmalade mewed.

Sidney stroked the velvety fur between the cat's pointed ears. 'Yes, you make an excellent point. Stay there, my friend. You are the only warmth in this house.' With Kitty absent and his mother issuing glacial chastisements and nothing else, Sidney's sole comfort was Marmalade.

Unless it was under Marmalade's ledger, there was no blank paper on the desk, so Sidney rummaged through the disorderly drawers. Dog-eared racing statistics jumbled together with tattered tradesmen's bills and gambling vowels. Cornelius's known debts of honour amounted to a staggering twenty thousand pounds, which Sidney must pay.

At last, Sidney located a piece of paper. He drew it out, slammed closed the drawer, and dipped the tip of his quill in the silver inkwell.

My dear friend, he wrote at the top of the page.

He stopped.

What could he say? Scrawling HELP ME in large letters was rather pathetic.

Sidney sighed, tossing down the quill. Ink splattered the page, spoiling it.

He cradled his head, with his brow pressing into his palms. Dammit – he'd failed at writing a letter to his friend, as he'd failed at almost everything after learning he was the new Earl of Eden.

Sidney's eyes fell again to Marmalade, who slept now, resting on his side. Under the fringe of the cat's ginger hair, the ledger displayed orderly lines of itemised expenses, listed in the neat hand of Mr Howes, the steward.

At the tip of Marmalade's twitching tail, however, Cornelius had scrawled a horse purchase for eight hundred pounds.

Horses and boxing had been his brother's life.

A tear slid down Sidney's cheek and splattered on the paper, rendering the word friend illegible.

Sidney recalled his fourteenth birthday, a brisk January day when he and Cornelius had ridden together. Mindless of the ice coating the laneways, Cornelius had galloped his chestnut stallion, while Sidney followed at a trot on his grey gelding Gallant – a birthday present from his father.

It was the first time his father had given Sidney *anything* enjoyable. Previous gifts had been books on military history, atlases of warfare, and guns. But even Gallant came with a price – the earl had ordered Cornelius to get Sidney up to snuff so he could accompany them on a gruesome fox hunt the next week.

All Sidney had wanted on his birthday ride was to enjoy the sparkling winter day. The ice-encrusted bare trees had glittered like ladies draped in diamonds; the snow-dusted yew branches were white gloved hands with splayed fingers. Robins picked at scarlet holly berries, and red squirrels scampered or nibbled nuts, their tufted ears twitching. Coal and woodfire smoke haloed every dwelling, from the vast expanse of red-brick Paradisum to the white-plastered cottages of the estate village.

Cornelius, far ahead, had circled back. 'Take that hedge with me, Sid,' he'd called as he thundered past. 'Get ready for when I return.'

Sidney didn't comply. Instead, he'd breathed. Crisp air had tingled his nose. He'd exhaled through his mouth, the breath-cloud like pipe smoke.

The hooves of Cornelius's horse had advanced. 'Dammit, get your horse to a gallop,' Cornelius yelled.

Sidney hadn't obeyed, and his older brother clamoured ahead, rose in his stirrups, and sailed over a hawthorn hedge into the adjacent snow-dusted field.

Cornelius had looped the fallow field and took the jump again, although his horse scraped its underbelly against the spiky-topped hedge and fumbled the landing.

Cornelius had yanked the reins and pounded to a halt beside Sidney. 'Grow some bollocks or put on petticoats, you cunt.'

'I don't want to hurt Gallant.' Sidney had stroked the gelding's gleaming grey neck. 'Or myself, for that matter.'

Cornelius had guffawed. 'Lord, wait until I tell Father what a fopling you are. If Gallant can't make a jump like that,' he'd said, nodding his head at the impossibly high hedge, 'he deserves to be shot.'

Sidney had recoiled, horrified. 'Don't say such revolting things, Cornelius.'

'Bloody hell,' Cornelius had sneered. 'Sometimes I wonder if you'll ever be a man.'

'The mark of a man,' Sidney had said cautiously, 'isn't taking foolish and unnecessary risks.' He'd continued with more confidence: 'The mark of a man is loving and caring for all of God's creation.' Sidney had swept out his arm, indicating the surrounding wonderland scene. His chest had expanded; he was rather proud of the wise words he'd conceived.

Cornelius had guffawed. 'Lord, if proper boys like Holbrook and Tyrold didn't defend you at Eton, you'd have been fagged to death by now.' He'd leaned forward in his saddle. 'The mark of a man is to be a *master* of God's creation. To show women and lesser creatures our strength and power. If a man doesn't do that, he's as worthless as a hunter who won't take a jump.'

Although every fibre of his being rebelled against his brother's speech, Sidney had silenced his tongue. No one in his family understood him.

'Besides,' Cornelius had continued, 'if I am to die of a broken neck because I reached ceaselessly for higher jumps, at least I shall die a man. A man in my prime, displaying my prowess.' He'd spurred his horse, yelling over his shoulder as he thundered down the lane, 'It's a fucking noble way to go.'

The memory had provided Sidney some comfort over the last weeks. As he'd told a distraught Butcher in the pugilist's damp cell at Newgate, Cornelius had died *his* definition of a noble death.

The visit to Newgate was the only thing Sidney had done well since he'd become Lord Eden. Guilt had racked Butcher, but the story had comforted him, as well. Sidney had left the prison with no shred of doubt that Cornelius's death was a dreadful accident.

Afterwards, Sidney had requested a two-shilling fine of the judge. He'd suffered a tongue-lashing from his mother for it, but he placated her with the news that Butcher and his sister sailed to Canada a week after the boxer's release.

Sidney had paid the ship fare himself.

He didn't tell his mother that.

It was hopeless to write to Tyrold when Sidney's mind wandered among ghosts and memories. With a deep sigh, Sidney stood, stretched his legs, and arched his back. He stuffed his hands in his pockets and strolled to a window.

It was the first day in weeks without rain. Pillowy clouds dotted the sky above the circular limestone Old Pond, set within a complicated knot garden of clipped yew. Lily pads floated on the pond's surface, sprinkled with elegant white flowers.

The water was as blue-green as Kitty's eyes.

Sidney rested his forehead against the cool glass. The diamond-shaped leading pressed into his skin.

He yearned for Kitty. He had done so since the moment he'd awoken from their last lovemaking to discover she'd left, and he had no choice but to follow her advice to manage on his own for some unspecified amount of time.

He knew he must honour her wishes, but he longed to go to her for comfort when the accounts weighed him down. Every evening, he wished Kitty's smile ornamented the other end of the expansive dining table rather than the cut-glass sneer of his mother. If Sidney could sink into Kitty's arms at the end of every day, the canopy of his father and brother's coroneted bed wouldn't hang so oppressively at night. Kitty's luscious curves and sweet caresses would heat the cold mattress.

More tears sprang to Sidney's eyes. He'd made Kitty promises he could no longer keep. Not his sacred vows – *those* he would honour until his dying day – but the other promises. Their quiet cottage life was an impossible dream. Simple Mr and Mrs Wakefield could never be. He and Kitty were the Earl and Countess of Eden now, and the well-being of many people depended on their fulfilling their responsibilities to the estate, to the extended family, to king and country.

Kitty had never agreed to such a life, and her letters implied she didn't want it. Apart from sweet stories of Ada-Marie, they contained only reminders for Sidney to prioritise his duty to his mother, not to visit Kitty in London, and not to announce their marriage, even to his friends. She'd repeatedly refused Sidney's entreaties to come to Hertfordshire. Her most recent letter, which Sidney had read after luncheon that very afternoon, cited Kitty's need to keep Ada-Marie in a familiar environment '*until everything is settled, one way or the other*'.

Which sounded so ominous that Sidney had at once resolved to write to Tyrold. Perhaps with John's guidance, Sidney could find a solution which balanced his own responsibilities with a life somehow still palatable to his wife.

Sidney turned from the window, determined to try his letter to Tyrold once more.

A clicking footstep sounded from outside the library. Sidney hastily wiped his cheeks.

He was too late.

'Crying again?' His mother stood framed in the door.

Sidney swallowed. 'Good afternoon, Mother. Do you want something?'

Other than to hound me?

She marched across the room and perched straight-backed on the edge of the stiffest of the crimson armchairs. Her black gown contrasted with the red leather like a crow beside the eviscerated innards of its fresh kill.

'I understand your Aunt Amelia called with your cousin Clara?'

'Yes, shortly after luncheon, while you were away. They were disappointed to miss you.'

Lady Eden snorted. 'Nonsense. They waited until they saw my carriage depart the gates before scurrying up from the parsonage.' She pursed her lips. 'What was the *true* purpose of Amelia's visit, Sidney?'

Sidney ground the toe of his Hessian boot, polished to a mirror finish by Cornelius's valet, into the scarlet and black Turkish carpet. His aunt had called to hint that she wished Clara could have the same sort of London Season *she'd* had in her youth. But, of course – Aunt Amelia had sighed – it wasn't possible on a vicar's income such as Sidney's Uncle Oliver earned.

'Sidney, answer my question.'

Sidney moistened his dry lips. 'Something about the London Season.'

'As I suspected. She wants you to insist I bring out that plain little Clara, who hasn't an ounce of beauty or of wit.'

'Oh, come, Mother,' Sidney said, defending one of his favourite cousins. 'That's hardly fair. Clara's pretty enough, and she's very sweet — and quite amusing when her mother lets her get a word in edgewise. She'd make you an excellent companion if you'd give her half a chance.'

Lady Eden glared. 'Well. I wasn't aware you had such a fondness for your cousin.'

Sidney's eyes trailed back to the blue-green water. 'There's rather a lot you don't know about me, Mother.'

It was the perfect opening, and he needed to tell his mother about his wife eventually, despite Kitty's protests.

He inhaled, readying himself.

His mother's voice cut into his intentions. '*That* would please Amelia no end.'

Sidney faced her. Lady Eden's eyes glinted, and her lips slashed across her hardened face. 'What would please my aunt?' His thoughts were still on Kitty.

'If Clara were to catch *you* in her claws.'

For a moment, Sidney didn't register her meaning. When he did, he chuckled. 'An impossibility, Mother.'

'Then why did you call off your engagement with Mrs Overton?'

'I didn't call it off.' Sidney leaned his back against the window. 'An engagement never existed. You have no authority to enter into matrimonial arrangements on my behalf.' The letter Sidney had written to Mrs Overton offered her his best wishes for her future health and happiness but explained that his heart had long been engaged elsewhere. He'd had no desire to hurt her. Her response had been equally honest: *'I don't hesitate to admit I'm disappointed, even more so now that you prove your integrity by not marrying for a fortune. So many men would – even if their hearts were otherwise engaged – that I have long since given up on wishing for anything more from a second marriage than to secure a truly respectable place in society for my beloved daughters. But I commend you for your honesty and wish you nothing but the best.'*

'Sidney,' his mother said, 'we *need* that money. You must go back to Eliza – she won't refuse you.'

Sidney gathered his breath again, readying himself to inform her of his marriage. 'Mother, I'd never marry a lady for her money. Every woman deserves a husband who loves and cherishes her. I cannot have such sentiments for Mrs Overton, because—'

Lady Eden smacked her palm against the upholstered armrest of her chair, curbing Sidney's speech. 'A marriage is a contract of business. Love plays no essential part in it. In fact, considering how you pine for that . . . that *woman*, your marriage will be much better off without any pretence of love. Best never to begin a charade if you don't intend to keep it up.'

The ticking of the pendulum resounded as Lady Eden's eyes flashed like gold daggers.

But something vulnerable lurked behind her icy front. Her heart was wounded, indeed.

Sidney sighed, his own heart aching for her. 'Father hurt you terribly, didn't he?'

Lady Eden started – an almost imperceptible recoil. 'No.' She lifted her chin. 'He couldn't.' A smirk played at the corners of her lips as her eyes fell to the ebony desk. 'I loa— . . . I-I *didn't love* him, so he had no power to affect me with his . . .'

She quietened and froze, except for the thumb of her right hand, which tapped against her gold wedding band.

'With his infidelity?' Sidney offered, hoping she'd address her pain. Had his father pretended to love her at one time? Had she surrendered a tender heart during their courtship, only to have it crushed by a man who flaunted his adultery?

Lady Eden folded her hands over her black silk lap and glared at the roaring fire. 'This is not a subject I shall discuss with you. You're just like him in that regard.'

Sidney longed to put a hand on his mother's shoulder, but he hadn't touched her in years, other than to assist her into a carriage or offer his arm to take her into dinner. He remembered too well how she'd rebuffed his few attempts at physical affection when he was a love-starved boy.

'I'm not at all like him, Mother,' he said, gently. 'And, for what it's worth, I'm sorry Father didn't cherish you as he should have. You deserved better.'

Lady Eden put her hand to her throat.

Sidney held his breath. Perhaps she would unburden herself.

But when she looked at him again, venom laced her eyes. 'For what it's *worth*? Your words are worth nothing. *You* are worth nothing. You won't even marry to help this family because of your *worthlessness* as a man, weeping for a whore and for a brother who never loved you.'

The words struck like a poisoned dart.

Dammit. Sidney knew better than to reveal his vulnerability. He'd learned to guard his heart as a child, but, caught up in sensing his mother's hidden sufferings, he'd offered her that tender organ, hoping she'd respond lovingly. But, of course, she hadn't. She never had before, so why would she now?

He waited until the waves of hurt receded enough to allow him to speak. 'Mother, did you *ever* love me?' he asked, his brow furrowed with his attempt to comprehend her animosity.

Lady Eden stiffened. 'I love you as a mother should love a child. I guide you with a firm hand to prevent your innate foolishness.'

Sidney walked to the hearth, pondering despite the ache in his chest. The fire crackled; the bottom of the logs glowed red as the yellow flames whipped, but the blazing heat reached only a semicircle around the hearth. It didn't penetrate the cold elsewhere.

Perhaps, if Ada-Marie's giggles and soft footfalls echoed in the long gallery outside the library, with Kitty's gentle voice crooning her replies, Paradisum

Park wouldn't feel like a mausoleum. *Kitty* loved Ada-Marie as a mother should love a child: she guided their daughter literally and figuratively, radiating love and warmth instead of vitriol and ice.

The tip of a log split and fell into the embers.

For eight-and-twenty years, Sidney had lived believing in his family's lie that he was inherently worthless. Now his mother's bitter words revealed the extent of her incapacity to accept love into her life.

Yet love was everything.

Love propelled Sidney to publish his books. Love drove him to offer his heart and hand to the woman he'd cherished secretly for years. Publishing his novels and marrying Kitty had made him sincerely happy and confident for the first time in his life. Those two actions were true to Sidney's nature, and his nature had worth.

Sidney would try once more to help his mother understand, and then she must either accept him or get out of the way of his happiness.

'A firm *guiding* hand,' Sidney repeated as he strolled away from the fire. He sat across from his mother, resting his elbows on the armrests and interlacing his fingers. 'Is that what you intended, slapping my face when I was five, merely because I asked for an embrace?'

Lady Eden's brows snapped together. 'I don't recall any such thing.'

It was a shadowy memory but burned into Sidney's mind. 'Nevertheless, it happened.'

She frowned. 'You misremember. There must have been more – some clumsiness or foolishness on your part.'

Sidney considered. 'Perhaps, yes. Certainly, I wasn't a perfect child. But I only recall being a small, distressed boy who felt my mother's arms would've made everything better. But you slapped me instead. It was as if the colour drained from my world.'

Lady Eden remained silent as she fidgeted with the strands of black beads draping her neck.

'I never asked again,' Sidney said as gently as possible. 'Not for an embrace, at any rate.'

Her eyes darted to his, and her hand dropped. 'If I was harsh, Sidney, it was because you were soft. Your father and I worried for you.'

Sidney raised his eyebrows. 'Worried? In what way, Mother? Did you worry I might have feelings? Emotions? That I might crave love?'

Lady Eden stared at her hands, resting like white ivory on her glistening black lap. 'We intended you to be an officer. A general who'd raise yourself to the peerage on your own account, as the Marquess of Wellesley has done – surpassing his own elder brother.' She looked up and met Sidney's gaze with narrowed eyes. 'In this way, you would've ennobled this family more. Can you perceive our disappointment at your lack of spirit?'

'I don't lack spirit, Mother.'

She looked him up and down. 'I see no evidence of it.'

'I defend what I believe in, but, more often than not, wars are fought for a cause I cannot champion: that of preserving power and wealth in the hands of an exclusive minority.'

'For the betterment of *all*.'

'I disagree wholly and completely.'

'A *writer*,' his mother hissed.

Sidney raised his eyebrows at her incongruous reply. 'Pardon?'

'A writer,' she repeated, spitting the words out as if they scalded her tongue. 'That's what you dared to tell your father when you were eighteen. "I want to be a writer, Mother and Father."' Lady Eden spoke in a high, mocking voice. 'What nonsense, I thought, but your father gave you a chance.'

'He didn't,' Sidney said.

'He *did*. He asked you to show him your writing.'

'Because he expected – oh, a military history tome, I believe. But I'd made it perfectly clear what I hoped to achieve with my writing: I wanted to bring joy to a hurting world. I wanted to provide a few moments of pleasure to readers who needed an escape from the troubles of life.'

'*Novels*,' his mother snapped. 'Worthless drivel.'

'There's much more than mere amusement to be gleaned from a novel, Mother. But, of course, Father didn't see it that way. He mocked me in front of Cornelius. I still recall his words: "I've never read a dafter load of rubbish".' Sidney leaned forward. 'I believed him. That's why I agreed to Father's compromise – the church, he said, since I was such a "weakling". For several years after, while I was at Cambridge, I wrote in secret, believing my stories and poems were foolish.' He took a deep breath and closed his eyes, evoking Kitty's sweet face, gazing up at him with loving devotion, as if he were her hero.

He'd be her hero.

Sidney released his breath and opened his eyes, locking his gaze with his mother's. 'But near the beginning of my curacy, I found someone whose heart overflows with love, and I knew innately I could trust her enough to show her my work. She helped me believe in myself again; she cleansed me of my family's poison.'

Lady Eden was stone-faced, other than her glinting eyes.

Sidney lifted his brows. 'Would you like to know who she is, this woman who saved me?'

'Not if it's a name unsuitable for a lady's ears,' his mother snapped.

Sidney's heart raced, but he steeled himself. 'Is Lady Eden a name unsuitable for a lady's ears?'

His mother's brow creased. 'You speak in riddles, Sidney. I've read none of your writing.'

'Well, as for reading my writing, you have the opportunity whenever you want it. Duffy and Ward published my first novel.' Sidney nodded towards a stack of three bound volumes on the corner of the ebony desk – a love story, released the week before and sent by Messrs Duffy and Ward along with a glowing letter expressing their pleasure in serving as the exclusive publishers of the works of Lord Eden. Tyrold said the novel was flying off the bookshop shelves, with gossip about Sidney and Kitty's known love affair and Sidney's sudden succession to the earldom fuelling its sales. It was the outcome

Sidney had dreamt of for years. It should've been a joyous occasion to share with his friends and with Kitty. Instead, it hardly felt real and certainly roused no joy while he was in this cold crypt of a house, with icy condemnation his primary companion. 'But,' Sidney said, staring intently at his mother, 'I do not speak of you. I meant Lady Eden, my wife.'

His mother's eyes flew open. For several ticks of the pendulum, their gazes locked again. When she spoke at last, her words lacerated the silence. 'You have no wife, Sidney.'

Sidney smiled. 'I have the best of wives. I was married in July, in Scotland, to the current Lady Eden, previously known as Miss Kitty Preece. I'm afraid you must add dowager to your title, Mother.'

His mother's expression filled with loathing. 'What foul lies you utter.'

Sidney tapped his fingers together. 'Not lies.'

She snarled like a vicious dog tearing at its lead. 'Take care of it. Annul this . . . this *atrocity* of a union. This *mockery* of a marriage. Divorce the slut.'

Sidney stiffened. 'Never speak of my wife like that. I love her devotedly, and I shall never desert her.'

'You care nothing for the honour and integrity of this family.'

'I care deeply about both honour and integrity. You and I have different ideas of what those two principles entail. And as for this family, you and Father taught me years ago what it was to "care nothing". You taught me so well, it's a wonder I survived with an intact heart.

292

If not for my friends and Kitty, I imagine it would've destroyed me.'

Lady Eden's face contorted. 'It would be better if it had,' she said through exposed, clenched teeth. 'Better you were dead than telling me this . . . this abomination means to fill my place.'

Sidney let the words flow over him, filling him with curious satisfaction. He'd married well, for Kitty would fill his mother's place with tenderness and sweetness. She was a true lady. 'If you don't like it, Mother, live elsewhere.'

Her eyes glittered. 'My son would turn me out of my own home?'

'Firstly, it is my house, and by extension my wife's house. Secondly, you may stay if you can be civil and respectful to Kitty.'

'It is a degradation for me to look at that woman,' she said, spitting out her words, 'much less address her.'

Sidney lifted his hands, palms out. 'Then you may not be around her, for I shan't expose her to your hate.'

Lady Eden's lips thinned. 'And where would you have me live, Sidney? Not the Dower House, I hope. You shan't exile me to a draughty cottage up the laneway from your *shameful* wife.'

A draughty cottage . . .

The words triggered Sidney. Paradisum Park was a vast, opulent, depressing mansion, an incessant drain on the estate's encumbered resources, with its army of staff and unceasing repairs. What did Tyrold once say? Something about not sinking money into silver and jewels but investing it so it could grow.

Maximise one's assets – that was it. A modern phrase, but one which suddenly made perfect sense. If leased to a wealthy tenant, Paradisum Park itself could become a *milch cow*, as Tyrold termed lucrative investments.

'No need to live in the Dower House, Mother.' As it happened, Sidney would much rather she not. The Dower House might not be a cottage in Devon, but it was still a cottage in the countryside, as Sidney had promised Kitty. 'You may have Eden House.'

The townhouse on Berkeley Square would serve his mother well. She was happiest in London, after all, and Sidney and Kitty could reside on Half Moon Street when Parliament was in session. Kitty could refurbish their rooms at Tyrold's to create a proper little home, and Sidney wouldn't care if others considered an earl and a countess living on one floor of a townhouse preposterous. As Tyrold had once advised, Sidney wouldn't give his pride more consequence than his common sense.

'Eden House?' his mother repeated. 'Am I never to see the countryside again?'

'You have friends, sisters and sisters-in-law,' Sidney said. 'Undoubtedly, you'll have ample invitations. Should you ever choose to accept my wife, and show her love, I suspect you'll find her willing to welcome you to our home, for she's the kindest soul that ever lived.'

'I would *never*.'

Sidney shrugged. 'In that case, enjoy Eden House. Maintaining the singular residence will help you live within your widow's settlements, which I shall insist on. If you will curtail your gambling and make do with one carriage rather than four, I think you'll find three thousand per annum more than sufficient. Perhaps I can give you a little extra if you're willing to bring Clara out in the spring.' Sidney smiled as he arose. 'Now, Mother, I have rather a lot of business to attend to.'

He sat down at *his* ebony desk, petted Marmalade, who miaowed as if emphasising Sidney's point, and took up his quill. After dipping it again in the inkstand, he traced over the smudged word *friend*. He knew exactly what he needed to write to Tyrold, for Sidney understood more about finances than he'd thought.

His mother's stiff black skirts rustled as she traversed the room. 'Since you exile me to London, I shall leave at once,' she hissed from the door. 'I cannot bear the sight of such a reprehensible son.'

Sidney didn't look up from his writing. 'Safe travels, Mother.'

She huffed, muttered, and departed.

After Sidney pressed his signet ring into the melted sealing wax on Tyrold's letter, he composed a list of all he must attend to in the upcoming days. Foremost among his tasks was ordering the draughts in the Dower House sealed. Kitty could redecorate later to her liking, but Sidney didn't intend to bring his beloved bride and his darling daughter to a chilly cottage.

Warmth would infuse their home.

20

On the fourth fine day after weeks of rain, Philippe insisted on Kitty venturing out.

'You are always in this room, *chaton*. It is not conducive to health.'

Kitty's shoulders slumped, but she replied blithely for Ada-Marie's sake, for Kitty played crossed-legged with her daughter on the white carpet of the ice-fortress bedroom. 'Damp weather such as we've had is also not conducive to health, Philippe.' She rested her hand on top of Ada-Marie's and marched a giraffe up Noah's ramp. 'That is why the animals go *into* the ark when it rains.'

'Ah, but it is not damp today.' Philippe threw open the window. Birdsong gusted in with the September morning breeze.

Ada-Marie lifted her head towards the freshness, a smile brightening her face. 'Please, may we go out, Mama?' she asked, employing the name she'd bestowed upon Kitty's return from Scotland. So that Ada-Marie wouldn't suffer too many disappointments at once, Kitty hadn't corrected her. But although Kitty had longed for years to hear Ada-Marie call her mama, her joy was stifled by the knowledge she must soon give her daughter up to Sidney and the future Lady Eden.

'Perhaps later, poppet.' Together, she and Ada-Marie dropped the giraffe into the hull of the ship, where a cow, a bull and a pair of dogs awaited. 'These animals need shelter first. Where's the giraffe's wife?'

If Kitty could re-engage Ada-Marie with the game, perhaps the child would forget about going outside. From Matilda's tales, gossip about Kitty and Sidney had increased rather than waned, and Kitty couldn't withstand stares and cutting remarks. Her emotions were more fragile than an eggshell.

Ada-Marie sighed and drew her fingers through the pile of wooden animals on the carpet. 'Here's the giraffe's wife,' she said listlessly, extending her hand with the long-necked wooden toy resting in her palm. 'You put her in.'

Kitty's heart twisted as she took the giraffe and dropped it in the ark. She couldn't keep Ada-Marie cooped up inside forever, no matter how devotedly she played with and read to her.

Ada-Marie stood. 'I'm tired of the ark for today.' She held her hands before her. 'Philippe, are you at the window? I hear a linnet. Is he eating the birdseed I put on the sill?'

Philippe led Ada-Marie to the window. As they murmured together, silhouetted in a rectangle of light, Kitty picked at a loose thread on her quilted silk dressing gown. She couldn't go out – not when she and Sidney were the subject of so much gossip. Any appearance would provide fuel at a time when discretion was essential. For now, Kitty must hide.

Throughout August, Sidney had written volumes of letters which spoke to his melancholy. He never mentioned divorce, but guilt, shame, and vague remorse about failed promises permeated every line. His evident misery articulated a regret Sidney likely didn't acknowledge.

But Sidney would acknowledge his regret eventually, which was why Kitty must save him from their debacle of a marriage. She had yet to determine how, other than maintaining their physical separation in the agonising hope that, with time and distance, Sidney would realise he must choose a suitable wife. Sadly, Kitty's plan to visit Mrs Overton failed because the widow had left town for the summer soon after Kitty and Sidney's return from Scotland.

Philippe snapped his fingers in front of Kitty's nose. '*Chaton*!'

Kitty startled out of her reverie. She hadn't noticed any movement, but Philippe and Ada-Marie stood hand-clasped beside her.

'We go out, *ma chérie*.' Philippe lifted Kitty's thick plait – the only way she'd worn her hair in weeks. 'And today, you dress up. You will feel better if you do.'

Kitty slumped more, her dressing gown sagging around her, and shot Philippe a silent plea.

But Philippe grinned. 'Today, Philippe has his way, for I wither without my art. Do you want Philippe to wither and die?' He pulled a face, crinkling his nose and bulging his blue eyes.

Despite herself, Kitty smiled.

'I wither too,' Ada-Marie said in a voice as quiet as the fall of a feather.

Kitty clutched her hand to her heart. 'Oh, Ada-Marie.' Awash with guilt, she gathered her daughter in her arms. 'My poor poppet, you and Philippe are correct. We shall go out this afternoon.'

As awful as it would be . . .

Philippe's eyes danced. 'Well done, *ma petite fleur*.' He rested his hand on Ada-Marie's fair head. 'Today, Philippe will dress you to match your *maman*. You will be two sunflowers – which is the flower most like the warmth of summer – and we shall eat a *pique-nique* in the Park. But first, we shall purchase *bonbons* at Mr Webb's *confiserie*.'

Ada-Marie's face shone like the sun. '*Allons-nous les manger pour le dessert*?' she asked, the words gliding off her tongue in her reedy voice as if she were a French child. Philippe had alleviated his boredom throughout August by teaching her several simple phrases.

Kitty appreciated his efforts. As the future adopted daughter of an earl, Ada-Marie must know French. Perhaps the child's flawless accent would impress Mrs Overton.

'*Oui*, we shall eat our bonbons for dessert,' Philippe agreed.

An hour later, Kitty stepped into the sun's glare dressed in a frothy yellow muslin gown. A brown velvet spencer warmed her arms and shoulders, and a jaunty gold capote bonnet topped her glossy ringlets.

Despite her cheery attire, darkness shrouded Kitty, but she drew her posture straight. Although it was better for Ada-Marie's future if the child wasn't seen in Kitty's presence, Kitty couldn't disappoint her.

And this might be Kitty's last picnic with her daughter. It was one final opportunity to make a memory which would sustain Kitty in the lonely years to come.

Ada-Marie's smile stretched wide when the sun splashed her face. She was a dainty primrose in a yellow velvet pelisse, clinging to straight-backed Nanny Ashcroft. Philippe had styled the child's hair into fine flaxen curls which peeked from under her bonnet's brim. A satin jonquil ribbon tied into a wide bow below one rosy cheek. Ada-Marie was the embodiments of loveliness, and it broke Kitty's heart to think she had so little time left with her daughter.

Philippe stood with a half-smile on his face, his sandy locks close-clipped and tidy under his tall-crowned black hat, and a picnic basket upon his arm. He placed his free hand on Kitty's shoulder. '*Mon Dieu*, this is a day such as one rarely enjoys in England.'

Although Kitty yearned to experience happiness as she once did, she just . . . couldn't. The warm sun oppressed her, yet the wind gusted too cold. Mount Street was busy; pedestrians stared as they passed the stoop, and each gawk penetrated Kitty's core, as if she had no defences left. A gentleman on horseback leered. An old lady in a sedan chair lifted an eyepiece. Three grey-gowned, white-aproned chambermaids clustered on the pavement looked at Kitty, clasped hands to their mouths in unison, and then bowed their bonneted heads together, as if sharing gossip.

Kitty put a hand to her throat. She couldn't do it. She opened her mouth to tell Philippe she needed to vanish back into the house and hide under the counterpane—

Philippe shook his head. '*Non, ma chérie.*' He spoke softly, as if he knew what she hadn't said. 'You do this for Ada-Marie, if not for yourself.' His grin broadened, and he spoke around Kitty to Ada-Marie. '*Où sont les bonbons*? We must follow our noses.'

Ada-Marie giggled, and they were off, although the sensation of exposure overwhelmed Kitty, like when she was fifteen and quivering naked before a multitude of aroused men.

Even before they arrived at Webb's Confectionery in Oxford Street, Ada-Marie skipped and swung from Kitty and Nanny Ashcroft's hands, declaring she could smell the sugar and sweet almond. The shop itself was a grand affair, fronted with huge bow windows displaying pastel confectionaries in towering pyramid mountains and agrarian scenes in candied miniature – moulded marzipan cows and sheep dispersed among chocolate cottages and spun-sugar meadows. A smiling man turned the crank upon a barrel organ outside the bright-blue double doors, filling the air with a tinny rendition of a cheery tune from *The Beggar's Opera*, and a frock-coated monkey tipped a droll hat to those entering and exiting the confectionery.

Porters in azure coats and snow-white breeches swung open the doors.

301

The clink of metal upon porcelain and the hum of conversation quietened as Kitty paused in the doorway, gathering her nerve. The shop burst with patrons seated at white-linen-topped tables, and every head seemed to turn in her direction. Ladies and gentlemen alike, eating ices with tiny silver spoons or lifting sugar-dusted confectionaries off delicate sky-coloured dishes, glanced up, then down, and murmured to their companions.

Kitty cringed, wishing she could shrivel and disappear. The Kitty Preece who would've marched into the shop with her bosom thrust forward blowing kisses to those who stared was another woman entirely. In her place was a broken shell, a mockery of a back-slumbred courtesan-countess with no place in the world.

'Why are there so many people in town in September?' she asked Philippe through her thickened throat, her voice as raspy as dry leaves. She'd hoped Mr Webb's shop would be relatively deserted.

Philippe narrowed his eyes. 'The constant rain, *je pense*. Perhaps these fine people do not wish to observe the discomfort of their tenants as the summer crops wither.'

Kitty's heart ached, remembering her cold, hungry childhood. What would the weather mean for the tenants on Sidney's estate? Would they require help and comfort? Would they worry about their children's health throughout the winter? As debt-burdened as the estate was, could Sidney afford the heavily taxed imported grain to supplement a poor harvest?

But such thoughts were the concerns of Sidney and his mother, who certainly wouldn't want Kitty's help.

The fate of the tenants was even more reason for Sidney to be free to recover his fortune through marriage. Kitty had nothing of tangible value to offer those who depended on the wellbeing of the estate. Love alone could not compete with money.

Right now, Kitty needed to purchase Ada-Marie's sweets and escape this shop. A sheltered picnic in Hyde Park to please Philippe and Ada-Marie was one thing, but Kitty couldn't tolerate much more display. Her tears hovered too near the surface, like water simmering before the boil.

A soft voice spoke in her ear. 'Miss Preece, welcome.' Mr Webb was a slight man in his early thirties, with light brown hair and kind hazel eyes. 'This must be your beautiful little girl.'

Kitty frowned. Was wealthy Mr Webb soliciting her good opinion to secure an *arrangement*?

The thought sickened her.

'Do you like marzipan?' Mr Webb asked Ada-Marie. 'I have some in the most delightful animal shapes which I think you would enjoy.'

Kitty tilted her head, confused. Mr Webb, who now took Ada-Marie by the hand, appeared genuinely interested in the child, although he'd never paid her any attention on previous visits. The shopgirls in pink and yellow gowns had attended to them before.

To Kitty's further astonishment, Mr Webb himself packaged up their marzipans and a rainbow selection of flavoured macarons which Philippe selected. But when Mr Webb waved his hand, refusing payment, Kitty's suspicions arose again.

Perhaps her distrust showed, for the confectioner blushed. 'Forgive me for taking a liberty, ma'am, but Lord Eden's novel . . .' Mr Webb hesitated, fiddling with the blue ribbon he'd tied around their box of confections. 'Miss Preece, I don't mind telling you the book was a balm for those of us with disappointed hopes. Reading how Charlotte and Mr Villeur found love despite the odds against them helped me believe what . . . what the lady I loved told me in June, before she married Lor— well, never mind.' He frowned. 'You see, she was already in love with *him* when I met her, so I hadn't a hope, but one day I shall find my own true love, like Mr Villeur in Lord Eden's book.'

Mr Webb's puzzling speech astonished Kitty so greatly she stumbled over her thanks for the treats. Whatever he was talking about, it was clear he had no interest in Kitty. It sounded as if the poor blighter loved another man's wife.

Kitty would be the same soon enough: hopelessly in love with another woman's husband.

As soon as Philippe placed the sweets in his basket, Kitty scooped up Ada-Marie and hurried out of the shop with eyes and murmurs following her. Again, tears threatened. She shouldn't have gone out. Once she survived the picnic, she'd return to Mount Street and never go out, ever again.

Ten minutes later, as Kitty spread a linen cloth near a Hyde Park willow tree fanning its filigree branches, a horseman approached from behind. His shadow fell

304

across Philippe, who knelt among the daisies and grass, uncorking a flask of pale-yellow lemonade.

Nanny Ashcroft, looking beyond Kitty's shoulder, bobbed a curtsy, her colour heightening, and dropped a loaf of crusty bread.

'Good day,' an icy voice drawled.

Kitty froze.

Gillingham.

She'd assumed him long since gone to the country. His presence was the last thing she needed today, but she'd get rid of him swiftly, somehow.

Kitty turned but didn't curtsy. 'Your Grace.'

The duke's hooded eyes trailed down her body, causing Kitty's skin to crawl. 'A picnic. How charming.'

Despite her depressed spirits, Kitty set her teeth. If he was angling for an invitation to join, he'd be disappointed.

Gillingham dismounted, swinging a booted leg over his massive black hunter. 'You, man,' he said to Philippe. 'Hold my horse while I walk with Miss Preece.'

Philippe pursed his lips. '*Monsieur le duc,*' he said haughtily as he poured lemonade into a tin cup for Ada-Marie. 'I am an *artiste*. I do not work in a stable. You must find someone else to 'old your big 'orse.'

Kitty nearly choked. Philippe had made *horse* sound decidedly like *arse*.

It would be hilarious but for the murderous glint which shot into Gillingham's eyes. Philippe could ill-afford to draw the duke's malice to himself, for there was a way well within English laws whereby a powerful enemy in possession of certain attainable information could send Philippe to the gallows.

Kitty needed to shift Gillingham's thoughts from her beloved dresser at once.

She smiled as warmly as possible. 'Your Grace, forgive me, but I'm enjoying a private picnic with my ward. I'm unable to walk with you, but if you call at Mount Street, *Matilda* and I would be most pleased to offer you tea.' She must be perfectly clear, so he wouldn't get an incorrect impression.

Gillingham's lips curled into a slow smile. He looked more wicked than Pantaloon in a harlequinade, but at least his sights weren't set on Philippe anymore. He leaned forward and whispered in her ear: 'Walk with me now. I shan't detain you long, *Lady Eden.*'

Kitty's hand flew to her mouth. How did he know?

Gillingham's evil grin deepened. 'It's best that we speak. We can remain here, in this grassy area. We needn't leave sight of your companions.'

Kitty acquiesced. 'I'll return soon, Ada-Marie,' she said, as calmly as she could muster. No doubt the duke had a nefarious purpose, but it was better to know her enemy's intentions than guess at them.

Philippe glowered suspiciously. Kitty shook her head at him, hoping he understood he mustn't involve himself.

She fell into step beside Gillingham, who led his horse by the reins with one hand and swung his riding crop with the other. 'Who told you?' she asked.

'No one told me. That frivolous bit of nonsense your husband published is practically an announcement of your marriage.'

Surprised, Kitty stopped walking. 'His novel *Salvation*? How so?' She hadn't read the published version, but she'd read many drafts.

The duke steadied his horse to a halt. The beast snorted, its velvety nostrils expanding with its exhalation. 'It is, of course, your love story,' he said, patting his hunter's ebony neck. 'The character of the noble-hearted seamstress Charlotte, with her blind daughter, is a thinly veiled Kitty Preece.'

Kitty fidgeted with the button at her throat. The surface similarities were more obvious now than when she had read Sidney's manuscript; she hadn't realised *then* how much she and Sidney loved each other.

Did this parallel explain Mr Webb's curious behaviour – and why he had engaged with Ada-Marie? Was the book the reason people stared and whispered? And if so, had everyone guessed Kitty was married to Sidney? Had Mrs Overton and Matilda read the novel? Would *Salvation* bring about the Preece sisters' ruination as surely as Kitty's marriage would?

Panic rose, compressing Kitty's breath. She needed a plan at once, but first she must rid herself of Gillingham. 'If you drew me from my friends to threaten exposure unless I shag you, you ruined your own scheme by telling me the novel announces my marriage, Your Grace.'

'That wasn't my purpose at all,' Gillingham said coolly. 'And you must call me "duke" now.'

Kitty furrowed her brow. 'I beg your pardon?'

Gillingham chuckled. 'Don't, Kitty.' Above the duke's tall black hat, a cluster of storm clouds swirled, inching their way into the blue sky. 'Don't beg my pardon, and don't call me your grace anymore. You are a countess now; you must learn our ways.'

Kitty's throat constricted. He was playing to her weakness, and it worked. If she tried for a hundred years, she'd never be a proper countess. It was a *rôle* too far removed for an urchin who had once rummaged in the muck under the shadow of the London Bridge. She wasn't a lady; she was a whore . . .

Kitty stiffened. *No.* She wasn't a whore. Not anymore. She'd be faithful to Sidney even after their inevitable divorce. She'd earn her living as a shopgirl or a chambermaid, but she'd never be a courtesan again.

Despite her distress, Kitty lifted her chin defiantly. 'Did you wish to speak to me to instruct me in aristocratic ways? My apologies if I'm not receptive. I'd prefer a different tutor.'

Gillingham smiled. 'Perhaps I requested the pleasure of your company simply because I enjoy gazing upon your lovely face.'

'Very well, you've gazed. Now I shall return to my friends.'

'No, stay. There *is* a reason I asked you to walk with me.' The duke's eyes flickered to Philippe. 'I want to ask you a question, and you'll answer unless you wish me to make enquiries about your impertinent manservant.'

Kitty stilled. It was a cruel world in which someone as vile at Gillingham wielded life-threatening power over a man as tender as Philippe. 'Why do you taunt me? Cannot you leave me and those I love alone?'

Gillingham lifted his brows. 'My girl, if you'd played by my rules, you would know that when I have what I want, I'm perfectly harmless. Pleasant, even, on occasion – and, certainly, I would've been exceedingly good to you. *But*' – his eyes glinted as he leaned forward – 'I despise being crossed. I play to win, my dear.'

Kitty rubbed her temples with her thumb and forefinger. She had so little strength left inside her. 'Please stop troubling me,' she said, rather feebly. 'I did you a good turn once. I refused your son's repeated offers of marriage for the sake of your family's honour. Can you not remember that now and let me be?'

Gillingham studied her with an impassive expression. 'Not yet. Answer my question first. Why did you succumb to an impoverished curate when you might've married *my son*?'

Kitty had expected a different enquiry. '*That's* your question?'

The duke bowed his head. 'You see I'm not a monster. I'm merely a bewildered father. Richard adored you. He would've treated you well. As my eldest son, he's many times your husband's consequence, and you would've been a duchess once I'm rotting in my tomb. Why give that up to turn around and marry Wakefield?'

'But the answer is obvious,' Kitty replied matter-of-factly. 'I didn't love Richard, and I love Sidney with all my heart.'

'Ah, but that is what I cannot work out. You didn't love Richard, but you respected his family honour. You *do* love Wakefield – I think even my foolish son suspected that – so why did you not respect his? Why subject a man you love to the same shame and ridicule which you spared a man who meant nothing to you?'

Kitty deflated as if Gillingham had struck her. The duke voiced her deepest pain. Her love for Sidney would be his ruin, rather than his salvation. The tears which had simmered all day boiled over at last. She covered her face and wept.

It was some time before she could speak. When she did, she gasped her words between sobs. 'All Sidney and I wanted was a quiet, simple life together in the country. No one would've shamed us for that – not for long, anyway. Cornelius was young, strong and healthy, so it didn't enter our imaginations that Sidney would succeed to the title.'

Gillingham extracted a handkerchief from his pocket. 'There, there,' he said, not unkindly, as Kitty wiped her face with the linen square. 'In that case, it's a damned shame how this has turned out.'

'A damned shame?' Kitty repeated, aghast. 'Is that what you call this *horror* I've lived for the past month and a half?' Rage bubbled through her sorrow; her face contorted, and she stomped her foot in the grass for emphasis. 'Damn you, Your Grace – this is all your fault. Cornelius was killed by the henchman *you* hired because you couldn't let me live my life.'

Gillingham put his hand over his heart. 'My dear girl, upon my honour, I had nothing to do with Cornelius Wakefield's death.'

'Your *honour*?' Kitty spat out the words. 'You haven't any honour.'

'Watch what you say.' The duke's voice was curt and clipped, and his fingers tightened around his horse's reins. 'If you're to live among our class, you must learn that a gentleman's honour is worth more than his life. I could call your husband out to answer for your words. I *should* call him out.'

Kitty crumpled, her spirit faltering yet again. Now her imprudence might get Sidney killed.

'I shan't call him out, this time,' Gillingham said, 'as you're obviously upset.'

'*Upset*? You f—' Kitty swallowed the insult. She inhaled, clutching the duke's handkerchief. Rouge and kohl had smudged the white linen, and, on top of everything else, her cry had induced hiccups, which did nothing for whatever shreds of dignity she might possess. 'Yes. I am, indeed, upset.' She rubbed her nose, smearing snot over the handkerchief's embroidered, strawberry-leaf-embossed G, and held her breath in spurts to ease her hiccups.

'My poor, beautiful girl,' the duke murmured some moments later, after the hiccups quietened. 'I think you regret this marriage.' He trailed his riding crop along Kitty's arm until she elbowed it off. 'You do realise you have the power to end it?'

Kitty raised her eyes. 'What power does a woman have to end a marriage?'

'In England, almost none,' Gillingham said, his voice as smooth as silk. 'But Scotland is another matter entirely.'

Kitty frowned. 'What do you mean?'

Gillingham's horse snorted, and the duke stroked the animal's neck. 'I assume your marriage was one of those preposterous affairs at a blacksmith's? Tell me, did a sham clergyman bind your hands and scrawl your names in a register? I'll wager he even wrote up a certificate, and presented it to you without so much as a mention of God or the law?'

Kitty eyed him warily. 'So what if he did? Scottish marriages are legally binding in England.'

'They are, indeed. It's how Richard hoped to marry you as well, so I investigated at the time. You would've been incontestably his legal wife in England – unless *you* wished to end it.' Gillingham half-smiled as he patted his horse. 'It's quite clever when you think about it, to put such power in the hands of the wife. After all, a woman must be hard-pressed indeed to end a consummated marriage.' He lifted his shoulders. 'Or exceptionally noble, as in your case.'

Another hiccup escaped. 'How do I end it?'

'Burn your marriage lines in the forge at the smithy where you married. The blacksmith will strike the record from his register, and your marriage will cease.'

Kitty narrowed her eyes, distrustful of Gillingham. 'How could it be that easy?'

'*Easy*?' The duke appeared astonished. 'It's not easy at all. The *bride* must willingly burn the marriage lines. If I'd dragged you back to Scotland after a marriage to Richard, you wouldn't have thrown your proof of union into a fire – and the brawny smithies would've no doubt come to your rescue if I'd attempted to force you.' He rubbed his chin as he stared into the distance. 'Although I heard bribes work on occasion.'

Kitty twisted the handkerchief as she pondered. It seemed too simple to be true, but the ceremony in Scotland had struck her as a humbug. Could the way to end it be similarly ridiculous?

If so, it was a convenient solution – and exactly what she'd hoped for. A quiet, scandal-free divorce would preserve her sisters' reputations and might enable Kitty to maintain a mistress–keeper relationship with Sidney, which would be a glimmer of joy in an otherwise bleak future.

She should ask someone else, but who? *Not* that beast Tyrold . . .

The duke intruded on her thoughts. 'I can help you. I can take you to Scotland.'

A bark of laughter escaped from Kitty; a hiccup chased it. 'Now we come to your true purpose. No, thank you, Your Grace. Nothing in the world would induce me to get into a carriage with you.'

'I will behave honourably. Take your manservant, if you don't trust me.'

Kitty shook her head, still scoffing. 'You aren't a self-less man. Eventually, you'd want something in return. You'd want *me* in return, and I won't be your mistress.'

Gillingham's eyes trailed Kitty's lips, neck and bosom before he again met her gaze. 'I shan't insult your intelligence by pretending I don't want you – one day, when you're willing to receive me – but desire isn't the only reason I offer to help. You're correct that my motives aren't selfless, but they aren't what you're thinking. The moment your marriage ends, I instantly receive something without touching your glorious body.'

'Indeed?' Kitty cocked an eyebrow. 'What do you receive?'

The duke angled closer, his sickly-sweet cologne permeating the air, which had dampened from the encroaching cloud cover. 'I receive that which is more important to me than anything else.' He breathed against Kitty's cheek. 'I receive preservation of rank. After all, what is all this,' he said, waving his hand down his body, 'compared with commoners, if the nobility doesn't preserve a sense of separation and mystique? Why, my peers and I might be no better off than our French counterparts twenty years ago. That is why it simply doesn't *do* for a courtesan to become a countess. The illusion of rank is too precarious.'

Kitty drew back. Illusion. She'd heard this same argument before, but from quite a different perspective . . .

Almost as if he perceived her thoughts, the duke continued: 'You know something about precarious illusions as well, Kitty. You and your sisters specialise in them. How otherwise are grubby-footed mudlarkers worshipped by men of rank and consequence?'

Kitty pressed the handkerchief to her lips. It *was* Matilda's argument. How uncanny to hear it from the duke, as if everything revolved around illusions of rank, of place, of worth . . .

'Well, my dear?' The duke tapped Kitty's chin with the tip of his riding crop. 'Do you want my help in extracting your husband from this misalliance? Shall we travel to Scotland together and save your beloved Sidney?'

Kitty smacked the crop away with the back of her hand. 'If I go, I shall travel alone.'

The duke's bottom lip jutted, much like a sullen child. 'You *might* think of me more fondly since I've freely given you helpful information.'

'It will take more than that for me to think fondly of you,' Kitty said, but her voice lacked spirit. She possessed the key to ending her marriage, but there was no joy in her success.

All the same, it must be this way.

She offered the duke his crumpled and stained handkerchief.

He didn't take it. Instead, he clutched her hand ardently. 'Don't dismiss me, you bewitching woman. Name your terms instead. I shall give you anything you ask.'

Kitty tugged her hand until he released it. 'We are at cross-purposes, Your Grace. The only thing I want from you is for you to leave me alone.'

His eyes flashed. 'This is the appreciation I receive for my help?'

'I'm not in the least certain it *is* help. Perhaps what you said is true, but—'

'You suggest I've lied to you?' There was a dangerous edge to the duke's tone.

Kitty capitulated, remembering his earlier threat to challenge Sidney. 'I suggest nothing.' There was no point in further discussion. As soon as her picnic finished, she'd somehow confirm the duke's story. 'Here's your handkerchief.'

Again, the duke didn't take it. His glittering eyes pierced Kitty as he studied her. 'Keep it,' he said at last. 'Despite your disagreeableness, my offer still stands to take you to Scotland. You may find you have reason to reconsider.'

With that chilling remark, Gillingham mounted his horse. He put a finger to the brim of his hat and trotted to the south, towards Rotten Row.

A brisk wind gusted. Overhead, the clouds churned, and Kitty shivered.

Philippe's voice called out, urging her back to the picnic. Kitty faced her friends, but her feet dragged through the grass as she returned, for her heart lay heavy in her chest.

21

By the time they returned to Mount Street two hours later, the steel-grey clouds covered the sun, and the wind was decidedly cold. Kitty peeled her gloves off numb fingers in the chilly entrance hall. Although it was only mid-afternoon, a servant had already lit the beeswax tapers in the sconces, and the flickering golden flames created honeyed halos on the carmine wallpaper. Two chambermaids arranged yellow chrysanthemums and scarlet dahlias in gilded vases – a reminder that it was a Thursday, the day Matilda opened the house to gentlemen and courtesans for a night of entertainment, dancing, cards and drink.

Kitty unfastened her brown spencer, quickly pushing its brass buttons through their velvety slits, desperate to dash upstairs and crawl under her counterpane with Ada-Marie, a storybook and a cup of rich chocolate whipped with steaming milk. While they snuggled, Kitty would determine who she could trust to confirm the duke's story.

Matilda emerged from the gold receiving room to Kitty's left. The outside cold was nothing compared to her frosty face.

'I must speak with you, Kitty,' she said, her lips thin. 'At once.'

Kitty's stomach knotted. Somehow, her sister knew.

She pressed a hand into her abdomen, as if she could dispel the sickening dread, and knelt before Ada-Marie. 'Go upstairs with Nanny Ashcroft and Philippe, poppet. I shall be with you soon.'

The girl flung her arms wide, enveloping Kitty in an autumn-fresh embrace, and planted a sweet-almond kiss on Kitty's cheek. 'I loved our picnic, Ma—' She hesitated, likely remembering Matilda's presence. '*Kitty*.'

Kitty's throat ached too much to permit a reply.

After Ada-Marie had climbed carefully up the stairs between Nanny Ashcroft and Philippe, Kitty wrapped her arms around her chest, hugging herself. Without her velvet spencer, her skin prickled with cold.

She faced her seething sister. 'Matilda, I can explain.'

Matilda jerked her head, indicating the room behind her. 'In *here*. Someone called specifically to hear what you have to say for yourself.'

Bewildered and nauseous, Kitty entered the receiving room. A blazing fire crackled in the gilded hearth, but its warmth didn't penetrate the icy glare of Lady Eden, who stood before it as black-swathed and veiled as one of Macbeth's witches, with one elegant hand resting on the mantel.

Kitty recoiled. She didn't possess enough strength for the countess's interrogation. She was too fragile after her afternoon out and her encounter with Gillingham.

She backed towards the door, but Matilda shut it, sandwiching Kitty between the ice-witch countess's glare and Matilda's frosty glower.

Lady Eden pointed a thin, black-gloved finger at a chair before her. 'Sit.'

Kitty limped forth and perched on the edge of the seat. The fire blazed too hot; the air scalded her right cheek. Her tears simmered again, but she could appease Lady Eden and Matilda swiftly by reassuring them she intended to dissolve her marriage with a trip to Scotland. 'I believe I know why you are here, my lady—'

'Naturally, you know why I am here,' the countess hissed. 'What other than the most horrendous of circumstances would compel *me* to enter a house like this and speak to someone like *you*?' Kitty flinched under the barrage. 'You took advantage of my son's noble heart and trapped him into an abomination of a marriage.'

Kitty curled in on herself, as if the countess had kicked her. 'Please let me explain.'

'Hold your tongue, girl.' Lady Eden lowered her voice, but the quieter words struck like daggers. 'Sidney weeps every day. He weeps because he made a terrible mistake which destroys the honour and integrity of our family *and* which spells his financial ruin.'

Ah, so Sidney realised Kitty was his ruin.

Devastated, Kitty pressed her hands together, pleading for forgiveness. 'Lady Eden, I'm so terribly sorry—'

'It's too late for that, isn't it? You've destroyed him.'

How many more wounding words could Kitty take before she crumpled to the floor, crying? She looked beseechingly at Matilda, who stood near the countess, wishing the sister who'd been a mother to her since she was eight would offer her solace.

But Matilda grimaced as if disgusted. 'After all I've done for you, Kitty, how could you betray me? You, who have always been my most faithful sister – the person I imagined would be by my side for the rest of my life, no matter what. Only *you* know the true price I paid.' Matilda faltered, put her hand to her forehead, and coughed.

Sorrow engulfed Kitty. Oh, how could she make Matilda understand? 'Matilda, I never meant to betray you, and I never would've left you without still shouldering my share of the financial commitment. Even after our marriage, Sidney intended to continue paying you for me. He and I were willing to sacrifice our own comfort to support you—'

The countess inhaled sharply. 'Indeed? And tell me, *Kitty*' – she spat out Kitty's name as if it tasted foul – 'why should my son sacrifice his comfort to support your sister?'

Kitty floundered, uncertain how to reply. Why indeed should Sidney do that? What had been the rationale? Something about Ada-Marie . . . something about Kitty's nieces . . . something about love . . .

'He l-loves me?' she said weakly, more as a question than a statement. The words rang hollow.

Lady Eden fumed. 'And so you repaid Sidney for his love by trapping him into marriage *and* by demanding he support your sisters when he can hardly support himself?'

'But it wasn't like that.' Kitty struggled to recall details, for it seemed as if those events had transpired in another life. 'Our love is sincere and mutual. We thought we'd manage in a way which wouldn't hurt anyone.'

'Selfish girl. You're lying.' The countess's face was pale with rage. 'You married Sidney because you wanted to rise above your station. To gloat at your sisters.'

'I swear that's not the case.' Kitty jumped up from her chair and knelt before Matilda. 'Matilda, I'd never hurt you.' She clasped her sister around the knees, burying her face in rose-scented silk skirts. 'You know I speak the truth.'

Matilda pushed her away; Kitty's bottom fell against the carpeted floor. 'Don't touch me, Kitty. You've wounded my heart. Do you not see what your impulsive actions will do to the reputation of this house, known for twenty years as a haven for gentlemen? What man will come here once word spreads that the Preece sisters are only out to trap their noble clients into marriage?'

Hunched upon the floor, Kitty wept into Gillingham's handkerchief. 'I'm so sorry, Matilda. Forgive me, Lady Eden. I realise I've injured you both, whatever my intentions were otherwise. Thus, I deserve everything you say to me, but I can *truly* make this right. I intend to travel to Scotland to dissolve the marriage at once.'

'You seek to mollify and deceive me with false promises,' the countess said bitterly. 'If you intended to dissolve the marriage, you might've done so any time these last six weeks.'

Kitty arose, pointing to the monogram on the duke's crumpled and stained handkerchief. 'No, because I learned only this very afternoon that it was within my power to do so. The Duke of Gillingham informed me. You see his grace's handkerchief here – we just spoke in the park. He offered to take me to Scotland himself, should I wish it, although I'd rather find my own way.'

Lady Eden's eyes darted from the monogram to Kitty. 'You truly didn't know you could dissolve the union?'

Kitty shook her head. 'I swear to you, I thought only Sidney had the power to end the marriage – and I thought he'd never do it unless I could make him think of his duty to his family before his duty to me. For six weeks, I've refused to allow him to announce our marriage, and I've dismissed his pleas to come to Hertfordshire.' It had hurt Kitty's heart every time. 'I thought with time and distance, he'd realise he must think of his family before me.'

The countess's expression lost its hostile edge.

Kitty's hopes lifted. 'Lady Eden, I never had malicious intentions. When I married Sidney, it was with the understanding that we'd live a retired life, buried in the country. We never, ever imagined how things would turn out.' Kitty glanced at her sister. 'Do *you* believe me, Matilda?'

Matilda nodded but remained silent as she turned her head towards the fire.

Kitty faced the countess. 'I shall make everything right, and if I' – she knitted her fingers together over the wrecked linen square she held – 'and if I still retain a bit of influence over Sidney, I shall encourage him to marry Mrs Overton, as you wished.'

The countess tapped her nails upon the mantel. 'I've perhaps wronged you, Kitty. You made a foul and reprehensible mistake, a terrible error of judgement, but I believe you do indeed now want the best for my son.' Her eyes fell again to Gillingham's handkerchief. 'The duke must like you. It's surprising he can spare days to take you to Scotland, with all the demands on his time.'

Kitty swallowed. 'We have no arrangement if that is what your ladyship implies. He wishes to help me in order to preserve the illu— to preserve the correct order of rank in society. He said it doesn't do for a courtesan to become a countess.'

Lady Eden's lips thinned into a tight smile. 'And very right he is, isn't he? If Gillingham deigned to offer his aid, you should accept.'

Kitty shook her head. 'No, my lady. I shall go with my sister instead. I–If you will travel with me, Matilda?'

Matilda stared at the crackling flames, her diamond earrings sparkling among her dark ringlets. When she looked up, her eyes blazed with a fire of their own.

'Naturally, I shall accompany you, Kitty. We'll depart at dawn, after tonight's entertainment. You must go upstairs and pack a valise.'

The hint of a smile twitched upon Lady Eden's lips. 'Very well. Soon this unpleasant business will be behind us.'

★

As Kitty trudged up the stairs after her interview with the countess, clinging white-knuckled to the rail for support, she struggled to drag one foot before the other. The longcase clock upon the landing whirled as she passed, readying itself to strike the hour. Each of the four chimes hit Kitty's ears like bullets.

She intended to crawl under her counterpane to rest with Ada-Marie for the remaining hours of the afternoon, but when she entered her bedchamber, she discovered only Philippe. He crouched before the white marble hearth, prodding at the red coals with an iron poker.

'Where's Ada-Marie?' Kitty's voice fell flat.

Philippe dusted his hands as he stood. 'She and Nanny Ashcroft went to the nursery for a short time so Philippe may care for his *chaton*. *C'est terrible*, this afternoon, and Philippe is to blame.'

Kitty's shoulders slumped. 'It doesn't matter. Nothing matters anymore.'

Philippe clutched at his chest. '*Ma chérie*.'

Kitty shuffled across the room and plopped on the edge of her mattress. 'I couldn't have hidden forever, Philippe,' she said, as she slid open the drawer of the bedside table and nudged aside her mama's shawl. Kitty's marriage lines rested underneath, exactly where she'd hidden them weeks earlier.

Philippe studied her with a frown. 'What do you look for?'

Kitty closed the drawer. 'Never mind.' She lay down and rested her cheek upon a silk pillow. 'I must entertain tonight.' That was Matilda's demand: a glorious return of courtesan Kitty Preece which would dispel any possible rumours about Kitty's marriage. 'And I cannot imagine how I shall survive.' Like a thick blanket, Kitty's emotions weighed her down, pulling her into her mattress, making her swollen eyelids heavy.

Philippe glided across the room and placed a warm hand upon Kitty's brow. 'Rest is what you need now.'

'But only for a bit, Philippe.' Kitty dabbed her runny nose with the duke's handkerchief and managed to squeeze a few more words through her aching throat. 'I must pack a valise . . .' Her voice trailed as the blissful oblivion of sleep began to dull her pain. She could escape into it for a few hours . . . a few hours before she must face her nightmare.

Philippe tucked the blanket under Kitty's chin. 'Rest now, *chaton*. Rest. Philippe will take care of everything.'

22

After overseeing the second day of repairs to the Dower House, Sidney sloshed through whipping rain down the stone-paved laneway to Paradisum, his greatcoat buttoned to his neck and his hat pulled low on his forehead. The storm had begun only a quarter of an hour earlier, but the still-saturated ground didn't absorb the new rainfall despite the last four days of fine weather.

As he walked, Sidney kicked at the puddles like a joyful child. The Dower House was in reasonable repair, with a sound roof and dry walls. Window and door replacements would remedy the draughts in the two-storey gabled brick building, and Sidney had reserved money in his new budget to purchase drapes, upholstery and wallpaper according to Kitty's preference. Before Tyrold located tenants for the estate house, Sidney would order the pianoforte from Paradisum's summer sitting room be moved into the light-filled Dower House parlour, which overlooked the mediaeval stone church and Uncle Oliver's parsonage. Ada-Marie should have an excellent instrument, but otherwise no part of Paradisum would infect the Dower House, which Kitty and Ada-Marie's presence would turn into a home.

Sidney quickened his pace, for once eager to return to the mahogany-panelled bedchamber he still considered his father and brother's room. He'd dress in dry clothes, eat in his room rather than at the cold dining table, and write to Kitty, because, at last, Sidney was confident of his success. He'd found a way to balance the responsibilities of an earldom with a quiet life.

That very morning, he'd received Tyrold's response to his letter from Monday. John had suggested a few tweaks to Sidney's plan, but, overall, the businessman approved. '*How gratifying to know you aren't an addle-pated numbskull, after all,*' Tyrold had concluded.

Galloping hooves pounding the laneway behind Sidney drew him from his thoughts, and he turned to face the very friend who'd occupied his musings. A rain-drenched Tyrold thundered towards him on his broad-chested stallion.

Tyrold reined the heavy-breathing beast to a halt. Water streamed over the brim of his hat, falling in front of flashing green eyes. 'Goddammit, Sidney. This marriage of yours will be the death of me yet.'

'Why?' Sidney asked, alarmed. 'What's the matter with Kitty?'

Tyrold swung his leg over his saddle and dismounted, landing in a puddle with a splash. His boots, trousers and greatcoat were caked with mud. '*She's* fine, for now, at least,' he said, over the noise of the rain, 'but *I've* had the devil of an afternoon. Kitty's manservant – the French *habilleur* you spoke of, I presume – paid me a visit around half past four. He's under the impression that your wife intends to abscond in the company of the Duke of Gillingham.'

Sidney recoiled. 'That's impossible. Kitty despises Gillingham.'

Tyrold raised the hand not holding his horse's reins. 'I know little else. The manservant formed his opinion based on observations and conjecture.' He reached into his sodden greatcoat pocket and withdrew a crumpled and rouge-stained handkerchief bearing a strawberry-leaf-encircled G. 'But he brought this for proof, lest I didn't believe him. It's the duke's handkerchief, which the manservant extracted from Kitty's hand after she wept herself to sleep this afternoon. He believes they intend to depart in the morning, if not sooner, but where or why, he could not say.'

Sidney's heart hammered as the rain splattered the handkerchief in Tyrold's hand. 'Then there isn't a moment to lose. I must call for my carriage at once.'

'Stop, Sidney.' Tyrold's eyes pleaded. 'My dear, dear friend, do not hasten to her side when her every action indicates she doesn't want this marriage.'

'She *does* want this marriage, John.'

Tyrold shook his head. 'I cannot believe it. She deserted you when you needed her the most. For six weeks, she has refused your entreaties for comfort and for aid, and now she abandons you for another man. Such aren't the actions of a woman who wishes to be a wife, Sid. I believe she intends to humiliate you into seeking a divorce, and I say let her go. You deserve better.'

Sidney's legs weakened as the truth of Tyrold's words glared.

Kitty had longed for a quiet life with Sidney, but initially, she hadn't wished to be his wife. He'd cajoled her into marriage with promises he couldn't keep, and now she looked for escape. She'd sought out Gillingham's assistance because the only legal grounds for divorce in Britain were a wife's abandonment or her adultery, and the duke was no doubt willing to assist Kitty with either action.

The rain battered Sidney as his head bowed and his shoulders hunched. Kitty thought he'd failed her. She'd assumed he wouldn't manage to balance his responsibilities to the earldom with their mutual desire for a quiet life. A better man never would've left Kitty in London. No doubt Sidney had disgusted her when he crumpled to the lavatory floor rather than standing up to his mother. How could strong, beautiful Kitty – who'd survived poverty and despair – admire a weak and weeping man? He should've fought for Kitty by announcing their marriage at once and demanding that his mother – and others – give her the respect she deserved. Kitty had fled because she thought she wasn't worthy, when she was the most precious thing in Sidney's life. Rather than let her go, Sidney should've demonstrated the strength of his love by holding her more securely and lovingly than ever . . .

He should have . . . *and* he still could.

Sidney's tense muscles eased as realisation dawned.

There was a time, not so long ago, when Tyrold's news would've destroyed Sidney. For nearly his entire life, he'd capitulated to feelings of inadequacy when faced with challenges. When his father had told him his writing was rubbish, he'd accepted it as fact. When his vicar had insisted Sidney's sole task at St George's was fundraising, Sidney had cast aside his dreams of pious purpose for daily tea with wealthy ladies who bade him to pray for their lapdogs' indigestion. When Kitty had suggested Sidney publish his novels, he'd dismissed her advice for six years, until the duke had threatened her safety and her happiness.

Sidney straightened his shoulders and met his friend's gaze with a bold confidence. 'I'm going to London to collect my beloved wife, and you'll not stand in my way. In fact, I expect you to speak of Lady Eden with the utmost respect in the future, John.'

Tyrold's black brows drew together. Lightning flashed and thunder crashed as the rain pounded them.

And then John's lips twitched into a smile. 'Damn, Sid. You've grown up.'

Sidney's chest swelled. Yes, he had – because of Kitty. His love for her had made him a man who fought for himself and for those he loved.

He wouldn't let his wife go unless she truly wanted him to, no matter what she'd done.

Twenty miles spanned the distance from Paradisum Park to Mount Street, most of it along the well-maintained Great North Road. Upon a good horse on a fine day, the journey lasted ninety minutes.

It was nearly three hours later – past ten at night – when the Earl of Eden's crested carriage drew up to the house on Mount Street. Sheets of rain sliced the gas lamps' glow as Sidney emerged, gripping his leather valise and sheltering under an umbrella. Hunch-shouldered men with tight-wrapped greatcoats dashed down the pavement, presumably rushing towards shelter, and hackney cabs sloshed along the waterlogged street.

'Return Mr Tyrold to Half Moon Street and stable the carriage and horses there,' Sidney yelled to his coachmen over the thrum of the beating rain. 'Mr Tyrold's servants will give you lodging, so don't go to Eden House. I shall remain here for tonight.'

Sidney had determined during the long journey that unless Kitty herself turned him away, he wouldn't leave.

Even if he found her with Gillingham – although he doubted he would.

The heavy handle of his umbrella pressed its weight into his shoulder as Sidney faced the Preece sisters' house.

Two of the greatcoat-clad pedestrians, their voices boisterous with drink, scurried up the stairs before him. Without knocking, they swung open the cherry-red front door. Light and music spilled from the entrance onto the front stoop.

Until that moment, Sidney hadn't remembered it was a Thursday, the evening the Preece sisters hosted their weekly entertainment. The house would be full to bursting, and Sidney didn't want an audience.

He hesitated, raindrops thrumming on the waxed canvas dome above his head. When a passing carriage sprayed a wall of water, he hopped onto the first step to dodge it.

With his boots firmly planted on the stoop, Sidney bolstered himself. Whatever arrangement Kitty had made with the duke, she'd likely done so because of the current of insecurity which ran through her, causing her to tolerate maltreatment from men and to reject Sidney when he praised her as a lady. But Kitty was Sidney's wife. He loved her, he needed her, and he was proud to be her husband. It was time for everyone to treat her with the respect she deserved.

Maybe an audience was *exactly* what Sidney needed.

Sidney ran up the steps, flung open the door, and stepped into the carmine hall.

From behind the closed door to the gold receiving room, a pianoforte played and the bustle of conversation hummed. In the entrance, the two gentlemen revellers who'd come in previously struggled with their wet greatcoats as Mr Dodwell waited. Although Sidney couldn't recall the gentlemen's names, their faces were familiar, and they apparently knew of him. One muttered something under his breath to the other; they both leered drunkenly.

They were ideal for Sidney's purpose. No doubt they'd spread ripe gossip quickly once they figured out how to unbutton their coats.

Sidney placed his valise on the floor, rolled up his dripping umbrella, and peeled off his rain-damp greatcoat. The Preece sisters expected formal attire at their evenings; fortunately, Sidney's black mourning suit of tight pantaloons and a fitted tailcoat – into which he'd rapidly changed as his coachman readied the carriage at

Paradisum – would detract from the potential affront of his gleaming Hessian boots. 'I'd like my bag taken to Lady Eden's room,' he said as he handed his valise to Mr Dodwell.

The butler's eyebrows shot to his hairline. The two gentlemen halted their greatcoat efforts, their mouths ajar.

Sidney blinked. 'Well, did you hear me, man?'

Mr Dodwell scrunched his forehead. 'D'ye mean Miss Kitty's room, m'lord?'

Sidney extracted a half-guinea from his waistcoat pocket for the poor fellow, for Sidney was using him rather abominably in order to put on a memorable show for the witnesses. Of course, the butler didn't yet realise Kitty was Sidney's wife. 'Refer to Lady Eden properly, man,' he scolded as he pressed the coin into Mr Dodwell's palm. 'Shall I find her ladyship in the drawing room?'

The butler's eyes widened at the coin. He slid it into his pocket and scratched his cheek, plainly confused. 'I want to assist your lordship, but I swear Lady Eden isn't here.' He brightened. 'But she *did* call this afternoon, m'lord.'

Sidney's mind swirled for a moment before awareness dawned like puzzle pieces fitting together. Of course. His mother was involved.

'You mean my mother, the *dowager* Lady Eden, who naturally called here to wait upon her daughter-in-law. I refer, however, to my lawfully married wife, whom it appears you still *incorrectly* know as Miss Kitty Preece.'

Mr Dodwell's jaw dropped.

The two gentlemen beside the butler choked.

'You *cannot* be serious,' one of the gentlemen said.

With his teeth clenched, Sidney advanced on his adversary. The closer he loomed, the more the man withdrew, but Sidney didn't stop until he'd backed him against the carmine wallpaper. 'I'm deadly serious.' The man's gaze faltered. 'I'll hear an apology for your impertinence against my wife *now*.'

The man tugged at his cravat. 'Forgive me, Lord Eden.'

'This time only,' Sidney said, dangerously. He backed off but glared at the other gentleman until that man's gaze fell as well.

That should do the trick. The news of Sidney and Kitty's marriage would spread throughout Mayfair within hours, punctuated with luridly exaggerated tales of Sidney's viciousness in protecting Kitty's honour. Hopefully, rumours of the dowager paying homage to the new Lady Eden by visiting the Preece sisters' home would enliven the *on-dit* as well.

It would serve Sidney's mother right.

Sidney almost chuckled as he smoothed his silk waistcoat, adjusted the cuffs of his black coat, and passed into the gold receiving room, on a mission to find Kitty.

A blast of steam greeted him. The room was dark; a roaring fire blazing at the gilded hearth and a few candles provided the only light. The close-pressed bodies of gentlemen in evening wear and ballgown-clad cyprians undulated in the shadows. Many courtesans frequented these evenings with their keepers, for there were few elegant events where gentlemen and their mistresses could frolic in company. Perhaps the heat suffocated by design, for some men had shed their coats and loosened their collars. Everyone imbibed heavily of the drinks footmen carried on silver platters, and the men tipped the servants freely.

Sidney was certain Matilda profited on these evenings. Gentlemen were caressed and pampered; drink lubricated their pockets, gold flowed generously, and play ran deep at the card tables. On the few occasions Sidney had attended in the past, usually with Holbrook or Lord Edward, he'd returned to Half Moon Street several precious guineas poorer, although he never gambled.

A young woman warbled love songs at the pianoforte. A single beeswax taper cast its glow on her face against the darkness as if an artist had painted her delicate features in chiaroscuro, and a drunken gentleman leaned over the instrument, ogling her mostly exposed bosom.

Sidney chafed. No doubt this was the employment Matilda had intended for Ada-Marie one day, as Kitty had confessed in Langholm. He dropped two gold coins in the girl's cup as he passed her.

Sidney didn't examine the shadows of the receiving room because Kitty wouldn't be in here. The Preece sisters held court in the grand drawing room. He accepted a flute of chilled champagne as he entered that dark-blue chamber, which was as vast as a ballroom. A string quintet played a buoyant waltz. A three-tiered crystal chandelier hung from the centre of the frescoed ceiling and sparkled with the light of many candles, illuminating two dozen couples swirling on the parquet floor but casting shadow on the embracing guests lining the walls, sharing armchairs, wine, kisses, and more.

Sidney sipped his drink, condensation on the crystal moistening his lips as the cold champagne fizzed in his mouth. Amy, Jenny and Barbara whirled on men's arms, their silk gowns glistening, but Kitty wasn't instantly visible. She typically commanded the room's admiration while devotees swarmed around her like flies to honey.

Tonight, a breathtakingly resplendent Matilda, attired in a gauzy gown of crimson silk, played that role.

Sidney raised his eyebrows, surprised by Matilda's beauty. Three red roses nestled in the centre of her low-cut bodice, and a single strand of pearls looped her neck. Her full lips were as red as cherries, but otherwise her face was refreshingly devoid of obvious cosmetics, making her skin shine like ivory. Her dark hair cascaded in thick waves down her back, rather than her customary bunched ringlets. Half a dozen drooling men encircled her, and she basked in the attention like a queen.

Undoubtedly, Matilda would know where Kitty was. As Sidney advanced towards her, around the edge of the room, heads turned in his direction. Either the two gentlemen in the hall had spread the word quickly, or other gossip fuelled the stares. Between Cornelius's violent death and the recently published novel, there was already much scope for *on-dit* regarding the new Lord Eden.

When Sidney had proceeded halfway along the crowded perimeter, an empathetic ejaculation – '*Good God, it's Wakefield!*' – caught his attention.

Sidney recognised the voice. It caused his pulse to pound at his temples.

He faced the despised old villain, whose customarily hooded eyes bulged in an empurpled face. 'Duke.'

Gillingham stood slack-jawed for a moment. Then he gulped rather heavily of his brandy and seemed to force a laugh. 'I thought you were in the country, Eden,' he said carelessly, as if that explained his odd reaction. 'Having abandoned your tasty wife.'

With difficulty, Sidney repressed a mental image of the duke flailing and grunting on top of Kitty. If Kitty intended to take Gillingham as a lover, she'd decided to do so for reasons she considered important, which she and Sidney must address together, as man and wife.

'Where is Lady Eden?' Sidney asked, as calmly as he could manage.

Gillingham's lips twitched. 'Am *I* your wife's keeper?'

Clearly, he'd intended the double entendre.

Sidney's good intentions vanished. He clenched his fingers around the stem of his glass. 'If you've touched her – or even if you only intended to – I'll cut off your shrivelled old bollocks. High time the world was rid of them.'

The duke's colour rose once more. 'You should be grateful if I expose her for what she is,' Gillingham said, spittle punctuating his words. Without his customary unctuous urbanity, the duke became a ridiculous old man, his face reddened with drink, his body oozing pomposity along with the putrid-sweet scent of his perfume. 'By God, boy, think the better of this marriage of yours. Kitty isn't worth losing the respect of your fellow peers.'

The duke's words instantly washed away Sidney's anger. Why on earth would Sidney care more for the fickle respect of a bunch of self-important, bullying aristocrats – such as Sidney's father and brother had also been – than for the love of the sweetest woman in the world?

Sidney tossed back the rest of his drink. 'Bah – you spout nonsense, old man. Kitty is worth a thousand of you.' He shot a carefully aimed poisoned arrow. 'Perhaps if you'd valued your own admirable lady's love while you still possessed it, you wouldn't be such an embittered, ridiculous arse now.'

Anger flared in Gillingham's eyes like paper on a fire. 'You're . . . you're a . . . a *fool* to make an enemy of me.' But the duke's voice floundered. Sidney had weakened his confidence, as he suspected he would.

Gillingham was the fool. Why was Sidney wasting precious time in inane conversation when he needed and wanted his wife?

But the music stopped before he could continue his search.

Clasped couples slid aside as Matilda glided to the middle of the room, her red-gloved arms spread wide. 'Good evening, my lovelies,' she purred. 'Would you like to see this evening's special entertainment?'

Cheers and clapping resounded.

Matilda slid a red finger along her pearl necklace and batted her long lashes. 'I'm afraid my performers find the room warm tonight. If the gentlemen have no objection, they'd prefer to remove their costumes as they dance.'

Applause thundered.

Matilda fluttered a lace fan. 'In that case, let the entertainment begin.'

Sidney needed to act before the performers emerged and threw the room into lust-fuelled chaos. He elbowed past the bodies which separated him from Matilda. 'A moment,' he said, loudly enough that his voice echoed.

Matilda's lips parted.

'Pardon the interruption,' Sidney said, addressing the company. 'I wish to locate my wife.'

Laughter erupted like a clap of thunder.

But Matilda wasn't amused. Her eyes fluttered over Sidney's shoulder, likely towards Gillingham, and her face hardened.

Sidney's eyes narrowed along with hers.

The laughter diminished to a few nervous titters.

Matilda painted a tight smile across her face. 'Good evening, Lord Eden.' She lifted her chin, and her smile broadened as her eyes slid over her audience. 'My lovelies, let us assist his lordship. Did anyone find a *wife* here tonight?'

Merriment erupted with more enthusiasm this time. The audience perhaps thought this was part of the entertainment, and Matilda evidently intended not to let Sidney speak again, for she waved her fan at the musicians.

If the performers came out, Sidney would lose everyone's attention. This was his moment to make a statement.

As the lead violinist drew his bow across his strings, Sidney dashed his champagne flute across the parquet floor. The crystal shattered, a collective gasp resounded, and the violin stopped.

He spoke severely to Matilda's back. 'Miss Preece, where may I find your sister Kitty, who is my lawful wife, and thus, the Countess of Eden?'

Matilda whipped around, a red flame, and the noise in the room became like the hiss of snakes writhing in every corner.

A sea of faces surrounded Sidney. Gentlemen he'd known for years – his father's acquaintances, his brother's friends, fellow students at Eton and Cambridge, parishioners at St George's – stared back at him, and he met their hostile, shocked, or amused expressions with a dare.

One by one, gazes faltered, and faces turned to stone.

A soft voice called, 'Sidney.'

Sidney's heart leapt. Kitty, his wife, his countess, stood framed in the doorway. She wore a dark green dressing gown – a simple thing, made of quilted silk and buttoned to her throat – and her long hair trailed over her shoulder in a thick plait bound with a green velvet ribbon. Her sweet face was rosy and soft.

She hadn't been at the party.

At that moment, Sidney knew with absolute certainty that whatever Kitty had planned with the duke, she didn't intend to commit adultery – not that he'd ever *truly* doubted Kitty's constancy. She didn't have an unfaithful bone in her body.

'Kitty.' It was as if only the two of them stood in the room, gazing at each other in front of the crowds. Sidney held out his arms, and, after only the briefest pause, she ran into them. He kissed her before everyone, long and deep, tilting her back as his embrace supported her.

When they stopped for air, she whispered against his lips. 'What have you done, Sid? Now everyone will know.'

Sidney nestled his nose next to her ear, breathing in her soapy freshness. His heart swelled in his chest, and his cock followed suit, unable to resist the curves of her body. 'I *want* everyone to know I have the most wonderful wife in the world.'

Around them, a servant cleaned the broken glass as the violins began the first vigorous notes of *'Eine Kleine Nachtmusik'* and a dozen young performers emerged wearing diaphanous, short-shirted gowns.

Kitty put her hand to his cheek. 'Sidney, we must end our marriage so that—'

Sidney kissed her words away. 'Answer me something,' he said, pulling back from her lips with reluctance. 'Do you love me?'

Her body softened. 'With my whole heart.'

Sidney tucked a loose strand of hair behind her ear. 'Then remain my wife, please.'

'How will we manage?' she asked, breathless.

'That we must discuss upstairs and in private.' And Sidney swung Kitty up into his arms.

She sighed against his chest.

The whispering crowds parted as he walked towards the door.

'I want to be your wife, Sidney,' Kitty said when they'd left the drawing room. 'But I don't know how to be a countess.'

Sidney shouldered open the door to the entrance hall. 'It took me a bit to discover how to be an earl, but you're made of sterner stuff than I am. You'll grasp countessing in no time.'

'Oh, Sidney,' Kitty said with a sweet giggle.

Sidney's grin deepened as heaved her more securely into his arms and mounted the stairs. 'My love, if you do in fact want to be my wife, what compelled you to arrange to run off with Gillingham?'

Kitty's eyes widened. 'Not with Gillingham. I intended to leave with *Matilda*, as I told your mother.'

'Ah, I knew my mother was involved. First lesson in being my countess: don't listen to my mother.'

'*First* lesson? Are there more?'

'Yes. Second lesson: my countess only takes orders from her earl.'

Kitty's eyebrows raised. 'You're very forceful tonight.'

'Forceful? I haven't even begun being forceful.'

Kitty's eyes brightened. 'Oh, Sidney, you're exciting me.' She clung tighter to him, pressing herself against his chest and nipping his ear, her tongue gliding into its folds.

Sidney crested the stairs and moved towards Kitty's room, his cock a throbbing rod in his trousers, bursting to possess her.

'Not my bedroom,' Kitty said. 'Ada–Marie is asleep in there.'

'Where then, wife? For I need to make love to you *now*.'

'Let me down,' Kitty demanded, her voice husky, 'and I shall show you.'

23

At the back of the attics was a gabled storage room where, as a child, Kitty had sought refuge when she'd first moved to Mount Street. The massive house had overwhelmed her, as did the endless hours of tutor-taught lessons designed to turn her and her sisters into faux young ladies – or, rather, into courtesans.

In the back attic, little Kitty would wrap her mother's blue shawl around her shoulders and clutch her knotted rag doll as she peered over the edge of a skylight. From that vantage point, London was a hazy rooftop-sea with pointed steeples rising above chimney smoke like the masts of dozens of ships. St Paul's dome was the vessel of a majestic queen.

The sight grounded Kitty. Their former Southwark lodgings – which, despite everything, she associated with her mama's love – had possessed a similar view of steeples and St Paul's from its grime-darkened window. Nothing else in her new life bore any resemblance to the years when Mama and Papa had lived, but when Kitty peered through the Mayfair skylight, she knew she was still *herself*, Kitty Preece, a London girl who'd fought to survive from her first infant breath, inhaling the city's stench and yet determining to cling to life with an iron grip, despite all the odds against impoverished children in one of the world's wealthiest cities.

That back-attic room was where she led Sidney now. It would be cold, but their love would warm it, and she needed it for the first time in years. Perhaps there she could ground herself again and discover if the indomitable Kitty Preece still existed underneath this new name and unwanted title, or if Kitty Wakefield, terrified Courtesan-Countess of Eden, had at last met her match. Defeated, in the end, by the fortress walls protecting illusions designed to keep wealth and power in the hands of a precious few.

Kitty's mind raced as she pulled Sidney by the hand, his strong fingers wrapped around hers. They hurried through the warren-like corridors of the top floor where the servants slept. The scandal was out. Whatever happened now, thank God there'd be no more hiding. The secrecy had depressed Kitty's spirits to near-desperation.

Then again, *the scandal was out*. The well-being of many people depended on how she and Sidney navigated the challenging road ahead. How would the gossip affect Kitty's sisters? Without Mrs Overton's money, would Sidney, like Papa, go to debtors' prison – or whatever equivalent happened to lords who couldn't pay their bills? Could his tenants survive after a bleak harvest without additional funds? Would Ada-Marie suffer as the adopted daughter of the notorious Lord and Lady Eden? Could their daughter grow into a respectable lady in the eyes of the *ton*, as Kitty had hoped, or would the scandal taint Ada-Marie's life, with men treating her with as much vulgarity as they treated Kitty?

The path forward seemed too twisted to traverse.

But Kitty wouldn't think any more about those things *right now*. Sidney was so close, his body heat offset the corridor's chill and sandalwood infused the air. After weeks of loneliness and despair, Kitty needed him. For a few hours, she'd put everything else aside so Sidney could cradle her in his secure arms.

They arrived at the entrance to the attics. Kitty rotated the knob of the plain wooden door. 'Through here.'

A narrow staircase rose before them. Sidney closed the door, plunging them into darkness.

And then he covered her – his mouth nuzzling her throat, his arm about her waist, his hand gripping her bottom – and drew her against his powerful erection. 'Here? Shall I take you on these stairs?'

Kitty was on fire, desiring the intense emotional and physical connection she and Sidney created when they made love.

'We could, but someone might overhear us, and I want to be entirely private with you.' Kitty found Sidney's lips and allowed his tongue to slide into her mouth. He teased her with its tip, only hinting at its capabilities. 'I had something else in mind,' she said when they broke for air. 'One more flight.'

Kitty led him up the narrow stairs with her hand on the wall to guide her, but Sidney took no such caution.

He embraced her from behind, kissing her neck and unfastening her dressing-gown buttons as they tumbled upstairs together. 'You cannot comprehend my agony,' he breathed against her ear.

She could comprehend it perfectly, as a matter of fact, especially as he grasped her breasts through her nightdress and teased her nipples.

Kitty swung open the door to the storage room. The rain battered the skylights, and wind whistled against the roof tiles, but some of Mayfair's street-lamp glow permeated the space despite the weather. Chests lined the sloping walls, with hatboxes sprinkled on top and tarnished mirrors leaning against them. A jumble of old furniture formed a rickety sculpture in the centre. The air was faintly musty, with hints of the rosemary, pepper and lavender scattered about to deter mice.

Sidney released Kitty. 'In *here*?'

Kitty's cheeks warmed. 'It's oddly special to me,' she said, shyly. She walked to the skylight, hoping for her view despite the weather, but the weaving lines of rain obscured everything. Perhaps she'd feel grounded again once the rain cleared.

Sidney slipped his arms around her from behind, and she melted into the comforting shelter of his embrace. 'Then it's special to me,' he said.

'I loved to come here when I was young,' Kitty explained as Sidney pulled aside her plait and kissed the nape of her neck. She leaned further back into his embrace, with her eyes rolling up behind her closed lids because his lips soothed and excited her simultaneously.

'I was frightened of the grandness of the rest of the house. This room reminded me of the lodgings we lived in with our mama.'

Sidney paused his kisses. 'It appears our grand surroundings frightened both of us when we were children. Perhaps that is why we long for a cottage now.'

'I suppose Paradisum is even grander than Mount Street?' Kitty asked, her voice wavering.

Sidney resumed kissing her neck. 'Oh, yes. It's dreadfully grand,' he said between caresses. 'It's also as cold as death and as black as the grave, for the whole thing is done up in the darkest wood, with drapery and upholstery the colour of fresh blood. It's a frightful pile of bricks, more like the ninth circle of hell than paradise. But it's exceedingly *grand*.'

Kitty's stomach sank. How could she ever be happy in such a place?

Sidney slipped her dressing gown off her shoulders, and it pooled on the floor at her feet. 'Thank God we'll have our cottage.'

Kitty started. 'What?' she asked, whipping around in Sidney's arms.

Without responding, Sidney kissed her bosom at the neckline of her nightdress.

Kitty wriggled, trying to get him to focus. '*Sidney*.'

He held fast with one arm and untied her nightdress ribbon with the other. 'Mmm?' he asked, cupping her breast and trailing kisses towards her nipple.

'What do you mean, we'll have our cottage?' Kitty attempted to ignore the fire building up inside her.

'Mustn't you manage your estate? Shouldn't you live in London during the Parliamentary Season?'

He looked up from his task, a playful grin on his beautiful mouth. 'My love, I *truly* don't wish to talk business or politics at this precise moment.'

Kitty tugged at his lapels. 'Stop teasing, Sid, and tell me what you mean.'

He groaned dramatically as he released her, but his eyes danced. 'I go to all the trouble to procure you a cottage, and yet I'm punished.' He settled himself on a tangled mound of old velvet and damask drapery under the other skylight and patted the space beside him. 'At least let me hold you while we talk, Kit?'

Kitty burrowed into the thick pile of fabric beside Sidney and laid her cheek on the fine broadcloth of his shoulder. He wrapped an arm securely around her.

When he spoke next, his voice was solemn. 'Kit, all teasing aside, I want you to understand you're everything to me. Not just my wife, but my inspiration and my strength. My whole world.'

Kitty nestled deeper into his embrace, her heart soaring.

'I shall uphold my duties to my family,' Sidney continued, 'but I shall do so in *my* way – putting you and Ada-Marie first. Even if my fortune were intact, I wouldn't subject you to Paradisum Park's gloom. You and I need our little cottage, as we planned, both for our sanity and to solve the problem of the debts. Thus, I've decided the Dower House will be our home.'

'The Dower House?' Kitty asked, confused. 'Isn't that meant to be your mother's home?'

'Yes, but she doesn't want it. Kit, it's perfect for us. It's a sweet two-storey brick house set within its own lovely garden. We shall still live on the estate, which means managing the lands and ensuring the tenants' well-being will be convenient. And I intend to write my novels, although likely I won't manage three a year now. The first one is selling better than I ever expected – enough to make a tidy sum – and Duffy and Ward will publish the next before Christmas. We can set aside part of my writing income to help your sisters and part for Ada-Marie.'

Kitty played with the folds of Sidney's cravat. 'I intend to sell my jewels for Ada-Marie.' She hadn't wanted Ada-Marie to go into the widow's care without money of her own. 'They're worth a fortune, and they mean nothing to me – apart from the pink sapphire set, I suppose, since you said you like it.'

There was a pause.

Sidney's chest trembled. Kitty raised her head, surprised. Was he crying?

But he wasn't. He was laughing silently, his left hand covering his eyes.

'What, Sid?'

'Nothing, my love, other than you never cease to amaze me. Yes, let's sell that rubbish from other men and invest the money for Ada-Marie and for our children to come. But definitely keep the pink sapphires so I can always remember my amazing wife is a hundred times cleverer and more sensible than I.'

Kitty settled back on his chest. 'You're very odd.' But she said it with a smile, for his praise warmed her heart. 'And I don't understand how living in the Dower House solves the problem of the debts.'

'Ah, yes. I can explain.' Sidney threaded his fingers in Kitty's hair. 'Living in the Dower House means we can lease Paradisum Park's house and parkland. There are many shockingly wealthy tradesmen who desire long-term leases on stately homes – and the grander, the better. Tyrold knows scores of them; he's constantly arranging such things. My mother and uncles won't like it, but I'm the head of the family now, and it's a sound business decision.'

Again, Kitty lifted her head and met his gaze. 'You won't be in debt anymore?'

He cupped her chin and ran his thumb over her bottom lip. 'It's not quite that simple. It will still take many years to pay off the debts – likely even more than I hope, for I doubt my mother will ever live within her widow's settlement. I shall never be a rich man, Kit.' He frowned, as if pondering. 'Well, I suppose rich is a relative term. What I mean is, you and I must always be careful to live well within our means, but with time and economy and John's help, I'm confident I can eventually restore the fortune in its entirety. The next Earl of Eden will inherit an unencumbered, profitable estate.'

'But surely you want the next earl to be your son?' Kitty asked, her voice cracking.

Sidney smiled tenderly. 'He may yet be. We don't know.'

Kitty's heart ached. 'If I could bear a child, Sid, I would've had one by now.'

Sidney touched her nose with his index finger. 'What did I tell you before on this matter?'

'That blood doesn't make a family.'

He entwined his fingers with hers. 'Look at us, Kit. We're a family now, although love binds us rather than blood. You and Ada-Marie – and our future adopted children – are all I need. Besides, the title is in no danger of not having an heir. I have six paternal uncles and all but one of them have sons. They'll be thrilled if I don't' – his voice changed, laughingly mocking – '"*produce a legitimate male heir of my own body*".'

Kitty rested against his chest, turning over his words as he played with her fingers. Could it be as Sidney said? Would their little cottage shelter them from vitriol and hate? If they still lived a relatively retired life as Lord and Lady Eden, would people eventually forget the scandal?

She turned her attention back to Sidney, intending to ask about his Parliamentary duties, but his furrowed expression stilled her tongue. 'What is it, Sid?'

He held up her hand. 'Why is this ring on your right hand?'

'Matilda made me put it there.' As she said the words, a tiny flicker of anger sparked within Kitty. Why did Matilda always determine how everything should be? But then Kitty recalled her sister's sacrifice, and she silently scolded herself for her disloyalty.

Sidney scowled. He twisted the ring off her finger and returned it to her left hand. 'Kit, with this ring you became my wife. God joined us together, and no man – or woman, even if it be mother or sister – will tear us apart. Do you understand?'

Enamoured with his conviction, Kitty's blood heated. Ever since the evening at Vauxhall, she'd found confident Sidney arousing. The length to which he'd go to defend their love, even after she'd told him she wasn't worth it, reminded her of one of her two purposes for coming to the attic room.

She needed his body.

'Good heavens, Sidney,' she said, breathing the words into his ear. 'Is this some of the forcefulness you promised earlier?'

His eyes gleamed as he clamped an arm around her waist and drew her against him. 'Is that what you want?'

'Oh, *yes*, darling,' she moaned, wilfully helpless in his strong, masculine embrace.

He grinned wickedly. 'Excellent. It's time for your husband to demonstrate his authority.'

'His *authority*?' Kitty sank into the drapery as Sidney's hard body pressed on top of her. She slid apart her legs to accommodate him. 'Does my husband have authority over me?' She scooped her hips, rubbing her swollen vulva against the erection in his trousers.

Yes.' He kissed her breasts over her gown. Her nipples stood erect, poking at the thin cloth. 'You must obey me.'

'The blacksmith in Gretna Green didn't say so.'

'I say so.' He looked up, and his eyes twinkled like starlight in the dimness. 'But never fear, for I shall hold myself to obeying you. As well as' – he gently cupped her breast – 'another vow which I said in the post-chaise: that as long as I live, with my body I shall worship thee. And *that*, Kitty Wakefield, is what I intend to do now.'

'Oh? And what am I supposed to do while you're worshipping, since I must obey you?'

He grinned. 'Lie back and let me.' He sat up, untying his cravat, and unravelling the linen strip. 'In fact, I shall ensure you don't move, for I'm not at all certain you'll obey.'

Kitty wiggled on the draperies, pretending to slink away from him.

Sidney grabbed her arm and pulled her upright, kneeling beside him. 'You are being intolerably naughty, wife,' he said, gazing heavy-lidded into her eyes.

Kitty leaned her head back, offering her neck to his kisses. 'Will you punish me?'

'A thousand times over,' he growled into her skin. 'Take off your nightdress while I undress.'

To tease him, Kitty inched the fabric up as Sidney removed his coat and unbuttoned his waistcoat. The hem had only reached her upper thighs when Sidney tossed aside his waistcoat, crossed his arms, and pulled his shirt over his head. His hard chest gleamed in the pale light.

'You're intentionally too slow – an *exceedingly* ill-behaved wife.' He tugged her gown up, sliding it above her face and tossing it aside. Kitty shivered in anticipation, her nipples hard in the cold attic. 'There. You're almost ready, my love.'

Kitty slipped two fingers between her legs. 'I'm *very* ready.'

He snatched her hand away. 'You are doing *my* job, and I won't have that.'

Kitty gasped as he clasped her wrists together and bound them with his cravat. 'Oh, Sid.' Her body throbbed for him. 'What are you going to do to me?'

'Everything.' He pushed her down on the drapery with her bound hands above her head. 'And you are going to let me service you.' He untied her velvet hair ribbon and loosened her plait. 'I like *these* gorgeous locks spread out like a fan, and these gorgeous legs' – he spread her in a vee – 'before me like an altar.'

Kitty purred, luxuriating in Sidney's caresses. The rain had slowed its beat on the skylight above them; it was a gentle thrumming now.

Sidney removed his boots and tossed them aside. 'If you move, I shall be forced to restrain you further.' He peeled off his trousers. 'So don't move.'

When lovers had bound Kitty before, she'd always experienced quivers of fear. This was different. She trusted Sidney wholly, so that there was nothing but excited anticipation when she lay vulnerable before him. He rubbed her body with his warm palms, from her neck, over her breasts, down past her abdomen, and along her thighs. She lay back, basking in her husband's ministrations.

Sidney's kisses glided over her tingling skin. Kitty was cold from the crisp air in the attic, but she was hot with fevered desire. Arousal intensified her senses

— the trickling raindrops resounded, the bunching folds of the thick drapery rubbed, Sidney's skimming fingers titillated, his lips thrilled as he worked his way from her hand to her shoulder.

His kisses fluttered along her collarbone.

His hand grasped her breast, pushing it up, kneading it.

His tongue skimmed her nipple.

Kitty whimpered.

Sidney looked up, a devilish grin on his face. Kitty lifted her pelvis, silently begging him to put an end to her exquisite misery, but he pushed her hips down with a splayed hand. 'Don't move unless I tell you to.' He administered to her breasts, giving soft kisses which sent electric thrills from her chest to her clitoris.

When his tongue encircled her nipple, rounding the hard peak, a moan ripped from her throat. She called out his name when he encased her, suckling her. Pleasure radiated throughout her body, but Kitty ached between her legs. If her hands were unbound, she would've stroked herself for some relief.

Kitty panted and squirmed. Sidney moved to her other breast, enhancing her need. A fire burned inside her, ravaging unchecked.

'I can't,' Kitty said, pleadingly. 'Sidney, I can't.'

'Can't what?' he murmured, moving down her abdomen with his kisses. The golden waves of his hair brushed her sensitive skin like a feather, teasing, tantalising.

'I can't wait any longer.' She lifted her hips. 'Please, Sidney.'

A smug smile decorated his gorgeous face. He leaned down, parted her folds with his fingers, and rounded the nub at the centre of her pleasure with his tongue.

Ah – there was the soothing balm Kitty needed.

His tongue flicked, and he sucked.

Not a soothing balm at all – it was more fuel for the fire.

Kitty cried out, for the shooting pleasure was simultaneously more than she could bear and yet not enough.

Sidney responded to her cry; he deepened his kiss, he inserted a finger into her, and the inside strokes and the flicks of Sidney's tongue worked in unison to send her closer and closer to the crest.

The summit soared high above her, and Sidney would carry her to it. There would soon be no holding back, even if she wanted to savour the moment, even if she wanted to prolong this paradise. Her tension tightened; her body couldn't stand it. She was writhing, moaning, helpless.

She was secure. She was loved.

Then she crested the peak. The pain of yearning vanished, wiped away like a sand formation by the tide, and in its place was only the ecstasy of release. Waves of rapture, coursing her body.

Kitty drove her fingernails into her palms and threw up her hips, trembling from head to foot from the force of her orgasm. 'Oh *God*, Sidney,' Kitty called out as pleasure split her, each pulsation a fresh peak of delight, until she shattered against the drapery. 'I love you so bloody much.' She panted the words, her body spent.

Sidney looked up, her legs framing his head. 'Don't relax too much. I'm not done with you, Lady Eden.'

Kitty wavered, for the name rendered her suddenly nauseous.

It must've shown in her expression, for Sidney rose, kneeling and rubbing her calves with his palms. 'That's your name now, my love. Neither of us wanted to be the Earl and Countess of Eden, but we are, and together we shall make the best of it.'

Kitty tried to believe his words, but her chest tightened. 'I don't think I can, Sidney.'

His palms moved up her legs. 'I didn't think I could either, at first. That's why I stayed away so long, although I wanted you every second of every day and night. In the end, it was the thought of you and of Ada-Marie that gave me the strength to see the path forward.'

The pressure in Kitty's chest didn't ease. Sidney couldn't understand there was all the difference in the world between a second son of an earl coming unexpectedly into the title and an urchin-turned-courtesan becoming a countess.

Then Sidney's fingers stroked her cunt. He was priming her for more, and he was succeeding, for sparks ignited. 'Please believe me, Kit.' His thumb rubbed her clitoris. 'Because Sidney the earl needs his muse every bit as much as Sidney the writer needs her.'

Kitty relaxed into the draperies with a sigh, physical pleasure easing her tension. After all, she'd allowed herself a few hours of hedonism, hadn't she? And that delicious orgasm was well worth a repeat . . .

As Sidney's tongue slipped into her – softer now, gentler than before, as if he were nursing budding flames – Kitty's lids fluttered. The rain had stopped. Perhaps the sky was clearing, for stars flickered between the sparkling raindrops on the skylight.

Kitty closed her eyes to focus on bliss. Sidney nudged her up the mountain again – higher, higher, close to the summit. Perhaps cresting it would be gentler this time, for the pleasure built in softer layers.

But Sidney's tongue deserted Kitty in her time of need.

She opened her eyes. He knelt between her legs, his hand manipulating his rock-hard cock.

'I want you on your knees,' he said, none too gently, as he pulled her up and flipped her over.

It wasn't a position Kitty had ever loved. It gave a man maximum enjoyment and a woman little, but Sidney had pleasured her and it was his turn now. She knelt on her elbows and knees. Her long hair fell about her like a curtain. She braced herself for a thrust.

It didn't come.

Instead, Sidney kneaded her tight shoulders. Kitty sighed, her muscles loosening.

He moved to the touch-starved skin of her back.

Kitty rested her forehead against her bound wrists. 'Oh, that feels so good.'

Sidney stroked her bottom. 'My God, my wife is luscious,' he groaned, sliding a hand over and under her hips, across her lower abdomen, and between her legs. His fingertips teased her clitoris.

Only then did he slip into her. Not fast and hard like other men had, but long and slow.

Kitty gasped, for his cock caressed her deep inside – unhurried, rhythmic strokes of a paddle into the currents of a river, urging Kitty forward as Sidney's fingers stimulated her nub, and his other hand braced her hip.

The depth of their connection was immense. He was so fully immersed, his bollocks pressed against her clitoris along with his fingers, spurring her to toe-curling heights. They were riding the currents together, and those currents were more intense with each stroke. Her body was no longer a gently flowing river; they rode like the tide crashing in, cresting as it had on the Thames at the London Bridge, when she'd scrambled up the slippery steps with Barbara to avoid being swept away.

Except the tide she rode with Sidney wasn't like that at all because this tide was safe, and even as Sidney tipped her into oblivion, and pleasure eradicated her reasoning and the all-encompassing waves swept her away and she pulsed her orgasm on his hard cock and called out his name, she knew once she'd ridden the crests, Sidney would catch her as she fell.

And catch her he did, after he joined her in orgasm.

He scooped her against his chest and laid her down on the drapery. The arms of the most wonderful man in all the world protected her.

The arms of her husband.

'My countess,' Sidney breathed.

Kitty shivered.

'Cold?' Sidney asked.

She was, although that hadn't caused the shiver.

She held up her wrists. 'Unbind me?' The rain had cleared; she needed to check the view and let it ground her.

He unknotted the cravat. 'You took that lesson on your husband's authority very well indeed.' He grinned as he unwrapped the linen and kissed her wrists. 'I look forward to when you tutor me about obeying my wife. I should be ready for instruction soon.'

Kitty smiled, despite her fluttering stomach. 'You might not be able to handle it, Sid.'

'Teach me until I master obedience – but let me rest first.' He leaned back on the drapery with an arm folded behind his head and closed his eyes.

Kitty kissed his forehead. 'You're an old man already.'

'Your old man, though,' he muttered.

She smiled and crawled over to her dressing gown with Sidney's semen moistening her upper thighs and her vulva still faintly pulsing its satisfaction. As she wrapped the quilted silk around her nude body, she rose and peered over the skylight edge.

She held her breath as she gazed beyond the raindrops.

The moon had set, and ribbons of stars streaked the black sky. Haze filtered up from the glow of lamps below, as if a layer of cloud still rested upon the street.

Beyond Mayfair's foggy brightness and the solitary domed tower of St George's Hanover Square, however, there was only darkness.

No steeples, no St Paul's.

Only a black void.

361

A tightness formed in Kitty's throat. She backed away from the window, her breath ragged, and crawled to Sidney's side. Only by burying her face into the hot skin of his shoulder and holding on to him could she dispel the horrid feeling that she was afloat in a black sea, with no sense of direction and no way to save herself from drowning.

24

Hours later, as the sky lightened to dark grey above the attic skylight, Kitty lay enveloped in her dressing gown with her head resting on Sidney's bare shoulder. She played with the spattering of light hair between the twinned rise of his upper chest muscles.

Two more exquisite lovemaking sessions had mellowed and calmed her.

Could she indeed be a countess, answering to 'your ladyship' without cringing? Would she survive a presentation at Court – and whatever unknown official duties countesses had? Was it possible to endure society's derision without her sisters constantly beside her?

Kitty's stomach coiled, and she nestled deeper into Sidney's shoulder.

Sandalwood, musk, warmth.

She and Sidney truly loved each other. But would that love be enough to give Kitty the strength she needed?

Kitty tucked her icy toes under Sidney's legs. The attic chill apparently didn't affect him. He sprawled nude and uncovered over the drapery, one arm wrapped around Kitty, the other folded behind his golden head. His magnificent cock lay satiated in the vee-shaped ridge of his lower abdomen. He was Adonis, relaxing in the wake of his sexual prowess.

His *considerable* sexual prowess. Kitty was pleasantly sore and spent – and exceedingly impressed. Clearly, Sidney hadn't exhausted his skills during their passionate honeymoon in Langholm.

Which really begged a certain question . . .

'Where did you learn to make love, Sid?' Kitty asked, still playing with his chest hair.

'Mmm?'

Kitty propped her chin on his shoulder. His eyes were closed. 'Are you asleep?'

His lids fluttered open, and he smiled drowsily. 'Not much. What did you ask me?'

'Who taught you to make love so well?'

Sidney combed his fingers through her hair as his smile deepened. 'A friend of my mother's.'

Kitty's eyes flew open. 'Of your *mother's*?'

'Indeed.' He gazed through the skylight at the fading stars above them.

Did he intend to elaborate?

'*Yes*?' Kitty urged, prompting him.

He lifted his brows. 'Oh – you want the particulars. That wouldn't be gentlemanly of me, Kit.'

An admirable and unsatisfactory response.

Kitty looked through her lashes. '*Please* tell me how you came to have an affair with your mother's friend.'

His eyes sparkled. 'Very well. I shall appease my wife's appetite for lurid details, but – seriously, Kit – I shan't mention her name, so don't ask.'

364

It was a disappointing but fair concession. 'I won't,' she said, nestling closer to him.

Sidney kissed the top of her head. 'The Christmas before I turned nineteen, my mother's friend hosted a magnificent Twelfth Night ball. After midnight, she slipped me a folded note scented with her perfume. Lily-of-the-valley, since I promised to provide details. When I read her proposition, my heart thumped so violently, I thought the room would hear its beat. Her husband stood not a yard away from me, speaking to my father. Not that either of them paid me any mind.'

Kitty's jaw dropped. 'She was married?'

Sidney frowned. 'Yes, but he was never faithful to her, Kit. After she bore him several children, she decided it was her turn to have some fun.'

'Did the affair begin that night?'

'It did, although I went to her room with some noble idea of saying I mustn't accept her advances, even though I wanted to. She reasoned my young conscience away in less than two minutes. Reasoned and . . . well, you can imagine. I was powerfully attracted to her, although she was more than twice my age.'

Kitty's first keeper had been thrice her age – five-and-forty to her fifteen. Although Kitty bore him no ill will, she harboured no sentimentality towards him either.

But Sidney was misty-eyed as he gazed at the sky, where the faintest hint of blue infused the grey firmament.

A tightness formed in Kitty's chest.

She raised herself up on one elbow, her hair cascading over Sidney's arm. 'I suppose she must've been very beautiful, if you were so attracted to her?' It was difficult to squeeze the words out.

Sidney caught her gaze. 'Her kindness attracted me, Kit. Like you, she's a true lady. Benevolent, gentle and loving to everyone, including her husband. I was an eighteen-year-old boy who'd known little kindness. She filled my heart.'

'You fell in love with her?' Kitty asked, heart-sore.

'I certainly thought so at the time.'

'And she fell in love with you?' The tightness returned to Kitty's chest. She regretted her promise not to ask the name of this woman who was Sidney's first love.

Sidney chuckled. 'Not in the least. She knew my love for what it really was: gratitude.'

The knot loosened a little. 'Did you tire of her?'

'No, she tired of me. She gently broke my heart after several months and sent me on my way, promising one day I'd find my true love.' He smiled. 'And she was correct. I found her.'

'Me?' Kitty asked shyly, although she knew the answer.

Sidney's eyes shone. 'Always and only you.'

Kitty's heart soared, but her curiosity about this mysterious lady wasn't satisfied. 'Do you think she ever took another lover?'

'Oh, yes. I was neither her first nor her last – merely one in a succession. She takes a different lover every year, and they are always very young men. Does this story shock you?'

Kitty considered. She was relieved the lady probably didn't harbour residual romantic feelings for Sidney, despite their on-going friendship. And why should it be so shocking that a lady was promiscuous? Women felt desire as much as men did.

'It doesn't surprise me much,' Kitty said. 'It's little different from the gentlemen who come here.'

'Her reasoning exactly. Her months with her young lovers, generally from Christmas until July, quite make up for her husband's infidelities – or so she claims when I enquire about 'her well-being. We're good friends to this day. She contributed generously whenever the vicar sent me round to ask her for money.'

'Does her husband know about her affairs?' This inverse to the life she once lived fascinated Kitty.

'He steadfastly pretends he doesn't; in turn, she steadfastly pretends not to know certain things about him. I suppose it's what works for them. Not for us, though, Kit. Never for us.'

'No.' Again, Kitty rested her cheek on his broad shoulder. 'You are the only man I want.' That much she knew, whatever happened.

She skimmed her fingers down the smooth central groove of Sidney's chest and rounded his navel. Whoever this woman was, if she was a friend of Sidney's supercilious mother, society must consider her a lady. If proper ladies behaved not quite respectably, what truly made a woman a lady? Was it, as Sidney believed, a benevolence and kindness, a generous and loving heart?

367

For now, Kitty stored those ponderings. She wanted to know more about Sidney's past. She'd often wondered if the rumours linking him to the wealthy ladies he visited were true, and it seemed perhaps they were.

'Sid, were there other lovers — for you, I mean — after this woman?'

There was a brief pause.

'Yes. My mother has many acquaintances, and word spread during my Cambridge years. Discreetly, but it still spread.' He brushed the back of his fingers on Kitty's cheek, petting her as he continued: 'Always matrons or widows. I never sought them out — they requested me because of loneliness or past hurts.' He lifted Kitty's hand, brought it to his lips, and kissed her wedding band. 'Young Sidney was perhaps not so different from a courtesan, eh?'

Kitty raised her head. 'You were a cicisbeo,' she said, rather astonished. Perhaps this explained why Sidney had always treated her respectfully. He understood something of the role she'd played. 'Did you mind?'

He furrowed his brow as he studied her palm. 'Usually, no. I was young and, well, eager to give vent to my virility, I suppose you'd say. But I longed for love.'

Kitty understood. She'd felt the same yearning for years, although she'd denied it until Sidney awakened those sentiments at Vauxhall. 'And after your Cambridge years? Did you have many affairs?'

'No.'

Kitty blinked. 'None at *all*?'

'None at all,' he replied with a smile.

'Prostitutes?' Kitty asked, hesitatingly. It didn't seem like something Sidney would do, but surely a young man with his passion wasn't celibate for six years.

'Good God, no. I've *never*.'

Kitty peaked her brows. 'So . . . nothing?'

'Nothing.' Sidney chuckled. 'You're surprised, but if you knew the reason, you wouldn't be.'

'Was it because you became a curate?'

'The curacy wasn't the primary reason, although, conveniently, many of my former lovers assumed so. Most men, spurred by Cornelius's gossipmongering, thought I never changed.' He grimaced. 'They believed I . . . er . . . serviced the ladies I visited, which would've been a violation of sacred trust.'

'But if your curacy wasn't the primary reason, what was?'

Sidney smoothed back her hair, a soft expression in his eyes. 'Because shortly after I became a curate, I saw a beautiful and tender-hearted lady holding her sister's baby, and, for me, Marlowe rang true: "*Whoever loved, that loved not at first sight*". You've been the sole possessor of my heart ever since, my loveliest Kitty.'

Kitty's fingers flew to her lips. 'Oh, Sidney.'

Sidney smiled. 'Now do you understand that you're my everything? And that you've been so for the last six years? My inspiration? My universe? My salvation?'

Like his novel . . .

Love overflowed from Kitty's heart. 'I do, Sid.'

'Be my countess?' he asked softly.

Kitty tensed, worrying her bottom lip. Matilda, St James's, and Sidney's mother's scornful face smothered her nerve.

But then she thought of Sidney. For some inexplicable reason, the most wonderful man in the world had chosen her six years ago, and he'd remained steadfast ever since. He needed her to complete him, and she loved him whole-heartedly. For his sake, she'd brave these treacherous waters.

With all the fortitude she could muster, Kitty nodded.

Sidney sat up, beaming. He pulled her into his lap and smothered her in kisses. 'We bring truth to the title at last, for our love is paradise, Lady Eden.'

Suddenly it was all Kitty could do not to retch. She'd made a mistake. She couldn't do this.

But she *must* do this.

Sidney released her to gather his clothes. Kitty knelt on the floor, hugging herself. 'It will be dawn soon,' Sidney said, tugging on his black trousers. 'Let's go awaken Ada-Marie. How delighted she will be.'

That brought a hesitant smile to Kitty's lips. Perhaps she simply must keep thinking of Ada-Marie to main-tain courage.

Sidney grabbed his crumpled shirt. 'Do you have a black evening gown, my love?'

'I have evening gowns in every colour,' she said, a bit peevishly. Evening gowns were the *uniforms* of 'ladies of the night', which was the type of lady Kitty truly was.

Sidney's head emerged from under his shirt with two creases between his brows. Perhaps he'd perceived the bitter edge to her voice.

Kitty forced a smile to reassure him. 'Why do you ask, darling?'

'Tonight, I shall take you to the theatre, but we should wear mourning. We'll see whatever is on at the Haymarket. It's not about the play – it's about the public appearance.' He pushed his foot into one of his boots. 'We mustn't allow rumours to fester. We shall demand respect and acceptance.'

Kitty's forced smile fell.

Sidney yanked on his other boot. 'We'll stay in Half Moon Street while the Dower House is readied. I intend to keep my lodgings there for when we must be in town. You can refurbish the rooms. Do you like that sort of thing?'

'I don't know,' Kitty said, weakly. 'Philippe decorates for me.'

'Perhaps Philippe can refurbish them.'

Kitty squeezed her arms tighter around her chest. 'Philippe won't come with me, Sid.'

'Why? Whatever do you mean? He's devoted to you.'

'A cottage life isn't for him,' she explained through a thickened throat. 'I shall encourage him to serve Matilda.'

If Philippe agreed, perhaps he could be a sort of peace offering to her sister. After all, he'd dressed Matilda the evening before – *la flamme de la passion*, he'd called her in her red dress – and the transformation had pleased Matilda. She hadn't said so, but her eyes had flickered constantly to her reflection when she'd visited Kitty's room before the gentlemen arrived downstairs, and her spirits had been so elevated, she'd allowed Kitty to sleep rather than attend the party.

Sidney flung his coat over his arm and offered a hand to assist Kitty up. 'As you think best, my love – but you must employ a lady's maid. I shall write up an advertisement for the papers tomorrow. Applicants will fall over each other dashing to our door, hopeful of a chance to serve the exquisite Lady Eden.'

Kitty pressed a palm to her abdomen. Sidney didn't realise how difficult it was to find maids willing to serve women of her reputation.

Sidney tugged her towards the door, as exuberant as a puppy, chattering something about how much his cousin Clara – who lived in the parsonage which neighboured the Dower House – would adore Kitty and Ada-Marie.

As they neared the top of the attic stairs, Kitty peered over her shoulder, hoping for a glimpse of St Paul's dome through the skylight.

But the sun had just crested the horizon, and its light stabbed Kitty's eyes.

She squinted, blinking, and stumbled as she felt her way down the stairs after her husband.

25

The next morning, breezes swirled the thin white inner curtains of Kitty's bedchamber like a lady's skirts on a dance floor. The crisp September air prickled Sidney's skin through his shirtsleeves as he sat in an armchair with Ada-Marie upon his knee.

His daughter clapped and swung her stockinged feet. 'Again, again, Papa.'

He laughed and started over, bouncing her to mimic a horse trotting, as he held her waist between his hands. She curled her little legs around his trousered calves and giggled.

'This is the way the lady rides,
Trit-trot, trit-trot.'

An increase to a three-beat canter.

'This is the way the gentleman rides,
Cantering, cantering.
But Ada-Marie's horse . . .'

His daughter squealed in anticipation.

'Goes galloping, and galloping, galloping away.'

When Sidney's galloping stilled, Ada-Marie rotated and knelt in his lap, patting his shoulders and neck with flat palms and splayed fingers, searching for his face. She pressed her hands to his cheeks and beamed. 'I like Ada-Marie's horse the best, Papa.'

Sidney kissed her forehead. 'Just as I hoped, mousey.'

He'd get his daughter a pony for Christmas, Sidney decided, and begin to teach her to ride. With trustworthy mounts and her resolute determination, in time Ada-Marie would learn to be a fine equestrienne.

She slid off his lap and crossed towards the bed with her hands held out. 'Mama?'

'I'm still here, poppet,' Kitty said from the bed, where she reclined against a mountain of pillows, a breakfast tray at her side. She cradled her cup of morning chocolate in both hands.

Ada-Marie crawled over the wide mattress where they'd all slept cuddled together until a half an hour earlier. 'Your horse isn't as much fun as Papa's and mine.'

Kitty held out her arm, and their daughter nestled against her breast. 'My horse?'

'Yours is the lady's horse, of course. The one that trit-trots,' Ada-Marie explained. 'May I have some chocolate?'

Kitty's brow furrowed as she guided her cup to their daughter's mouth. When her gaze lifted, Sidney smiled, hoping to reassure away her self-doubt about being a lady.

In response, Kitty's mouth widened into a too-bright grin which didn't reach her eyes.

She was attempting to hide her trepidation from him.

Sidney leaned back in his armchair, rubbing his stubbled chin as Kitty spread raspberry jam on thick toast for

Ada-Marie. His wife was the bravest and most generous lady in the world. She was pushing aside her fear and misgivings for the sake of Ada-Marie and himself.

She likely thought he didn't know how much effort she was exerting.

But he did.

And he wanted to ease her burden in any way he could. If he must, he'd remind Kitty a thousand times a day of the strength of his devotion. In time, she would understand his love wasn't a reflection of Sidney's steadfastness, as she now believed, but of her own remarkable worth.

A sharp rap sounded on the door.

'Miss Matilda,' Ada-Marie said, her mouth full of her toast.

Kitty visibly paled.

Sidney stood. 'I'll speak with her, Kit. You and Ada-Marie enjoy your breakfast.' Kitty needed love and comfort, not Matilda's harassment.

The knock sounded louder.

Sidney pulled his coat on over his shirtsleeves and waistcoat. He combed his fingers through his hair, but his morning stubble would have to remain.

He opened the door and stepped into the hall rather than allowing Matilda in.

'Good morning, Matilda.' He closed the door behind him.

She drew back, pressing her hands against the smooth silk of her pale orange skirts. 'I want to speak with my sister.'

'Speak to me instead. Aren't I the reason you're here?'

Two red spots enflamed her cheeks, and her bosom heaved with quick breaths.

'Come,' Sidney said, offering his arm. She was angry; Sidney should get her away from Kitty's door in case she yelled. He'd encourage her to support Kitty and accept their marriage, which would bolster Kitty. 'Walk with me, my sister.'

She glowered. 'Do you mock me when you call me that?'

'Not at all. But I insist we speak elsewhere so as not to trouble my wife. Kitty has had a rather difficult few weeks. She needs support and kindness now, such as she *always* provides to others.' He nudged out his elbow. 'Take my arm, Matilda.'

'I don't need your help to walk, Sidney.'

He dropped his offered arm. 'Where can we have privacy?'

She nodded towards the opposite end of the corridor. 'My room.'

Sidney followed her.

Matilda's rose-scented bedchamber was as red and dark as Paradisum. A fire burned in the carved mahogany hearth, roasting the room.

Once inside, Sidney stood near the door, while Matilda paced her scarlet carpet.

'So, you mean to go on in this way?' she asked. 'Pretending there's no problem with your morganatic marriage?'

Sidney squared his shoulders. To dispel her antagonism, he must tread carefully but firmly. 'Not morganatic, Matilda. That would imply Kitty hasn't a right to share my title, which isn't the case. Kitty is a countess now, and if we conceive children, they will be lawful heirs to the honorifics, et cetera.'

Matilda stopped pacing and stood by the hearth, her orange gown mirroring the flames. 'You know what I meant. Your marriage is unnatural.'

'I object to that term even more strongly than your last choice.'

She huffed. 'You're exasperating me, Sidney. Call it what you will, but answer my question. Do you mean to pretend there are no problems?'

Sidney crossed his arms. 'It depends on what you mean by problems, Matilda. If you are asking if I intend to deny my wife or be ashamed of her, my answer is an emphatic no. Not only do I love her more than my own life, but I consider her my superior in every way. She has maintained astonishing goodness despite horrific challenges.'

Matilda's nostrils flared. 'As have I and all my sisters.'

'I want to believe in your goodness, Matilda, but some of your choices make it hard to do so.'

She reddened. 'You mistake common sense for cruelty.'

Sidney remained silent.

Matilda coughed, closing her mouth and rubbing three fingers along her throat as if trying to smooth away a tickle. 'Does Kitty want to be a countess?' she asked at last. 'Is she happy, Sidney?'

Therein lay the rub.

Sidney gathered his breath. 'In time, I hope that Kitty—'

'*In time*?' Matilda interrupted. 'So, you admit, as I knew, that my sister is *not* happy. Yet, from your privileged position, you seek to assure me that everything will be well. What does a cosseted lordling know of life's trials?'

Sidney bristled. 'I wasn't as cosseted as you imagine.'

Matilda scoffed. 'No doubt, *my lord*. I shan't attempt to argue about your hardships anymore, for you certainly know best, being a man. Let me tell you, though: my other sisters and I will suffer for your folly. You've destroyed our impeccable reputation as courtesans who look and dress like ladies, but who know our place. Nothing scares off gentlemen faster than the fear of being trapped into marriage, and without our wealthy clients, we have nothing. We will starve to death, as my parents did.'

Whip-smart Matilda, who likely possessed safes as full of jewels as Tyrold's was full of banknotes, seemed in little likelihood of starving to death.

Nevertheless, Sidney replied mildly. 'I'd never allow my sisters and their children to starve. If nothing else, you have a home at my estate.'

Matilda seethed. 'That is all you have to say? No pretend apology even?'

'I have nothing to apologise for,' Sidney said, lifting his shoulders. 'I *could* profess that you possess as brilliantly ruthless a business mind as my friend Tyrold, and you're likely able to turn everything you touch to gold, but you've already expressed how little you value my opinion.'

She narrowed her eyes. 'Don't try to flatter me.'

Sidney disguised a snort of laughter as a cough. Matilda *was* like Tyrold if the term ruthless flattered her.

Still, the conversation was in danger of descending into bickering. It was time for clarity.

'Matilda, you and I both want the best for Kitty.' At least, Sidney hoped Matilda did. 'Trust me to provide that. With Kitty's graciousness, poise and wit, she'll transform into a spectacular countess as soon as she believes she can – and she'll believe in herself more quickly with the support of her adored eldest sister. If you love her, let her flourish.'

Matilda's jaw clenched. 'She'll wilt, not flourish. Our kind aren't meant to inhabit your world as equals. No one will allow it.'

Sidney shrugged. He'd offer one more olive branch. 'I disagree. My novel is tremendously popular; it has primed everyone with a romantic streak to accept our love story. Come with me and Kitty when we attend the Haymarket Theatre tonight, and you'll see.'

'No, thank you,' she snapped. 'I have no wish to witness my sister's public humiliation.'

The evening might not be a resounding success, but it certainly wouldn't be a humiliation after Sidney's show of strength last night.

His patience with Matilda had worn thin. She was exactly like his mother, determined to set herself against their love. 'You think everyone will be as bitter as you, but you're wrong. And as for those who are bitter, all Kitty and I must do is face our *enemies* with confidence, and they'll falter.'

Matilda's eyes widened. She'd caught his implication. 'Is that what I am? An enemy?'

Sidney held out his hands, palms up. 'I certainly hope not, but your actions will determine the answer. And if you are, you mayn't be near Kitty.'

Matilda noticeably shivered. Or perhaps shuddered. Or shook with anger.

Whatever it was, Sidney was weary of conversation with yet another disparager. 'If you're cold,' he said, opening the door to let himself out, 'the blue Kashmir shawl you took from Kitty at Vauxhall would complement your gown very nicely indeed.'

After he'd closed the door on her hateful expression, Sidney paused in the corridor to steady his emotions before returning to Kitty. Hopefully, he'd find a way to bring Matilda as an ally, eventually. She was important to his beloved wife.

But, like his mother, Matilda must get out of their way if she couldn't accept their happiness. The hate and prejudice of others wouldn't poison Kitty and Sidney's love.

That evening, Philippe propelled Kitty to the full-length mirror in her dressing room.

'Do you like it, *chaton*?'

Kitty's black gown of tussore silk possessed a square neckline, puffed sleeves and a moderate train. The lustre of her pearl earrings glowed in the candlelight. Philippe had smoothed her hair into a tight coil, with a few modest curls at her forehead. He'd topped her coiffure with a dainty lace cap.

Kitty felt sick, as if she might regurgitate the chicken she'd nibbled at dinner. Her stomach had been unsettled for weeks, but tonight was the worst of all. If only this dreadful evening were over, rather than beginning. All Kitty wanted was to survive the next few hours of humiliation. Then she'd hide inside for days, if she could. Or at least until Sidney dragged her out again.

'Do you like it?' Philippe repeated.

'Please don't make me wear the cap.' Kitty's voice squeaked.

'You are married now, *ma chérie*. You wear the cap.' Philippe cupped her face between his palms and drew his brows together. 'And I won't hear any more nonsense like, "I'm not respectable, so I don't deserve to wear a pretty little cap". You must follow your heart now, *chaton*.' He tapped his index finger against her chest. 'At the end of your life, you won't look back and think, "I should've cared more about what bitter and judgemental people thought of me." You will think, "Thank God for every single moment I lived true to my heart"'

Kitty wished it could be that easy. 'But what if their opinions wear me down?'

Philippe released her face and peered with her into the mirror. 'You mustn't let them. You must believe in your worth, even when others don't see it.' His blue eyes twinkled. 'But enough lessons from Philippe. Do you wish to know the name of tonight's creation?'

Kitty nodded, not wanting to disappoint Philippe.

'I call it *La Comtesse de la Valeur*.'

Kitty frowned. 'The Countess of Valour? Is that a French tale?'

'*Non*,' Philippe said, grinning. 'It's your tale. But I must explain, for you do not yet comprehend how clever Philippe is: *valeur* means both value, or worth, *and* valour, or bravery. Thus, tonight – and for always hereafter – you are Kitty Wakefield, *née* Preece, the Countess of Worth and Bravery. *La Comtesse de la Valeur*. I have decided it fits you better than Lady Eden, for paradise is boring. In paradise, there is nothing to challenge us to grow and learn.' He waggled his brows. 'But I have no doubt paradise is what you make in bed with the gorgeous Lord Eden. Did you know Philippe shaved your husband's beautiful face today? *Mon Dieu*, he is a work of art. If Philippe had the dressing of him, he'd never dress him.'

Despite her anxiety, Kitty couldn't repress a giggle. 'You are truly incorrigible.'

Philippe held out her black fur-trimmed cloak. 'Follow your heart,' he said, emphasising each word with a shake of his index finger. 'Promise Philippe?'

Kitty half-smiled. 'I promise I'll *try*.'

Philippe offered his arm. 'That will do for now. First step, we follow your heart downstairs to your magnificent lord.'

Sidney waited in the entrance hall, wearing a black evening suit and tall-crowned hat. He swept off his hat in a courtly manner and bowed as Kitty came down the last flight of stairs on Philippe's arm. 'Lady Eden, my dearest love.'

Kitty slipped her gloved hand into the crook of Sidney's arm.

Do this for his sake. Follow your heart. Know your worth. Remember Ada-Marie.

Surely *one* of those thoughts would get her through the evening.

But her queasy stomach didn't settle, even after Sidney sat beside her in his crested carriage and sheltered her in a firm embrace.

'There's nothing to fear,' he said, confident and golden as he always was now.

Kitty didn't reply.

The carriage swayed forward on the mile-long journey to the Haymarket. Out the window, lamplighters reached up their long poles and sparked Mayfair's gaslights. The hexagonal globes blazed in the amber evening light.

If only it were the return journey, travelling from the theatre to Half Moon Street, where they'd settled Ada-Marie and Nanny Ashcroft earlier in the evening. Ada-Marie was likely sleeping already, curled up in bed like a pink and gold shell. Kitty longed to slip under the sheets beside her.

Sidney broke her thoughts. 'Kitty, there's something I want to ask.'

'Yes?' Her throat was tight.

'Why did you and Matilda intend to leave London? What was your aim?'

'To travel to Scotland,' she responded listlessly.

'But why?'

Kitty sighed. She might as well tell him how close she'd come to ending their union. 'To dissolve the marriage by burning the certificate in the blacksmith's forge.'

Sidney's face darkened like a thunderstorm. '*What*?'

He was angry, and Kitty sought to calm him quickly. 'I understand now that you don't want a divorce, but at the time, I thought—'

'Oh, my sweet love. I'm not cross with you, but why did you think a marriage could be dissolved in such a way?'

Kitty's heart pounded. 'Gillingham told me so.'

'And you believed him?'

'Not at first, but when I mentioned it to your mother shortly after, she acted as if . . .' Kitty stopped herself, understanding at last. 'They lied. It's not true. One cannot end a Scottish union by burning the certificate, can one?'

'No, Kitty. A Scottish marriage is as legal as an English one, and dissolving it requires the action of the ecclesiastical courts or an act of Parliament – and a husband may only bring forth a bill of divorce if his wife commits adultery or abandons him.'

'Then in what way—' Kitty clamped a hand to her mouth. Indignation rose, dispelling her queasiness. The duke had taken her for a fool. No, she'd been a fool to listen to a single word from him. Did he seriously think he could've seduced her? Kitty might not believe

384

herself worthy of her new title and position, but she *still* had no intention of letting the viperish Gillingham slither into her bed. She'd have kicked his bollocks into his throat first.

And as for her mother-in-law . . .

Kitty tightened her hands into fists. 'My God, your mother and Gillingham were working together. She planned to send Gillingham after me so he could abduct me. She wanted you to think me unfaithful.'

Sidney spoke through clenched teeth. 'No doubt she believed it would destroy my spirits so I'd agree to an annulment or seek a divorce. And not so long ago, it would have. But not anymore.' Sidney kicked at the floor of the carriage. 'Damn her. Damn them both. That's why that bloody devil Gillingham was so unsettled to see me last night.'

'She sent him to abduct me from my bed, didn't she?' Kitty asked, appalled. 'Or she thought I'd be entertaining, so that *everyone* would see him take me away and believe I went of my own accord. She never intended for me to leave with Matilda . . .' Kitty's throat constricted. The countess and the duke must've laughed at her gullibility.

'Something else bothers me.' Sidney glared out the carriage window, where more purple than orange streaked the evening sky. 'The way Matilda looked at Gillingham, over my shoulder—'

'Not Matilda, Sidney.' Kitty clasped his fisted hand. 'She's not involved in this. Your mother must've deceived her, for she loves me too well. She sacrificed everything for me.' The sister who'd taken violence and abuse intended for Kitty wouldn't have betrayed Kitty to violence and abuse.

Sidney frowned.

What could Kitty say to make him believe her?

As she thought, the carriage swung to the right, off Piccadilly onto Haymarket. Then, with a neigh from the horses, it jolted to an abrupt halt.

Kitty lurched forward, falling.

Sidney's arm caught her before she plunged to the carriage floor. He pulled her back to the seat.

'What in the devil?' He reached to open his door.

The window on his side exploded. Kitty screamed, throwing her arms up, shielding her face from a barrage of glass shards.

Sidney grunted, as if stricken by pain. He doubled over, and something hard thudded against the floor of the carriage.

Kitty's window shattered in another torrent of glass. Her cheek stung. When she put her black-gloved hand to her face, stickiness smeared her skin.

She and Sidney were under attack.

Noises and motions slowed, as if Kitty moved through a dream.

Hisses and jeers.

The jerking flames of handheld torches streaking the black-purple dusk.

Yelling.

The whistle of a whip.

The carriage rocked.

Everything swirled, and the doors burst open on both sides. Hands yanked at Kitty's limbs and pulled her away from Sidney, out of their carriage. Into the arms of a mob.

'Kitty!' her husband yelled, although she could no longer see him.

'Si—' A hand clamped over her mouth.

Kitty flailed and kicked, trying to get her feet on the ground. She swayed like a hammock in the pungent arms of the rioters. Clammy bodies pressed in with suffocating closeness, clawing at her cloak, her hat, her gown.

Her cloak choked her neck. A rip of fabric enabled her to breathe again, but as the cloak fell away, so too fell Kitty: out of her captors' arms and face down onto the unforgiving cobbles.

She couldn't breathe. Darkness enveloped her.

Something grabbed her feet and yanked, dragging her across horse muck and street slime and far away from the carriage. She covered her face with her gloved hands, trying to protect it from the rocks and the filth.

Her captor turned a corner.

If Sidney still called her name, Kitty couldn't hear it anymore.

26

Claw-like hands dug into the flesh of Kitty's upper arms and dragged her to her feet in a narrow alley off Haymarket. Two wiry women of indeterminable age, haggard but strong, shoved her against a brick wall and pressed their tattered rag-clad bodies into Kitty. The sides of the alley loomed overhead, choking out the last light of evening and casting coal-black shadows over the face of a third ruffian, a squint-eyed, sinewy man with a ragged, grey-streaked beard.

One woman wheezed, exhaling putrid hot gin-breath on Kitty's cheeks. 'Think you're better than us?'

Although her muscles ached from her fall, Kitty writhed, struggling to free herself so she could run back to Sidney, for the roar of the mob sounded around the eastern entrance to the alley. But the women's jagged nails cut like serrated glass deeper into her flesh as they pressed her harder against the wall.

What was the mob doing to Sidney?

'Sidney!' Kitty's throat throbbed from the force of her scream.

The second woman slapped a suffocating hand over Kitty's mouth.

Kitty twisted, but Gin-Breath aided her companion's efforts by clamping her palm around Kitty's neck.

Gin-Breath grinned wickedly, with a flinty glint in her eye. 'I'll squeeze if you keep wiggling like a fish.'

Kitty stilled. The women were hard-faced criminals, prepared to do whatever it took to survive on London's violent streets, and Kitty knew better than to under-estimate them.

The second woman, who bore a cluster of warts on the side of her nose, guffawed. 'Not so high and mighty now, are you? Nor should you be. Trussed up like a gentry mort, but you earned it moaning on your back, same as any whore.' She grasped for Kitty's pearl earrings.

The squint-eyed man cuffed Wart-Nose's cheek with the back of his hand, and she stumbled and dropped onto the pavement.

Kitty gasped for air as Wart-Nose's hand fell away, but Gin-Breath retained her vice-like clamp on Kitty's throat.

The man grunted at Wart-Nose, who sat splay-legged on her bottom, rubbing her cheek in the shadows. 'No stealing.'

'I were just touching them.'

He growled at her before focusing his squinty eyes on Kitty. 'Ain't you a dimber mort. Come with me, doll, and I'll show you what a real man can do.' He grabbed his groin.

'No rape neither,' Wart-Nose said as she rose to her feet, her hand pressed to the wall. 'No thieving, no murder, no rape. Those was our orders, and you know it.'

'I ain't said nothing about rape.' Squinty thrust a clammy hand down Kitty's bodice and leaned over her. 'Women like her want it all the time. Don't you, sweetheart?' A brown-toothed smile scored his face, stretching his streaky beard.

Kitty didn't have time for a drunken oaf who clearly underestimated her. Sidney needed her protection.

She steadied her wobbling legs, drew up her strength, and kneed the man's crotch with all her might.

His squinty eyes widened, his hairy jaw dropped, and he collapsed, doubled over and grunting.

The women cackled.

'That's shown you, hasn't it?' Gin-Breath said, her claws still cutting into Kitty's arm and neck. 'Get out of 'ere, you great lobcock, and lick your wounds like the dog you are.'

'He'll like that,' Wart-Nose crowed. 'Licking his own bollocks.'

The women looked at Kitty with new respect.

Wart-Nose pressed her verrucous beak close. 'Knew you was one of us, pet.'

Kitty tried to turn her cheek, but Gin-Breath's clamp tightened. The women possessed the herculean strength of hard-working labourers, while twenty years of luxury had softened Kitty. She couldn't best them.

Instead, she attempted to appeal to their feminine hearts. 'Please let me go to my husband.' Her voice was hoarse from Gin-Breath's throat-grasp. 'Something hit him in our carriage, and he's hurt. It might've been a bullet—'

"Tweren't no bullet.' Gin-Breath squeezed tighter. 'A pebbly rock, that's all. Your man won't be roughed up no worse than you. No rape, no murder, no stealing.'

Kitty panted in her effort to breathe, the tip of her tongue jutting out of her mouth. 'Who said these things?' She gasped rather than spoke the words. 'No rape, no stealing? Who put you up to this?'

Wart-Nose sneered. 'We can't tell you the name, but 'twas someone as wants you to see yourself for what you really are. You don't belong in no crested carriage. You're a back-slums girl, born and bred.'

Gillingham, no doubt.

Kitty seethed. The duke had carried his perverse obsession with her too far.

'Never mind if you won't tell me,' Kitty said, still gasping for breath. 'I know who ordered this. He's as black-hearted a villain as ever lived. You serve the devil when you serve him.'

Squinty grumbled from the shadows. "Tweren't no man. A woman ordered it. A lady, by the looks of her.'

Sidney's mother, then.

That knowledge hurt. Terribly.

When Kitty had discovered her mother-in-law wanted to assist Gillingham's seduction, it had infuriated Kitty. But this devastated her. The dowager Lady Eden truly would stop at nothing – even physically harming her own gentle-hearted son – to destroy Kitty and Sidney's marriage.

Where would this end?

Sidney's *death*?

Shoved against a wall, beaten and bruised, Kitty surrendered her spirit. Tears ran in rivulets down her scratched and scraped cheeks, stinging her wounds. She couldn't fight Gillingham, Lady Eden, Matilda and society anymore – not when Sidney's life hung in the balance. Kitty's strength reserves had withered, leaving her as dry as a desert.

This wasn't supposed to be her life. She should've never allowed Sidney's idealism to awaken longings she didn't deserve. The alternative – if she'd remembered her place and insisted on a mistress-keeper relationship – flashed before her. On evenings like this one, she'd wait in her jasmine-scented bedroom, dressed in lace and silk. In front of a crackling fire, she and Philippe would play *vingt-et-un* together until a footman announced Lord Eden's arrival below. They would've readied the room by tucking the cards away, snuffing half the candles, scattering rose petals on the silk sheets, and pouring Sidney a glass of fine brandy. Kitty would've draped herself on a chaise longue while Philippe arranged her cascading curls and lace. Then Sidney would've entered, and Kitty would've melted his cares away . . .

And so they would've continued until Sidney tired of her, as keepers always do. No depth, no longevity, but an arrangement accepted by society.

Kitty wouldn't be in an alley, covered in shit and mud, with everyone hating her. Sidney wouldn't be in pain, suffering at the hands of a violent mob his mother had ordered.

A flame of fury against her own folly awakened her withered spirits. She was *absurd* to have attempted to rise above her station. Ludicrous, laughable. A daydreaming little girl without a bit of sense in her head.

Kitty's tears swelled, blurring the shadows of the alley, and she opened her mouth and screamed. 'You fucking fool, Kitty Preece!'

The women fell away, slack-jawed.

Without their arms supporting her, Kitty's legs wobbled. She collapsed onto her bottom, struggling for air and rubbing her aching throat.

She half-cried, half-screamed at the startled women. 'I'm bloody well done with this.' She yearned for a release from this agonising hurt, this horrible situation she couldn't escape. 'I'm not a countess. I'm not a lady. I never was and I never will be.'

In the thin rectangle of dusky light at the western end of the alley, a carriage drew up with the soft whinny of horses. A figure emerged, leaning out the door.

A figure wrapped in a blue shawl.

Kitty's heart leapt to her throat. *Mama.*

With an airway suddenly too tight to speak, Kitty smeared her gloved hands over her cheeks, staggered to her feet, and stumbled down the alley.

The apparition turned up her face, and a street light cast its glow across her features.

Not Mama – but Kitty's heart soared, nevertheless.

'Matilda,' Kitty said, blubbering like a baby. 'Matilda.'

From the carriage step, Matilda held out her arms. 'Kitty-cat.'

A burst of energy infused Kitty. She pined for her sister's embrace. She picked up her long filthy skirts and ran towards the blue shawl.

'*Kitty*!' Sidney's voice yelled from the other end of the alley. 'Thank God, Kitty.'

Kitty ceased running and glanced over her shoulder.

Sidney limped forward with one hand pressed to the wall. Stumbling. Obviously in agony.

Kitty's heart broke. Her audacity had brought this attack on him. Tears stung again, and her throat tightened, rendering speech even more impossible.

'Kitty.' He tottered, floundered, and stopped only a yard or two into the alley. 'Come home with me, my love.'

Home? What home? They were six weeks married, and they hadn't made a home together yet. Their marriage was death, violence, hate, and the ruining of many, many lives.

'Come home with *me*, Kitty-cat.' This time it was Matilda's voice, soft, gentle, familiar, comforting. A voice that had once harmonised with Mama's, singing the younger sisters to sleep in the rickety attic bed. A voice that had filled the void after Mama died.

Kitty returned her gaze to her sister. Matilda's arms reached out, draped in Mama's shawl, and they were the arms that nurtured Kitty through childhood illnesses, through hunger-pains, through nightmares.

Matilda's arms were the ones which could save Kitty from the nightmare she now faced.

Kitty looked back at Sidney. Necessity loosened her aching throat enough to speak. 'Take care of

Ada-Marie, Sid,' she called out, projecting her voice although it hurt. 'Tell her I love her, but my home is with my sisters.'

If any part of Kitty's heart remained unbroken, it shattered then.

'No, Kitty—' The words were strangled, choked.

But Kitty turned her head and fled to her sister's embrace. She burrowed her face into Matilda's rose-scented shoulder. Mama's blue shawl enveloped them as they tumbled together onto the backward-facing seat inside the carriage.

The driver called to the horses, and the vehicle churned into motion like the rocking of a cradle.

Kitty sobbed onto her sister's bosom. The softness of Mama's shawl shielded her from feeling or seeing anything of the horrible world. 'I'm so sorry, Matilda. I'm so sorry.' Her words bubbled through saliva and snot. 'I wish none of this had ever happened. I was silly and foolish, and I want to go home.'

Matilda rubbed Kitty's back. 'There, there, Kitty-cat,' her sister said, coughing as she spoke.

Kitty's tears amplified. 'And through it all, my dearest Matilda has been unwell for months. I should've taken care of you and not thought of my own selfish dreams.'

'I'm glad you see reason at last,' Matilda said. 'You've created a bloody disaster, but fortunately we still have some friends who'll help us.'

Matilda's harsh words startled Kitty's tears away. Brow furrowed and blinking, Kitty lay with her head on her sister's shoulder under the shawl.

It wasn't Mama's thick, raw wool shawl at all. This one was as soft as down and as smooth as liquid: the shawl Sidney had wrapped around her at Vauxhall on the evening Kitty chose to kiss him, setting all these terrible events into motion.

A fresh tear rolled down Kitty's cheek. She deserved Matilda's harshness.

'Lady Eden arranged for a mob to attack us.' Kitty sniffled and wiped her nose with the back of her filthy glove. 'No doubt with Gillingham's help.'

A familiar deep chuckle rumbled like a waking dragon from the other side of the carriage.

Kitty's heart stopped.

'My dear girl,' the duke's voice drawled, 'I must give credit where it's due. Tonight's fun was entirely your sister's clever thinking.'

Kitty's blood turned to ice.

She whipped her head up, shoving Matilda's arms off and recoiling against the upholstered side of a dark carriage – clearly *not* the Preece sister's pale blue landau with its ivory silk interior. In her desperation, she hadn't registered her surroundings before collapsing into her sister's embrace.

Unfortunately, Kitty's ears hadn't fooled her, for Gillingham laughed in the forward-facing seat, dressed in buckskin breeches and a caped greatcoat, with his legs spread wide and his riding boots firmly planted on the inky carriage rug. He steepled his gloved hands over the hefty silver dragonhead top of an ebony walking stick.

Kitty clenched her fists, shaking from head to foot. 'You *betrayed* me, Matilda? To violence and abuse?'

Matilda lifted her palms defensively. 'Only to demonstrate what will happen repeatedly if you leave the sphere in which you belong.'

Flames coursed through Kitty's blood. 'You'll hire mobs to attack me and Sidney?'

Matilda dropped her hands and crumpled up the Kashmir shawl where it cascaded into her lap. 'N-No. Only this once, to show you how foolish it is to pretend to be a lady. Everyone will despise you.'

Kitty's hackles rose. 'You don't know that everyone will despise me. So far, the only hate Sidney and I have encountered is from the two people who ought to love us the best.'

As the spontaneous words burst from her mouth, Kitty savoured their truth. Besides Gillingham, who was meaningless scum and therefore irrelevant, only Matilda and Lady Eden loathed their marriage. Others had reacted very differently indeed.

Grumpy, grouchy John Tyrold, who hardly cared for anything but money, had assisted them repeatedly because he knew Sidney loved Kitty devotedly. Philippe believed in Kitty and Sidney's love so much that after years of helping Kitty shield her heart, he now demanded she follow it – to *Sidney*. Ada-Marie didn't loathe their marriage. She celebrated her parents' love because it bound their family together. Mr Webb the confectioner said Sidney's novel – which was a version of *their* love story – gave him hope after heartbreak.

When Kitty and Sidney were together, there was warmth and security, honesty and kindness. Love and goodness blossomed. They gave each other strength; they supported each other's dreams.

Awareness dawned like the brightness of the sun rising through the skylight that same morning: Matilda had become jealous and selfish over the years, demanding possession of Kitty's heart by trying to cast out Ada-Marie and Sidney.

Kitty stared unflinchingly into her sister's eyes. 'Matilda,' she said steadily, 'if the tables had been turned, I *never* would've impeded your joy. I would've celebrated it. Sung it from the bloody rooftops, danced about it in the damn streets.'

Gillingham grunted, but Matilda lifted a faltering hand to her parted lips. 'But, Kitty, you *aren't* happy.'

Kitty lifted her shoulders. 'Not fully happy yet, but I was trying to be. Consider, Matilda: Sidney and I were less than two weeks married when our world turned topsy-turvy. We can't snap our fingers and figure everything out at once.' As Kitty spoke, blinders lifted. She'd been far too hard on both herself and Sidney. She'd almost thrown away the two greatest gifts of her life because of the misguided notion she didn't deserve them based on the circumstances of her birth, despite adhering to principles such as integrity, loyalty and generosity her entire life. Kitty placed her hand on her sister's knee and softened her voice. 'I love Sidney so much, Matilda. Don't you see that? He completes me, and I complete him – like two halves of the same coin.'

The duke grunted again – for all the world like a pig.

Matilda's lips turned down. 'But I *need* you, Kitty.'

'I say,' the duke scoffed. 'This is tedious.'

Kitty snapped. 'Hold your maggoty tongue, you pestilence, and let me speak to my sister.'

Gillingham's hooded eyes opened rounder than two guineas, and his thin lips slackened, but he said nothing.

Kitty returned her attention to Matilda. 'I know how much my love means to you, Matilda. But this isn't the way to retain it. If you force me to choose, you'll lose me. But if you celebrate my marriage, not only will I never desert you, but you'll gain the devotion of a brother.'

'It will never be the same.' Tears streamed down Matilda's face. 'Why must you change everything? *I* sacrificed for *you*.'

For the first time in twenty years, guilt didn't paralyse Kitty. 'Thank you for protecting me when I was very small, Matilda. That man was a savage villain, and, like me, you were an innocent child. He hurt you horrifically, and that is not fair. It will never be fair that you suffered in such a terrible way.'

Matilda's face crumpled. Her shoulders hunched, shaking. 'Oh, Kitty.'

Kitty held out her arms, and this time Matilda fell into them. 'It will never be fair,' Kitty repeated, rubbing her sister's back. 'But there's also my side to the story, Matilda. For thirteen years, I gave my body to whomever you told me to because I thought I owed you. That's not fair either. It's time we both stop allowing one man's cruelty to define our worth.'

As Matilda's sobs lessened, Kitty pulled back slightly to view her sister's tear-streaked face.

'Matilda, for years I didn't believe myself worthy of much. But I was wrong. I'm honourable, loyal and kind. I *am* worthy. I'm my own woman, ready to navigate the challenges of life with the husband and daughter I chose, even if I fall occasionally. Even if sometimes I'm sad. And, yes, even if people are cruel, spiteful, or jealous. For the sake of love, I shall show the world that Kitty Wakefield is a lady.' Kitty lifted her chin, remembering what Philippe had told her earlier. 'She's *la Comtesse de la Valeur*, in fact.'

Matilda's blue eyes grew round. She searched Kitty's face as if looking for more answers.

Kitty knew exactly what her sister needed to hear: the bad and the good. 'And let me tell you something else, Matilda. Somewhere along your way, you lost sight of what's important. You're better than the bitter woman you've become. You are better than *him*,' she said, jerking a thumb at Gillingham, 'and better than all those who cut you down. You are Matilda Preece, a self-made businesswoman, who raised her sisters from extreme poverty to vast wealth. You are Matilda Preece, and you are a *lady* worthy of happiness as well. Don't forget it ever again, do you hear me? And if anyone dares to tell you otherwise, you tell them to talk to your sister, the Countess of Eden.'

Matilda's eyes widened more. She blinked, paused.

Then her shoulders quivered, and a whisper of a giggle escaped her lips. 'My sister, the Countess of Eden?'

Kitty smiled. '*Yes.*'

They clasped each other again.

'But enough of this,' Kitty said, squeezing Matilda once more. 'I'm covered in filth – and still *exceedingly* cross with you, Matilda, because the mob hurt my beloved Sidney, and it's all your fault.'

Matilda twisted the shawl. 'Forgive me, Kitty-cat.'

Kitty scowled, a bit playfully, but mostly seriously. 'I will forgive you eventually, Matilda, but not tonight. Right now, I shall get out of Satan's coach, in part because even Gillingham's profuse use of cloying perfume doesn't cover the brimstone stench he emits. But mostly because I want to find my darling husband and take care of him.'

Kitty reached up and banged her fist against the carriage roof.

A resounding *whoa* reverberated outside, and they rolled to a stop.

Kitty rose, sticking out her tongue at Gillingham as she did so. 'As always, duke, I found your presence as welcome as the plague. Rot in hell, will you?'

The duke's jaw tightened, but he didn't speak. Kitty had bested him.

She laughed.

'Wait, Kitty-cat.' Matilda held out the shawl. 'Take this. You'll get cold otherwise, for you haven't a wrap . . . and it's yours, anyway.'

Kitty's heart filled her chest as she took the shawl. 'I love you, Matilda. I'm *furious* at you, but I love you always and forever.' She made a kissing gesture with her lips. 'And if my face weren't covered in horseshit, I'd kiss you a thousand times.'

Matilda giggled again.

Kitty enveloped herself in the soft-as-down shawl and put her hand to the door.

Only to have it yanked away as Gillingham whipped her back, hurled her on the seat beside him, and, with his booted foot, thrust her into the corner, pinning her torso with the force of a battering ram.

Kitty gasped for breath, pulling in vain at the boot to remove it.

Matilda lunged forward, but the duke drew back his arm and threw his walking stick. It hit Matilda's chest with a thud and knocked her into the far seat. As she wheezed and coughed, two footmen entered the carriage and confined her.

'That show of sisterly affection was dreadfully moving.' Gillingham smirked at Kitty, his voice cold and evil. 'But I'm afraid *you* aren't the Preece sister getting out of my carriage.'

'Let me go, duke,' Kitty rasped. 'You cannot abduct me.'

Gillingham chuckled. 'We'll discuss what I can and cannot do on our journey together. Thomas and Jack, see Miss Preece home.'

As the footmen dragged her out, Matilda bawled. '*Kitty*! — I'm so sorry. I'll find Sidney.'

Kitty flailed, trying to free herself. But the duke ground his heel into the vulnerable softness of her abdomen, knocking the breath from her afresh.

'Going to Eden will do you no good, Matilda,' Gillingham called out as Matilda's head disappeared out the door. 'I'm taking your sister to a *secret* place, known only to my coachman and myself. Jack, close the door and tell the driver to make haste.'

The footmen slammed closed the door.

The carriage lurched forward.

Gillingham settled back into his corner of the seat, yet again grinding his heel into Kitty's bruised and battered torso. 'You've been a difficult conquest, you little bitch, but that will make my reward all the more satisfying. I'm going to fuck your impertinence out of you.'

Between the swaying of the carriage – the horses were at a near-gallop, although they must still be in Mayfair, and the vehicle swung wide around corners – and the duke's boot grinding into her gut, Kitty heaved. This was the last straw after a turbulent evening.

She retched, spewing her scanty chicken dinner over the duke's boot.

27

Sidney's swollen knee throbbed with every footfall as he jogged raggedly west on Mount Street covered in crowd-thrown mud, with his hat long lost.

He should've stopped a hackney when Kitty drove off in the unmarked black coach with its team of six horses, but without thinking of his knee, he'd run the shortest route possible to the Preece sisters' house. In normal conditions, he'd easily outrun a carriage in traffic. Thanks to his injury, these weren't normal conditions. Kitty and Matilda must've long since arrived back.

Sidney pounded upon the cherry-red door, expecting trouble.

The door swung open. Philippe stood framed in the light, his blue eyes wide and his freckled face as grey as ash. '*Grâce à Dieu!*' He called over his shoulder: 'It is Lord Eden, *ma rose*. Thank God.'

An unexpected welcome.

Philippe clasped Sidney's hand, pulled him inside, and slammed the door closed.

Matilda was sprawled across the lower stairs, weeping. She arose in a flurry of orange silk. 'Forgive me, my brother. I made a terrible mistake.'

Sidney's heart raced. Something was dreadfully wrong. None of this was as expected. 'Where's Kitty?' he asked, panicked.

No one replied. Matilda fell to her knees, wailing into her hands. Philippe knelt beside her and rubbed her back.

The world spun. Sidney clutched his chest. 'My God, is she dead? Answer me this bloody moment.'

Matilda spoke through her sobs. '*He* has her. Gillingham has her. And I don't know where he took her. And I'm so very sorry . . . I never, ever should've played any part in this horrid scheme. I should've celebrated you as my brother.'

The world stopped swirling, and a level of normalcy returned to Sidney's breathing. Kitty was alive, which mattered more than anything. She needed immediate rescue, but her life wasn't in danger.

Rescue required rational thinking and quick action, not hysterics and moaning.

Sidney glared at Matilda. 'I take it you were involved in the attack on our carriage.'

'Please forgive me, Sidney,' she pleaded, still on her knees before him.

'Dammit, you don't get off that easily, and I haven't time for forgiveness now, Matilda. But it *is* time we work together.' Sidney held out his hand to assist her up. 'Did the duke take Kitty to Grosvenor Square?'

Matilda shook her head vehemently. She pulled herself up and drew in a ragged breath. 'Definitely not his house in town. His exact words were that they'd take a *journey* to a *secret place*, known only to himself and his coachman. It could be anywhere.'

Sidney pressed his palm to his forehead. The carriage was a light travelling vehicle with a team of six high-bred horses, designed for speed . . . but not necessarily for distance, unless the duke intended to leave immensely valuable animals at a posting house. Sidney should've known the moment he saw the conveyance that it wasn't headed to Mount Street, but he hadn't been thinking then. He'd think now.

A place known only to the duke and his coachman . . . a sort of secret lair, undoubtedly for illicit affairs, the sort of thing Gillingham would steadfastly want to keep from his family . . .

A weight suddenly lifted from Sidney's shoulders.

Of course. The duke wasn't as stealthy as he thought; just as . . .

But there was no time for such thoughts now, nor could Sidney dwell on the twisting in his gut – worry over the discomfort he'd have to cause a friend. Discomfort and worry were nothing compared with saving Kitty.

Sidney stood tall. 'Gillingham's wrong. He's not the only one who knows its location.'

Matilda's eyes widened hopefully. 'You know it?'

'No, but I know someone who does. And if she's not in town, I will find her in Kent. Matilda, please order your travelling carriage and your best horses. *At once.*'

Matilda rang the bell and issued orders in another flurry of orange silk, but this time, it was an efficient flurry.

Philippe rested his hand on Sidney's shoulder. 'I shall accompany you, my lord.'

Sidney patted Philippe's arm, his heart filling with gratitude for the man who'd cared for Kitty so well for so long. 'Thank you, Philippe. I appreciate the offer, but please stay here and comfort Matilda instead. I shan't be alone.'

Fifteen minutes later, four white horses pulled Sidney in Matilda's light blue landau, with its creamy leather top up, to the front of one of the grandest houses on Grosvenor Square. Despite his throbbing knee, Sidney jumped out and banged the lion knocker on the dark green door.

The supercilious butler opened it. His eyes widened as he took in Sidney's filthy attire, and his nose elevated to the sky. 'May I . . . help you . . . Lord Eden?' His tone indicated he'd rather clean a bog house than assist Sidney with anything.

But at least Sidney's elevation to an earldom meant the butler didn't pretend not to recognise him.

'Yes, you can help me.' Sidney encroached on the doorstep, nearly toe-to-toe with the unyielding servant. 'You can get out of my way.'

The butler gasped. 'My *lord*—'

'And tell me' – Sidney brought his face up against the man's – 'if the duchess is at home.'

'I would never . . .' The butler scowled until his lips formed an upside-down u. 'How highly irregular, sir!'

'Nonsense, Harper,' a laughing voice chimed from beyond the servant. 'Lord Eden is always a welcome guest when I'm at home.'

The tension in Sidney's shoulders eased. Thank God she was in town. No voice other than Kitty's could be more welcome.

He pressed past the butler into the white marble hall. Tapers shone in golden candelabras, illuminating Her Grace of Gillingham, who stood at the bottom of the sweeping staircase with one slim hand resting on the gilded newel post. Her pale pink gown pooled around her feet, and her silvered brown curls framed her face under a lace cap.

Sidney swallowed, again disliking disturbing her. It wasn't the duchess's fault she'd married a monster.

Still, she knew what Gillingham was, and Kitty needed rescue.

Sidney bowed. 'Good evening, duchess.'

She held out her hand. 'I've wanted to see you for an age, Sidney, because I so enjoyed your lovely novel.'

Sidney squeezed her fingers, as soft and cool as ever. 'Thank you, but—'

'—But you're not here to chat, are you?' She half-smiled, wistfully.

'No, Clarissa.' Sidney spoke low, so as not to be overheard. 'I've come to ask an enormous favour. And haste is essential.'

He gazed into her dark brown eyes. Their sparkle dulled, diminished, although the ghost-smile still hovered on her lips.

A pause.

She nodded. 'Do I need my cloak?'

'Yes. And a valise.'

Her delicate brows raised. 'Indeed, my sweet?' A hint of playfulness threaded her voice.

Despite the gravity of the occasion, Sidney's cheeks warmed. '*And* your maid.'

The duchess's smile deepened, losing its sorrow and displaying the dimple in her left cheek. As Sidney knew well, she never let herself remain unhappy for long. 'I'll bring a footman,' she said with a wink. 'He can sit with the driver and not invade our privacy, for I think you must have a great deal to tell me, my poor Sidney.'

A lump formed in Sidney's throat. The urge to sob out his sorrows in her soft embrace overcame him. 'I do.'

She patted his cheek. 'Tell me all on our journey, and I shall help.'

As he'd done countless times before in the duchess's presence, Sidney wished his mother were as kind as her friend.

He lifted Clarissa's hand to his lips, inhaling her scent as he kissed her fingers.

Lily-of-the-valley.

She'd worn it for years.

28

Gillingham didn't flinch when Kitty's vomit splattered his foot and leg. Instead, he chuckled. 'I enjoy seeing you under my heel, Kitty.' He removed a handkerchief from his greatcoat pocket and pressed it to his nose. 'You smell revolting, of course, but you're remarkably attractive even when covered in shit, blood and vomit – your natural state, one presumes, when you mudlarked to earn your bread.'

Kitty wiped her damp chin on her shoulder. Although the duke's boot constricted her lungs so she could barely breathe, retching had felt cleansing. She'd swallowed back that bile for weeks.

Now her mind was steady and her body calm.

She must escape.

She'd succeed. It was only a matter of *how*.

'We rarely ate bread.' She wheezed, forcing herself to speak through the pain. Gillingham could hurt her body, but he wouldn't damage her dignity. She'd leave him in no doubt of her opinion: he was a fool and a villain. 'The scarcity of British wheat twenty years ago and the prohibitive taxes on foreign grain made bread too expensive. Perhaps you recall supporting those taxes? They protected the interests of landowners like yourself. No doubt your pockets grew plumper while poor people like my parents starved.'

The duke laughed through his handkerchief. 'Good lord.' The carriage veered to the right. Over Gillingham's shoulder, the city lights thinned as the thrum of the fast-paced hooves rang slightly hollow. They were crossing the Thames on Westminster Bridge. Through the duke's window, the pearl shimmer of a rising moon illuminated Lambeth Palace's turreted square towers. 'What great big thoughts you have, my girl.'

He mocked her, but he didn't daunt her. As a courtesan, she'd never spoken her opinions frankly to any gentleman but Sidney. Now she was a countess, and she'd speak her mind, especially about the plight of the poor.

'I'll happily share more "great big thoughts" if you'll remove your foot and allow me to *breathe*.'

And jump out of the carriage the moment it slows . . .

Gillingham shook his head. 'No, my dear. We'll stop at the turnpike soon, so my foot will remain exactly where it is until the horses are galloping on the open road.' He pointed a finger of the hand not covering his nose. 'And don't imagine you'll escape then. This team is the fastest in England. They travel twenty miles an hour at peak speed. You'll break your pretty neck if you jump from the carriage.'

Undeterred, Kitty raised her eyebrow. 'They can't run that fast forever.'

'No, but we'll be at our destination before they tire.'

Ah, so the duke wasn't taking her far. Kitty had listened to a *lot* of horse talk from gentlemen over the years – it was far more interesting than other favoured topics, like cockfights and gout. Even the best team couldn't maintain top speed for an hour. Thus, their destination must be within twenty miles of the city. A distance Kitty could walk before sunrise if she must.

But she wouldn't have to. She still possessed her pearl earrings, and they'd be more than enough to hire a chaise at a posting house or cajole a kind-hearted farmer into hitching up his waggon in the middle of the night.

The carriage slowed, then stopped. The duke thrust his boot harder.

Kitty needed a plan to get out of the carriage in one piece, but first, she wanted *air*.

After the driver paid the toll, he called to the horses, and the carriage lurched forward at an impossible speed. The galloping hooves drummed against dense dirt, not stone, and only moonlight illuminated the outside darkness beyond the carriage lights.

They were south of the city.

'Now will you remove your boot, duke?'

'Of course.' He lifted his heavy leg. 'You see how reasonable I am.'

Kitty gulped a lungful of air when the pressure left her abdomen. She released it slowly, relishing the freedom of movement and joy of breathing.

'You're not reasonable. As I've said before, I knew you were a monster the moment you sent poor sweet Richard to war so you could steal me.' She patted her aching torso to check for damage. Her bones seemed more bruised than broken, but when she returned to London, she'd have Sidney send for his friend Dr Mitchell to be certain.

Gillingham leered. 'Did him good, I've no doubt. And, at last, it will do me some good as well, Kitty.'

'Call me Lady Eden.'

The duke snorted with laughter as he leaned back into his upholstered corner, with his thighs spread over two-thirds of their shared bench seat. 'How I'm looking forward to putting you back in your place soon.' He stroked the bulge in his breeches with his free hand.

Kitty grimaced. Disgusting. 'I'm rather surprised you haven't rubbed your needly little erection on me already, as you did at Vauxhall.'

The duke yanked his hand off his crotch and glared. 'I'd fuck you now if your odour didn't repel me. In fact, it's amusing that you complain about my fragrance when you reek worse than a pigsty.'

Kitty laughed. Thank God for the muck covering her. No wonder the fastidious nobleman had only touched her with his boot.

To offend him further, Kitty flicked the chunks of regurgitated chicken off her filthy black skirts towards his buckskin breeches and wiped her gloves on the upholstered space between them. 'Personally, I enjoy how my vomit offsets your perfume. What do you call it? Putrid pears?'

'I receive *many* compliments on this fragrance,' the duke said, as belligerent as a bull. 'It's gardenia and lily, among other scents. My parfumier mixes it according to my preference.'

'Next time, choose a fragrance he mixed according to *his* preference.' Kitty folded her hands in her lap. 'Now, tell me, duke, what's your motivation for committing a criminal act tonight? You know perfectly well I've recommitted to my marriage.'

'You're *supposed* to be *mine*.' Gillingham crumpled his handkerchief in his fist, apparently abandoning his efforts at covering his nose. 'You committed to *me* first.'

'We've discussed this before. I made no such commitment.'

'But I want you.' The duke glowered like a sulky child. 'I *desire* you. I need to have you.'

Kitty rolled her eyes. It was useless to tell a man like Gillingham that people don't get everything they want. 'So, this comes back to your cock controlling your thinking, is that it? I warned you at Vauxhall you'd do better to think rationally. I suppose your speech about illusions was nonsense to mislead me into trusting you?'

'No, not nonsense.' He picked petulantly at a button of his greatcoat. 'Your husband's novel is dangerous rubbish, romanticising equality between the classes, and if your marriage is successful, it would further the treacherous falsehood. I cannot allow it.'

'*Allow* it? The success of my marriage has nothing to do with you, duke. My beloved Sidney won't divorce me because you've abducted me or raped me.'

'It won't matter if he divorces you or not,' Gillingham said with relish. 'The damage will be done the moment rumours spread – and they *will* spread – that the new

414

Lady Eden abandoned her marriage not two months after the wedding for a passionate affair with the Duke of Gillingham. Everyone will see the fairy-tale bride for what she truly is: a sordid piece of filth.'

A vein pulsed in Kitty's temple. Sidney's fellow peers *would* scorn him for rumours of an affair.

His writing dreams would suffer if the rumours disenchanted his readers . . .

The gossip would poison Ada-Marie's future . . . and wound Kitty's sisters, whose reputations depended on their loyalty to their keepers.

Then Kitty bolstered herself.

No. None of that would happen.

There wouldn't *be* any gossip because Kitty wouldn't permit it. Even if she must crawl to London on her hands and knees, Kitty would be in town before the sun rose. Tomorrow, she, Sidney and Ada-Marie would infiltrate every corner of Mayfair. They'd ride on Rotten Row; they'd drink frothy milk at the dairy farm in Green Park; they'd savour ices at Mr Webb's; they'd listen to the ballad girl on the corner of Park Lane for an hour. In the evening, Kitty and Sidney would again go to the theatre. *This* time, they'd watch the bloody play.

And although Lord and Lady Eden might be swollen and bruised from an angry mob's *random* attack – as Kitty would ensure the rumours claimed – everyone would witness the newly-wed earl and countess's ardent, devoted love.

The only question was *how* Kitty would achieve her freedom. The carriage moved much too rapidly to jump, especially in her bruised state. Until it slowed, Kitty might as well attempt to appeal to Gillingham's reason.

If he had any.

'Rape is a capital offence,' she said, as calmly as if she were discussing the weather.

The duke snorted. 'It needn't be rape.'

She narrowed her eyes. '*If* it happens, it will be utterly against my will, and therefore, rape.'

'In that case, it's your word against mine, in a court of my peers, who all know what you are. Face it, my girl, you haven't the reputation to claim innocence.'

'I'd not be so confident if I were you.' Kitty lifted her chin. 'My past keepers – who are your peers – would attest to my impeccable loyalty.'

The duke's thin lips curled into a smile so evil, Kitty faltered. 'Let me be perfectly clear, Kitty. My peers wouldn't send me to the gallows if I raped a hundred courtesans in Hyde Park in daylight and *The Times* printed my sworn confession. You *do* understand that, don't you?'

Kitty swallowed, almost losing her spirit. He was likely correct.

Nevertheless, he wouldn't defeat her.

Kitty racked her brain, trying to think of something else which might encourage him to turn back. 'Very well, but Sidney can bring you to trial for adultery – for a criminal conversation.' This was information she'd gleaned from gossip over the years. Wives belonged to their husbands according to the law; therefore, a man could sue another man for damaging his property by committing adultery with his wife.

Gillingham chuckled. 'I can give him tit for tat.'

Kitty frowned, unable to make sense of his reply. 'What do you mean?'

'I've loathed your husband ever since a Twelfth Night many years ago when – after he'd attended *my* ball, drinking *my* wine, and eating *my* food – he stuck his prick into *my wife*. I should've gelded him.'

Kitty froze, wide-eyed and blinking. Gillingham's wife was Sidney's first lover.

She clapped a hand over her mouth and shook with silent laughter. While Gillingham strutted around like a pompous cockerel, his wife – her last keeper Richard's mother – annually sought virile and enthusiastic young men to fill his vacant spot in her bed. Good for the duchess!

The duke stared out the window, his cheeks undulating as he ground his teeth. 'I discovered several sickening love letters your husband wrote my wife, in case you think I haven't proof.'

'But surely' – Kitty's voice wavered because of her suppressed mirth – 'you wouldn't submit your wife to such humiliation?' She pressed her fingers to her lips, lest her mouth betray her amusement. It might enrage the duke into violence if he knew how utterly hilarious she found this revelation.

The duke observed her keenly. 'I won't have to. The threat will be enough. Besides, your hypocrite of a husband wouldn't want either you or my wife shamed with a *crim con* case, as noble as he pretends to be. We both know he won't do anything.'

But Sidney *might* do something. His occasional spurts of hot-blooded anger (Kitty really *must* teach him to control those) might compel him to duel the duke. As much as Gillingham and Sidney despised each other, they'd likely both shoot to kill.

It was another reason for Kitty to save herself as soon as possible.

Clearly, there was no reasoning the duke out of his determination to commit a crime, so Kitty must perfect her escape plan. Unquestionably, the duke's physical strength was superior to her own; if she located a weapon, it would help ensure her successful getaway when the carriage stopped.

She cast her eyes down, discreetly investigating the carriage doors. The handles were a simple rotation lever on both sides.

'You're upset,' the duke said, his voice intruding on Kitty's thoughts. 'It troubles you to learn your precious Sidney doesn't believe in the sanctity of marriage after all, doesn't it?'

Kitty lifted her brows. Apparently, her wavering voice and cast-down eyes misled the duke. She *could* pretend she was upset and attempt to deceive Gillingham into trusting her and thereby relaxing his guard when they stopped. But she relished the opportunity to shame the old man.

'I'm not in the least bit bothered to learn my husband made an error of judgement in his youth. The past is in the past. Sidney matured into the worthiest of men – noble, honourable and willing to listen, learn and adapt – unlike *you*, who behave like an overin-dulged, dangerous baby. Instead of doing good with your powerful position, you're cruel, hateful and sulky.'

'Talk like that's going to earn you my hand across your face, you bitch,' the duke snapped, squeezing his fists. 'I should've brought rope to tie and gag you, but I thought you'd be reasonable.'

'No, you thought I'd be *malleable*, like I was yesterday in the park. You exploited my trust while I was in a state of terrible melancholy, or I would've seen through your motives more clearly than a window after cleaning day. Did you really think you'd carry me away and seduce me successfully? That *I'd* ever want *you*?'

'I told you to shut your mouth,' Gillingham seethed.

Kitty remained silent out of choice. He hadn't cowed her, but she couldn't waste time on fruitless bickering when she needed to focus on locating something she could use as a weapon.

She leaned her head against the curtained side of the carriage. With her left hand, she explored the pockets within the upholstery.

There was nothing. Not even a travel-chess box or a deck of cards she might throw, much less a proper weapon.

Kitty tapped her foot against the carriage rug as they sped past a cluster of houses and a steepled church. Oil lamps blazed at a brick inn. White-tipped, conical-roofed oast houses nestled on the edge of a field where hops grew on tall wooden frames.

The village vanished in the blink of an eye as the horses sped on.

Kitty suppressed a sigh, racking her brain. Could she throttle the duke? Thrust *her* foot, in its thin-soled satin evening slipper, into *his* gut? Grasp at his greatcoat pockets, hoping to find a small pistol, as gentlemen sometimes carried?

The ideas were silly, but there had to be *something*.

Could Kitty choke him with the shawl warming her shoulders – the shawl Matilda had returned just before Gillingham hit . . .

Kitty's eyes flew wide open.

The ebony walking stick, with its hefty silver dragonhead, was *somewhere* in the carriage.

She squinted, peering into the shadows of the backward-facing bench.

Then she smiled.

There – the black wood blended into the seat crevice, but the dragonhead glinted faintly in a corner.

Perfect. Not only would Kitty escape, but she'd also give the duke his just dessert for hurting her sister.

Kitty tallied her resources.

A pair of valuable earrings to hire a coach.

A shawl to keep her warm.

A weapon within her reach.

And an undefeatable attitude.

It would do.

Kitty tensed, readying herself for the first sign of the carriage slowing.

With no warning, Gillingham's foot thrust into her stomach again, knocking her breath away.

'Why?' she wheezed, in tremendous pain. Her lungs burned.

The carriage rolled to a stop.

'Because we're here, and the gatekeeper must open up for us – and you're a devious bitch looking to escape.'

Of *course*, the duke would restrain her *before* the carriage slowed. Kitty should've hit him when she'd had the chance . . .

But, no, because if her attack failed, the consequences would be severe. Kitty couldn't afford to underestimate her enemy. Their carriage conversation revealed the extent of Gillingham's sense of prerogative and the depth of his depravity. He might kill her in a blind rage.

If Kitty had another chance, she'd time it exactly right and reach for the weapon just before the carriage slowed. She couldn't bungle this, and she had to get his foot off her.

Outside the duke's window, torches lit the stone walls of an ancient gatehouse. On the other side of the towering metal gate would be perhaps a mile's drive – at most – through parkland. If the duke got her into a house filled with loyal servants, there would likely be no escape.

'I've been beaten several times tonight,' Kitty said, weakened from the pain of his boot. 'I hurt. Terribly.' That was the truth. 'I'm in no condition to fight, emotionally or physically.' That wasn't true – yet. 'Please remove your boot.'

'In a moment.'

The gate creaked open, and the horses galloped forward again. This time, their hooves produced dull thuds and the carriage wheels crunched over gravel.

The duke removed his foot. 'If you're hurt, it's your fault. I wanted to be kind and companionable with you. You brought my anger upon yourself.'

Kitty nearly exploded, but it wasn't yet time to attack the duke. 'You're a vile man, without a kind fibre in your body. Even when you have what you want – me, your prisoner, locked into your . . . your secret estate or whatever this is—'

'My hunting lodge.'

'. . . Even *then*, you haven't an ounce of humanity.'

The duke snorted. 'I intend for you to receive a warm bath and a proper meal as soon as we are through my door. That's kindness, isn't it? You'd like a bath and food, wouldn't you?'

'Actually, I would.' *When I return to Half Moon Street*, she added silently.

Gillingham smiled. No doubt he envisioned himself as beneficent. 'You shall have them – within my sight the entire time, of course. You'll see I treat you well when you're a good girl. I shan't desert you, Kitty, even after I've had you tonight. You'll be my mistress, and I shall lavish you with luxury beyond what you can imagine, my dear.'

Kitty tensed her muscles, readying herself as the carriage rounded a bend. She wouldn't wait for it to slow. Gillingham's boot wouldn't catch her a third time. The dim glow of house lights shimmered on her side of the vehicle. Through the duke's window, there was darkness beyond the circle of the carriage lantern.

She'd escape out of his door as soon as she'd gauged her movements, for she must grasp the walking stick without a stumble . . .

Meanwhile, the duke's boots remained firmly planted on the carriage rug, which was good.

The rustle of wool and a rush of air alerted Kitty to a different method of attack: Gillingham lunged with his whole body.

But Kitty was primed. She dodged him, springing to her feet with the agility of a tiger, despite the still-moving carriage. *For Sidney*, she thought as she seized the cane. *For Ada-Marie*; she drew back her arm. *For Matilda*; she aimed for Gillingham's face.

And for myself.

She exerted all her physical might and swung the hefty metal top.

It landed with a satisfying, bone-shattering thud against his cheek.

The duke crumpled, falling sideways on the bench with bulging eyes. The dragonhead had ripped into his skin; there was a lightning flash of jawbone in a sea of dark liquid where his cheek had been. He gurgled and clawed at his high shirt collar. Blood bubbled on his thin lips.

'I am *not* a "good girl".' Kitty drove the cane double-handed into his gut as he'd done to her with his boot. He grunted, spewing blood from the force of the thrust. 'I'm a goddamned lady, and don't you *dare* trouble me or anyone I love *ever* again, you "sordid piece of filth".' Kitty thrilled at throwing Gillingham's own insult back at him.

She tossed down the cane, rotated the latch on the carriage door, and plunged into the darkness as the carriage jolted to a halt.

29

Almost two hours after Sidney last saw Kitty in the alley, the pale blue landau stopped on the gravel drive before Gillingham's timber-framed hunting lodge. The moon hung high in a star-strewn sky, casting a silver hue on the hearty oaks and elms surrounding the two-storey, gabled house.

The crisp night air cooled Sidney's overheated brow as he leapt from the carriage, ignoring his throbbing knee, where a goose egg-sized bulge strained against his trousers.

He held out his hand to Clarissa.

She shook her head. 'My footman will assist me. Find your wife and keep your temper with Gillingham. It won't help Lady Eden if you're imprisoned or exiled for murder, my sweet boy.'

Sidney limped-ran towards the house, his boots crunching in the gravel as the horses whinnied behind him. A rabbit scampered out of the grass and crossed the path, its white tail bobbing in the moonlight. The scent of woodfire infused the night, smoke rose from a massive brick chimney, and light flickered behind the diamond-pane leaded windows.

Someone was inside the old lodge. A surge of hope filled him. Clarissa had guessed correctly.

Without knocking, Sidney threw open the heavy wooden door. It crashed against the inside wall of a low-ceilinged, white-plastered entrance vestibule.

A thin-faced old manservant carrying a taper popped his head around an oaken interior door. 'Are you the surgeon, sir?' he asked, holding out the candle to illuminate the chamber. He drew back, evidently taking in Sidney's bedraggled and filthy evening clothes.

A *surgeon*? Was Kitty hurt?

'I'm the *husband*. And if Gillingham injured my wife . . .' Sidney squeezed his fists, shaking in fury.

The servant's eyes widened. 'Sir—'

Sidney didn't wait to listen. He shouldered past the man into an exposed beam hall, furnished in the dense, dark wood style of the seventeenth century. A fire roared in a vast brick hearth. A blanket-swathed body lay on a leather sofa turned towards the fire, and a mob-capped elderly maid tended to it with a wadded, reddened cloth.

Kitty.

Sidney clamped his hand to his pounding heart.

Please, not *Kitty.*

Dear God, let Kitty be well.

He inhaled, strode forward, and peered over the back of the sofa.

Sidney exhaled, relieved. The duke – not Kitty – lay bloodied and bloated with his face half-flayed.

Then terror seized Sidney. If Gillingham looked like

that, what horrendous accident had befallen him? And *where* was Kitty?

Sidney spoke through clenched teeth. 'By God, you foul beast, what have you done with my wife?'

Gillingham grimaced, as if in pain. His engorged purple lips and shredded cheek quivered as he coughed. Blood tinged his teeth pink. 'What have *I* done with your hellcat wife?' His voice was raspy and hoarse, and his words garbled. 'Look at what *she's* done to *me*.'

Sidney's tense muscles eased. Behind him, skirts rustled. He turned, his hopes soaring, but only Clarissa stood at the door, smiling wistfully as she loosened her hat.

Sidney returned his attention to the duke. 'Kitty did this to you? But how?'

'With my walking stick.' Gillingham gurgled, one hand to his throat. 'Beat me to a pulp and left me for dead. How did you find me, Eden?'

Sidney, with laughter swelling his chest, ignored the question. 'What a magnificent wife I have! Where is she?'

'Damned if I know. She ran off. My gamekeeper has searched this last hour to no avail.'

Kitty was likely seeking a way back to London.

'You,' Sidney said to the thin-faced man. 'Saddle the best fresh horse in the stable at once. And while I ride out and find my wife, assist my driver in tending to my carriage horses. I want them ready to return to London within the hour.'

The servant looked to the duchess, who nodded and waved him on.

'You'll pay for this, Eden,' Gillingham wheezed, his voice strained. 'I'll bring the law down on you and Kitty for attempted murder.'

Clarissa's laugh chimed.

The duke's face blanched under his purple bruises.

'Nonsense, Harold.' Clarissa's skirts swished as she crossed the room. The maid retreated, allowing the duchess to come around to the fire side of the sofa. Clarissa gazed upon her husband like an affectionate mother at an impish child. 'You'll do no such thing. Only the people in the room, Matilda Preece and the *new* Lady Eden will ever know any of this happened – unless I decide to tell my brother, that is.' Clarissa's brother, the Duke of Amesbury, was as kind as Clarissa – and more powerful than Gillingham. Sidney had long suspected Clarissa had sway over her husband through her brother's protection. 'For everyone else's benefit,' the duchess continued, 'you had a nasty fall from your horse, riding at night after drinking too much.'

The duke tugged at his loose cravat. 'Clarissa – how——?'

She laughed. 'Oh, dearest, I've known about this cave of yours for twenty years. You get up to all manner of foolishness here, don't you?' Her smile deepened. 'That – among other things – will cease. You and I shall have several long talks as I nurse you over the upcoming days.' She tilted her head, her silvered curls bobbing under the brim of her lace cap. 'Dear, dear. That gash will leave a nasty scar across your face.' She turned to the maid. 'Plenty of hot water and a needle and thread, please.'

The duke choked. 'Good God, Clarissa – wait for the surgeon.' He clutched white-knuckled at the rim of the sofa.

The duchess's musical laughter chimed. 'No need, dearest. My needlework is exquisite.'

The thin-faced manservant re-entered. 'Your horse . . . rather, his grace's horse saddled for you, sir.'

Sidney jumped to attention.

Wherever Kitty was in the Kentish countryside, Sidney would find her. He'd comfort her, console her, caress her. Promise never to fail to protect her again. Plead for the honour of telling her daily he loved her, in whatever kind of arrangement she wanted. Because she was his everything.

Sidney bowed his head. 'Thank you, Cla— . . . duchess.'

Then he ran, ragged but resolved. Outside, into the night, towards a powerfully built, dappled draught horse. He grabbed the animal's reins and . . .

'Sidney?'

Clarissa stood behind him on the moonlit path, her white hands pressed splay-fingered against her abdomen.

'Yes?' Sidney asked, impatient to leave.

She gathered a breath, hesitated, and spoke. 'Tell your wife I shall visit her as soon as I return to London.'

Her words rendered Sidney speechless. Under normal customs, a duchess would ask a countess to visit *her*. But under *truly* normal circumstances, a society leader like Clarissa, admired everywhere, would have nothing to do with Kitty.

'She resides on Mount Street, I believe?' Clarissa asked. 'The large corner house with the red door?'

Sidney blinked. Would Clarissa indeed visit the Preece sisters' home?

'Sidney, don't gawk, my sweet. Answer me.'

He recovered his voice. 'Not at Mount Street anymore. You can visit her at my lodgings on Half Moon Street. That is, *if* I can convince her to stay with me, despite the hell she's lived through tonight.'

'Half Moon Street then.' Clarissa pressed her palms together. 'I shall ensure your wife has nothing to fear from Harold anymore. Please tell her she can trust me. As you know, my influence is broad – on my husband and on others.' Clarissa smiled. 'I shall make a little pet of her, as I did you once upon a time. But I shan't drop her after a Season.'

Warmth filled Sidney's chest. 'Thank you, Clarissa.' Favoured treatment from the Duchess of Gillingham would guarantee Kitty's acceptance *everywhere*.

'She must be quite something, from the way you and Richard speak. He writes to me about her, although he *oughtn't*, I suppose. He misses her dreadfully, but he realises she was never truly his. I know what he feels.' The duchess cast down her eyes. 'You were always lovely, Sidney. One of my favourites.'

'You say that to us all,' Sidney teased, although a lump formed in his throat.

Clarissa frowned. 'No, Sidney, I don't. You were special. I didn't let you go because I tired of you. I let you go because you were in danger of stealing my heart, and I keep my heart loyal to Harold.' Her eyes twinkled with laughter again. 'For better or worse.'

Sidney reached out; she laid her cool palm in his. 'He doesn't deserve you, Clarissa.'

She smiled, showing her dimple. 'I'm fine, Sidney, my sweet.'

For the second time that night, Sidney brought her hand to his lips.

'I'm glad you found happiness,' she said as he kissed her.

Sidney pressed her fingers. 'She's my true love.'

'Then go.' The duchess reclaimed her hand and shooed him away. '*Go.*'

Again ignoring his aching left knee, Sidney raised his foot into the stirrup, swung his leg over the saddle, and galloped in pursuit of his wife.

Kitty eyed the moon warily as she trudged on the field side of a hawthorn hedge which ran along the road back to town. The near-full orb was still high and bright, cradled among clouds of stars such as one never saw in London, but once it set, darkness would descend and finding a farmer's house would be near impossible.

Although Kitty struggled to walk in the muddy fields, she stayed off the road. For some time, a man on horseback – a servant of the duke's, no doubt – had pursued her. Other than the blue shawl shielding her from the cold night air, Kitty's only solace was the apple she munched – the last of three she'd gathered from an orchard after crawling under the hedge surrounding the duke's hunting grounds.

An owl hooted. With a rustle of wind and wings, it swooped from the hedge. Kitty jumped back, startled. The bird glided soundlessly away, sweeping over the hops growing on their high wooden frames.

Kitty nibbled at her apple core, savouring the last of the sweet-tart juice. With a sigh, she tossed the core into the hedge.

Her stomach rumbled as she marched on. The farmer who tended these tidy fields must live *somewhere*.

Hooves thundered down the road on the opposite side of the hedge. The duke's man had returned. Kitty scowled as she pulled her shawl over her tangled hair – amazingly, her lace cap was still attached – and clamped it with a fist under her chin, seeking both to warm herself and to blend with the shadows. How long would this servant pursue her?

A call resounded in the night-quiet: '*Kitty! Kitty!*'

It was *not* the duke's man.

It was her precious, beloved husband.

Kitty yelled Sidney's name with all her might, although her throat and torso ached.

The horse galloped closer.

'*Sidney!*' she called again, running to the hedge. She fell on her hands and feet and wiggled through the interlacing scratching branches, yanking her shawl as she went.

Would Sidney hear her before he passed?

She emerged on the other side, with her shawl-covered hands clutched over her yearning heart. Sidney's horse shone silvery white, pounding down the ribbon-road in the moonlight.

'Sidney.' Her voice was a whisper-squeak because her throat clamped at the sight of her love. 'Darling Sidney,' she said, her mouth as dry as sand.

'*Kitty!*' Sidney reined in his horse. It neighed, grinding its hooves to a halt in a cloud of road dirt.

Sidney swung off the saddle in one swift motion, like a golden arc.

He stumbled towards her with glistening eyes. 'My love.'

Bruised and torn – but far from shattered – Kitty dashed into her husband's arms and pressed her black-gloved palms to his cheeks, framing his beautiful face.

Sidney lifted her off her feet, and she wrapped her mud-soaked legs about his waist.

She kissed him, drinking Sidney's gorgeous taste. Love, security, strength, and vigour.

Her heart took flight.

When the essential need to breathe forced them apart, Kitty unwrapped her legs and placed her feet on the ground, although the world seemed to wobble under her. Sidney supported her with an arm tight around her waist. He smoothed back her hair with his warm palm.

'My love,' he said. 'My dearest, most wonderful, most marvellous love. You've been through hell tonight, my poor angel – and I'm so sorry I failed you. I'll die before I let anyone harm you, ever again, Kitty. Please grant me another chance. Permit me to convince you a thousand times a day of my love and devotion.'

Kitty squeezed him close. 'Oh, Sidney, none of this was your fault, darling. And, oddly, now that we are safely together, I'm not altogether unhappy about how events unfolded. I learned a thing or two about myself tonight.'

He lifted his brows. 'You learned that you are perfection itself, in every way?'

'Very nearly, yes.' Kitty giggled, he laughed, and they tightened their embrace. 'In earnest, though, I learned to be grateful for the opportunity fate has granted me. Whatever good *this* Lady Eden can do in this magnificent but hurting world, she'll do with her whole heart.'

Sidney gazed at her as adoringly as if she were a goddess in a temple – an exceedingly pleasant sensation, and quite familiar to the countess who was once London's most desirable courtesan.

The difference, of course, was that Sidney worshipped Kitty even when muck covered her from head to foot, and she stank like the Thames itself.

'My wife is a worthy lady, indeed.'

Kitty scrunched her nose. 'I shan't argue.'

And again, he stole her breath with a kiss, squeezing her close on the moonlit path. She wrapped her arms around his broad shoulders, enveloping them both in the warmth of the Vauxhall shawl.

It triggered a memory.

When Kitty disengaged from the kiss, she laughed.

A smile danced on Sidney's lips. 'What's so amusing?'

'A curate and a courtesan wooing in the moonlight,' she explained. 'Do you remember? Gillingham said that when he mocked us at Vauxhall. It was truer than I realised at the time, but it's not at *all* true now.'

'It's not?'

'No,' Kitty said, her heart triumphant. 'We're an earl and a countess wooing in the moonlight.'

She gave herself over to another of her husband's kisses.

Her own lady. Her own choice.

Exhilarating pleasure.

30

Christmas Eve 1813

Kitty draped the folds of a velvet garland trimmed with oranges, cinnamon sticks and tinkling silver bells across the back of one of the cream silk sofas in the Dower House drawing room. She inhaled, luxuriating in the aroma of citrus and spice. 'Perfect. It smells, feels *and* sounds like Christmas. A garland especially for Ada-Marie.'

The crackling fire reflected in Sidney's smiling eyes. Kitty and Sidney had created the garland together, after kissing Ada-Marie and Tess goodnight as the cousins snuggled under their feather counterpane.

It was the last touch to the festive decorations in the charming room, now ready to host half of Sidney's uncles and their families for tomorrow's festivities. Ivy garlands draped the wainscoting on the butter-coloured walls. More ivy swathed the doorways and decorated the creamy marble mantel. Red-berried, glossy-leafed holly hung across the tops of the daffodil silk curtains. The small chandelier, with its dozen beeswax tapers, bore greenery, fruits, nuts and mistletoe.

Sidney, dressed in formal evening clothes of a dark tailcoat and white satin breeches, walked behind Kitty, wrapped an arm about her waist, and pressed his warm body to her back. He held a twig of mistletoe aloft as he trailed kisses from the top of Kitty's head, down her cheek and into the curve of her shoulder.

'I confess,' his voice rumbled into her neck, 'I'm as eager as our girls for tomorrow morning. Will Ada-Marie like her pony and Tess her mare, do you think?'

Kitty smiled. '*Like*? You'll have some difficulty getting them to stop riding and come to church.'

'They shall ride to church.'

'All fifty feet from our stables to the church door?' Kitty asked with a laugh. The churchyard was beyond the low brick wall of the snowy Dower House garden.

Sidney brushed away a loose tendril of Kitty's hair, his attention still on her neck. 'Yes. And once we're there, Clara will convince them to come in.'

Kitty's heart filled her chest as her husband continued his ministrations to her neck and shoulders. It would be just as Sidney said, for his cousin Clara adored Ada-Marie and Tess like the sisters she'd never had, although Clara was nineteen and preparing for her first London Season in the spring. Kitty would bring her out with Clarissa's guidance while Sidney fulfilled his Parliamentary duties.

Although Kitty loved their country life, the Season would be splendid fun: a brief return to London's thrills and a chance to see her sisters and Sidney's friends, who'd become her own friends over the autumn. Sidney had leased their own small townhouse from Tyrold because his income from book sales permitted it.

But as amusing as London would be, better yet would be when Parliament closed, and they returned to their snug house in the country. Sidney flourished while writing; Kitty adored housekeeping. Together they cared for their tenants and the land and loved their girls. It was a peaceful and purposeful life.

Kitty's fairy tale, come true.

Sidney's arm left Kitty's waist. He tucked the twig of white-berried mistletoe into the bodice of her green silk evening gown.

'Am I meant to wear mistletoe between my breasts for the ball at Paradisum?' Kitty asked. The ball was the reason they'd dressed up; they'd promised their tenants they'd attend. Carriages had rolled towards the big house for the last hour. The amiable, munificent Waldings were already popular in the neighbourhood.

'Yes, wear it for *my* convenience, for I want to kiss you frequently tonight. Needless to say, other men mayn't touch it.' Still behind her, Sidney rummaged in his pocket. 'And the mistletoe isn't the only thing I want you to wear.'

Cool metal slipped around her neck.

Kitty put her hand to the necklace as Sidney fastened the clasp. It was a strand of gems in a riviere style, resting so close to her neck she couldn't see their colour. 'Oh, Sidney, darling.' She didn't say he didn't need to; she wouldn't challenge his choice. They were careful with their money, but nothing was as dire as they'd once supposed, and Matilda made clear she'd never take a penny from Sidney – even reimbursing the three hundred pounds he'd given her in July and the thousand he'd paid to Gillingham – so everything Sidney's books earned was theirs to spend, save and give as they wanted. Two of his novels had sold with profound success, Duffy and Ward would publish the third before Easter, and Sidney's new manuscript grew thicker daily. Kitty turned and threaded her arms around his neck. 'Thank you.'

His amber eyes twinkled. 'Can you see it?'

'No, but I love it all the same.'

'Sit with me, Kit.'

'It's nearly ten. We promised the Waldings we'd come . . .'

But despite her protest, Kitty let her husband pull her onto the cream silk sofa, for she loved nothing better than his embrace. She perched on Sidney's lap and arranged her dark green skirts around their legs.

Sidney drew her close and sighed happily, his breath soft on her cheek. 'All I ask is a few more minutes alone with my wife before I share her with a multitude of covetous eyes, so that I may remind her why no other man is as wonderful as her husband.'

Kitty's pulse increased. 'And how will you do that without tangling my hair, Sid? Look at how beautifully Grace curled it.'

Philippe now served Matilda, but Kitty's new maid, hired from the workhouse, had learned rapidly and enthusiastically. Providing Grace with a better life *also* warmed Kitty's heart.

Although Kitty wasn't especially devout, over the autumn, she'd embroidered a quotation from Corinthians

439

and hung it at her dressing table. She read it several times a day: '*But by the grace of God I am what I am*'. She and Sidney weren't awash in wealth or influence, but what Kitty could do for those less fortunate, she would do.

'I have no intention of tangling your pretty curls,' Sidney said. 'Your mind dashed to improper places, while mine was perfectly innocent. I want to show you how wonderful I am by reading you my latest composition, "Lines Composed to my Wife, Daughter and Niece as they Cuddle by the Fire on Christmas Eve". However, if you want something else, I'm happy to oblige. As for your hair, it looks best when it's tumbling over our pillows, but if you want to protect it, I'll gladly lie back on this sofa and let you use me however you please.'

Kitty giggled. 'It's tempting. When we return from the party, I want you to carry me upstairs and tumble my hair everywhere you choose. But for now, read me the poem.'

Sidney removed a folded paper from his waistcoat pocket. Kitty snuggled closer as his gentle voice read his poetry. It evoked the moment, earlier that day, when she, Ada-Marie and Tess sat on the same sofa. Their six-month-old wolfhound pup Bouncer – a gift to the girls from Tyrold when they'd left London in early October – snored and twitched before the fire, exhausted from a walk with Sidney and Tess, and Marmalade purred in Ada-Marie's lap as the little girl's dimpled fingers stoked his fur. 'He's vibrating, Mama,' Ada-Marie had squealed. 'Like the strings of the pianoforte.'

Kitty wiped a tear from the corner of her eye when her husband finished reading his poem. 'It's beautiful, Sidney. It's perfect.'

Sidney lifted her chin with his thumb. 'An ode to my three perfect ladies.'

Kitty kissed him long and deep, with her heart full.

They settled against the cream upholstery, their arms entwined, as the flames flickered.

'You showed me, you know,' Kitty said. 'You showed me no other man is as wonderful as my husband.'

He grinned. 'With my poem?'

'With the *first* poem you ever wrote me, with this poem now, and with everything you've done in-between and continue to do daily. You're my generous, kind, whole-hearted, sensitive Sidney, of whom I'm exceedingly proud. The most wonderful man of all time.'

Sidney beamed like a delighted boy. 'Because my Kitty – the most wonderful lady of all time – makes me so.'

Kitty closed her eyes as her husband cradled her in his secure embrace. 'She's your everything.'

'That you are.'

Historical Note

I adore learning social history from novels; thus, it is my mission with The Gentlemen of London series to provide a high degree of historical accuracy. In writing *A Courtesan's Worth*, I researched a long-time fascination: the lives of Georgian sex workers. My depiction of the Preece sisters is based upon reading accounts of many Georgian prostitutes and courtesans, but my biggest influence was undoubtedly the salacious memoirs of Harriette Wilson.

Harriette was one of the reigning courtesans of the Regency. But as she aged into her thirties, men who'd loved her deserted her, and she relied on an annuity from the Duke of Beaufort (whose son was once Harriette's besotted lover). When Beaufort revoked the annuity after some years, Harriette was destitute.

Destitute – but in possession of a resourceful mind.

She was a brilliant, witty woman – a voracious writer who'd recorded much of her life in letters and diaries. Therefore, when deprived of her income, she sought an eager publisher and issued an ultimatum to her former lovers: pay her two hundred pounds, or she'd write them into her soon-to-be-published memoirs.

Many sent banknotes by return post, leaving us wondering what we missed out on. But others, including the Duke of Wellington, disdained her offer. The Iron Duke allegedly declared 'Publish and be damned', which is perhaps why Harriette describes him thusly on one occasion in her memoirs: 'Wellington was by now my constant visitor – a most unentertaining one, Heaven knows! and, in the evenings, when he wore his broad red ribbons, he looked very like a rat-catcher.'

Like fictional Kitty, by the age of fifteen, Harriette was already in a line of work graced by her elder sisters. Her first (known) keeper was the Earl of Craven, who, at twice Harriette's age, didn't impress the teenager with his staid ways, his ratty cotton nightcap, and his obsession with a past trip to the West Indies.

While Harriette wouldn't have known this, it might interest Jane Austen's fans to learn that the voyage Craven droned on about nightly bore a heartbreaking connection to the Austen family. Cassandra Austen's beloved fiancé, the Reverend Thomas Fowle, accompanied his cousin Lord Craven as chaplain on that ill-fated expedition to earn money for his marriage. Sadly, Fowle died of yellow fever in February 1797 and never returned to England, devastating Cassandra, who remained unmarried for the remainder of her life. The death impacted Craven as well. When the earl discovered his cousin had left behind a fiancée, he was distraught, declaring he never would've asked Thomas to accompany him if he'd known of the engagement. Perhaps Craven bored Harriette with obsessive accounts of the expedition because he still mourned his friend and cousin?

While many details of Kitty's life are figments of my imagination, I tried to paint the life of a Georgian courtesan with a historically accurate brush. It was unquestionably an exciting existence, but the fame and wealth were short-lived, and the occupational hazards significant. Men were sometimes violent: Harriette describes a time when Frederick Lamb (brother to the future prime minister, Lord Melbourne) strangled her nearly to death when she refused his advances. Additionally, a courtesan often bore many children whose fathers provided for them or not, depending on whim. Others, like Harriette, never had any children, possibly due to an early encounter with venereal disease.

There is historical precedent for Sidney and Kitty's union; courtesans did, on rare occasion, marry into the *haut ton*. Harriette's younger sister, Sophia, married Lord Berwick and subsequently snubbed her courtesan sisters, who occasionally amused themselves at the opera by spitting down from their box onto Lady Berwick's hair. Courtesan/actress Lavinia Fenton, who originated the role of Polly Peachum in *The Beggar's Opera*, famously became Duchess of Bolton in 1751, after being the duke's mistress for decades. The prominent Whig statesman Charles James Fox married courtesan Elizabeth Armistead in 1795, after they too had lived together for many years. These marriages were scandalous and met with varied success, but because of my research into them, my imagination created what

I hope are historically plausible obstacles on Kitty and Sidney's path to happiness.

On another note, I owe a debt of gratitude to my lovely sister-in-law Kristen for her assistance in developing the character of Ada-Marie. Like Ada-Marie, Kristen was blind at birth from congenital cataracts and has lived her entire life with significant visual impairment and occasional total blindness between many surgeries. She is also in every way the most remarkable of women, both professionally and personally. While congenital cataracts was only one of many reasons for blindness in the Regency era (illness and accidents were perhaps the leading causes), I wanted to base Ada-Marie on the experiences of someone I know and love.

The earliest successful cataract surgeries date from the mid-eighteenth century, but it is highly unlikely this surgery would've been performed on a four-year-old in 1813, given the enormous risk of infection. The prevailing concern for any parent of a blind child at that time would've been – as it is for all parents and all children, in all times – supporting the child so he or she could live a full and independent life.

And such a thing was entirely possible. For centuries, blind children who had access to supportive adults or philanthropic charities were taught trades to support themselves – and those who showed any musical inclination or ability were often encouraged to take up an instrument, as there was ample employment for musicians before the invention of sound recording. During the Regency, people would have frequently encountered blind musicians from buskers to ballroom violinists to cathedral organists, like the blind composer and organist John Stanley (1712-1786), Master of the King's Music to George III.

But beginning in the eighteenth century, the education of the blind expanded beyond trades and music. An early inspiration in new, enlightened thinking about blind people and classical education was Nicholas Saunderson (1682-1739). Saunderson lost his sight at age one from smallpox, but rather than encouraging him towards a trade or musical career, Saunderson's father taught him arithmetic. Through hard work, a heightened tactile sense and the use of his apparently remarkable memory, Saunderson went on to become a brilliant mathematician and popular teacher at Christ's College, Cambridge and, ultimately, the Lucasian Chair of Mathematics (a position also held by Isaac Newton, Stephen Hawking and only sixteen others since its creation in 1663).

In the mid-eighteenth century, philosophers first widely pondered how the blind might learn to read. Talented young French musician Mélanie de Salignac (1744-1766), who was born blind, taught herself to read music and letters by a self-developed method of tactile print. Her success inspired the great philosopher Denis Diderot, who wrote a treatise arguing that the blind should be taught to read using a universal tactile system.

After the time of this novel, Diderot's treatise would inspire Louis Braille (1809-1852) to create the system of tactile print still in use today – but even before Braille,

Valentin Haüy (1745-1822) developed a wide-spread system of raised letters to teach blind students, directly inspired by Maria Theresia von Paradis (1759-1824). Paradis was a blind Austrian musician and composer and a good friend of Mozart. Like Mélanie de Salignac, she had developed her own system of raised letters for reading. Haüy refined her method and employed it with great success when he opened the world's first school for the blind in 1785, which is still in operation in Paris today. Britain followed Haüy's example in 1791 with the Royal School for the Blind in Liverpool (Edinburgh and Bristol soon followed). Although the British schools were at first still largely trades-based, the Liverpool school has the distinction of being the world's first school for the blind founded by a blind person, namely Edward Rushton (1756-1814), a sailor, poet and abolitionist.

Perhaps some of my readers might wonder why, if such possibilities existed for the blind, Ada-Marie was left in a basket outside Dr Alexander Mitchell's maternity hospital. In developing this aspect of the plot, I considered the impossible choices faced by working class or unwed mothers at the time. In my mind, Ada-Marie's birth mother wanted the best for her child, but she didn't have the means to provide it. Therefore, she left her daughter not at a workhouse or orphanage, but on the doorstep of a philanthropic physician (as established in book one of this series, *A Lady's Risk*), hoping Alexander would ensure her baby received the best possible chances.

It is my hope that *A Courtesan's Worth* accurately depicts Kitty and Sidney's understanding of the possibilities available to Ada-Marie, and their knowledge that with support and means, these possibilities could become reality. Like all parents, they love their child fiercely; thus, in development of the plot, I always considered how Ada-Marie's wellbeing would have affected their decision-making.

Acknowledgements

Like all novels, *A Courtesan's Worth* would not exist without a support team, and I want to offer my heartfelt thanks to mine: my critique partner, Jessica Bull; my mentor Suzy Vadori; my agent Kate Nash and her team; my editor Sanah Ahmed and her team, especially Jade Craddock; my wonderful draft readers; and my husband Tim and our children, Benjamin and Susannah.

But my biggest thanks of all goes to you, my readers! Your enthusiasm for these characters means the world to me. Like Sidney, I hope my novels bring you joy.

Don't miss the next steamy, heartwarming and
unputdownable Regency from Felicity George . . .

A Debutante's Desire

Available to pre-order now!

'A heart-warming and richly emotional debut that shines with sparkling wit, passion and fun'
NICOLA CORNICK

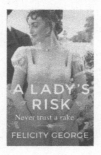

Never trust a rake . . .

Lady Margaret has devoted herself to taking care of her young siblings and the estate while her half-brother fritters away the family fortune. Upon Edwin's death, she learns he has left them destitute and, worst of all, at the mercy of a notorious and cruel rake.

Lord Nicholas would much rather be pursuing women for quick sport than taking care of a headstrong debutante without any prospects, as well as her siblings. But Edwin saved his life once, and now he owes him a debt. Fortunately, all he has to do is find Meggy a husband, and his debt will be paid.

There's just one issue: Meggy is *nothing* like what he'd imagined. And the more time he spends in her company, the more he begins to wonder whether he's met his match . . .

www.ingramcontent.com/pod-product-compliance
Ingram Content Group UK Ltd.
Pitfield, Milton Keynes, MK11 3LW, UK
UKHW022321280225
455674UK00004B/403

9 781398 715943